THE PUZZLED
MYSTERY ADVENTURE
SERIES

BOOKS 1-3

P.J. Nichols

For my son, Justin,
You are so awesome.

PUZZLED

THE PUZZLED MYSTERY ADVENTURE SERIES: BOOK 1

CHAPTER 1

While fiddling with a couple of twenty-sided dice in his left hand, Peter took another glance at the clock above the blackboard. It now read 1:36, only three minutes later than the last time he had checked. As always, Peter was incredibly bored by Mr. Pendleton's Grade 7 geography class.

"Isn't it amazing?" Mr. Pendleton said. "Doesn't the complexity of nature just fascinate you beyond belief?"

Peter's teacher seemed obsessed with taking simple and easy concepts, and stretching out the explanations as long as humanly possible. Today, he was trying to illustrate the difference between a tsunami and a tidal wave. And in an attempt to make it easier to understand, he had drawn dreadfully awful sketches for his audience of uninterested twelve-year-old boys and girls.

"So as you can clearly see," Mr. Pendleton continued, "these are two completely different things. You would be shocked to know how many people, even grown-ups, confuse the two."

Peter looked up at the clock again. Somehow, it had only managed to move ahead by another four minutes. That meant he still had twenty minutes here, followed by an hour of an even more boring math class.

Peter was by far the cleverest student in the class. He was actually the top grade seven student in the school, and most likely had one of the highest IQs in the entire town. His mind worked like a super computer, easily understanding even the most complex things. When he was nine or ten years old, he had tried over and over to help others see how easy it was to learn. But he had given up on that by the time he turned twelve.

Since school provided nothing interesting or challenging for him, he kept his mind busy by playing complex games and solving puzzles and riddles at home.

To try to distract himself from the clock, he started looking around the room at the other twenty-three students. In particular, he focused on the girl sitting two rows in front of him. Nicola had been attending the same schools as Peter since they were in kindergarten, but she sure had changed in the last few months. She was much taller and thinner now, and exactly eighty-seven days ago, had shown up at school with braces.

Peter and Nicola used to play together when they were in elementary school, back when no one cared about whether their friends were boys or girls. They even walked together to junior high for the first few months. But a new school meant new friends, and Nicola's new group decided that Peter was too *weird and geeky*, and that she was better off staying away from him.

His daydreaming was brought to an abrupt stop by Mr. Pendleton. "Peter, could you please rejoin us all on planet Earth for a minute?" his teacher said. "We would be very gracious to hear, in your own words, what causes a tsunami. Not a tidal wave, a tsunami."

Peter was fairly embarrassed that Nicola was now looking his way, so he got ready to give a *textbook answer* to the question, one that would cause no giggles or glares. But just as he was about to speak, his elbow accidentally bumped the dice off his desk.

"C'mon Peter," Mr. Pendleton said. "You know you're not supposed to bring toys to class."

This caused at least half of the class to start laughing, the exact thing Peter had been hoping to avoid.

Red-faced, he bent down to pick them up. But just before his hand got there, the kid sitting in the desk beside him decided to kick them away. "You heard him!" the kid said. "No toys!"

They rolled a couple of meters and stopped directly under Nicola's seat. She picked them up right away, but wasn't sure if she should return them to Peter or give them to Mr. Pendleton.

"Nik, what are you doing?" one of her ditsy new friends asked loudly. "I wouldn't touch those if I were you. You don't know where they've been!"

Nicola spun around to look at Peter, but he was already staring down at his lap. She'd known him for a very long time, and didn't like seeing him suffer like this.

Mr. Pendleton walked down her row and took the dice from her hand. "Thank you, Nicola," he said. "Peter, you may collect these after school today. And don't worry, I won't play with them or break them or anything like that."

The class had a good laugh over that one too. Peter could feel his face getting even redder than before. He had a very pale complexion to begin with, and it quickly changed color whenever he got even slightly anxious. His current level of embarrassment was enough to make it almost purple.

With the dice ordeal finally over, Mr. Pendleton got ready to continue his lecture. But for some reason, he couldn't recall where he had left off. "Now where were we?" he asked himself aloud. "Hold on a minute, everyone. I need to check my notes."

Mr. Pendleton started filing through the mess of papers on his desk. And while he searched, students here and there began chatting quietly with each other.

Then the bell rang, and everyone packed up and headed out of the room. All twenty-four of them were going upstairs to math class next.

Peter joined the procession. What surprised him was that Nicola grabbed the dice off the teacher's desk on her way out. Of course, she did it in a way that none of her new friends noticed.

CHAPTER 2

Peter walked through the door of his math classroom just as the bell was ringing. Although he loved numbers, formulas, and calculations dearly, he really hated Mrs. Baird's class. She had quickly noticed Peter's math skills during the first week of school, and now used him as her *go to* student whenever she wanted to hear the correct answer. And on top of that, she had moved him to the front row, right in front of her desk. That way she could ask him to help grade quizzes and things anytime he finished his work early.

As he took his seat, he noticed the dice were in his desk. Nicola must have found a way to put them in there when no one was looking.

"Hey geek!" he heard from one of the jocks in the back row.

Peter was no stranger to being teased, especially by the guys on the football and basketball teams. But since they were so much bigger than him, he did whatever he could to avoid any type of confrontation. As he had done so many times before, he ignored their name-calling again today.

"Can't hear us, geek?" another one said, much louder

this time. "Oh, I guess you think you're too smart to talk to us, right?"

Thankfully, Mrs. Baird walked into the room, so the jocks immediately stopped teasing Peter. They didn't want to risk getting detention after school today, as that would mean they would miss their beloved sports practice.

Today's math class was so slow and boring that Peter felt himself nodding off a few times. Mrs. Baird's monotone voice seemed to magically lull kids to sleep.

When there was about thirty minutes left in class, his teacher walked toward the door. "I need to make a few photocopies," she said. "While I'm gone, please continue working on pages 118 and 119, QUIETLY."

Within seconds of her departure, Peter felt the familiar sting of being hit by a spitball. He wasn't sure why they were called spitballs, as they were actually just tiny pieces of crushed up paper. These little paper balls were wetted with spit, put in the end of a drinking straw, and shot out like bullets by blowing through the straw.

But Peter wasn't going to give whoever fired the spitball the satisfaction of a reaction, so he pretended nothing had happened.

"Next one's going to be extra wet, loser!" one of the boys yelled. "And this time I'm aiming for your ear!"

Peter pulled his collar up as far as possible, hoping it would reduce the chance of the next one hitting his bare skin.

"Grow up, guys!" one of the other kids yelled in Peter's defense.

Peter recognized Neil's voice immediately. Neil was the scatterbrained kid, who also had very few friends at school. Like Peter, Neil was the victim of regular teasing, so he was just trying to stick up for one of his own.

"You want one instead?" one of the boys asked Neil. "I'd be happy to help!"

"If you do, you'll regret it!" Neil yelled back, standing up at his desk.

"Wow!" the leader of the jocks said to his buddies. "Aren't you so big and tough! Oh, we're soooooo scared!"

Before it escalated any further, the door opened and Mrs. Baird walked back in. The spitball culprits managed to hide their straws in time, but Neil was caught standing up. Mrs. Baird instantly assumed that Neil had been causing some type of problem.

"Neil Bannister!" she said loudly. "You clearly were NOT paying attention when I told you to work quietly. So you have just earned yourself detention with me after school today. That's lucky for me, as I have tons of paperwork that I need help sorting."

Neil sat down without saying a word. Mrs. Baird was famous for doubling detention time for anyone who tried to argue with her.

"Show's over. Back to work, everyone," she said. "Unless any of you would like to join Neil after school?"

Everyone, jocks included, quickly picked up their pencils again. Mrs. Baird then began to "monitor" everyone's effort, which meant she walked slowly up and down the rows with her arms crossed.

But the monotony was broken up by a loud clap of thunder outside.

"Oh, not again," Mrs. Baird said, with a concerned expression on her face. "What on earth is with this crazy weather?"

Everyone looked out the window and watched the strange weather phenomenon. It was something which seemed to be occurring more and more regularly during the past few months.

"Maybe they'll cancel school again. Maybe we can go home early," Nicola said to a friend sitting close by.

In the span of only fifteen seconds, the clear sky became as dark as night. Then a powerful wind started howling, and rain hammered down.

These sudden and extreme storms only lasted about five minutes, but were causing irreparable damage to buildings, homes, crops, and shops. And weather experts couldn't explain what was causing them.

The lights suddenly went out. It looked like the storm had knocked out the power again. Peter smiled. They were probably going to be sent home early today.

A few minutes later, the rain let up, the wind subsided, and the blue sky opened up. The school principal then came into each class quickly and announced that school was cancelled for the rest of the day. Everyone was to pack up and head home quickly and safely.

Cheers of joy could be heard around the room. Peter even noticed Mrs. Baird smile after hearing the announcement.

Peter jammed everything into his backpack and darted for the door. He was planning to stand just outside the classroom door, and thank Nicola about the dice on her way out. But Peter was accidentally blocked by Neil. Neil was on his hands and knees picking up papers which had fallen on the floor when he had tried to pack up too quickly. Peter gave up on his race for the door, and helped Neil pick up a few handfuls of loose notes.

"Here you go," Peter said to him. "And thanks for standing up for me."

"No biggie," Neil replied. "I hate those guys too." Once Neil had managed to stuff everything back in his bag, he bolted for the door. "And this storm just got me out of detention!"

As Peter walked out of the front doors of the school, he surveyed the mess. These sudden storms always left puddles and mud on most of the roads. It was going to make today's trek home slow and messy.

"It's muddier than it looks!" the principal shouted as students exited the school.

Peter had used his older brother Bradley's snazzy new mountain bike today. But he had taken it without asking, so he made a mental note to himself that he would need to give it a good cleaning when he got home.

He slowly and cautiously walked through the sloppy mess toward the bike rack. But when he got there, it was obvious that a huge amount of mud had gotten into the chain. There was no possibility of riding it home.

"You've got to be kidding me!" Peter said to himself. He was not looking forward to pushing Bradley's bike through the muck for the entire 1.56 km trip home.

CHAPTER 3

After ten minutes of mumbling and complaining to himself, he was finally getting close to the intersection he had to cross to get to Beaverbrook Street. Peter looked up as he approached the crosswalk, to double-check that there were no cars coming.

There weren't any cars in sight, but something else caught his eye. There was a very old man standing on the side of the road just before the intersection. Peter knew he had never seen this old guy before, and couldn't fathom how someone could end up lost in the middle of the day. Despite the fact that Peter just wanted to walk right past him, he remembered all of the lessons his parents had taught him about helping those in need. He felt more or less obligated to offer some assistance.

"I suppose I'm going to have to help this old weirdo," Peter muttered under his breath, making sure he said it quietly enough that the old man couldn't hear him.

The man appeared to be holding some sort of paper or map in his hand. That likely meant it was just a simple case of needing directions. The man had also noticed Peter approaching, and was clearly getting ready to ask something.

Peter decided to initiate the conversation. "Sir, are you lost?" he asked. "Maybe I can help."

After a brief pause, the old man replied, "Well, I do suppose I'm lost. But whether or not you can help is really a different question altogether."

Peter was a little surprised by this answer. "Try me," he said to the old man. "I've been living around here my entire life."

The man pushed the paper, which was a map, quite close to Peter's face. "I'm trying to get to the library. Central Library, on Leeds Street," he said.

Without even glancing at the map, Peter quickly answered, "Oh, it's easy to get there. Just keep going down this road until you—"

But the old man interrupted Peter with a loud, gross grunt. It was like he was preparing to spit or cough or something. Then he pointed at his right leg, which was thinner and shorter than the left one.

"I know *how* to get there," the old man said, "but there's no way my legs are going to walk me that far. If I have to walk more than half a kilometer, I'll collapse on the spot!"

The old man took a couple of very awkward steps to demonstrate his point. And as Peter watched him limp, his mind began doing what it did best, calculate.

Thirty seconds later, Peter offered up a newer and better suggestion.

"Okay, then how about this?" Peter said. "Seventy meters down the road, you'll see the entrance to Mr. Wilden's farmhouse. Mr. Wilden is about eighty or so now, and he gets picked up every afternoon at around three by Mr. Wright, his neighbor, to go for coffee. They always head to the little coffee shop on Kade Boulevard, which is less than two hundred meters from the door of the library. And I'm sure they would let you ride in with them if you ask."

The old man listened intently. He nodded his head while listening, and a grin began to appear across his face.

"That's a fantastic idea," the old man said. "And you thought it up so quickly. You're a clever boy."

The old man began slowly limping down the road toward the Wilden house. Peter could no longer see his face, which meant he couldn't see he was grinning from ear to ear.

CHAPTER 4

About fifteen minutes after his encounter with the old man, Peter finally made it back home. His house looked like it had escaped today's storm relatively unscathed.

Peter's family lived in one of the larger homes in an area of town where everything had been built over twenty years ago. It was a sturdy and practical two-story house, with really ugly off-white stucco on the exterior walls. When Peter was five or six, he was regularly scolded for picking off the stucco. There were a few patches on the wall that he had picked almost bare.

Without checking to see if anyone else was home, he pushed Bradley's bike through the gate and into the backyard. Peter knew how angry his older brother would get if he found out Peter had borrowed his new bike without asking. He turned on the water for the outdoor garden hose, grabbed an old rag from the garage, and started scrubbing away at the mud. Peter was the *meticulous* brother, and Bradley was the *anything goes* brother. A quick cleaning would be enough to fool Bradley.

To help distract himself from this incredibly boring task, Peter decided to count how many seconds he had been doing it for. Even before his second birthday, Peter had fallen in love with numbers. He would count anything and everything he could.

His count was now up to 846, which he knew was exactly fourteen minutes and six seconds. Peter had always wondered why his mind had to be computing or calculating something.

He finished cleaning the bike and started pushing it into the garage. Just before he got there, he saw his younger sister skipping and whistling happily toward him. Sophia, or *Princess Sophie*, as she liked to be called, was quickly approaching her ninth birthday. Despite being fairly irritating and unbelievably ditsy, she always happily tried Peter's puzzles and games. Most of the time, she couldn't even understand the rules of the games. And she never even came close to solving any of the puzzles. But no matter how hard or confusing it was, she never gave up or complained.

"Brad's going to kill you when he finds out you used his bike!" she said to him in her high-pitched voice.

Playing it safe, Peter decided to get Sophia on his side. "He'll never know," he said, "if you don't tell him. And if you promise not to tell him, I'll take you to the mall on Saturday morning."

He figured this proposal had close to a hundred percent probability of being accepted. Sophia would never turn down the chance to go to the mall.

"Really?" she squealed in excitement. "Okay, I promise! But if you don't take me first thing on Saturday morning, then I *will* tell him, and he'll beat the crap out of you!"

Peter realized that borrowing Bradley's bike today had been a mistake. He would stick to using his own from now on. He knew two hours at the mall with his bratty sister was going to be a bore, but it was the only way to avoid Bradley's angry wrath. Peter knew Bradley wouldn't hurt him by using kicks or punches. Bradley would do something much, much worse. He would break one of Peter's puzzles or games. And those were by far his most prized possessions.

CHAPTER 5

At precisely 7:37 the next morning, Peter walked out the front door to head to school. If he rode, he would be able to delay his departure until 7:52. But since he wasn't sure if the roads were still muddy or not, he chose to walk.

Just like every other morning, Peter began counting the number of steps it took to reach the end of the street. He knew it would take him an extra three or four steps today, as he had to walk around a small puddle of water at the end of the driveway.

He got to the corner on step 153. He knew he'd be taking another nine hundred or so more before reaching the intersection. After about eight minutes of walking, he noticed someone standing at the intersection again today. As he got closer, he quickly realized it was the same person as yesterday. And not only that, but the man looked as if he were waiting for Peter's arrival.

"Now this is a getting creepy," Peter said to himself as he got closer and closer to the old man.

Wanting to steer clear of any danger, Peter stopped walking when he was about two meters away from him.

With a tinge of sarcasm in his voice, Peter asked,

"Lost again, sir? This is a pretty small town. It's tough to get lost in the same spot twice."

It appeared as if Peter's words had gone in one ear and out the other, as the man's expression didn't change one bit.

After a fairly long pause, the old man replied, "Lost? No. In need of your assistance again? Yes."

"My assistance?" Peter said hesitantly. "What do you mean?"

Peter took a few more steps back. He wanted to ensure that he was well out of the old man's reach.

"Don't run away!" the old man begged. "The reason I need your help is... well... I need some puzzles solved."

"Puzzles?" Peter said, having trouble hiding his interest. "What do you mean? And why me? You could ask anyone."

"Because you," the old man said, "are very clever. Remember the question I asked you yesterday? You were about the two hundredth person that I asked that exact same question to over the last six months. And none of the previous people were able to help.

Peter backed up even further. Now this old guy was making him feel really, really uncomfortable.

"Wait! Please wait!" the man begged, even more desperately than before.

Peter looked the old man directly in the eyes. "Just tell me what you want. And why," Peter said. "I have to get to school. I'm going to be late."

"As I just said," the old man explained, "I want you to help me solve some puzzles. Why? Well, I can explain all the details in due time. For now, I'll leave you with this."

The old man put a small cardboard box on the ground.

"Young man," he said, "you are very smart. But I only

need your help if you are *exceptionally* smart. Try to solve this puzzle. If you can't solve it, then you'll never see me again. But if you can solve it, then I will *need* to see you again."

Then the old man turned around and slowly started to limp away.

Peter looked down at the box. He nudged it a few times with his foot. Once he had convinced himself that it wasn't some type of explosive, he made the decision to look inside.

"I hope there isn't something like a dead frog in here," he said jokingly to himself.

He used his foot to open up one of the flaps on the box. And its contents intrigued him significantly.

CHAPTER 6

Peter squatted down so he could get a closer look at what was inside. The box contained only three things. There was a carrot, a blue felt-tip marking pen, and small piece of paper with something written on it. He removed the paper from the box and stood up. The message was even more bizarre than the contents of the box.

Your tools: This box, a carrot, a blue felt marking pen
Your task: Make a rabbit change color.
(But you CAN NOT color the rabbit with the pen!!)

HI READER! (^_^)
QUITE A BIZARRE PUZZLE THAT PETER HAS TO SOLVE, ISN'T IT?
BEFORE READING ON, SEE IF YOU CAN COME UP WITH THE SOLUTION!

"This just keeps getting weirder and weirder," Peter said to himself.

He read the note again, thinking about how absurd

the whole situation was. He had just been asked by an old guy, who came out of nowhere, to make a rabbit change color! But Peter couldn't refuse a puzzle, regardless of whom or where it came from. He immediately started considering various possibilities of how to approach this one.

"I suppose," he said to himself, "I could use the felt pen to color the inside of the box, and then drop it on a rabbit. Then while it jumps and flips around inside, the ink will get all over it. That would make it change color."

Peter smiled smugly about his brilliant plan. But a few seconds later, he dismissed it.

"No, no, no," he said to himself. "That won't work. The ink would dry on the box before I'd have a chance to drop it on a rabbit."

Beads of sweat started to form on Peter's forehead, and his hands became clammy. His hands always got cold and wet like this when he was concentrating. Peter paced around the box, holding the pen in one hand and the carrot in the other. He mumbled to himself as he considered other possibilities. Then he stopped suddenly and raised both arms in the air, like a marathon runner who had just crossed the finish line.

"Ladies and gentlemen, I believe we have a winner!" Peter blurted out. "And it didn't even take me three minutes."

Beaming with pride, he put the carrot and felt pen back into the box and picked it up. He started jogging toward Mr. Wilden's farm, just down the road. He quickly ran up the front steps and rang the doorbell twice.

"Mr. Wilden!" Peter shouted, well before Mr. Wilden had even come to the door. "Mind if I play with your rabbits for a bit?"

"Who goes there?" asked Mr. Wilden. His hearing aids were not turned on, so he hadn't heard what Peter had said.

"It's Peter!" Peter said loudly, as Mr. Wilden slowly approached the front door. "Can I play with your rabbits for a while?"

"My rabbits?" Mr. Wilden said, looking a little confused. "Aren't you too old to be playing with rabbits?"

Peter thought up a suitable response quickly. "It's for a school science project," he said. "And it won't take long."

Mr. Wilden seemed convinced enough by this explanation. "For school, eh?" he said. "Sure. Knock yourself out!" Then Mr. Wilden turned around to walk back to his sofa.

Peter was moving as fast as he could now. He was excited to put his brilliant plan into action.

"Over there looks good," he said to himself, eyeing a muddy spot beside the shed.

He placed the carrot on the ground. Then he turned the box upside down, and gently placed it over the carrot. He took the pen, lifted up one end of the box, and carefully propped up that end with the pen. He had just created a beautifully simple rabbit trap.

"And that," Peter proudly announced, "is what you do to catch yourself a rabbit!"

Peter knew Mr. Wilden had at least thirty rabbits in or around his barn. That was the reason he had chosen to come here in the first place. He picked a light-colored one and carried it over to his trap. He placed it down gently, and then just like he had predicted, the rabbit quickly went for the carrot. It bumped the felt pen on the way in, causing the box to fall and trap it inside.

Peter then put his foot on top of the box, making it impossible for the rabbit to escape. He crouched down and put both hands on top of the box, and then lightly slid it back and forth a few times. He did this gently to ensure that the rabbit inside wouldn't be hurt by his little stunt.

After about thirty seconds, he lifted up the box. The mud-covered rabbit hopped away, with the end of the carrot hanging out of its mouth.

"Viola!" Peter shouted, impressed by his handiwork. "That was a piece of cake!"

Peter sat down on a log in front of the shed, and kept watching until the rabbit had gone behind a small bush. "That was too easy," Peter said aloud. "Too bad that old guy didn't have something harder."

"Be careful what you wish for," said a voice from behind him.

Peter spun around quickly. The old man was less than two meters away, smiling and rubbing his hands together.

"Hey, wait a second," Peter said to the old man. "I know you didn't follow me here. I would have seen you behind me."

"So?" the old man replied, putting his hands in his pockets and shrugging his shoulders.

"So... that means... you got here before me," Peter answered. "But how did you know I'd come here?"

"Because," the man answered, taking a few steps closer to Peter, "I am also extremely good at solving things. I knew you'd come here because that's exactly what I would have done."

"Okay, okay," Peter said, standing up so he could be at

eye level with the old man. "But why do you care? Who are you? Are you a salesman from a toy store or magic store or something?"

The old man let out a giggle, which turned into a roaring laugh. Then his laugh became hoarse, and ended in a disgusting cough. Peter was worried for a second that the old guy was going to have a heart attack right then and there.

Once the old man had caught his breath enough to speak, he sat down. "I most certainly am not a salesman," he said, still straining a bit to breathe properly. "This is not about money, Peter. It's actually an extremely serious matter th—"

"Peter?" Peter said, rudely interrupting the old man mid-sentence. "How do you know my name?"

The old man was unfazed by the interruption. "I heard you say it when you were calling for Mr. Wilden," he replied. "Peter, give me fifteen minutes of your time, after school today. That's all I ask. Just hear me out. I'll be waiting for you by the big sign on the side of the highway. You know, the *Welcome to Clearville* sign. You certainly don't realize it right now, but your help is needed by more than just me. It's needed by everyone."

CHAPTER 7

Peter ended up arriving at school more than an hour late, but managed to give the principal a very believable excuse. He made up a little tale about what had happened while walking his sister to elementary school. He told the principal that his sister had tripped and scraped her knee badly, so they needed to go to a nearby home to ask for help.

All day at school, Peter found himself pondering the meaning of the old man's comment. Although he was confident in his ability to solve puzzles, he had no clue at all how his skill could be *needed to help everyone.*

"And your homework," Mrs. Baird said, "is to finish all of the review questions on pages 121 through 124."

The bell rang and Peter robotically started packing his bag. But he shot back to attention very quickly when he heard Nicola's voice. She was standing right in front of him, and looking directly at him.

"Hey, Pete," she said. "You've always been a whiz at math, right? Do you think you could, um, give me a hand with this homework? I mean, um, if you're not busy…"

Before she had a chance to retract her request, Peter anxiously answered, "Sure! Sure! But, I've gotta meet someone after school, for like, twenty minutes or so. But I could meet you after that."

Nicola's impatient friends were staring daggers at her from just outside the classroom door. "Cool," she said. "So, uh, just come to my place when you're done. At say, like, four or so? Thanks, Pete. I owe you one."

Peter noticed that his heart was now racing and his palms were cold and sweaty. Even though he knew Nicola was only looking for a way to get her homework done quickly, deep down he hoped he could find some way to get her to become his girlfriend.

Not wanting to waste any time, Peter stuffed everything in his backpack and bolted out the door. He wanted to get through his meeting with the old man as quickly as possible. He had to make sure he wouldn't be even a minute late to get to Nicola's after.

CHAPTER 8

At three fifteen, Peter arrived at the arranged meeting place, the area near the *Welcome to Clearville: Population 4500* sign on the highway into town. The old man was supposed to be waiting there for Peter, but hadn't arrived yet. Peter looked around as he walked through the dirt and tall grass, wondering which direction the old man would come in from.

"Why on earth does he wanna meet me on the side of the highway?" Peter asked himself. "There's absolutely nothing here."

"And the fact that there is nothing here," the old man suddenly said, catching Peter completely by surprise, "is precisely why I chose it."

Peter quickly spun around to face the old man. He was definitely not there five seconds ago. It was as if he had appeared there out of thin air.

"How did you...?" Peter said, in complete and utter shock. "What are you? Some sort of magician?"

"C'mon Peter," the old man laughed. "We both know magic isn't real. It's just smoke and mirrors. Please don't disappoint me by saying you can't figure out where I was."

Since Peter was quite proud of his ability to solve things, he quickly began thinking. He scanned the area nearby the old man, and his mind raced through all of the various possibilities. One by one, he quickly eliminated the improbable ones.

Before sixty seconds had elapsed, he had pieced it together. Peter pointed toward the long and narrow mirror which was lying face down in the dirt and grass. The old man had obviously been holding up the mirror and hiding behind it.

"You were doing nothing more than just standing behind a mirror," Peter said. "And since the terrain around here all looks the same, the reflection of the ground in the mirror blended in with the surroundings perfectly. You were hiding behind the mirror while I walked down the road."

Peter stood proudly with his hands on his hips, and continued, "So am I right, or am I right?"

The old man starting applauding, but with very long and slow claps. He was not congratulating Peter on a job well done, but instead seemed to be mocking him. Peter became quite irritated, and took a few steps closer to the old man.

"What's your problem?" Peter asked him. "You said you needed me to solve puzzles, right? And I just did. And now you're laughing at me?"

The old man didn't even flinch, but simply returned Peter's glare. "On a scale of one to ten," he said, "with ten being very difficult, this silly little trick of mine would be... let's say... a two. Only a two!"

Now both angry and confused, Peter threw his arms up in the air. "Stop right there!" he yelled at the old man. "Silly little trick?! Two out of ten?! What on earth are you talking about? Look, I think I've played along with your games for long enough. Either you tell me exactly what's going on, or I'll run to the nearest house I can find and call the cops. I'll tell them some weird old guy is wandering around and scaring kids."

The old man sighed and put his wrinkled hands in his pockets. He looked slowly up to the sky, and then back at Peter. "Alright," he said calmly. "I owe you an explanation. Peter, this is not about me. Nor is it about playing silly games. It's not a game at all. It's actually very, very serious. I need your help. No, let me rephrase that. *We* need your help. And by we, I mean everyone. So let me start from the—"

"Hold up!" Peter replied, cutting the old man off. "I'll be honest with you too. I like the fact that you are into puzzles. I've never met anyone who likes them as much as me. But solving puzzles and being *needed by everyone* are two completely different things."

The old man stayed quiet, waiting for Peter to continue.

"But when we met this morning," Peter said, "I promised you I'd hear you out. So hurry up and tell me your story, before I change my mind."

They walked a few meters to a place where there were some piles of dirt large enough to sit down on. Peter motioned for the man to sit down first, and then sat beside him.

CHAPTER 9

"I'll try to make this as short and simple as possible," the old man said. "But it won't make sense unless I explain everything, from start to finish.

"You have obviously noticed the awful storms that have been occurring more and more frequently recently. And you are probably aware that meteorologists, from all over the world, have been unable to come up with any explanation about what's causing them.

"Well, the laws of nature are actually not the only things that influence the weather. As far-fetched as this may sound, many aspects of weather are controlled by supernatural beings.

"For the sake of simplicity, let's call these supernatural beings *weather gods*. These weather gods are the only reason that life on our planet, and countless other planets, has been able to survive.

"Here's how it works. For each inhabited planet in the universe, one weather god is sent for a span of fifty years. While there, they do everything in their power to limit the devastation that the environment can cause. They change the direction of hurricanes, shorten the length of droughts, and even reduce the magnitude of earthquakes. They use their powers to help keep planets habitable, and ensure the creatures on those planets remain safe.

"But each planet is very different. Most are quite small, and many don't even have seasons. Obviously, those ones are extremely easy to manage. Those are the places that all weather gods hope to go to. It's like a fifty-year holiday, where they rarely have to do any work.

"On the other hand, Earth is one of the most challenging and difficult planets to be sent to. Because of its size and the complexity of the environment here, it's unbelievably hard to manage.

"Earth's current weather god is named Zoltan Screed XVI. Zoltan is very young, well at least as far as weather gods go. And Earth is his first assignment. However, Zoltan never expected to be sent here.

"Zoltan is quite clever, but incredibly lazy. And Zoltan knew how the planet assignments were made. He knew that once every fifty years, the twelve lead weather gods held an anonymous vote in a secluded chamber. They wrote their votes on small pieces of paper, put them in a special box, and the votes would be counted the following morning.

"So Zoltan snuck into the chamber at night and changed some of the names. But he was caught. And as a punishment, he was assigned to Earth.

"Since it was a punishment, Zoltan put very little effort into his work. He quickly noticed that when he did very little, the weather caused horrific damage. And in a very sick way, he felt some sort of satisfaction watching the people of Earth suffer."

The old man paused. For the last few minutes, Peter

had seemed very distracted.

"Peter," he said, "you clearly have somewhere else you want to be, don't you?"

"What do you mean?" Peter replied.

"You have looked at your watch seven times since I began telling this story. Seven times. School is out for the day, and you're too young to work. So my best guess is that you are going to meet someone. Probably a girl, right?"

Peter tried to hide his embarrassment, but the old man had just hit the nail on the head.

"My story is nowhere near finished," the old man said, "but I have a better idea."

The old man reached into his small bag and pulled out a DVD.

"Take this home," he said to Peter while handing it to him. "Watch it. I never expected someone like you to believe any of this without some kind of proof. Well, this is your proof. If it convinces you, then come back here at the same time tomorrow."

Peter quickly put it into his bag. "Okay," he replied, checking his watch again.

"Now off you go to your girl!" the old man said. "But remember to watch the DVD! Tonight!"

"Don't worry," Peter answered quickly while running to his bike, "I will!"

It was only 3:37. He'd easily make it to Nicola's before four o'clock.

But while riding toward her house, he didn't feel the anticipation and nervousness that he usually did before talking to Nicola. Instead, he couldn't stop thinking about the amazing story he had just heard.

"Worry about that later," he said to himself. "Don't

blow your chance with Nik!"

CHAPTER 10

Time at Nicola's went by way too fast. He spent just over an hour helping her out with math and joking around. Hanging out with Nicola seemed so easy and natural when her new friends weren't around.

As he rode home, he tried to convince himself that one day Nicola would ditch her new friends and become his girlfriend. He already knew all of the places they would hang out together.

He got home just before five thirty. Surprisingly, no one else was back yet. His mom and dad were probably busy at work and had to stay later than usual. And he figured that Bradley and Sophia were most likely with friends.

"Lucky!" he said to himself. He knew this was his chance to watch the DVD the old man had given him, as he wouldn't be able to if anyone else was home.

He took the DVD out of his backpack and put it on the coffee table. He wasn't exactly sure how he felt about watching it. The whole idea of a supernatural being destroying the world by altering the weather was absolutely preposterous. Peter had a scientific mind, and would only believe claims supported by evidence and facts. But despite all of his doubts, he couldn't deny his intrigue.

"Well, here goes nothing," he said while putting it into the DVD player.

The video began with the old man standing next to the *Welcome to Clearville* sign. It was exactly the same place Peter had met him earlier that afternoon. The camera was completely still, so Peter guessed that the old man had set it up on a tripod or something.

"This video is being shot with one camera," the old man said, *"which will run the whole time, without being stopped. Trust me, there will be no camera tricks."*

About thirty or forty meters behind the old man, a tall man wearing a hooded cloak walked in from the left.

"The man standing back there is Zoltan," the old man said. *"He may not look scary, but let me assure you that what you are about to see will terrify you. Anyways, let's start the demonstration. As you can see, Zoltan is standing over there, by himself, in the middle of the field. And it's exactly noon. If you don't believe me, look at the shadow being cast by the population sign. The weather is clear and sunny, which you can obviously see for yourself."*

The old man then turned around and yelled to Zoltan, "Zoltan, a demonstration please! How about a... a sudden storm! Rain, wind, thunder, lightning, the works! But take it easy on the hail. I don't want the camera to break."

Zoltan nodded his head and lifted his arms into the air. He yelled something up at the sky, but it wasn't in any language that Peter was familiar with. Zoltan kept looking upwards, as if he were ordering the sky to do something.

Within seconds, huge black clouds filled the sky. A powerful wind immediately followed the clouds. Then the loud and heavy rain started.

Peter's jaw dropped. Less than a minute earlier, he had been looking at a clear and sunny day. Now he was watching an intense storm. It was impossible. It was absolutely, completely impossible. But the camera had never stopped. There were no tricks. So what had just happened?

"That's enough Zoltan!" the old man said.

Zoltan lowered his arms and looked ahead again. The rain and wind died down within seconds, and the clouds quickly vanished.

The old man, soaked by the storm, walked up closer to the camera.

"That is just a small portion of what Zoltan is capable of," he said. "He can do anything he wants with the weather."

The old man turned around to face Zoltan again. "Let's see a tornado!" he said. "I want to make sure Peter is one hundred percent convinced! But not too close by. Do it over there somewhere, where nothing will get damaged."

Just like before, Zoltan raised his arms and began mumbling incoherently at the sky.

About twenty seconds later, an enormous tornado formed about one or two kilometers away from them.

"Hold on, Peter," the old man said. "Let me zoom in the camera so you can get a better look."

As the camera zoomed in on the tornado, it became clear that this was the real thing. And it wasn't just any tornado. It was a very, very strong one.

Peter went to pick up the remote so he could stop the DVD, but it slipped right out of his hand and fell back on the coffee table. The mix of excitement and fear had made his hands sweat like crazy.

Zoltan then stopped the tornado, and the old man approached the camera once more.

"A picture is worth a thousand words," he said. "Meet me again tomorrow, and I'll finish my story."

CHAPTER 11

The next day at school, Peter kept replaying in his mind what he had seen on the DVD. He was still trying to wrap his head around the fact that supernatural beings existed. He couldn't decide if he was more amazed or more terrified. Peter wished he had his own supernatural power right now, so he could use to it to speed the clock up to three o'clock.

But Peter would have to wait. Wait and wait and wait, until the clock slowly ticked its way to the final bell of the day.

When it finally did, Peter made a beeline for door. He was the first kid out of the front doors of the school, and was on his bike less than ninety seconds after the bell had rung.

* * *

The old man was standing beside the sign when Peter rode up. Huffing and puffing from how hard he had pedaled, he jumped off his bike, and let it fall to the ground. "I'm all ears," Peter said.

The old man took a deep breath and looked at the curiosity in Peter's eyes. He knew he would have Peter's full attention for the remainder of the tale.

"As you saw clearly in the video," the old man began, "Zoltan can use the weather to do anything he pleases. But his sick and twisted mind led him to *cause* destruction instead of prevent it. He started playing some kind of game with himself, where he tried to make each new storm stronger than the previous one. The more powerful he made them, the more people suffered. And the more they suffered, the more he enjoyed it.

"And that's where I came into the picture. I joined together with representatives from numerous other countries, and we pleaded for mercy. We offered Zoltan anything he wanted. Any extravagance he could imagine. Unfortunately, material goods were of no interest to him.

"Thankfully, he did provide us with one window of opportunity. He said that he would stop the destruction, his only form of entertainment, if we could provide him with an equally satisfying entertainment. Believe it or not, games and puzzles were that entertainment. And since I was the best at making challenging ones, Zoltan selected me to be the one to create his puzzles. As long as I filled Zoltan's days by providing him with challenging new games and puzzles, he left the people of earth alone.

"But Peter, this started over twenty-five years ago. Look at me now. I'm old. For the last couple years, my mind hasn't been what it once was. Zoltan's boredom with my substandard puzzles over the last two years has caused him to go back to the only other form of entertainment he knows, causing destruction by messing with the weather.

"I need someone to replace me. I've been searching for ages. For over half a year. And finally, I've found my replacement. You."

"Your replacement?" Peter answered in disbelief.

"Exactly," the old man said. "You can take over for me. You can become the one who makes the puzzles. And then Zoltan will stop causing all of these storms. People will be safe again."

Peter was speechless. He was overwhelmed. But before he could respond, he needed some time to think.

"Sleep on it," the old man said, as if he had just read Peter's mind. "Come back tomorrow and tell me your decision."

CHAPTER 12

The next day after school, Peter went to meet the old man again. The ball was in Peter's court now, so the old man waited patiently for Peter to speak first. But in his mind, he already knew what Peter was about to say.

"I'll do it," Peter said.

The man approached Peter with a smile and shook his hand. "Well, first things first," the old man said. "Allow me to formally introduce myself. I'm Leonardo Alexander Winchester."

"So you do have a name," Peter joked. "Nice to meet you, Mr. Winchester."

"The pleasure is all mine," Mr. Winchester responded. "And I look forward to getting to know you better. But first, let me tell you some good news. I actually met with Zoltan last night. And I told him I was ninety-nine percent sure I had found my replacement."

"And how did he react?" Peter asked. "I bet he laughed his head off."

"Actually, he was quite excited by the idea," Mr. Winchester said. "But he will only allow you to replace me if you can solve a series of puzzles. And Zoltan himself will create them. He will make eight puzzles for you, and each one will be harder than the previous one. If you can solve all eight, then you will officially replace me. And the date for these challenges has been set. Exactly fifty days from today."

"Fifty days?" Peter replied, not sure if that was a long time or a short time.

"And I managed to get him to agree to two terms," Mr. Winchester continued. "Both of which will help our preparations go more smoothly. Number one: He has agreed to cause no more destruction for the next fifty days. And number two: He has agreed to allow you to recruit three people to join you."

"Join me?" Peter blurted out, feeling a little offended.

Mr. Winchester looked Peter directly in the eyes, wanting to make sure that he had Peter's complete attention. "You are exceptionally clever," he said. "There's no arguing that. But different types of puzzles require different types of skills. Not all of them are solved by brains only."

"I'm not following you," Peter replied, fairly confused.

"Well let me explain it this way," Mr. Winchester continued. "Some puzzles will require more than just intelligence. Some might need strength. Some might need patience. Some might even need things that one person could not do on their own. So you see, you *need* a team."

"A team?!" Peter said. "How and where am I going to find people so quickly? It took you forever to find me. What do you expect me to do? Ask people from school? Ask my relatives?"

Mr. Winchester crossed his arms behind his back and took a deep breath.

"That, Peter," he said, "is precisely who you will ask."

"And how do you propose I persuade them to help me?" Peter said, still quite frustrated.

"I can promise you one thing," Mr. Winchester replied, giggling a little. "Getting three people to join you will be, by far, the easiest part of what lays ahead. So off you go. Once you have assembled your team, the training can begin."

CHAPTER 13

Peter woke up at the crack of dawn the next morning. He looked at the list of potential candidates he had tried to write the night before. He had three columns on his list, one for each of the three types of people he was looking for. He wanted one person with strength, one who was very careful and precise, and one who could think out of the box. He had written four or five names in each column.

He picked up a pen and started crossing off any people he thought would refuse his request. That left him with only two or three in each column. Then he went through the remaining names one by one, thinking about how well he really knew each person.

More quickly than expected, Peter was down to only one name in each row. He had Bradley for *strength*, Nicola for *careful and precise*, and Neil under *think outside of the box*.

Peter figured it was going to be easy to get Neil on board. Even though Neil seemed to always be in his own little world, Peter considered him a close friend. Neil had the habit of talking about the weirdest things at the oddest times, so he was regularly teased by other kids.

Peter was also the target of teasing, so they had formed some sort of bond.

* * *

Peter left home eight minutes earlier than usual, and was now waiting just around the corner from Neil's house.

A few minutes later, the front door opened and Neil walked out, carrying nothing but his lunch bag. When he was almost at the end of his driveway, the door opened again. Neil's mom ran down the driveway and gave Neil his backpack. Peter guessed that this kind of thing probably happened a lot.

Whistling happily as he walked, Neil was heading straight to where Peter was standing. But since Neil wasn't paying attention to anything around him, he hadn't noticed Peter at all.

"Hey, man. What's up?" Peter said, trying not to startle or surprise him.

After finally noticing Peter, Neil responded, "What are you doing here? Your house is the other way."

Peter knew Neil wasn't being rude. This was just another example of how he often spoke before thinking.

"I just thought we could walk in together today," said Peter.

Neil made no attempt to answer Peter. He also showed no expression about whether or not he was happy to walk to school together with someone for a change.

Peter started the speech he had rehearsed earlier. "You remember when you brought your yo-yo to school last week?" he said. "And you did all of those cool tricks? Well, I was up in the attic yesterday, and guess what? I found some old yo-yos up there. I brought one with me. I

44

thought you could check it out and tell me what you think."

"A yo-yo?" Neil replied enthusiastically. "Sure! Let's see it. I wonder if it's a ball bearing one or not? I doubt it, since it's old."

Peter had no idea what Neil was talking about, but he played along. He pulled the yo-yo out of his backpack and handed it to Neil. "Here it is," he said. "What do you make of it? Is it usable? Or should we just throw it out?"

"Wow!" Neil replied excitedly. "This is old school! People stopped using this type, like, five or six years ago." Neil unwound the string and looked at it carefully. "The string is frayed. But if I change it, it should work. Hold on, I think I've got some extras in my bag."

Neil squatted down and opened up his overstuffed backpack. He started digging through it to find a yo-yo string.

"I left the other yo-yos at home," Peter said. "But you can have them too if you want. Why don't you come over after school today? You can check them out. If you want them, they're all yours."

"Really? Are you sure?" Neil replied.

Of course, Peter didn't really have any more yo-yos at home. He just needed an excuse to get Neil to come over.

CHAPTER 14

Peter had trouble paying attention to anything at school for the entire day. He had been continuously rehearsing how to approach Nicola. The final bell of the day was going to ring in just over four minutes, so his nerves were causing his palms and armpits to sweat profusely.

"Chill out," he whispered to himself. He kept reminding himself to stick to the plan.

As soon as the bell started to ring, Peter jumped from his seat and walked directly over to Nicola. She had only just started to put the first of her books in her bag.

"Hey Nik," Peter said, trying to mask his nervousness. "You know that big biology project that's due next month? Mr. Wittbaker said we can do it alone or in pairs, right? Do you wanna go with me? I mean... I'll like... do most of the research. You could be in charge of making the poster."

"Really?" Nicola replied happily, clearly realizing that the offer was a generous one. She knew she would get an *A* if she did the project with Peter. "Yeah, sure," she said with a smile. "But, you know, I'm not so good at science."

"Don't worry," Peter replied. "So... can you come over to my place at four or so today? I'll show you what I've done so far. And I'll explain about the poster and stuff."

"Yeah, no problem," Nicola said as she started toward the door. "First math help and now science. You're the best!"

So both Neil and Nicola were now set to come over to Peter's place after school. The first part of his plan had worked.

CHAPTER 15

Peter rode home as quickly as he could, getting back at 3:17. He needed to have the house to himself when Nicola and Neil arrived. His parents would still be at work, and Bradley had basketball practice today, so that only left Sophia to deal with.

Peter had a simple and clever plan to get Sophia out of the house for a while. At three forty-five, he went up to her room and said he had a favor to ask. He told his sister he really felt like a chocolate bar, but was too lazy to ride all the way to the convenience store to buy one. If she would ride there and buy one for him, then he'd give her enough money to buy some stuff for herself too.

Sweets were few and far between at their house, so she gladly accepted. Peter knew the trip there and back, at her speed, would take at least forty-five minutes.

* * *

Neil rang the doorbell just before four o'clock, and Nicola got there shortly after. Peter didn't have much time to waste, so he got right to the point.

"Look guys," he said, "the real reason I asked you over today has nothing to do with yo-yos or a biology poster."

"What do you mean?" asked Nicola.

"C'mon, follow me," Peter said, leading them into the family room.

Peter had already set up the DVD, so all he had to do was press play. And after it finished, he retold the story he had heard from Mr. Winchester. He tried to cover all of the important points as quickly as possible.

Peter had expected a lot of questions, but got none. They both appeared overwhelmed by the seriousness of what they had just seen and heard. Before Peter even had a chance to ask them if they would help or not, they told him they wanted in. It was almost like they felt they really had no choice. They had just seen what would happen if they didn't try to help.

"But I haven't asked Brad yet," Peter said.

"Brad?" Nicola said excitedly. "Is Brad going to be on our team too?"

Peter had heard the girls at school talking about his *cool and sexy* older brother. Apparently Nicola was also one of his adoring fans. But Peter would have to deal with that later.

"I think I have a plan about asking Brad," Peter said. "I'm going to tell him that we are training for some kind of big athletic competition, and that we want him on our team. I'll tell him it's a really big one, and that people from all over the country will come to compete. Knowing Brad, he'll jump at the chance to enter something like that. There's nothing he loves more than winning something and then bragging about it."

"But what if he checks it out and finds out it's not real?" Nicola asked.

"I know how to fool him," said Neil. "My cousin, the one in university, is majoring in media and design. He could create a believable poster in his sleep! He's got all of the software on his computer at home. I'm sure he'd do it for us. Well, if we pay him, I mean. And if we pay him enough, I bet he'd make a fake website too, just in case Brad tries to check it out online."

Peter gave Neil a high-five.

"Awesome plan!" Peter said. "But how long will it take?"

"For the right price, I can get him to do it tonight," Neil answered.

Peter ran upstairs. He had a hidden stash of money in his sock drawer, which he had earned from delivering newspapers and mowing lawns.

"Okay, here's all the money I've got," he said. "There must be least fifty or sixty bucks in total. But don't offer it all right away. Start at like twenty or so. And if that's not enough, keep offering more and more."

"Cool," Neil replied. "He'll probably go for twenty, but we'll see. Anyway, you just leave it to *the Neilster.*"

Neil went to the front door and started tying up his shoes. Once he was out the door, he turned around and yelled, "I'll be back with your poster before you go to bed!"

CHAPTER 16

The next morning, poster in hand, Peter walked out of his room and down the stairs. When he got to the kitchen, Bradley was alone at the table. The bowl of cornflakes in front of Bradley was big enough for at least three people.

"How's it going?" Peter said.

Bradley responded with only a grunt, and then went back to stuffing his face with cereal.

"Hey Brad," Peter said, sitting down on the other side of the table. "I gotta ask you something."

"No, you can't borrow my bike," Bradley replied coldly, without even looking up from his food. "I'm going to Jason's house after school today, and you know how far away he lives."

"I don't wanna use your bike," Peter said quickly. "Actually, I need your help."

"My help?" Bradley laughed, causing some cornflakes to spray from his mouth. "With what?"

"There's a new outdoor sporting competition," Peter said. "It's called the *Brains and Brawn Championship*. Actually, I've already signed us up for it. I figured since you are the strongest guy in school, and I am the smartest, we could win it in a breeze."

"The what?" Bradley said. "Never heard of it."

"You haven't?" Peter asked. "What about all of the posters that are up all over town?"

Peter unfolded the poster and put it on the table in front of Bradley. Neil's cousin had done a great job. It looked very authentic.

"Like I said, it's new," Peter continued. "It's a pretty big thing, too. It's a national competition."

Bradley looked more intrigued now. "You mean reporters will be there and, like, interview us and stuff?" he asked.

"You got it!" Peter answered. "Well, I mean, as long as we win."

Bradley held up his hand to Peter for a high-five. "Petey, my friend," he said. "You know I never lose. This will be a piece of cake."

Peter gave Bradley the high-five he had been waiting for, and then sat down and poured himself a bowl of cornflakes. Their little white lie had worked perfectly.

CHAPTER 17

At three forty-five that afternoon, Neil came over to Peter's home. Shortly after, Bradley walked out of the house to join them on the front porch. Peter spent a few minutes lying to Bradley about how each four-person team in the *Brains and Brawn Championship* was required to have one girl.

A couple minutes past four o'clock, they watched as Nicola casually walked up the driveway. "Hey Pete, hey Neil," she said while starting up the stairs. Then she saw Bradley sitting behind them. She greeted him in a completely different tone, "Hi, Brad. Remember me?"

Bradley smiled, but didn't say anything back.

Nicola then sat down beside Bradley, and tossed her hair to one side. "C'mon Brad," she said. "You remember me, don't you? You used to pull my pigtails and make me cry."

This comment made all three boys laugh a little.

"Well look at me now!" she continued, standing up and twirling around once. "Sure have grown up, haven't I?"

Bradley watched as Nicola posed in front of them as if she were in a fashion show. "You're gonna be popular when you get to high school," he said. "You're already hotter than most of the chicks there now!"

"Oh?" Nicola giggled, still trying to appeal to Bradley. "C'mon… Now you're teasing!"

Peter stood up and turned around to face everyone. He reminded them that the date of the competition was only seven weeks away. When Nicola heard Peter say that they would be practicing regularly for the next seven weeks, which would mean countless hours around Bradley, she looked like she had just won the lottery.

"This competition is going to be a lot harder than we think," Peter said at the end of his little speech. "But if we prepare well, I think we have a good shot at winning. We start training tomorrow morning. Be at the entrance of Meeks Park at ten. Mr. Winchester will be waiting there for us."

When Peter finally crawled into bed at around midnight, he couldn't stop worrying about how long his crazy lie to Bradley would hold up. When would he have to tell Bradley the truth? And how would he tell him?

CHAPTER 18

The following day, which was Saturday, Peter intentionally arrived at Meeks Park twenty minutes early. He needed a chance to talk to Mr. Winchester before Bradley got there. Mr. Winchester had already arrived, and was setting up some folding chairs under a large tree.

"Before Brad gets here," Peter said hurriedly, "there's something important I need to tell you. In order to put this team together on such short notice, I had to... uh... tell a couple of little white lies."

"Little white lies?" Mr. Winchester responded.

Peter spent the next ten minutes giving a rushed explanation about how Bradley was under the impression that they were preparing for a competition. Mr. Winchester listened carefully to the whole story.

"So you have to go along with it," Peter said at the end of his explanation, "or else he'll quit. And I don't know anyone who could take his spot."

Mr. Winchester nodded his head a few times, and then replied, "I see. Although I'm going to be training your team, you are the leader of it. If you want me to play along with this lie, then that's what I'll do."

55

"Okay," Peter said, not really sure what else to say. "Thanks."

"No need for thanks," Mr. Winchester said back quickly. "It is *I* who should be thanking *you*. If you had turned down my request, then Zoltan would—"

"Hey Pete!" a voice called from behind them. "Didn't you say ten? You're early, aren't you?"

They spun around and saw Neil standing there, wearing baggy shorts and an oversized T-shirt. As Neil approached, he put out his hand to Mr. Winchester.

"You must be the super old dude that Peter said is going to train us," Neil said while shaking Mr. Winchester's hand. "Oh, by the way, I'm Neil."

Peter hung his head and looked at the ground. He couldn't believe the ridiculous comment that had just come out of Neil's mouth.

"Young Neil," Mr. Winchester said politely. "I am indeed the person who will be training you. But what exactly is a *super old dude?*"

Neil giggled, and took a seat on one of the folding chairs.

Very shortly after, Bradley came roaring toward them on his mountain bike. He pulled the back brake hard, causing the back wheel to lock and kick up dust as he ground to a halt just a couple of meters away. He looked at his watch and triumphantly announced, "Made it here in less than six minutes! I guarantee you won't find anyone else this fast in the entire town!"

Mr. Winchester stepped forward and shook Bradley's hand. "You must be Bradley," he said. "Peter has told me a lot about you. With you on this team, we can surely..." Mr. Winchester paused suddenly, as if he were uncomfortable about what he was going to say next.

"Win this... this... competition."

"You bet, dude," Bradley answered, shaking Mr. Winchester's hand so hard that Peter thought he was going to pull the old man's shoulder out of its socket.

"So I guess we are just waiting for Pete's sweetheart to show up now, right?" Neil said.

Peter's ears instantly turned red. Even though most of the other kids in grade seven knew about his crush on Nicola, Bradley certainly didn't. Now it had just become public knowledge.

"Oh, so she's your little girlfriend then, is she?" Bradley asked in a sarcastic tone. "Well, I guess she must be a lot geekier than she looks."

Before Peter could figure out how to respond, they all spotted Nicola walking their way. She was arriving fashionably late by about five minutes. And her outfit and make-up today made her look at least sixteen years old.

Being the only gentlemen in the group, Mr. Winchester walked up to greet her as she approached. "Young lady," he said. "If your mind is even a fraction of your beauty, then you will be the secret weapon that will propel this team to victory."

Nicola felt her cheeks turn a shade of pink. She was hoping that Bradley didn't notice, as she was trying to maintain her *cool and casual* look.

"It's a pleasure to meet you, Nicola," Mr. Winchester continued, lightly shaking her hand.

Nicola sat down on the remaining seat, and Mr. Winchester stood in front of them. "I'm not going to waste your time," he said. "And I'm not going to try to make this sound easier than it is. This competition is going to be very, very hard. You may all look confident right now, but without the proper training and practice, you won't have a chance. You either do this right, or you don't do it at all."

Peter, Nicola, Neil, and Bradley looked back and forth at each other. None of them spoke, which meant they all agreed to take this seriously. But they had no clue how hard their training was going to be.

CHAPTER 19

Their first two weeks of training went by in a flash. They were meeting on Tuesday and Thursday afternoons, plus all day on Saturdays and Sundays. Mr. Winchester had created a training regime that covered the skills he figured they needed the most. They worked on strength and endurance, calculation, perception, and teamwork.

The strength and endurance training was extremely hard for everyone except Bradley. Mr. Winchester explained that some of the challenges would involve some type of pushing, pulling, running, jumping, or lifting. Bradley knew this was his forte, and he loved showing off as much as he could while training. He was always the first to finish any race, and he could lift more than Peter, Neil, and Nicola combined.

"Bradley, Bradley, Bradley," Mr. Winchester said one day after Bradley had finished an obstacle course before the rest were even half-done. "You are built like an ox, but you can run like the wind." This comment, and other similar ones, made Bradley beam with pride.

The calculation training was a breeze for Peter, but was not going so well for the rest of the team. In one of their first calculation training sessions, they were given a pile of thirty small metal blocks, all different sizes and weights. The task was to divide them up into three piles of exactly equal weight. And it had to be performed without the use of any type of scale. Less than thirty seconds after starting, Bradley threw his arms up in defeat and sat on the ground.

"Out of my league!" he announced. "Pete, you got this one. I'll save my energy for the ones that require some strength."

Right after Bradley said that, Mr. Winchester suddenly grabbed Peter's left arm and twisted it behind his back.

"Ouch! Let go!" Peter screamed. "How do you expect me to solve this puzzle when it feels like you're gonna break my arm in half?"

"Let go of my brother, old man!" Bradley yelled, standing up and coming toward Mr. Winchester. "Or I'll pound the crap out of you!"

Mr. Winchester had no intention of hurting Peter, so he let go and spun around to look at Bradley. "We all know Peter is good at these kinds of things," he said in a stern voice. "But as you just witnessed, he was completely useless when I distracted him. You can't depend on him all the time. If Peter loses his concentration, or gets hurt or something during one of the challenges, what are you going to do? Give up? Quit?"

Bradley was fuming. It looked as if he was ready to punch Mr. Winchester in the face. "Look, old man," he said.

Mr. Winchester was also quite upset now, so he quickly responded, "Don't *look old man* me Bradley. I am preparing you so that you can win this thing. If you are planning to give up whenever something looks a little too hard for you, then you have no hope of winning. We don't need any quitters on this team."

Mr. Winchester then walked over to one of the nearby park benches and sat down.

Nicola had been silent throughout the entire ordeal, but she decided to speak up. "I think someone better go and apologize to him," she said. "He wasn't trying to break anyone's arm or make anyone feel stupid. He just wants us to win. Think about how hard it must be to try to teach all of this stuff to us."

"She's right," said Neil, without thinking through how silly his next comment was going to sound. "He's the best coach that money can buy."

"OK, I'll do it," Bradley said first. "I suppose I started this. I'll go fix it."

The others watched as Bradley walked over and sat beside Mr. Winchester. No one could hear what was being said, but less than three minutes after sitting down, Bradley and Mr. Winchester shook hands. Then they both stood up and walked back to the group.

CHAPTER 20

The perception training was their biggest challenge, as none of the four truly understood what or how they were supposed to practice.

In one of the early training sessions, Mr. Winchester asked Neil to open his hand. "OK, let's practice perception for a while," he said to them.

"Dice?" Neil replied, as Mr. Winchester dropped them into his hand.

"The task is very simple," Mr. Winchester continued. "Roll these two until you get a total of seven. That's it."

Neil looked at the other three, not really knowing what to say. He shrugged his shoulders and shook the dice in his hand. Then he rolled them on the ground.

"Did you do it?" Mr. Winchester asked.

Neil looked at the dice. "No," he replied. "I rolled a six and a two, for a total of eight."

"Good math, Einstein," Bradley joked.

"Shut up, Brad!" Neil said back quickly.

Peter jumped in, "C'mon guys. Rolling dice is simply about odds. The odds of rolling a seven are one in six. If you roll six times or more, it's highly likely one of them will be a seven. Neil, pass me those."

Peter rolled a pair of twos. On his second try, he rolled a ten.

Bradley snatched the dice out of Peter's hand before his third attempt. "You guys have no luck," he said. "Leave it to a *real* man to roll a seven."

Bradley rolled an eight. He tried again, but still couldn't get a seven. "Third time lucky!" he proudly announced, holding the dice high above his head.

"You should just give up!" Nicola said loudly. "I guarantee you will not roll a seven this time, or the next time, or the time after that."

"And how could you, little girl, possibly know this?" Bradley asked sarcastically.

"Because if you look closely at those dice," she replied, "you'll see there are no odd numbers on them. They only have twos, fours, and sixes. So you'll never, ever get a total of seven."

Bradley twirled the dice around in his fingers. Once he realized what Nicola was saying was true, he turned to Mr. Winchester and said, "You tricked us, old man! These aren't real dice."

"I most certainly did *not* trick you," Mr. Winchester replied firmly. "If you recall, I put two objects into Neil's hand. And I did not call them dice. It was Neil, followed quickly by the rest of you, who made that assumption."

"That's still pretty tricky though," Neil added, a little flustered about his mistake.

Peter was hoping to put a stop to what seemed like the start of a tense moment. "Calm down, guys," he said. Unfortunately, he hadn't spoken as boldly or loudly as he should have. It appeared as if this argument was going to escalate.

Nicola was the only one still seated. She

uncharacteristically yelled, "Shut up and sit down! It seems to me like you *boys* have had your pride hurt by a *girl.* You guys are pathetic. Think about what happened? Before giving those two dice to Neil, Mr. Winchester said we were going to work on perception. Perception! If you had been listening, you would have known to look more carefully at the dice, instead of just rolling them over and over."

The boys sat back down. They were shocked by Nicola's sudden character change, and also embarrassed by their careless mistake.

Mr. Winchester cleared his throat and then announced, "Thank you, Nicola. I can see you will be needed to keep these boys honest. And boys, let this be a lesson to all of you. We all have weaknesses. I can only hope that all four of you don't share a common one."

"Why are you lecturing *me?*" Bradley asked in an angry tone. "I'm the muscle on this team. Not the brains. I'll leave the geeky stuff to these three."

"Who are you calling geeky?" Neil said, standing up and taking a step toward Bradley.

Bradley stood up too. "You, you geek!" he replied. "And Petey and his little geeky girlfriend!"

Peter needed to do something to calm everyone down. But he was too late, as Neil had already pushed Bradley hard in the chest. Bradley didn't fall, but had to take a couple of steps back to keep his balance.

Once Bradley was standing up straight again, he walked toward Neil. Just before he got close enough to hit him, Nicola jumped between them. "STOP!" she screamed at the top of her lungs. "Please just stop!"

Despite how badly he wanted to throw a punch, Bradley wasn't going to risk hitting a girl to try to get at

Neil. Peter seized the opportunity and quickly said, "Look, I don't care who's geeky and who isn't. What I care about is winning. C'mon, guys. If we spent as much time practicing as we did arguing, we'd be a team to reckon with."

Although this fight had been temporarily averted, Peter wondered how they were going to get through the next six weeks without ripping each other's heads off...

CHAPTER 21

They were now into their third week of training. They had actually made some vast improvements during the first two weeks, but their perception skills were still quite lacking. In an effort to try to help them learn how to notice things better, Mr. Winchester decided to start with a perception challenge today.

He had explained that Zoltan was a big fan of paths, mazes, and *finding the exit* challenges. He wanted them to understand the fact that many of their challenges would require noticing something different than what they thought they were looking for.

Today's perception task was going to help them with this. They were standing at the start of a straight path, about twenty meters or so in length. It was lined with high hedges on both sides. There was a large mirror at the end of the path, with a big red square taped on it. All they had to do was run down the path and touch the red square.

"Peter, give it a go!" Mr. Winchester announced. In the past couple of weeks, the old guy was starting to talk more and more like a teenager.

"Are you sure you can run that far?" Bradley said in a

high-pitched voice.

Mr. Winchester turned to Bradley. "We all know you are the fastest," he said. "But this time it's not about speed, it's about perception. C'mon, support your team."

Bradley was a little taken aback by these strong words, but not enough to apologize.

Mr. Winchester looked back at Peter. "There's no starting gun," he said. "You may begin whenever you are ready."

Peter started to run down the path. Actually, it was more of a jog than a run. He was looking all around him to spot the trick that was hidden somewhere in the next twenty meters. He wanted to make sure he didn't step through a tripwire or fall into a camouflaged hole in the ground. His eyes darted everywhere as he slowly and cautiously jogged down the path. He could also see his reflection growing in size, which meant he was running out of time to spot the trick.

"Where's the stupid trap?" Peter asked himself as he jogged past the halfway mark.

He looked back up at his reflection again. He was less than five meters away now, so he could see the red square clearly.

He slowed down a little, and then realized the one place he hadn't checked yet, *up*. "What's going to fall on me, old man?" he said to himself while looking up.

Unfortunately, his upward inspection didn't reveal anything. There was nothing up there other than the blue sky and a few thin clouds.

He was almost at the mirror now, so he slowed to a walk for the final meter and a half. He was just about to put out his hand to touch the red square when his face and his knee simultaneously banged into something.

Peter brought up his hands and felt a large, thick pane of glass in front of him. The trick was simpler than he had thought. Mr. Winchester had set a clear pane of glass twenty centimeters in front of the mirror. The trick was that the red square could only be touched if Peter were to move or break the glass.

"Okay, I get it," Peter said. "Make sure you always carry supplies, right? Things like a hammer or whatever."

"This challenge can be won without breaking or moving anything," Mr. Winchester answered. "Remember, it's about perception."

Peter was stumped. He had no clue what to do next.

"Allow me to demonstrate," Mr. Winchester said. "Neil, Nicola, Bradley, follow me."

Mr. Winchester, followed by the other three, started walking along the path. About two meters before reaching the end, he stopped and turned to his right. Then he casually walked through a twenty-centimeter gap in the hedge. Shortly after, he reappeared between the glass and the mirror.

"You were too preoccupied looking for a complex trick or trap," he said. "You walked right past the gap without even noticing it. If you look too hard, you'll miss the easy ones."

Peter followed the others through the gap, shaking his head in disappointment.

"Shake it off, Petey," Bradley said while patting him on the shoulder. "I would have run past it too. I bet Neil and Nik would have done the same. Don't beat yourself up."

"Thanks," Peter replied. Unfortunately, Bradley's words of encouragement did little to make Peter feel any better. But at least Bradley was finally offering up some positive comments.

CHAPTER 22

After a long, slow, and boring week of school, it was finally Friday again. Peter couldn't wait for their weekend training to begin. The puzzle solving and camaraderie were becoming more and more fun as time went on. And on top of that, he would get to spend close to twelve hours in the presence of Nicola over the next two days.

Peter ran for the door the instant the bell rang. He was planning to be the first out again today.

"Hold on, Peter," Mrs. Baird said. "I need to talk to you for a minute before you go home."

"Me?" Peter asked, sounding a little irritated.

"Yes, you," she replied sarcastically. "You don't see any other Peters in this room, do you?"

Peter could hear the jocks having a good laugh about that one. "Enjoy your date with the teacher!" he heard from one of them as they left the room.

Peter sat back down at his desk. Once most of the students had left and the room became quieter, Mrs. Baird approached him.

"Thank you for staying," she said. "Actually, I just wanted to remind you about tomorrow. Remember a few months back when I asked you if you could help tutor math to the weaker students on Saturday mornings?"

Peter recalled the conversation. He also had a feeling about what she was going to say next.

"Well, your name is on the list for tomorrow," she said. "It's only two hours, from nine to eleven. So we'll see you tomorrow morning, Peter. And thank you for volunteering to help."

"Okay, Mrs. Baird," Peter replied politely. But inside, he was cursing himself for having agreed to do it in the first place.

Although he was upset that they would have to cancel their morning training tomorrow, he tried to convince himself that being able to train in the afternoon was better than nothing. He would need to phone everyone when he got home to tell them about the change in plans.

Peter got on his bike and started heading home. But as he approached the corner of Beaverbrook Street, a new plan popped into his mind. He would still phone Neil and Mr. Winchester, but decided to drop by Nicola's place and tell her in person. Basically, he had just created a convenient excuse to go and see her.

* * *

He could feel his heart rate speed up as he got closer and closer to Nicola's home. Even though he saw her all the time now, today was different. Neil and Bradley wouldn't be there. This would be the perfect chance to finally ask her out.

The cul-de-sac Nicola lived on was right in front of him, but Peter was way too nervous. He decided to do a big loop through other streets to give his nerves a chance to calm down. He actually ended up doing the loop a total of four times.

Now he was finally ready, and he knew exactly what he was going to say. After telling her about tomorrow, he was going to casually ask her to go out for a movie and dinner next Friday.

"Don't chicken out again," he said to himself, finally riding up to Nicola's house.

He got off his bike and leaned it up against one of the trees in the front yard. He knew Nicola was always outside when it was sunny, so he decided to just walk through to the backyard without ringing the doorbell. If she was in the backyard and he rang the doorbell, she wouldn't be able to hear anyway, right?

When he got to the side of her house, his heart almost stopped. Bradley's bike was leaning up against the side of her house! Peter couldn't believe his eyes. His mind started racing. Was Bradley putting the moves on Nicola? Was he that much of a loser? Or maybe they were secretly going out already, and just hiding it so they wouldn't hurt Peter's feelings.

One thing was for sure. He couldn't be seen by either of them right now. He had to get out of there. But at the same time, he needed a peek at what was going on in the backyard. As quietly as possible, he edged closer and closer to the back of the house.

Just before he got to where he would have been able to see them, he heard Bradley's loud, stupid voice. Peter couldn't make out exactly what Bradley was saying, but it was probably another one of his many stories about how strong or cool he was. And then he heard a happy giggle from Nicola. From the tone of her laugh, Peter deduced that she obviously was crazy about Bradley. They were either already a couple, or were going to be soon.

Peter had heard enough. He tiptoed back to his bike, and quietly pushed it to the end of the cul-de-sac. The he got on and started peddling home in a depressed trance.

When he finally got home, he forced himself to call Neil and Mr. Winchester to tell them about tomorrow. Then he walked upstairs and locked himself in his room.

CHAPTER 23

The next morning, Peter managed to get to tutoring on time, but was literally shaking from how angry he still felt. He looked so flustered and distracted that Mrs. Baird asked him numerous times if everything was okay.

He couldn't believe his backstabbing brother! How could Bradley just come and steal his girlfriend? Well, she wasn't technically his girlfriend yet, but he was getting closer and closer to finally asking her out on a date. But with Bradley in the picture now, everything was ruined! He couldn't compete with Bradley. Bradley was cooler, taller, older, better at sports. He didn't stand a chance.

"Peter?" Mrs. Baird said while lightly tapping him on the shoulder. "If you're not feeling well, that's one thing. But if you do feel fine, then you can't just sit there and ignore everyone's questions. Either help the other students, or go home. You're being very rude to everyone who came here today."

Peter wanted to snap at her, but knew he would regret it later if he did. "I'm sorry, Mrs. Baird," he said. "I barely slept last night, and I have a really bad headache. I want to help, but I just can't seem to concentrate on anything today. Maybe you're right. Maybe I should go home."

"Alright," she replied. "If that's what you feel is best."

"I'm really, really sorry," he repeated. "I promise I'll come in twice next month to make up for today."

Peter left the classroom and started walking down the empty hallway. When he passed Bradley's old locker, number 418, he punched it hard.

"Girlfriend thief!" he yelled, without stopping to see if anyone had seen or heard him.

He got on his bike and started toward Meeks Park. It was only a quarter past ten, so he had almost two hours to figure out what to say to Bradley and Nicola when he got there.

Peter started pedaling harder and harder, until he was going as fast as he could. He saw the turnoff to the park coming up, but since he had no reason to get there this early, he just kept going straight.

"I hate you Brad!" he screamed to the top of his lungs. "I hate you! I hate you!"

* * *

Twenty minutes later, Peter was totally exhausted. He had been riding south on the highway out of town, and was actually pretty close to the neighboring city of Stoneburg now. Plus he was unbelievably thirsty. He knew there was a gas station coming up soon where he could buy himself a soft drink, so he kept heading in the same direction.

A few minutes later, drink in hand, Peter watched the cars roar by on the highway. "Screw them!" he yelled, kicking his bike over intentionally. He had just decided not to go at all today. He was still way, way too angry.

CHAPTER 24

It was almost twelve thirty, so Neil, Nicola, and Bradley had been patiently waiting for Peter at their usual rendezvous point at Meeks Park for quite a while. Mr. Winchester was of course there too, but he was off near the river setting up a few things for training. Everyone was starting to get concerned, as Peter had never been late before.

"What should we do?" Nicola asked the two boys. "Maybe his bike got a flat or something. Why doesn't one of us ride toward his house and see if we can find him?"

"Well I'm definitely the fastest," answered Bradley. "I can make it home and back in, like, twelve minutes or less."

"OK, go for it," Nicola said. "Me and Neil will wait here. But whether you find him or not, make sure you come back right away."

"Be back in a flash!" said Bradley as he mounted his bike. He then put on quite an impressive display of speed as he rode away.

"You know, it's really not like Peter to be late," Nicola said to Neil. "I mean, I've like known him my whole life, and I can't remember him ever not being on time."

"Well there's a first for everything, right?" Neil replied. "But I wouldn't worry. Anyway, Brad will be back before you know it."

* * *

Bradley sizzled down the highway. No sign of Peter anywhere. Then he leaned hard to make the sharp left onto Beaverbrook Street. But Peter was nowhere to be seen. When he skidded to a stop in the driveway, he checked his watch.

"Ladies and Gentlemen!" he announced to the non-existent audience. "I believe we have a new record! Five minutes and twenty-five seconds!"

Peter's bike wasn't in the garage, so Bradley figured that meant he wasn't at home. "I wonder where the little wiener is?" he asked aloud.

* * *

Peter had spent the entire afternoon biking around aimlessly, occasionally stopping here and there to grab a snack or use the washroom. But he made sure to stay clear of any places that Neil, Bradley, or Nicola might come looking for him.

He knew his parents would get angry if he wasn't home for dinner, so he started to head home at about half past five. He ended up arriving home at 5:53, just a few minutes before their regular dinner time.

As he was slowly pushing his bike up the driveway, his mom came running out of the front door. "Peter, we've been worried sick!" she said. "What happened? Are you okay?"

"Huh?" Peter mumbled in reply.

"Nicola came here twice," she continued. "Neil phoned half a dozen times. And Bradley rode all over town looking for you. We were just about to call the police!"

"I'm fine," Peter replied without looking up. He was trying to think up a quick lie to explain his vanishing act.

"You're fine? That's it?" his mom asked angrily.

Peter had thought of his lie. "Actually, after the tutoring," he said, "Mrs. Baird asked if I would mow her lawn for five bucks. Her husband hurt his back or something like that. Anyway, I need the money and I felt a little sorry for her, so I said okay."

Peter's mom didn't reply. She stood with her arms crossed, blocking his path to the door. When Peter finally looked up at her, she could immediately see the distress in his face. Although she knew he was lying through his teeth, something had obviously happened that a young boy wasn't comfortable telling his mom about. She stepped aside and let Peter walk past her into the house.

"And I've got a stomachache," he said while walking to his room, "so I'm gonna skip dinner."

CHAPTER 25

Peter woke up as early as possible the next morning. He had to make sure he was out of the house well before Bradley got out of bed. He was going to just bike around and kill time, and then show up for their training at exactly ten o'clock. He still didn't know what he was going to say to Nicola and Bradley, even though he'd played through countless scenarios in his mind last night.

He ate and dressed quickly, and then walked out the back door out at 6:52. Was three hours of riding around, with no real place to go, going to be long enough to think?

* * *

When Peter arrived at the park entrance, Neil, Nicola and Bradley were all waiting there for him. Mr. Winchester was sitting on one of the benches by the river.

"You're alive!" Neil yelled, as if he were acting out the scene of a sci-fi movie.

"Pete!" Nicola said while running toward him. She was hugging him even before he had a chance to speak. "Are you okay? I was soooo worried."

"Yeah, man. Me too," said Bradley. "You weird out or something yesterday?"

"Me?" Peter said quietly, stuck for words. It was the first time in his life that Nicola had hugged him. But if she liked Bradley so much, then why was she hugging Peter? Now he was even more confused.

"Anyway," Nicola said, finally releasing her hug after a good ten seconds or so. "You're alright. And that's all that matters!"

"Yeah, I'm cool," Peter replied, feeling re-energized by the big hug.

"And more importantly," Bradley said, "Happy thirteenth!"

Peter had been so busy obsessing about Bradley and Nicola that he had forgotten his own birthday.

"Happy Birthday!" Nicola announced loudly. "Here you go!" She reached in her bag and pulled out a small present.

"We all pitched in," said Bradley. "And then on Friday after school, I went to the mall and bought it. But Nik was worried that I'd lose it before today. You know how messy my room is, right? Anyway, so after I bought it, I went straight to her house to give it to her for safekeeping."

Peter felt ashamed now. Bradley wasn't secretly dating Nicola at all. The only reason he was at Nicola's house was to drop off Peter's present. Peter had just spent the last forty hours worrying about nothing.

"Open it, man!" yelled Neil. "You're gonna love it!"

Peter ripped off the wrapping paper and opened the small box. It was a brand new digital wristwatch.

"That's quite a nice watch," Mr. Winchester said while he walked over to join the group. "You can test it out right now, as the first part of today's training is a timed challenge."

CHAPTER 26

The next month or so of training went by quickly for everyone, and Mr. Winchester was pleased with their progress. School was now out for summer, so they would be training every day for the final week. They only had six days to go, so Mr. Winchester was giving them harder and harder tasks to try these days. This morning's challenge was going to be their hardest to date.

"Good morning, everyone," Mr. Winchester said. "In order to simulate the real thing, I will be only watching this time. Everything you need for the challenge is in that box over there by the tree, and the instructions are in the envelope pinned to the tree. Good luck."

Mr. Winchester took a few steps back, and sat on a tree stump that would give him a clear view of everything. "And before you ask," he said. "Speed does count, so get a move on it!"

They quickly jogged over to the tree. While Bradley opened the box, Peter took the envelope off the tree and removed the note inside. He read the notes' contents aloud slowly and clearly.

Task: Get all 6 plastic rings to the opposite side of the river.
Tools: A 5-meter rope, a rock
Rules: Nobody touches the water
Time Limit: 15 minutes

HI READER! (^_^)
CAN YOU SOLVE THIS PUZZLE?

Peter quickly pushed the start button on his new watch. Bradley removed the plastic rings, rope, and rock from the box. Each ring was roughly the size of a dog collar and the thickness of a hot dog. The rope was thick and heavy. And the rock was approximately the size of a baseball. In silence, all four of them looked back and forth between the items and the river in front of them.

Peter estimated the river as being somewhere around ten meters across. It was slightly narrower in a few places, but nowhere was it any less than seven or eight meters wide.

Neil spoke up first. "Brad, you're pretty strong," he said. "Think you could throw them over?"

Bradley tossed one of the rings back and forth between his hands a couple of times. "No way," he said. "They're too light."

Nicola was holding one end of the rope. "And how are we supposed to use the rope?" she asked. "It's not long enough."

"You aren't supposed to be able to get it right away, Nik." Neil said rudely. "It's called a *challenge!*"

"Shut up, Neil!" Peter said angrily. He didn't have any time to play peacemaker right now. "If you have a suggestion, then speak. Otherwise, keep your mouth shut."

Peter glanced at his watch. Over two minutes had already elapsed.

"Well, I'm pretty sure I could chuck the rock over," Bradley suggested. "It's round, so it'd be easy to throw." But after realizing how useless that would be, he put the rock down and looked to Peter for a better idea.

A total of four minutes had gone by, and they still didn't have a feasible plan. Peter picked up the rope and turned toward the other three. "The rope has to hold the answer," he said to them.

"Hey Pete," Neil said a little hesitantly, recalling Peter's comment about when he should and shouldn't speak. "Remember when we were on that camp? And we didn't have enough rope to put up our tarp? Then, Mr. Davidson unwound the rope, and showed us it was actually made of three thinner ropes?"

Peter looked at Neil. "Bingo!" he shouted. "Neil, you start unwinding it. Once you're done, tie the ends together. Then we'll have a fifteen-meter rope."

Peter felt his heartbeat speed up. They were onto something. But they only had nine minutes left. "Think Peter, think," he said to himself. "Figure it out. What are you missing?"

Nicola timidly decided to offer a suggestion. "Pete, there are trees along both sides of the river," she said. "Couldn't we tie it to one of the trees?" But then she realized this wouldn't lead to anything, so she backpedaled. "But wait, I guess that wouldn't help."

Peter turned to face Nicola. "You might be onto something," he said. "Let's roll with it."

Peter's eyes were darting around like mad, trying to spot the solution that hadn't come to mind yet. He kept looking back and forth between the rings, rope and trees.

"Only six more minutes," Nicola said nervously while looking at Peter's watch. "We're running out of time. We gotta try something."

"The rock," Peter said to himself, pacing around in a circle. He picked up the rock and pulled it within inches of his face. "Stupid rock! What am I supposed to do with you?"

And then, like magic, the solution came to him. He turned to Bradley, who was sitting cross-legged on the ground. "Brad, tie one end of the rope to the rock, and then throw it across the river!"

"Why?" Bradley asked. "How's that—"

"Just do it!" Peter yelled, cutting him off.

Slightly over four minutes remained. Peter turned to Neil and said, "Neil, me and you are gonna climb that tree. You hold the rope, and I'll carry the rings."

"Rock tied up Petey!" Bradley said from behind them. "Now watch this sucker fly!"

He threw it with such force that the entire high school baseball team would have been in awe. It easily cleared the river by a few of meters.

"Neil!" Peter yelled impatiently. "C'mon, let's go!"

Neil started up the tree first, with the rope held tightly in one hand. Peter put the rings on his left wrist, and started up behind Neil. Once Neil was about two meters above the ground, Peter said to him, "Okay, that should be good enough. The rest of the work will be up to our good old friend, Mr. Gravity."

He carefully passed the rings up to Neil and said, "Neil, put the rings on the rope, and then hold it up as high as you can."

Neil did as instructed. Just as Peter had hoped, the

rings were sliding down the rope.

"And whenever they start to slow down," Peter added, "shake the rope a bit, and that will keep them moving."

Neil only had to shake the rope a couple of times, as the rings seemed to be sliding down quite smoothly. In less than a minute, they had slid the entire length of the rope.

The instant the rings reached the other side of the river, Peter glanced at his watch. "Game, set, match!" he yelled in celebration. "And we still have two minutes to spare!"

Down below them, Bradley gave Nicola a high-five. Peter and Neil also joined them for more high-fives as soon as they had made their way back down the tree.

"You're the man!" Bradley said to Peter, pointing at Peter's chest. "The man!"

They all turned around to see Mr. Winchester, who was still sitting on the tree stump. Just as Bradley was about to brag about their performance, Mr. Winchester stood up, and spoke first.

"I am impressed," he said. "You just might have it in you to win this thing." Mr. Winchester looked at his watch, then back at the group. "Let's call it a day. You've earned yourselves an afternoon off. See you tomorrow morning. I'll have something much harder ready."

HI READER! (^_^)
ENJOYING THE PUZZLES? WANT MORE?
HEAD OVER TO MY WEBSITE (pjnichols.com)
YOU'LL FIND SOME REALLY COOL, HEAD-SCRATCHING PUZZLES THERE!

CHAPTER 27

The next morning, it was clear to Peter and his team that something was wrong. It was twelve minutes past their meeting time, and Mr. Winchester still hadn't arrived. Since he had never been late before, they all started to assume the worst.

Just before ten fifteen, Mr. Winchester finally came into view. He was about a hundred meters away, and appeared to be walking very slowly. Realizing that something was not right, they all ran over to him.

"Mr. Winchester!" Nicola said. "Are you feeling okay?"

"Well, I'm not dead," he replied in a weak voice. "But my joints hurt so bad that I might as well be."

Nicola put her hand on his forehead, and immediately realized that he had a very high fever. "You're burning up!" she said. "We need to get you home to bed."

"Just a slight fever," he replied stubbornly, a bit embarrassed by the worry he was causing them. "I'll be fine once I..."

But before he could finish his sentence, he collapsed onto his knees. A few seconds after that, he toppled over sideways. His eyes were glazed over and his breathing was erratic.

"This is serious guys!" Nicola yelled in a panic. "Brad, call an ambulance! Pete, take off your shirt, run to the river, and soak it in cold water! Neil, go and stand by the corner of the road so the ambulance doesn't miss the turnoff!"

Mr. Winchester was in no state to respond, but he smiled on the inside. Nicola was usually the most timid and shy member of the team, but she had just taken over in a moment of crisis. Maybe they would have a chance against Zoltan after all...

CHAPTER 28

Late that afternoon, Mr. Winchester finally regained consciousness. He was in the ICU at Stoneburg Memorial Hospital. Clearville had no hospital, so the ambulance had to take him to the neighboring city of Stoneburg. Since it wasn't that far away, they rode their bikes there after Mr. Winchester was picked up by the ambulance. After almost eight hours of waiting and worrying, they saw a doctor walking their way.

"Are you family?" Dr. Rollins asked while approaching them. "Are you his grandkids?"

Peter stood up first and shook Dr. Rollins' hand. "Actually, we are his students," he said. "We aren't even sure if he has any family. He's never talked about a wife or brother or kids or anything."

"I see," Dr. Rollins responded. "Well first of all, I must commend you on your prompt action. Calling the ambulance certainly saved his life. But Mr. Winchester is a very, very ill man. I won't go into all of the technical terms right now, but some of his organs are failing. He will need numerous tests done, but he is currently far too weak to run any tests on. So we will have to wait a few days before doing anything."

"Can we see him?" Nicola asked, wiping off some tears with her sleeve.

"You may see him," Dr. Rollins said, "but you won't be able to speak with him. The medicines we are giving him make him very sleepy. He won't be able to carry on any type of conversation. But the good news is that he is currently not in any pain. Anyway, hopefully he will be coherent enough to start talking again within the next week or so."

When they heard the phrase *week or so*, they looked at one another. Everyone was thinking the same thing. For the final five days of their training, they would no longer have a teacher.

Peter felt an additional fear, due to the fact that he still hadn't told Bradley the truth. He was hoping to have Mr. Winchester explain it to Bradley on their final day of training. But now Peter would have to be the one to tell him.

Dr. Rollins took them to the large window in front of the ICU. They could barely make out the old man's face, as he had all sorts of tubes and tape attached to him. After a minute or two in silence, they thanked the doctor and walked toward the front door. Once they were outside, they sat down at one of the picnic tables nearby the entrance.

"This training and stuff has been fun," Neil said. "But, well, seeing him like this... I guess I feel kind of responsible for what happened."

"It's not your fault, Neil," Nicola said. "For all we know, maybe he hasn't been feeling well for days, or even weeks. He just loves training us. He didn't want to let us down."

"More than anything, he wants to see us win," Peter

added. Then he paused. He knew this wasn't the best time to explain everything to Bradley. "And since he can't come to watch us, all we can do is go and win this thing, and then march in here with the trophy!"

"You got it Petey," said Bradley, patting Peter on the shoulder. "Let's win it for the old man! Neil, Nik, you in?"

Neil and Nicola looked at each other, and then back at Peter. They both nodded. There seemed to be a silent understanding between them that Bradley didn't need to hear the truth quite yet.

"But who's gonna finish our training?" Nicola asked.

Peter wanted to say something to keep his team confident. "You leave that to me," he assured them. "We'll meet up tomorrow to train. Same time. Same place."

CHAPTER 29

The next morning, Peter outlined what they would do for the final four days. "So here's how it's gonna work," he said. "We are going to create puzzles for each other. You know, tough ones for the other three people to try to solve. But they *must* be solvable, okay?"

Everyone seemed fine with Peter's plan.

"So today we split up and spend the day making our puzzles," he continued. "We'll do mine tomorrow, Nik's on Thursday, and Neil's and Brad's on Friday."

"Cool," Bradley said. "But I can't imagine I'll be able to think of anything that will stump you."

"C'mon Brad," Peter said quickly. "We've been training like crazy for almost two months. Plus you've been watching me do puzzles since I was, like, two years old. I'm sure you can come up with something."

"Well, I'll give it a shot," Bradley said, although not sounding quite as confident as Peter had hoped.

"Alright guys," Peter said. "Go and get started. You've got all day. And let's up meet at the hospital at six to see how Mr. Winchester is doing."

CHAPTER 30

It was a very long and tiring day for all of them. After splitting up in the morning, no one came up with anything for the first few hours. But somehow, everyone managed to complete their puzzles by midafternoon.

As they had agreed on at the start of the day, they met up outside the hospital front doors shortly before six o'clock.

Peter walked up to the counter while the other three sat in the lobby. "Excuse me," he said softly to one of the nurses. "We are here to see Mr. Winchester. He's in the ICU."

"Just a moment, please," the nurse responded. After looking through some paperwork and typing something into her computer, she looked back up at Peter. "Actually, Mr. Winchester was moved out of the ICU this afternoon. He's now in C-wing, room 202. You can go up to see him, but no more than two at a time in the room. And in all likelihood, he'll be sleeping. If he is awake, he might not be able to respond very well. He's medicated quite heavily."

Peter politely thanked the nurse, collected the rest of his team, and they walked upstairs and down the hallway toward C-wing. Peter and Nicola decided they would go in first. Once they were inside, they could see that Mr. Winchester was not doing well. They didn't know his actual age, but with all the machines hooked up to him, he looked close to eighty. His eyes were closed, so they pulled up the two guests chairs as close as possible to his bed.

Nicola put her hand on Mr. Winchester's forehead. It felt cold and clammy. Peter and Nicola looked at each other, not knowing what to do or say next.

Peter leaned in and put his mouth close to Mr. Winchester's ear. "Mr. Winchester, it's us. I mean, it's Peter and Nicola," he said. "Oh, and Neil and Brad are just outside the door. I don't know if you can hear us or not, but, uh…"

Sensing Peter's nervousness, Nicola tried to help. "We came to tell you that we are not quitting," she said. "You are an awesome leader. You taught us so much."

"He probably can't hear us," Peter said, taking her hand. He was hoping to prevent Nicola from breaking out into tears again. Unfortunately, it didn't work. "Maybe we should just head home and visit him again tomorrow."

Peter should have been focused on the old man, but was selfishly thinking about how he and Nicola were holding hands so naturally. It was almost as if they were a couple. He gently put his arm around her waist as they walked out of the room.

With Nicola crying so hard and Peter thinking about how much longer to keep his arm around her waist, neither one noticed that Mr. Winchester had opened his eyes and was now smiling.

CHAPTER 31

The challenges they had designed for each other were all unique and tough to solve. Peter was extremely pleased by how these final three days went. His team was beaming with confidence. After finishing Bradley's challenge at about 5:00 p.m. on Friday, they started talking about heading to the hospital.

Peter made a suggestion about today's visit. "There's no sense in all of us going to the hospital again," he said. "He's probably still sleeping, and he can't respond to us anyway. Why don't you guys head home, and I'll just go in quickly by myself."

They were all tired and hungry, plus a little nervous about their big day tomorrow. They agreed it was a good plan.

Peter started riding to the hospital. He was really hoping that Mr. Winchester would be awake today, as he needed some last minute advice.

* * *

When he entered the hospital room, he was surprised to see that Mr. Winchester was not only awake, but also sitting up. Peter quickly spotted an envelope on the bedside table with *To Peter* written on the front. Mr.

Winchester was still too weak to talk, but was able to point at the envelope and whisper, "open it."

The handwriting looked shaky, leading Peter to guess that Mr. Winchester had written it by himself. Peter read the note to himself silently.

Dear Peter,

Zoltan came to the hospital today. You are to be at the base of Mt. Silverhead at 8:00 a.m. sharp tomorrow. Good luck.

Your friend,

Leonardo

Peter was very familiar with the Mt. Silverhead area. It was one of the most mysterious and intriguing places in the whole country. Like certain places in Egypt, it had once been inhabited by some type of ancient civilization. Zoltan must have chosen this area for their upcoming challenges because he was planning to use some of the old structures or buildings. And since most of the area hadn't been documented yet, it meant Peter had no way of guessing what kinds of puzzles they might encounter there.

Peter put the letter in his back pocket. "We are as ready as we'll ever be," he said.

Mr. Winchester coughed a few times, and tried to clear his throat. Then he somehow managed to quietly say, "I know."

Knowing how weak his teacher was, Peter began to speak without pausing. All the old man needed to do was to listen. "I need your advice, Mr. Winchester," he began. "I have no idea how to tell Brad the truth. If I don't say anything, he'll realize something is wrong when we meet at Mt. Silverhead tomorrow. But if I tell him tonight, you know, explain all about Zoltan and the weather gods and stuff, then he'll call me a liar and quit. I've thought about what to do over and over, but I can't figure out what's best. I have to tell him tonight, but if I do, then he—"

"You lying loser!" a voice said from behind Peter. He turned around to see Bradley standing there. Red with anger, Bradley continued, "I came here to tell you we decided to go for pizza tonight, but instead I learn you've been tricking me the whole time!"

"Brad, wait," Peter begged, hoping to reason with him.

"Shut up!" Bradley yelled, loud enough to be heard by most of the people in C-wing. "I'm out of here! And you can forget your stupid competition! Or whatever it really is!"

"Please, hold on," Peter begged again. "Just hear me out. It'll make sense if you hear the whole story. Neil and Nik already know everything."

Bradley was now in the hallway. He turned around to face Peter again. "Pete, I told you to shut up!" he yelled. "I don't want to hear another word out of your lying mouth. If I do, then I'll hit you so hard that you'll be staying in this hospital too!"

Bradley stormed away. Peter hung his head in defeat, and turned around to face Mr. Winchester. Peter shook his head, frustrated by how stupid and naive he had been. Not just about the lying, but about thinking that he and his silly team had a chance against Zoltan. And with Bradley out, the chance of success was now definitely zero.

Mr. Winchester picked up a pen and wrote something on the paper on his bedside table. Peter picked it up and read it.

You can do it without Bradley.

Unfortunately, Mr. Winchester didn't really believe what he had just written on the note. He only did it in a desperate attempt to prevent Peter from quitting before tomorrow even arrived.

More than anything, Peter wanted to talk more with his mentor. He needed to hear more words of encouragement. Unfortunately, the old man's eyes were already closed.

Peter headed for the pizza shop. He had to explain to Neil and Nicola what had just gone down at the hospital.

CHAPTER 32

Neil and Nicola listened intently as Peter explained what had just happened in Mr. Winchester's hospital room.

"So Brad's out," Peter said at the end of his long and detailed explanation. "And I don't think we have any hope of doing this without him."

"Well I'm still in," Neil said, "I think we can do it."

"I'm not quitting either," added Nicola.

Peter smiled. At least he wouldn't be on his own tomorrow morning. "But I just wish Brad would have let me tell him the whole story," he said. "He left so quickly. I had no chance to explain. If I had, maybe he wouldn't have quit."

"If he wants out that bad," Neil said, "then I say forget him."

"Don't talk like that!" Nicola responded quickly. "Brad worked just as hard as you did for the last two months." She turned and looked back at Peter. "Maybe I should talk to him. He might listen to me if—"

"Thanks Nik," Peter said, cutting her off, "but if you knew how stubborn Brad could be, you'd know he's beyond reasoning with. We are a team of three now, like it or not. I wish Brad were with us, but he's not. So we just to have to live with it."

Neil stood up and flexed his biceps. "Tomorrow morning," he said. "We are going show this Zoltan that we can handle anything he can throw at us! No sweat!"

Upon hearing the word *sweat*, Peter looked down at his palms. They were sweating so profusely that the beads were running down his arms and dripping on to his lap. He smiled and looked back up. "Sweat or no sweat," he said, "we'll give him a run for his money."

"You got it!" said Nicola enthusiastically, happy to see Peter looking somewhat positive again. "Now let's all go home so we can get some sleep. We need to be as sharp as ever tomorrow."

They left their money for the pizza on the table, walked out the door, and hopped on their bikes. Even though they'd all be home in time to get plenty of sleep, all three knew that tonight was going to be one of those long nights spent worrying and staring at the bedroom ceiling.

CHAPTER 33

Before going to bed that night, Peter decided to make one final attempt at getting Bradley back on their team. He knew Bradley wouldn't talk to him, so he figured a letter was the only option left. He grabbed a pencil and a blank sheet of paper, and began writing.

Brad,

I know you're angry. If I were you, I would be too. I shouldn't have lied. But I did, and I can't undo that now. Don't blame Neil or Nik. It was my idea, not theirs.

Here's the DVD I got from Mr. Winchester a couple of months back. It's a video of Zoltan demonstrating his powers. Please watch it. I'm sure it'll convince you.

We really need you tomorrow. We won't be able to do this without you. We have to be at the base of Mt. Silverhead by 8:00. That's where

Zoltan will have the 8 challenges waiting for us.

Peter

He taped the note to the DVD, and walked quietly toward Bradley's bedroom. He pressed his ear to the door, and could hear Bradley snoring away like a chainsaw. He slid the note and DVD under the gap at the bottom of the door. Now all he could do was hope.

CHAPTER 34

When Peter got out of bed at six thirty the next morning, he felt nowhere near refreshed. He figured he had only slept a total of about two hours. He walked past Bradley's bedroom door on his way to the stairs. He slowed down as he passed the door, wondering if Bradley had noticed the note and DVD yet.

As Peter ate his cornflakes alone at the kitchen table, he found himself suddenly obsessed with the size, shape and contours of his spoon. He started to picture all of the different things a teaspoon could be used for. Once he'd come up with about eleven or twelve, he suddenly realized he had finished his cereal, and there was nothing left in his bowl but milk. He slapped his cheeks a couple of times in an effort to make himself more awake.

He made two peanut butter and jam sandwiches, which had been his favorite lunch for as long as he could remember. Then he grabbed a few juice boxes, some cookies, and a granola bar, and put everything in his backpack. He had no idea how long today was going to be, and wanted to make sure he had something to eat when he became hungry.

Shortly after seven o'clock, while the rest of his family were still in bed, Peter quietly left through the back door and got his bike from the garage. He pushed it to the end of the driveway, trying not to make any noise, and then began riding.

* * *

There was a large sign on the main road indicating the turnoff to the mountain. The narrow road connecting the main road to the mountain was an old dirt one, about two hundred meters long. Peter couldn't see any bicycle tracks in the dirt, which meant he was the first to arrive. He decided to wait near the sign for the rest of his team to get there.

Peter kept looking around while he waited, hoping to catch a glimpse of Zoltan. "I wonder what he looks like..." Peter said to himself, remembering how Zoltan's face was blocked by a hood in the DVD. "Maybe he's got the face of a lizard or something."

Peter giggled at his silly train of thought, which was actually being brought on by excessive nervousness. In an effort to calm himself down, he sat cross-legged on the ground, closed his eyes, and started taking some slow, deep breaths.

CHAPTER 35

About fifteen minutes later, Peter spotted Nicola and Neil riding his way. He kept hoping to see Bradley, but knew this was merely wishful thinking.

"Ready to rock, Pete!" Neil said while skidding to a stop to Peter's left. "Let's show this Zoltan guy who the boss is!"

Neil was either unrealistically confident, or was just trying to mask his fear by making ridiculous comments.

When Nicola came to a stop just in front of them, Peter thought she looked different today. There was nothing different about her hair or clothes or anything like that. But her face looked pale and expressionless. Her shoulders hung. She looked terrified.

"Hi," she said while getting off her bike. "I suppose this is where we say something encouraging to each other." After a short pause, she continued, "And then we walk down that path to our doom."

Both Neil and Peter were speechless. Each was waiting for the other to respond first.

Nicola cracked a smile and slapped them both on the back. "You guys are so lame!" she yelled. "I'm just joking!"

After propping their bikes up against some trees, they stood shoulder to shoulder at the start of the path. Peter then began walking first, and Nicola and Neil followed a few steps behind. No one spoke. The only sounds were those coming from the dead leaves being crushed under their shoes as they walked.

After a couple minutes of walking, they spotted a single white envelope hanging from the branch of a tree. Peter nervously took the envelope off the branch and slid out the letter that was inside.

CHAPTER 36

With Neil and Nicola looking over his shoulders at the note, he nervously read the message aloud.

Follow this path to the entrance. Your challenges lay beyond it. In order to get to them, you'll have to choose the right entrance.

You'll see three identical staircases, leading to three identical doors. While one of those is the real entrance, the other two open up to rooms filled with thousands of bees. Your tool is a magnifying glass, and you'll find it hanging from a tree at the end of the path. And you may also use anything that nature has provided.

"Don't try to figure anything out till we see it first," Nicola said supportively, taking Peter's hand. "Let's not get ahead of ourselves."

As they continued along the path through the dense forest, Peter found himself daydreaming a little. He kept thinking about the fact that he and Nicola were holding hands again, and couldn't help but wonder if he would ever kiss her. And maybe if he kissed her, she'd become his girlfriend. And if she did, then they could walk around hand in hand at school all day...

But he quickly shot back to reality when they reached the end of the path. As promised, the magnifying glass was there. Neil removed it from the tree and inspected it for a few seconds. Then he handed it to Peter.

"Okay, here's how we play this," Peter began. "I take the middle one. Neil, you got the left. Nik, the right. When you get to your door, wait till I tell you what to do. *Do not* touch it unless I tell you to."

Thirty seconds later, they were all standing at the top of their respective steps, staring at the identical light green doors in front of them.

"First," Peter said loudly, "put your ear on the door and listen for any sounds, like buzzing or something."

They all put their ears up against the doors, hoping it would give them a clue about which was the correct one.

"Nothing here," said Neil.

"Nothing here, either," said Nicola. "Quiet as can be."

"Same for me," added Peter.

After pausing a few seconds to gather his thoughts, Peter explained the next course of action. "Okay, now kneel down and try to look under the crack at the bottom of the door. Tell me what you can see. One by one. Nik, you go first."

Nicola lay flat on the ground, trying to get in the best possible position to view under the door. "Hard to see," she said. "Looks like a garden or something. Or maybe grass and trees? But the gap is too narrow, I can't really say for sure."

"Okay. Neil, you're up," Peter said quickly.

Neil twisted and turned into various awkward positions while trying to look under the door. "Same here," he said. "All I can say is there's lots of green inside."

Peter was already lying on the ground. He also found it next to impossible to get his eye close enough to the ground to see anything. After cursing a few times, he stood up. He realized that Zoltan wasn't going to make any part of this easy.

Peter pulled the magnifying glass from his back pocket. He looked over to Neil and Nicola, who were still awaiting their next instructions.

"Guys!" he yelled. "What do you think we're supposed to use this for?"

"The only thing I've ever used one for was to burn caterpillars when I went camping," Neil answered.

"Burn caterpillars?" Peter replied, glaring at Neil.

But Neil's comment had given Nicola an idea. "He might be onto something," she said. "I remember, like, a few months ago, watching something on TV about bees. People in this remote village were, like, using smoke to get bees to leave their hives. And then they cut down the hives for the honey. If we could—"

"Set a small fire near each door," Peter said, finishing her sentence for her, "the smoke would bother the bees enough to make them start buzzing around!"

"And then we listen to see which door has no buzzing behind it," Neil added. "And bang! We're in! Okay, you guys start piling up dead leaves in front of the doors. And I'll use my *expertise* to get the fires going!"

They quickly put small piles of leaves in front of each door. Then Neil effortlessly used the magnifying glass to focus the sun's rays. He had all three fires going in no time at all. They used their hands to waft the smoke through the narrow gap between the doors and the ground. A couple of minutes later, both Peter and Nicola could hear the angry bees buzzing around like crazy. Neil heard nothing behind his door. Neil gave them the thumbs up, and they ran over to join him.

"You do the honors, Nik," said Peter, gesturing for her to open the door. "It was your idea."

She twisted the knob and slowly pushed the door open. Behind the door lay a small room. It actually seemed more like a garden than a room.

"We're in!" Neil said, holding up his hands to receive high-fives.

Even though he had just told Nicola to lead the way, Peter mindlessly stepped through the doorway first. He was nervous, and didn't realize that he was blocking Neil and Nicola from coming in behind him.

"Make some room for us too, Pete," Nicola said playfully. She put her hands on Peter's waist, and gave him a soft nudge forward.

Once inside, they looked around. The ground was grass, and there were some bushes and a couple of big trees. It was almost as if they were standing in a park surrounded by walls. Neil quickly spotted the next envelope. It was hanging from a branch on the tree closest to the door.

CHAPTER 37

Neil took the envelope off the tree, and read it slowly for everyone to hear.

Let me explain what lies ahead. There is a series of 8 challenges. Each one is significantly harder than the previous one. If you can, somehow, manage to solve all 8 before sunset, then you win, and you will replace Mr. Winchester.

And I'm sure Leonardo has already pointed this out, but many of these challenges will appear quite intimidating, or even scary. If you would like to quit, simply retrace your steps back to this room. You may then leave through the same door you just entered.

But if you do choose to quit, then you had better prepare yourself for catastrophic events, unlike anything you've seen even in your worst nightmares.

So let's start! Once you walk past the bushes and trees, you'll come to a long corridor. Halfway down that corridor, there is an envelope containing the instructions for your first challenge.

"You won't see us run out of here like a bunch of babies!" Neil screamed at the sky, as if he thought Zoltan were floating somewhere above them.

"Settle down," Nicola said quickly. "Don't get all worked up. You'll need every bit of energy you have."

While Nicola was calming Neil down, Peter confidently strode toward the corridor.

"C'mon," Peter shouted back at them. "What are you waiting for?"

CHAPTER 38

They approached the start of the long, narrow corridor. They could see the door at the end of the corridor, and the small table halfway between them and the door. On the table lay the envelope that Zoltan had just mentioned.

"Let me grab that," Neil said, starting to make his way toward to the table.

"Wait!" Peter yelled, grabbing Neil by the shirt. "There could be some kind of trap between here and there. We take it slow and steady, just like we practiced."

They prepared to start the *corridor technique*. This was a cautious method to move safely down any road or path. They had spent a lot of time practicing it during their training. First, they locked arms. This ensured they would be able to help each other immediately should any one of them slip or fall. If Bradley were there, his job would be to walk backward behind them and make sure nothing surprised them from the back. Today, they would have to periodically check behind them to make up for Bradley's absence.

Nicola was on the left, Peter in the middle, and Neil on the right. Nicola's job was to scan the left wall. Neil would scan the right wall. And Peter would check the floor and ceiling. Before each step, all of them had to say "clear." Although it was very slow, it guaranteed they wouldn't miss any hidden traps.

Four minutes later, they finally reached the table. Thankfully, they hadn't met any surprises on the way.

"Better safe than sorry, right?" said Peter.

Neil picked up the note and read it to Peter and Nicola.

For your first challenge, which lies beyond the door at the end of the corridor, your instructions are simple:
1. Enter
2. Close the door tightly behind you
3. Find your way through

They finished their way to the end, using the *corridor technique* the entire way. The room they were about to enter looked extremely dark. After they walked through and closed the door behind them, they realized it was pitch black.

"Oh, great," said Nicola, her voice a little shaky. "Just what I needed. Zoltan must have spied on us and found out that I'm afraid of the dark."

"Don't worry, Nik," Peter said. "You'll be fine."

"I hope so," Nicola said, searching around in the dark until she managed to find Peter's hand. "But how are we supposed to find the exit?"

"Zoltan has just taken away our best sense, *sight,*" he continued. "That means we have to use our remaining four senses. So let's start with *touch*. Put your hands on the door we just came through. Feel around until you can find it."

After a little bit of touching at the air and turning around in circles, all three found the door.

"Neil," Peter said, softly nudging Neil to the left with his elbow. "You are going to move along that wall. Go slowly and carefully. Shuffle your feet along the ground. Keep one hand on the wall, and the other one out in front of you. Nik, you do exactly the same in the opposite direction. And take it slow. There's bound to be traps somewhere."

Neil and Nicola did as told, carefully moving along the wall in opposite directions.

"Pete!" Neil yelled about a minute later. "I just got to the corner of the room. Should I turn around and come back? Or head down along the next wall?"

"Keep going," Peter answered. "But go *slowly!*"

"Roger that," Neil replied.

"Hey Pete, me too," Nicola said. "Okay, I'll do the same as Neil."

"Oh man!" Neil suddenly screamed.

"What? What happened?" Peter yelled in reply, wishing he had a flashlight or something to see what was going on.

"I'm fine," Neil said, "but the floor over here just suddenly ends. It's like a cliff or something. I almost fell over it."

"Nik! Stop!" Peter yelled with urgency in his voice.

"Okay!" Nicola replied. "Hey, my side's the same. The floor just comes to an end suddenly."

"Okay, good job so far," Peter said. "Somewhere over there, there must be a path or bridge or something to get across. Get on your knees, put one hand on the ledge, and then start crawling along it. As soon as you find something, shout."

Peter impatiently waited for one of them to say something.

"Ouch!" Nicola yelled suddenly.

"Ouch back!" Neil said back to her.

"Bad news, Pete," Nicola said. "Neil and I just bumped into each other." If they had just bumped heads, that meant they had met somewhere in the middle. Neither had found a path or bridge.

"Gimme a minute to think," Peter said.

Peter ran through different options in his mind. "I guess using *touch* on its own isn't going to be good enough," he finally announced. "So let's try *sound*. Lay on your stomachs, with only your heads over the ledge. Then make short, loud noises and listen carefully to the echo."

They got in position, and Neil went first, yelling "Hey!" About two seconds later, it echoed back. Nicola didn't know what word to use, so she just copied Neil. She got the same result.

"All I can say," Neil said, "is that it's a *long* way down."

"Now take all of your change out of your pockets," Peter instructed. "We're going to use it to find the bridge."

They both fished through their pockets and took out whatever change they had.

"Ready!" Neil shouted. "Now what?"

"Drop one," Peter explained, "and then count how long before it lands at the bottom of the pit."

Neil did as instructed. Then he yelled back to Peter, "About four or five seconds!"

"Okay, good," said Peter. "Now move carefully along

the ledge, in opposite directions. Every meter or so, drop another coin. When you hear it land quickly, stop and tell me."

"Oh I get it," said Nicola. "If it lands quickly, that means it's landed on the bridge, right?"

"Yup," Peter answered.

They both started. On his seventh or eighth coin, Neil stopped and yelled, "Pete! I think I found it!"

"Okay," Peter replied. "Drop one more just to be sure."

Neil did as told. "This is the spot!" he yelled.

"Awesome!" Peter said back. "Nik, slide along until you get to where Neil is. I'm gonna make my way over to you guys."

Peter shuffled along the wall, turned the corner, and made his way to the ledge. Then he kneeled down and crawled along until he bumped into Neil.

"Hopefully the bridge isn't too far down from the ledge," Peter said. "I'm going to hang my arms over and see if I can reach it."

Lying on his stomach, Peter reached down with both arms, but there was nothing there. "I can't reach it," he said.

"Why don't I try?" Neil suggested. "My arms are a lot longer than yours."

"No," Peter replied, a fresh thought popping into his mind. "Neil, you wearing a belt?"

"No. Why?" Neil replied.

"I am," said Nicola, taking off her belt and passing it to Peter.

Peter leaned over the ledge again, dangling the belt in one hand. He heard the clank as the belt buckle made contact with the surface below. He then jerked the belt up and down a few times, listening carefully as he did so.

"There's something down there," Peter said. "And I can't say this for sure, but it sounds like a bridge made of wood. I'll go down first, but you'll have to help lower me. It's a pretty big drop. Once I'm sure it's safe, I'll help you guys down."

Lying on his stomach, Peter hung his legs over the ledge, with Nicola and Neil holding his arms tightly. He slowly slid down further and further, until his toes made contact with the surface below.

Within a minute or so, Peter had helped both Neil and Nicola down as well. He hoped that the hardest part of this challenge was now done.

"This bridge seems pretty narrow," Peter said. "And I can't feel any railings. We crawl across very, very carefully."

After crawling for a few minutes, Peter's head hit the hard rock wall at the end of the bridge.

All three stood up, and put out their hands to feel for the wall.

"No door, though," said Nicola.

"It's probably up above, so we gotta climb up there first," Peter said. "Nik, you're the lightest. Neil and I will boost you up."

They boosted Nicola up first. Then Peter helped Neil up, and finally they helped pull Peter up.

"I'm assuming that the exit side is the same as the entrance side," Peter said. "But we'll still go slowly, just to be sure."

They carefully crawled their way along the ledge until they found the side wall. Then, keeping one hand on the wall, they stood up and shuffled to the corner. Then they turned and shuffled along until they felt the cold metal of the door.

"Voila!" Neil screamed. "We found it!"

Peter felt around until he found the doorknob. He twisted it and pulled open the door. The light which came through was blinding, as they had been in absolute darkness for the last twenty minutes. Shielding their eyes, they walked through the door.

CHAPTER 39

What lay in front of them now looked extremely similar to one of the most traditional and popular amusement park attractions, a *house of mirrors*.

Neil spotted the envelope taped to the entrance of the maze. He opened it quickly and began reading the note inside.

> *I suppose this challenge needs no explanation at all. All you have to do is navigate your way through this maze. Oh, but that would be too easy, wouldn't it? So I'm imposing a time limit. You have 5 minutes, starting now.*

They looked up at the large digital clock on the wall behind them. Just as Zoltan's note had explained, the countdown began. They watched it count. 4:59, 4:58, 4:57...

"I'll go first!" Neil yelled, remembering all of his childhood visits to the house of mirrors at the local fair. "I'm really good at these!"

"Hold on!" Peter said abruptly, grabbing Neil by the wrist to stop him. "We all go in together, and we stay together. You can't just run ahead. If you get through on your own, how are you going to explain to us how to find you?"

"Oh yeah, you've got a point," Neil responded, looking a little deflated. "But at least let me lead."

"Fine," Peter answered. "You can go first, but remember, no running ahead."

The maze looked no different than any typical one from a county fair. There were lots of windows. There were lots of mirrors. And there were lots of long, twisting paths with tons of corners and dead ends. Neil was leading at a quick pace. Unfortunately, Peter didn't share in Neil's confidence to find the exit so easily. About half a minute after they had started, they were once again standing at the entrance. They had obviously made a wrong turn somewhere. The clock was down to 4:18.

Neil was frustrated, but quickly got ready to start again.

"Slow down!" Peter yelled. "We'll never find our way through like this. We need a way of marking our path as we go, to make sure we don't make the same mistake twice."

"You mean like a trail of breadcrumbs?" Nicola asked.

Peter took off his backpack and smiled at Nicola. He pulled out the plastic bag with his two sandwiches in it.

"A trail of breadcrumbs," Peter said, "is precisely what I mean."

Neil took the lead again, followed by Nicola, and Peter brought up the rear. Every few steps, Peter ripped off a chuck of bread, and dropped it on the ground. But they quickly ended up at the entrance again. Now the clock was down to 3:52.

Peter wanted to keep his team positive. He knew these mazes were simply a process of elimination. Eventually, they would run out of *wrong* paths, and find their way through.

"Look guys," Peter said. "Now we know which path *not* to take. This time we head down somewhere with no breadcrumbs. Eventually, we'll find it."

At the first fork in the road, where the breadcrumbs showed they had already tried the left, they went right. Peter starting dropping more pieces of bread again, feeling like his plan was working fine. But shortly after, their new path rejoined one that already had breadcrumbs on it. It appeared as if they were caught in some sort of a loop.

They carried on like this for about two minutes. The clock was down to 1:49, but everywhere they went was covered in breadcrumbs. There were no untaken paths remaining.

"Stop for a second," Peter said, a little short of breath and somewhat disorientated. "There must be more than meets the eye to this maze. One of the mirrors or windows can probably be moved. So this time, try to push on every single pane you walk by. Yell as soon as one moves."

They hurriedly began with this plan. Neil was trying all of the panes on the left side, and Nicola the ones on the right. Peter followed behind picking up the bread, to make sure they didn't take the same path more than once. Unfortunately, this didn't provide them with the exit.

"Look at the clock!" Nicola said. "Only fifty-eight seconds left! Now what?!"

Peter heard her, but didn't want to waste any of the

remaining seconds replying. He needed to think.

"On your hands and knees!" Peter yelled. "Feel around on the ground for trapdoors! There's gotta be one somewhere!"

They frantically crawled around, but found nothing. The clock was down to 0:24.

"No!" Neil screamed, not wanting to accept defeat. He kicked one of the panels near him, which was obviously made of thick, shatterproof plastic.

Nicola sat on the ground and leaned back against one of the mirrors. It looked as if she was going to cry.

The countdown continued. 0:19, 0:18, 0:17. Just then, Peter hit on an idea.

"Instead of pushing," he yelled, "try to *slide* them!"

They madly ran everywhere, trying to see if any of the panels would slide. 0:11, 0:10, 0:09.

Miraculously, the one of the mirror panels Neil was testing slid to the right.

"Found it!" Neil screamed. "C'mon! C'mon!"

They bolted through the opening, tripping over each other. 0:04, 0:03, 0:02. They made it out just before the count reached zero.

CHAPTER 40

They were now standing in a three-by-three-meter room with a brick floor. In the center of the room was an enormous pile of keys. The top of the pile was almost up to their knees. And there was another white envelope, which this time was resting on top of the key pile.

While walking up to the keys, they all took notice of the single door on the opposite side of the room. It had a deadbolt on it above the doorknob.

"Uh, guys," said Neil. "It would appear this is a *find the needle in the haystack* game."

"Looks like way," Peter replied. "But let's take a look at the note first."

Peter slid the note out and read it aloud.

Keys! Keys! Keys! Don't you just love keys! You may not believe this, but there are exactly 1000 keys here! Only one key can open the lock, but I'm sure you have figured out that much already. But what would be the challenge in simply trying key after key after key? You may try only 10 keys. Only 10!

Peter crushed the note in his hand and threw it at the pile.

"Don't get frustrated," Nicola said. "We'll figure it out."

"I've always hated these kinds of games," he responded. "*Find the right one* games. To be honest, I really suck at them."

Neil walked over to check out the lock on the door. It looked like a standard deadbolt that you'd find on the front door of any home. He knelt down to inspect it more closely.

"Well how's this for starters?" he suggested. "Tons of those keys are way too fat to fit in this lock."

"You're right," Peter answered. "So first, let's throw out all of the ones that won't fit."

They began picking up handfuls of keys and sorting through them one by one. They threw all the ones that looked too fat back toward the entrance, and the others they put into a new pile.

This task turned out to be much more tedious than they had thought. It took them close to twenty minutes to finish, and their checks became less and less careful as time went by. When they had finally sorted through every single key, the new pile looked about thirty percent the size of the original one. That meant they had somewhere in the ballpark of three hundred keys remaining. So their odds of guessing were now one in thirty. Not good enough yet.

"So what can we try next?" Neil asked, knowing that they were still nowhere close.

After a few minutes of awkward silence, Peter thought of something to try. "I think I have an idea," he said. "First, we need to find the longest and skinniest key here."

They all began fishing through the pile, holding on to any really long and narrow keys. After a few minutes, they lined up the keys they had selected. There were only nine in total, so it was pretty easy to spot the longest one.

"Game on!" Peter said.

He took the key and slid it into the lock. Then he picked up a second key, and used it to scratch a mark on the shaft of the first key. It marked exactly how far the shaft had gone in. Then he pulled the narrow key out, and showed it to Neil and Nicola.

"Now we know the exact length of key we are looking for," he said. "Let's search for ones with the same shaft length. There can't be that many."

This also took a little longer than he had expected. But once they were done, they were down to around forty or fifty.

"Odds are getting better, eh?" Neil said. "About a one in five chance now!"

Although one in five was way better than the original one in a hundred, it was still too risky. Peter paced around the room, talking quietly to himself.

"I think I have an idea," said Nicola, who had been fairly quiet for the past little while. "Look how some of the keys have one or two really high notches. There's no way that they'll fit in the lock."

They carefully lined up all the keys on the ground, and removed the ones with any high notches. There were only about thirty left now. Since Peter had used up one of their ten attempts when he put the skinny key in the lock to measure the shaft length, they had nine chances left. Their statistical probability of guessing correctly was about thirty percent.

Peter was stumped about what to do next. He decided it was time to test their luck. "This may sound crazy," he said, "but I'm going to give it a try. Maybe I'll have beginner's luck, right?"

Peter randomly picked up one of the keys and took it over to the door, his hand shaking as he slid it in slowly. The key went in smoothly, but it wouldn't twist. He pulled it back out and threw it away.

Neil and Nicola both remained silent. They weren't sure if Peter was pondering a new idea or not.

Then he picked up another one and tried it. But it was not the right one either.

"Well, the odds were against me anyways," Peter said. "Maybe one of you will be luckier."

Nicola had been counting the remaining keys. There were twenty-seven left.

They sat on the ground and looked at the keys. After a few minutes of pointlessly staring at the small pile, Peter took the initiative again.

"I've tried three already," he said. "So now you both choose three each, and see if you can get lucky."

"Are you sure, Pete?" asked Nicola, shocked by Peter's risky proposition. "Maybe there's something we missed."

After a long pause, Peter replied, "You might be right, but we seem to be out of ideas."

Even though they were just choosing randomly, it took over five minutes for them to pick their keys.

Neil went first. He slid his first key in very nervously. With his eyes closed, he tried to twist it. No luck. The same happened with his other two keys.

Nicola then walked up to the door. She took her first key and rammed it into the keyhole. When it wouldn't twist, she then started jiggling the key around in the lock. Once she had convinced herself that it wouldn't budge, she pulled it out and tried her two other keys. They were also the wrong ones.

Peter gave Nicola a pat on the back, and turned back to the remaining keys on the floor. There were twenty-one left. He had a better chance of guessing someone's birth month than picking the right key.

Peter closed his eyes and put his hand to the ground. He picked up the key his hand landed on. He spun around to face the door, but lost his balance a little, and the key slipped out of his hand. It bounced a couple of times on the stone floor, and landed on the doormat in front of the exit. Peter swore once, and then picked it up and went to stick in the lock.

When Peter's hand was a few centimeters from the deadbolt, Neil suddenly jumped in front and blocked the lock with his hand.

"Neil? What are you...?" Peter said. He had no clue what Neil was up to.

But Neil was grinning from ear to ear.

"What are you smiling about?" Peter asked him.

"Step aside, my dear friend," Neil said with a bit of swagger in his voice. "And allow *yours truly* to solve this one."

Peter took a few steps back. Neil bent down, lifted up the doormat, and triumphantly threw it off to the side. On the ground, where the mat had just been, lay a single key.

"Dudes!" yelled Neil. "Isn't this where everyone hides their spare key? Now am I the man? Or am I the man?"

Nicola started jumping up and down in excitement.

"Neil, you rock!" Peter yelled. "Now unlock that

sucker!"

Neil picked up the key. Without any hesitation, he put it into the lock and twisted it. They all heard the click they had been waiting for. Neil grabbed the doorknob and opened the door.

"Boys and girls!" Neil announced. "Three down! Five to go!"

Peter recalled the part of Zoltan's first note that said the challenges would get progressively more difficult. Although he would never admit it to Neil or Nicola, he was terrified of how hard the *five to go* were going to be.

CHAPTER 41

The room they had just entered seemed like some type of dungeon or cavern. It was large, fairly dark, and the air was cold. And the room was completely empty.

The floor of the room was very unique though. It looked like a giant checkerboard, made of eighty-by-eighty-centimeter stone squares. And every square had a large, yellow *1*, *2*, *3*, *4*, *5*, or *6* painted on it. At first glance, it appeared there were no patterns or order to the numbers.

They did a quick count of the floor. It was eight squares wide and fourteen long.

"Where do you think he put the note this time?" Neil asked, hoping to shed some light on how this game was to be played.

While Nicola and Neil looked around for the note, Peter concentrated on the numbers on the floor in front of him. His gut told him that some type of mathematical calculation would show them the right way across.

"Hey, what's this?" Nicola asked. She had just noticed a small box on the ground. It was near the door they had just come through.

"Only one way to find out," said Neil. "Open it up."

Nicola picked up the box and opened it. There were a few small dice inside, but no note.

"Only dice?" asked Neil. "How are we supposed to know what to do with them?"

Nicola took the dice out of the box and looked at them carefully. They were typical six-sided dice, the same as you would use with any board game.

"Mr. Winchester told us this might happen," Peter said with a concerned look on his face. "He said some of the challenges might come with no instructions, and that figuring out what to do would be part of the challenge itself."

"Well dice are only good for one thing, right?" Neil said. "Why don't I roll one and see what happens?"

Neil picked one out randomly, and rolled it gently on the ground beside where he was standing. He had rolled a two.

"Maybe that means I have to walk across by stepping on only the squares with twos on them," Neil said hesitantly. "What do you think? Should I give it a try?"

"Don't see why not," Peter answered. "But go slowly, just in case you're wrong."

There was a *two* right in front of Neil. He slowly put the toe of his right shoe on the square. He kept the other ninety-nine of his body weight on his back foot. Then he gradually shifted his weight to his front foot. Since everything seemed safe, he lifted his back foot and brought it into the square too.

"This ain't so hard," Neil said. "All I have to do is go from *two* to *two* to *two*, until I get to the other side."

The next *two* was diagonally ahead to the right. Feeling fairly confident now, he bent down and jumped with both feet together to the next square. But the instant his feet lifted from the first stone, it immediately dropped away. It fell into some type of deep pit lying below. Nicola and Peter tried to look down, but it was too dark to see where it had fallen to. Then they all heard a loud crash when the stone smashed into the floor of the pit. Judging from the length of time that had elapsed, Peter figured it was at least three or four meters deep. That was deep enough to cause broken legs, or possibly even something worse, to anyone who fell into it.

Neil gulped. "Well, no turning back, eh?" he said, his face now drained of all confidence.

"Neil, stop there for a sec," Peter instructed. "Nik and I are going to figure out the easiest way for you to get across, and then we'll guide you."

Peter and Nicola carefully looked at the entire board, specifically at the *twos*. They guided Neil, one block at a time, until he was safely across.

"You're up, Nik!" Neil yelled from the other side.

Nicola grabbed a die and rolled it. It was a four.

Peter took her hand before she had a chance to step on the closest *four*. "Let's plan out your path before you start," he said.

There was only one way to get across on the *fours*. Once Nicola had made it to the other end, she gave Neil a big high-five.

Now it was Peter's turn. He rolled a three. There were a lot of *threes* on the first half of the board, but very few on the second half.

"There's no way across on the *threes*!" he shouted. "Well, unless I can jump 1.6 meters. Which of course I can't!"

"Then why don't you roll again?" Neil suggested.

It seemed like a reasonable idea, so Peter picked up

the same die and rolled it once more. But the instant it touched the ground, every square with a three on it fell at the exact same time. When those squares crashed into the pit below, the boom was unbelievable and the ground shook.

"Uh oh, guess I shouldn't have done that," Peter said.

He turned away from the checkerboard filled with holes and looked down at the dice. It was a six.

"One way or another," he yelled to Neil and Nicola, "I've gotta get across on the *sixes*!"

He managed to get about halfway across before he found himself stuck. There was a huge gap between him and the nearest *six*.

"You can do it!" Neil yelled. "Just jump there! It's not as far as it looks!"

Peter looked at the big void in front of him. He didn't agree with Neil at all. "No way, Neil," he said, his voice cracking with fear. "I'll end up at the bottom of that pit!"

Peter sighed. He wasn't prepared to make a leap of faith to the next *six*. Unfortunately, he had no other choice. He looked around again. There were no *twos*, no *threes*, no *fours*, and a giant space before the next *six*.

"There's gotta be a better way," he mumbled to himself.

He was panicking now. He couldn't turn back, nor could he go forward. And the dark pit beneath him was the last place he wanted to end up. Peter was close to hyperventilating. He needed to calm down. He sat down and started to take deep breaths.

"What is he doing?" Neil asked Nicola. "Why doesn't he just try to jump? I mean, like, that's his only choice, right?"

"Because he can't," Nicola replied sharply, her eyes

starting fill up with tears.

But Peter was still thinking. He was hoping to find a better solution. "Stupid six!" he yelled at himself. "Why couldn't I have rolled a one, or a five?"

And just as easily as that comment had come out without thinking, the solution came to him too. He stood up and smiled at Neil and Nicola.

"May I ask you," he said loudly, looking very relaxed, "how we get six?

"Huh?" Neil said to Nicola. "He's not making any sense. What's he talking about?"

Before they could even try to answer, he announced, "By adding one and five, that's how! If I put one foot on a *one*, and the other on a *five*, that makes six! I won't fall!"

"But how do you know?" Nicola said. "What if you're wrong?"

But somehow Peter wasn't worried. He looked around at the nearby *ones* and *fives*, and spotted a place where he knew he could land one foot on each.

Peter looked up in the air. "C'mon math, save me, man!" he yelled. Then he bent he knees, and pushed off hard. He simultaneously landed his left foot on a *one* and his right on a *five*. He raised both arms up in celebration. "Yeeeees!"

Neil and Nicola both started cheering.

"You did it! You did it!" she screamed.

Peter finished making his way across. Nicola had another huge hug waiting for him the second he got there. Neil gave him a few hard pats on the back.

Once they felt they had done enough celebrating, they started walking up the stone steps toward the exit.

CHAPTER 42

The exit led to a tunnel, which seemed to be gradually going down. They followed the tunnel deeper and deeper, and eventually it took them to somewhere cold, stinky, and mucky. They were now at the bottom of an old well. It was just like the ones that people in the old days used to get their water from by using buckets and ropes. The brick walls of the well rose up to the ground high above them. Peter guessed they were at least five meters down.

"Anyone good at climbing?" Neil asked, not really expecting to get a response.

Peter touched the walls. They were all covered by a thick layer of slippery moss. Climbing was not going to be an option.

At some point, there had been a ladder mounted inside the well. But all that remained of that ladder now were the holes in the wall where it had originally been attached.

They had been so focused on looking up and around that it took a few minutes before anyone noticed the box and note on the ground. Neil picked up the note and maneuvered it until he had enough light to make out the words on it.

Feel free to use any of these tools to assist you in getting out of this well. You don't want to be stuck down here for too long!

"That's all?" asked Nicola, hoping it had said more.

"Yup, that's it," answered Neil. "Well, let's open up this box and check out what's inside."

They looked inside the metal toolbox. There were screwdrivers, wrenches, a tape measure, a level, some rolls of rope and string, plus various nuts, bolts and screws.

"Well he left us lots of tools," said Neil, "but no wood or anything to build with."

"So there must be something else that we can use them for," said Peter.

They began sifting through the toolbox and pulling out items randomly. Then they would talk about how each one could possibly help them out of their current predicament.

"I think I might be onto something," Neil said. "Lots of the things in here, especially the screwdrivers, are long and skinny. I could slide them into the holes, and use them as hand and footholds to climb up. You know, like a rock climber would."

Neil took out a few of the screwdrivers and started jamming them into holes. They slid in quite easily, and the handles stuck out about ten or twelve centimeters. Once he had four firmly in, he grabbed the two higher ones with his hands, pulled himself up, and put his feet on the two lower ones. He then steadied himself, pulled one out, and reached up to put it in a higher hole.

"What do you think?" he asked. "I could just keep

working my way up like this."

"But how do you move the ones you're standing on?" Peter asked back. "And if you ever lose your balance, you'll come crashing down."

Neil paused, but decided to try continuing up a little further. Unfortunately, Peter was right. He could get the ones he was holding with his hands in and out easily, but pulling out the ones he was standing on was impossible. He gave up and hopped back down.

Peter grabbed a rope from the box. He knew that leverage could help pull and lift heavy things, even a person's body weight. But he was lost about how to set anything up without someone being up top.

* * *

Twenty minutes later, there were still at square one. They were at the bottom of an empty well, with no feasible way to get out.

"Man!" Peter yelled in frustration. "Is he planning on letting us starve to death down here?"

"Calm down, Pete," Nicola said softly. "Remember what Mr. Winchester taught us? That when you're completely stumped, take a few steps back, and look at it from a different perspective."

There wasn't enough space to take even one full step back, let alone a few. But what Nicola was suggesting certainly wouldn't do any harm. They all leaned back against the wall, hoping a solution would somehow present itself to them on a silver platter.

"Doesn't matter where I look, or how I look at it, a well is a well," Neil said. "Or a hole. Or whatever you wanna call it."

Peter tried to ignore Neil's comment. He wasn't ready to give up yet. He stared straight ahead at the moss-covered bricks.

He held his glare at them, trying not to even blink. Just before his eyes started to water from keeping them open for so long, Peter noticed something he hadn't seen before. On one part of the wall, there was an almost unnoticeable thin line, which had little or no moss on it. The line started on the ground, and went up about half a meter.

"What have we here?" Peter asked as he moved closer to touch it.

The closer he got, the more clearly he saw it. There was a very narrow gap in the moss, which was just wide enough that Peter could slide his fingertips in. This was clearly something worth investigating more closely.

"Gimme a hand, Neil," he said. "This has gotta be some kind of door or something. Let's see if we can get it to move by pushing or pulling."

Neil knelt down next to Peter. They both squeezed their fingers into the crack.

"On the count of three, we pull," said Peter. "Ready… One, two, three!"

They both felt something shift. They took their fingers out and looked at the wall again. They could see clearly now that this was not part of the wall, but was actually a tiny door. They pulled and pulled, eventually managing to get it open. Once they had it open a full 90 degrees, Peter lay flat on the ground to look through it.

Peter slid into the fifty-by-fifty-centimeter opening. Then he wriggled through a narrow tunnel, which was at least ten meters long. Once he was finally through and standing on the other side, he yelled for Neil and Nicola to join him.

"I am so glad to be out of that gross well," said Neil

once he was through.

"Not as happy as I am!" Nicola added. "Look at me. I'm all covered in slime!"

"C'mon! What's a little slime?" Peter laughed.

CHAPTER 43

They spent a few minutes trying to help each other get as much of the slime off as possible. Then they looked around to see where they had just arrived. They were on a fairly narrow ledge, which was about a meter wide. There was a long ladder which led from the ledge down to something below.

They peered over to get a better look at what was down there. It appeared to be a large, square swimming pool. As they looked down, they noticed the water in this pool begin to spiral. Within a couple of minutes, the force of the spiraling increased rapidly, and it became an incredibly powerful whirlpool.

Before anyone started down the ladder, they spotted the note taped to the wall. Nicola was the closest to the note, so she grabbed it and read it aloud.

This challenge doesn't require much explanation, does it? You can see the raging whirlpool below. You can see the ladder that will get you to it. And you can also see the ladder on the opposite side that that will take you to the ledge with the exit. All you have to do is make your way across!

"Better go down and see how big that thing really is," said Neil.

Neil started down the long ladder first. He had only made his way down about five or six rungs when the ladder made a loud creaking sound. He froze, and squeezed his grip on the ladder even tighter.

"Oh, man!" Neil yelled in fear. "The bolts holding this thing to the wall must be all rusted or something. It feels like it could give way at any time!"

Once he was convinced the ladder was sturdy enough to keep going, he cautiously continued his descent. The ladder creaked and moaned with every step. When he was about halfway down, Nicola got ready to start.

"Hold on!" Neil yelled up at her. "It's too weak for more than one at a time! Wait till I'm off, and then start."

Both Peter and Nicola watched nervously. Neil made it to the bottom, looked up, and waved.

Nicola started next. Since she was only about two-thirds of Neil's weight, the ladder remained quiet. But just past the halfway point, she heard a snap. Then she felt the ladder shake a little. One or two of the rusted bolts had just broken off. Even though she knew moving slowly and lightly was important, fear took over. She descended the final few meters as fast as she could.

"Sorry Pete!" she yelled up to him once she was at the bottom. "I panicked!"

Now it was Peter's turn. He was worried about how long the ladder was going to be able to support his weight. As he moved from rung to rung, the ladder made all sorts of noises. It was only a matter of time before another bolt would snap, and Peter desperately wanted to be off the ladder before that happened.

But the snapping noise Peter feared came sooner than expected. He had only come down a couple of meters before a blot snapped, causing a big jolt in the ladder. He stopped, hoping this wasn't the beginning of a chain reaction that was going to bring the whole thing crashing down. Miraculously, the ladder remained fixed to the wall.

A few rungs past the halfway mark, the ladder creaked again, really loudly this time. It wasn't going to hold up for much longer.

Peter looked down. There were still another seven or eight rungs. It looked like just over a meter and a half to go.

"Jump off, man!" Neil screamed. "Do it now, before it breaks!"

Peter knew he didn't have a choice. He could see Neil and Nicola below him, trying to find the best place to stand to be able to catch him and break his fall. When it looked as if they were both ready, he loosened his grip and let himself fall from the ladder. Neil and Nicola were ready for him, and his landing actually went quite smoothly.

"How nice of you to drop in," Neil said with a smirk on his face.

"Very funny," Peter replied. "Nice catch."

"When you two are finished flirting," Nicola said, "could you take a look at the big whirlpool in front of you, and start thinking about what to do?"

Big was an understatement. The pool was eight by eight meters in size, and the whirlpool in it went right up to the edges. The water was moving with such force that the mist continually splashed up on them, and it was so noisy that they could barely hear each other. There was another small ledge on the opposite side, similar to the one they were currently standing on. And they could see the ladder on the other side which would take them up to the exit. But there were no ledges on the sides. They were going to have to, somehow, go through the vortex of water in front of them.

They could see all sorts of thing floating in the whirlpool. There were buckets, tree limbs, and even some really odd items like tennis balls and toys. The floating junk whizzed around in the whirlpool, progressively getting closer to the center of the spiral. Things were then sucked toward the black center where they disappeared from sight.

"That thing's a death trap," Neil said, swallowing hard. "It's too strong. We'd all get sucked to the bottom and drown."

"No one's gonna drown, Neil," Nicola said, noticing Peter was deep in thought.

Peter remained silent, so Nicola took charge. "Let's start by grabbing whatever we can as it goes by," she said. "Maybe there's something useful in there."

Over the next five minutes, they amassed quite a collection. They had pulled out pails, empty pop bottles, a tire, some shoes, and even a small shovel. They looked at their haul, but nothing seemed to hint at a way to get across a ferocious whirlpool.

Peter got the impression they were waiting for him to suggest something. But instead of giving instructions, he asked for help. "I'm not seeing it," he said. "I mean, like, how can any of this junk help us get across?"

Neil noticed something move near the exit. He

grabbed Nicola and Peter, and quickly pointed it out to them. None of them saw what, or who, was just there. But what was left behind was clear. Next to the exit, a digital clock was now hanging on the wall. The timer on the clock was set to five minutes. Before anyone had a chance to comment on how short five minutes was, it began to count down.

"Neil, Pete, look!" Nicola said hurriedly. "Only five minutes! What are we gonna do?"

Peter quickly became flustered. The clock was ticking down, and the pile of junk in front of them contained nothing useful. He started talking to himself. "C'mon, Peter," he said softly. "You can do this. Think man, think. You can't go though it without drowning. And you can't go around it. So that leaves going over it. But how do we get over it?"

Neil and Nicola kept fishing items out of the whirlpool, hoping to find something helpful before the time ran out.

"Over it. Over it," Peter repeated. "But how?"

Peter's concentration was interrupted by a loud jolt. The ladder he had come down about ten minutes ago must have just lost another bolt.

Nicola's eyes instantly lit up. "You've gotta be kidding me!" she yelled. "Guys! Get over here! I think I've got it, but we have to hurry!"

"Really? How?" Peter said.

"Actually, it's easy," she explained. "We rip the ladder off the wall, lay it across, and we will have ourselves a bridge!"

The clock now read 1:55, which meant they really needed to hurry. On the count of three, they all pulled hard, and the ladder broke free from the wall. Then they held the bottom of the ladder, and let the top fall down until it banged down hard onto the opposite ledge. Their bridge was ready.

"One at a time!" Nicola ordered. "It'll never hold all three of us!"

Neil went first, crawling across on his hands and knees. It was much more awkward than expected. When he was finally across, the clock was down to 1:02.

"Neil! Go up the next ladder to the exit! Now!" Peter yelled. "C'mon! Start climbing!"

Neil started up the ladder, but it was also in very poor shape. He knew they would have to climb up cautiously.

Neil got to the top at about the about the same time Nicola had finished her way across the bridge. Then Nicola started climbing up and Peter began on the bridge. But time was running out.

"Only thirty seconds left!" Neil yelled. "Hurry!"

Nicola was about halfway up the ladder. "I'll make it!" she yelled. "But Pete doesn't have enough time!"

The ladder became shakier and noisier. A few bolts had already snapped.

"I'm across!" Peter yelled from below, but he couldn't start his ascent until Nicola was on the ledge.

As soon as Nicola was within reach, Neil grabbed her arm. "Pete! Start now!" he yelled down. "I've got Nik!"

Neil pulled Nicola up on the ledge, and they both looked down to watch Peter's progress.

The ladder was literally falling to pieces. But there wasn't enough time left to climb slowly, so all he could do was race up it and hope for the best.

He was getting close to the top when he heard the noise he was dreading: the loud crack of the remaining bolts giving way. The ladder tore from the wall and started to fall to the ground below.

Peter knew he was a goner. Now it was time to scream.

But out of nowhere, two hands grabbed his arms. The ladder kept falling, but Peter was being held tightly by Neil, who was leaning far over the edge. The only reason Peter didn't pull Neil down with him was that Nicola was using whatever strength she could muster to hold Neil in place.

Neil managed to pull hard enough for Peter to get one hand up to the ledge. Then they heaved with all their might until he was all the way up. Without even bothering to look at the clock again, they dove through the open exit door.

CHAPTER 44

"Nik! That was awesome!" Peter yelled, hugging her tight and lifting her up off the ground.

"No kidding!" said Neil. "How did you figure it out? Me and Pete had no clue what to do."

"I don't know... I..." Nicola replied shyly, cheeks turning a little red.

The victorious trio was now full of confidence. They saw the envelope on the floor in front of them, with the words *Final Challenge* printed on it. Peter picked it up and pulled out the note. The message for their final challenge was very, very short.

> *Your final challenge is simple: Find the exit.*
> *Find your way out.*

"Find the exit?" Neil asked. "That's it? And I thought the final one was gonna be, like, all complicated or something."

"Not so quick, Neil," Peter replied. "The easier it looks, the harder it probably is."

They looked around the massive room they had just entered. It appeared to be some sort of warehouse, maybe fifty meters wide and at least a hundred meters long. But there was no system of organization in this giant storage room. Some things were stacked and divided neatly on high shelves. Other things were just in massive piles, almost like they had been dumped there from above.

"It'll take too long to search for the exit in here as a group," Peter explained. "Let's split up. We can cover more ground that way."

"Sure," replied Neil. "But who goes which way?"

"Wait," said Nicola. "I don't like this splitting up thing."

"What do you mean?" Peter asked.

"If we split up, and something happens to one of us, no one will be there to help. It's too risky," she said.

"What about you, Neil?" Peter asked. "We all have a say in this."

"I say we split up," Neil replied. "I'll go on my own, and you two go together. We'll cover twice as much ground that way." He paused a few seconds and then continued, "Plus that will give you two lovebirds a chance to kiss while you search, right?"

As soon as Neil finished that remark, Nicola hit him hard in the shoulder with right hook.

"Ouch!" he screamed in a high-pitched voice. But Neil had learned his lesson.

Peter and Nicola started heading along their wall, and Neil in the opposite way down his. It was only a matter of who would find the exit first.

In less than a minute, Peter and Nicola had reached the corner, so they turned and started walking along the long wall. What stood in front of them was completely impassable though. There was a huge mountain of junk, which looked to be at least five or six meters high.

"Keep both eyes open, Nik," Peter said, taking her hand to help her feel safe. "Although this looks like nothing more than a pile of garbage, there's probably something hidden in it. Some trick or hint or clue or something. We've just gotta spot it."

"Okay," Nicola replied, happy to be hand in hand with Peter again. "Maybe something in the pile points to the exit."

"So what we should do," Peter said, "is look for things that are different or out of place."

* * *

Neil had also reached the corner on his side, and had turned to start up the long wall. What lay in front of him was very different from what Peter and Nicola were facing. Along the entire wall was a row of large, identical wooden crates. Each crate was about two meters high, and there was no gap at all between them. When he took a few steps back to get a better look at them, he counted at least fifty.

Neil walked up to one of the crates. He tried to see if he could push or slide it, but it was way too heavy. And the crates had been nailed shut, so there was no way of opening them.

"What I need to do," Neil said to himself, "is find the clue that tells me which one is hiding the exit."

He walked back about ten meters so he could look at the crates from a distance. They were all identical. And both the ground in front of each crate and the wall behind each one had no special markings.

Stuck for ideas, Neil decided to continue walking past the crates and head for the far wall. That way he could meet up with Peter and Nicola, and get them to come and check out the crates. He was sure that Peter would have some way of figuring out which one the exit was hiding behind.

* * *

Peter and Nicola were slowly walking along the edge of the massive junk pile. They had decided against trying to climb up it, as they didn't want to risk spraining an ankle. They walked in silence, as searching for hidden clues required an incredible amount of focus and concentration. It took a good five minutes to walk past the whole thing.

"Anything?" Nicola asked.

"No," Peter responded, shaking his head in frustration.

"But don't forget this pile could be nothing more than a distraction to throw us off," she said. "The exit could be on Neil's side."

"Maybe you're right," said Peter. "But you know I hate *maybes.* And I'd really hate it if we just walked past the clue without noticing. Let's walk over there and look at it from further away. Maybe we'll spot something we missed.

They walked back a few meters and surveyed the pile again. Nothing seemed to stick out at first. But after taking a few more steps back, Peter thought he spotted something.

"Look toward the left of the pile," said Peter. "Over there, about two meters up from the ground. See where that hockey stick is horizontal? And on both sides of it, see those two wooden beams? Don't you think it looks like a big capital *H?*"

Peter gently twisted Nicola's head so she was facing in the right direction.

"Sure does!" she answered. "And look up there," she said while pointing diagonally up and right of the *H*. "There's an *A*. Well, I think that's an *A*."

They both scanned for more letters, figuring they would eventually be able to spell out a word. They managed to find six letters in total, three *As* and three *Hs*, but couldn't make any sense out of them.

"We've got a bunch of *As* and *Hs*," she said. "But that's it. That doesn't spell anything, does it?"

Peter ran up to the junk pile and kicked a cardboard box as hard as he could. It went flying across the floor. Then without saying a word, he took Nicola's hand. He started walking past the junk pile toward the part of the wall they hadn't checked yet.

While walking, Peter angrily said, "Nik, the letters do spell something. They spell *HA HA HA*. Zoltan's laughing at us! Man that guy is really starting to bug me!"

He looked up at the ceiling and yelled at the top of his lungs, "Ha ha ha! Very funny! You're quite the comedian!"

Realizing Peter was shaking with anger, Nicola squeezed his hand tighter. Then she lightly touched the side of his face with her other hand. When Peter looked down from the ceiling, Nicola's big eyes were focused right on his. For a brief instant, Peter forgot about where he was and what he was doing. He just stared back. His tension quickly drained, and his confidence returned.

"Let's go win this thing," Peter said to Nicola. "We'll continue along the wall till we meet up with Neil. He must have found something over there."

* * *

Neil had made it to the end of the long wall, and

turned at the corner. He knew it wouldn't be long before he'd meet up with Peter and Nicola. The end wall itself was completely bare. As he started along it, he saw Peter and Nicola coming his way.

"Come here!" Neil said excitedly. "I think I know where the exit is! But…" After a short pause, he continued, "But it'll be way easier to show you than to tell you. Follow me!"

They quickly ran over to Neil and let him lead the way. Within a couple of minutes, they were standing in front of the crates.

"So which one is the door behind?" Nicola asked.

Neil sighed, and then turned to face them. "That's the problem," he said. "One of them *must* be hiding the door, but I have no idea which one. I thought maybe you'd have some way of figuring it out."

"Let's do it," Peter responded quickly, anxious to get this final challenge solved as soon as possible. He walked up to one of the crates to see how sturdy it was.

"No dice, Pete," said Neil. "Those things can't be moved or opened."

"We can't open all of them," Peter replied. "But if we can figure out which one is hiding the exit, I'm sure we can find a way to pry it open enough to squeeze through."

"And when exactly did you become so big and strong?" Neil said jokingly, while squeezing Peter's right bicep.

They stood back a fair distance from the crates, hoping they could spot something that Neil had missed. After a few minutes of pacing back and forth, Neil broke the silence. "I'm still not seeing anything," he said. "If there's a clue in there somewhere, then it must be invisible."

Nicola's expression showed that she felt the same as Neil, but Peter appeared to be in his own world. Neil and Nicola were very familiar with this type of silence. They knew it meant Peter's mind was busy contemplating and calculating. Peter looked at the boxes, then at the floor, and then at the wall. After a few minutes of thinking, he turned around suddenly, and looked over at Neil and Nicola. They were familiar with this look too. It meant he had a plan.

"Don't you see?" he said. "The whole time, we've been looking from one vantage point."

"One *what* point?" Neil replied. "What's a vantage point?"

Peter rolled his eyes. He wasn't in the mood for giving a vocabulary lesson. "We've been standing out *here*," he explained, "looking at the crates over *there*. What we need to do is stand on the crates and look out here."

"Huh?" Neil said, still not understanding what Peter was getting at. "Why?"

"Trust me," Peter said.

The two boys helped boost Nicola up on top of one of the crates. There was no way either of them was going to be able to get up there with her. It was too high, and she wasn't strong enough to help pull them up.

"We can't get up there," Peter said, "so you're gonna have do this on your own."

"I'll try," she replied.

"Just look out. And look down. And look over there," Peter said. "The clue is hiding somewhere. Take your time. Don't worry. You can do it."

She started with a scan of the floor area just in front of the boxes, but it was nothing more than a brick floor. There were a few different colors of bricks, but none formed any shapes, letters, numbers, arrows or anything useful. Next she looked further out, about five or six meters away from where she stood. The ground was still made from the same bricks, but she could see that the position of the bricks was no longer random. She guessed that the bricks had been placed to form symbols or letters on the ground. The expression on Nicola's face made it clear that she had found something.

"I knew it!" Peter exclaimed, giving Neil a high-five.

"One looks like an arrow I think," she said. "No, wait. Maybe that's not an arrow. No, it's not… Maybe it's a letter. It is! It's an *A*! And hold on, there's another letter over there. An *H*!"

Peter enthusiasm instantly vanished. Those two letters could only mean one thing. Zoltan had left them another *HA HA HA* message on this side too.

"It spells *HA HA HA*, doesn't it?" Peter asked.

Nicola scanned the floor further to her right, and found the other *H*s and *A*s. Peter was right. "Yeah," she replied.

Peter kicked one of the crates, badly stubbing his toe while doing so. Then he swore in pain and hopped away on his good foot. Neil helped Nicola down, and then she explained to him how they'd found the exact same message in the pile of junk on their side.

Neil and Nicola looked in Peter's direction, but neither said a word. Peter wasn't hopping anymore, but he was still limping a little. He definitely shouldn't have kicked that crate so hard. A few minutes later, he walked back to them. The serious expression on his face gave them the impression he was all business.

"We are not going to give up yet," he said. "Back to the drawing board. Back to formula. Back to step one.

Whatever you want to say. But we *are* going to find the exit, and soon."

CHAPTER 45

"So what should we do next?" Neil asked, expecting that Peter had already come up with a plan.

"We've looked along all the walls, and there's no door anywhere," Nicola said. "Well, unless it's behind one of the crates. But if it is, we still don't know which one."

"Whoever said an exit has to be on a wall?" Peter said. "We made the assumption that we're looking for a *typical* door on a *typical* wall. Looks like we were wrong. Let's go look everywhere else in here. The exit is hiding somewhere. C'mon! Let's go find it!"

This little pep talk seemed to have worked, as both Nicola and Neil were eager and energetic to get started again. They began walking through the massive room. They navigated their way around the boxes, shelves, and piles of junk. Whenever one of them spotted something promising, they all stopped to check it out. But twenty-five minutes later, after they had covered the entire place, they still hadn't found anything. No exit. Not even a clue as to where the exit might be.

"Man, this is frustrating!" Peter yelled. "What are we missing?"

Neil and Nicola stayed silent. They knew Peter wasn't

really asking them, but was just letting off some steam. Peter then began thinking aloud again, mumbling indecipherably in a soft voice. Neil and Nicola both sat cross-legged on the ground and faced away from Peter. They didn't want to cause any distractions.

"How many places can you hide an exit?" Peter asked himself. "I mean, it's either on a wall or on the floor, right? And we checked those, right? And the only place we can't see is behind the crates. But if it were behind a crate, then we surely would have spotted the clue by now, right? So it's gotta be somewhere else then. But where?"

Peter paced around in a small circle, his eyes darting everywhere. He kept mumbling away, getting more and more agitated by the minute.

Then all of the sudden he stopped pacing and put both hands on his head. He looked up and yelled, "How could I have been so stupid!"

He bolted as fast as he could past Neil and Nicola. They quickly stood up and chased after him.

"Don't you guys see?" he yelled back at them while running. "Where's the one place we didn't look? The one place you'd *never* look for an exit?"

"What do you mean?" Nicola replied. She kept running as fast as possible to try to catch up.

After about thirty seconds of sprinting, they arrived where Peter had been headed. They had come all the way back to the entrance.

"Uh, Pete," said Neil. "I hate to crash your party, but this is the entrance, buddy. We need to find the exit."

"Think about it," Peter said, still breathing heavily. "The one place you'd never, ever look for an exit is here. Right next to the entrance."

Neil looked at Nicola. They both had no idea where

Peter was going with this.

"Come closer, guys," Peter said. "Look."

Neil and Nicola approached the door. Neil spotted it first. About fifteen centimeters to the right of the doorknob, there was a second doorknob, painted perfectly to camouflage it against the brick wall. Neil grabbed the camouflaged handle and tried to twist it, but it was locked.

"I don't get it," Neil said. "There's a door hidden here, but it's locked. What are we supposed to do? Look for the key?"

"No," said Peter, taking Neil's hand off the camouflaged doorknob and putting it on the other one. "That perfectly camouflaged doorknob doesn't open the exit door. It's actually the handle of the entrance. That's why you can't open it. Don't you get it? What we *assumed* was the entrance is really the exit."

Neil and Nicola still weren't following him. "Let me explain," he continued. "Remember when we walked in here at first? The door closed behind us, right? And none of us watched carefully as it closed. Why would we, right? Then we looked around for the note. So we probably moved a little. By that point, the door on the wall behind us, or at least the only one we saw, we naturally figured was the entrance."

"Hold on," said Nicola. "So are you saying that the doorknob in Neil's hand, the one that we thought was the entrance door, is actually for the exit?"

"You got it!" answered Peter, crossing his arms in satisfaction.

"Then open it!" Nicola yelled excitedly. "What are you waiting for?"

Neil twisted the knob. It wasn't locked. They had

found the exit.

CHAPTER 46

Of course, they were now standing back on the ledge where they had exited the whirlpool room. Since they had already completed this challenge, they were a little confused about what to do next. But the answer was, literally, written out for them on the ground. Someone had just finished painting *Follow the arrows* in yellow paint. And every meter or so, there was another yellow arrow pointing them in the right direction. They followed the arrows as instructed, which took them along the entire length of the ledge. The final arrow pointed to the wall at the end of the ledge. As they approached the wall, they spotted a hidden door.

"This Zoltan sure likes his camouflaged doors, eh?" Neil said jokingly.

"But at least this one we didn't have to search for," Peter replied.

Peter grabbed the doorknob and twisted it. Then he stood aside, motioning for Nicola and Neil to walk through. He never would have been able to complete these challenges without their help. As they walked through the door toward victory, they were hoping to see a big *Congratulations* sign or something. Or maybe

Zoltan was going to be waiting for them in person.

They were finally outside again, at the top of the mountain. A long, windy path lay directly in front of them. They guessed Zoltan was probably waiting for them at the bottom.

Neil raised his arms in the air. "Victory sure does taste sweet!" he yelled.

Peter jokingly slapped him on the back, and then they both turned around to hug Nicola.

"We did it!" Nicola yelled. "We are quite the team, aren't we?"

"This may sound a little cheesy," Peter said, beaming with pride, "but I never doubted our chances for a minute. I knew we'd win!"

Arms around each other's waists, they started down the path. Then they chased, pushed, pinched, and tickled each other, singing and laughing the whole time. They looked like a group of kindergartners playing during recess.

"You know what?" said Nicola. "We must have really tired out that Zoltan guy. He was supposed to make eight challenges for us, right? But I just re-counted in my head, and I'm pretty sure we only did seven."

Peter froze. "Stop walking! Now!" he yelled.

"Stop walking?" asked Neil. "Why? What are you so worried about?"

"I said STOP!" Peter screamed. He ran in front of them and held out his arms to block them. "This isn't *just a path*. This is the eighth challenge. He was trying to trick us into thinking we'd already won. But, it's not really over yet."

"Gimme a break, Pete," said Neil, pushing past Peter's outstretched arm. "Remember the note? It said that was our last challenge."

"Yes, I remember what it said," Peter said, "*Find the exit. Find your way out.* Don't you see? We found the exit, but that was only the first part. The second part must be getting down the mountain."

"You're paranoid, man!" Neil said, walking backward down the path. "We won man! We—"

And then Neil suddenly vanished. Of course he didn't really vanish. He had fallen into a large hole.

"Neil!" Peter shouted, running together with Nicola up to where they had last seen him. "Hold on!"

They looked down at Neil, who was lying at the bottom of some sort of pit. As they leaned closer to see how far down he was, the ground gave way, and they both fell in too.

They had just been deceived by one of the oldest and most primitive tricks in the books, *a hole in the ground, hidden by sticks and leaves.* After a day of amazingly complex and difficult puzzles, they got fooled by something unbelievably simple.

"Anyone hurt?" asked Peter, not being able to see them clearly yet. His eyes were still adjusting to the relative darkness of the pit.

"I'm fine," replied Nicola. "But I think I landed on Neil."

"I'm okay too," said Neil. "And Nik, it's a good thing you're light, or else you would have busted my leg."

"So what did we just fall into?" Neil asked, feeling around for the wall.

"Not sure," replied Peter, as his eyes slowly adjusted enough to see a little. "But I don't plan to be in here for long."

They carefully examined the walls of the pit, looking

for anything that would give them a way to climb out. It was way too deep to boost someone out of, and the walls were too smooth and slippery to climb. They were stuck.

"Check by your feet," said Peter. "There must be something in here we can use to help us get out."

Unfortunately, the only things on the ground were the leaves and sticks that had been covering up the hole. It didn't take long for them to realize that this wasn't a puzzle at all. It was simply a trap. A trap with no way out. And it could have been avoided if they had been a little more careful.

Peter sat down. He felt a mixture of disappointment, anger, and confusion. Not only were they going to be defeated by Zoltan, but they were also now stuck in a hole, in the middle of nowhere. And there was no way out.

As time passed, the already dark pit grew even darker. It wouldn't be long before it would be pitch black. Peter kept reminding himself about the rules, which were that they had to complete the final challenge before sunset. If they didn't, then Zoltan would win, and the destruction which he had promised would start again.

Peter felt a hand pat him on the back. "I screwed up, man," said Neil. "I blew it for all of us. Now we are stuck down here. Man, I was so stupid!"

Peter didn't know how to reply. He still couldn't believe that Neil had ignored his warning and ran ahead.

Not knowing what to say to each other, they all sat down. Then suddenly, their depressing silence was broken. They heard the rustling of leaves up above. Someone, or something, was coming their way.

"Help us!" screamed Nicola. "Down here! Help! Help!"

They all looked up, but since it was so close to sunset, they couldn't see much. Then a very bright light, from some type of flashlight, was shone into their eyes.

Nicola waved her arms frantically and yelled, "Help us! Please! We're stuck!"

Whoever was holding the flashlight had no intention of speaking. Instead, he or she dropped the flashlight into the hole. It landed near Neil's foot. He quickly picked it up, and aimed it upward to see who their rescuer was.

But all they saw was a hand, which was holding something small. The hand then let go of whatever it was holding, and it began fluttering down slowly. As it got closer to them, they realized it was an envelope. After it landed, Neil aimed the flashlight directly at it. It was a small envelope, just like the ones they had received all of their puzzle instructions in. Peter took the note out, and softly read its contents.

So close. You did quite well. 7 out of 8. But close is not good enough.

Anyway, now 3 of you are trapped in this pit, and the fourth will soon become lost in the darkness. So unless you can miraculously pull a rabbit out of a hat, (or should say out of a hole - ha ha ha) then I suppose you lose!

Peter crushed the note into a ball, and threw it on the ground. Not only had they lost, but now their faces were being rubbed in it.

"What does he mean by the *fourth* person?" Nicola asked a couple minutes later.

"He must mean Brad," Peter replied expressionlessly. "I guess Zoltan has no idea that Bradley quit on us before we even came today."

But all of the sudden, Peter's face changed. "Hold on a second," he said. "If Zoltan just watched three out of four people fall into this hole, then that means someone else must be up there. And they must be close by. We know it's not Brad. It must be a hiker or camper or something. Anyway, I don't care who it is. If someone is up there, they can help us get out!"

All three of them began screaming for help as loud as they could. Neil aimed the flashlight up, hoping to make their location easier to spot. After a few minutes of yelling, they paused to catch their breath. Then they heard footsteps coming quickly their way.

A face appeared over the ledge. "Figured you couldn't win this thing without me!" said Bradley, dropping a rope ladder down to them. "Hurry up and climb! Zoltan hasn't won yet!"

"Brad?!" Peter exclaimed in utter disbelief. "How did—"

"Mr. Winchester came to see me today," Bradley yelled down, cutting Peter off. "Anyway, there's no time to talk now! C'mon, climb! We can still win this if we hurry!"

One at a time, they frantically climbed up the rope ladder. Sunset was very, very close. When all three were out, Bradley quickly passed everyone headlamps, which he had already turned on. These headlamps would make it easy to see the path out in the darkening forest.

"Never come unprepared!" Bradley said while pointing at his huge backpack. "Okay, let's go! Run in single file! Follow my steps exactly! We don't want you falling in any more holes!"

Bradley led them down the path. He had dropped bright yellow markers on all of the other hidden pits he had passed on his way up. As long as they stayed away from those markers, they'd be able to make it down safely. Peter could see quite a few markers ahead of them, meaning they would have had no chance at all without Bradley's help.

Peter needed an explanation for Bradley's timely arrival. "What do you mean he came to see you?" he asked Bradley as they weaved their way between the traps. "How did he get out of the hospital?"

"No clue," Bradley replied. "He just showed up at our house at about lunchtime. He made me watch that DVD, and then he begged me to come out here."

"But we'd already started," Peter said back quickly. "Why would—"

"Not to join you," Bradley said, cutting Peter off again. "He said he was convinced that Zoltan would pull some trick to prevent you from winning. He wanted me to come out here and watch for anything suspicious."

"You mean he thought Zoltan was gonna cheat?" Peter asked.

"Something like that," Bradley replied. "Anyway, so I put all our outdoor gear in a backpack and rode out here. And after walking around the mountain for an hour or so, I spotted some guy in a hood setting up traps."

"A hooded guy?" Peter asked as they ran past the last of the traps. "You mean Zoltan?"

"I guess," Bradley replied. "So I hid in the bushes, and watched where he set the traps. Once he got far enough away, I marked the ones I remembered. And then I just hid and waited for any sign of you guys."

"And when you heard us screaming," Nicola said

loudly from behind Peter, "you ran over to help!"

"To help?" Bradley said back, giggling a little. "You mean to *save* you! But how did you manage to fall in the only hole I missed? I mean, like, what are the odds of that?"

"Look!" Neil yelled. "There's the exit!"

The exit was less than fifty meters away now. It was actually nothing more than a gate at the end of the path. They all sprinted, using whatever energy they had left. They needed to get through that gate before it was too late.

They burst through the gate and collapsed on the ground in exhaustion. A tiny sliver of the sun was still visible on the horizon. They had made it in time.

Peter stood up first. He aimed his headlamp toward the road. A short distance away, two people were standing and looking their way. One was Mr. Winchester. How he had managed to get out of his hospital bed was a mystery of its own. And the other was Zoltan. Neither of them moved, so Peter took it as a hint that they were expecting him to walk over.

He approached them quickly. He really wanted to see the face of this supernatural being close up. But Zoltan's face was once again hidden by a large hood. Just before Peter got to them, Zoltan shook Mr. Winchester's hand. Then without saying a word, Zoltan turned and walked away.

"Well done, Peter," Mr. Winchester said in a raspy voice. "I am so pleased, and honored, to have you take over for me. You're perfectly capable of keeping Zoltan entertained. People will be safe again, thanks to you."

He handed Peter a small box. Peter opened it and looked at the two things inside. One was a key, and the other was a piece of paper with an address written on it.

"There's a shed at that address," Mr. Winchester said. "And you can open it with the key. Inside the shed, you'll find everything I've ever used while creating puzzles for Zoltan. Notes, sketches, tools, everything. That's where I came up with, created, and stored all of my puzzles. Use anything you can. I'm sure it will help."

Mr. Winchester appeared to have tears forming in his eyes. He turned and started limping slowly away. To where? Peter had no idea.

CHAPTER 47

Peter looked up at the clock on the far side of the classroom. He still had sixteen minutes left of listening to Mr. Pendleton's boring geographical explanations. Since Peter had the same teachers again for almost all his Grade 8 classes, he was used to these yawn-inducing geography lessons. Then he shot a glance over to Nicola. She winked at Peter again, for the twelfth time that class.

"And this may be straying from the textbook a bit," his teacher said. "But haven't you all noticed those nasty storms seemed to have become a thing of the past?"

No one was sure if that question was being asked to the class, or if Mr. Pendleton was just rambling away and killing time until the bell.

"I spoke with a friend at the weather bureau," he continued, "and he informed me that nothing out of the ordinary has happened for two months."

Peter counted Nicola's thirteenth wink. He couldn't wait to get out of school today. They were now officially a couple, despite all of her friends' objections. And since today was Friday, they were going to the movies after school. They would watch a mystery again, hoping something in the movie would provide them with some inspiration or ideas to use on their next puzzle for Zoltan.

Then tomorrow, Peter and Nicola would spend the day at the secret little hideaway holding all of Mr. Winchester's supplies. They went there every Saturday, often staying until it was time to head home for dinner. They used Saturday as their day to prepare Zoltan's weekly puzzle. And if they could get it ready quickly tomorrow, Peter knew they'd spend the rest of the afternoon telling stories and hanging out. He wondered if tomorrow would be the day he'd finally get enough courage to try to give Nicola a kiss.

Neil kicked Peter's chair. "Sleeping again, Pete?" he asked. "Or just daydreaming about your girlfriend?"

Peter looked up. Other than Neil, he was the only one left in the room. Nicola was standing at the door with her arms crossed.

"Oops," Peter said. "Must have dozed off."

He ran to the door and put his arm around Nicola's waist. They started walking together to their final class of the day, math. Unfortunately, they still had sixty minutes, or three thousand and six hundred seconds, of school left before they could head to the theater.

"I've got an awesome idea for the next puzzle," she said as they walked upstairs. "Wanna hear?"

"I certainly do," he replied. "But not here. If people hear you talking about that kind of stuff, they'll think you're as weird as me!"

Nicola giggled. The bell had already rung, so they were going to be late for class. But on a good note, they only had 3555 seconds of math left to go.

REALLY PUZZLED

THE PUZZLED MYSTERY ADVENTURE SERIES: BOOK 2

P.J. NICHOLS

CHAPTER 1

"Haven't you ever paddled a canoe before?" Nicola asked playfully, amused by the fact that Peter couldn't get their canoe to do anything other than constantly go in a big circle.

"Gimme a break!" Peter replied while laughing at himself. "Don't tell me that you now expect your boyfriend to be good at sports, too?"

* * *

Nicola had been allowed to join Peter's family for their annual summer camping trip at Starlight Lake National Park. She had begged her mom for months to let her go. She used the fact that she was now fifteen and about to enter high school as her main bargaining chip. Plus she played the "and you've known Peter's dad since you were six card." Clearville was a pretty small town. Her mom had attended the same schools as Peter's dad for thirteen years, and they were even in the same class a number of times.

Peter's older brother Bradley had decided not to join the annual trip this year. He was signed up to compete in the big district triathlon at the end of September, and he had told his parents he wanted to stay home and train for it. But Peter knew the truth: Having the house to himself was what Bradley was really after. Bradley was a partier. And since the family camping trip was booked for the last week of summer break, Peter had no doubt that Bradley would invite everyone he knew over for a huge bash. He was actually so worried about it that he had removed all of his puzzles and games from his room, and locked them away safely in the attic, out of sight of Bradley's friends.

Since Bradley had talked his way out of going on the trip, the six-seater family van had enough space for one more. So Peter's parents had decided to also let Sophia, his twelve-year-old sister, invite a friend along. Of course she chose Anita, her best friend for as long as everyone could remember. And Anita's home was only three houses down the road, so both sets of parents were friends as well.

* * *

"Wait, I think I just figured it out!" Peter proudly announced as he tried desperately to aim their boat in a straight line for the first time.

"No you didn't!" Nicola answered, laughing so hard that she made a loud snorting sound. "Now we're going sideways!"

It was hard for Peter to believe that he and Nicola had been dating for two years now. For the first few months, he constantly worried that someone bigger, stronger, and cooler would show up and sweep her off her feet. Nicola was incredibly attractive, but luckily for Peter, she was completely disinterested in the strong and handsome jock type. Whenever a guy approached her and asked for a date, she simply said, "Already got a boyfriend." And that was that.

Peter decided to give up on his feeble attempt at looking macho while paddling, and handed Nicola the other oar. He intentionally passed it to her in a way that splashed her with as much water as possible. Nicola responded by rocking the boat to one side so quickly that Peter almost fell overboard.

After they both became tired and sore from maneuvering their canoe around the lake, they slowly started to make their way back to the shore. But instead of taking in the amazing view, Peter and Nicola were pondering what to do for Zoltan's weekly puzzle.

Since taking over as Zoltan's puzzle-maker two years ago, the weekly routine had remained the same for Peter. Zoltan was to be provided with one interesting, challenging, and creative puzzle per week. The weekly puzzle needed to be completely ready by eight o'clock on Sunday morning, regardless of the season or the weather. Nicola had, of course, offered to help Peter with this immense task, whether that meant coming up with ideas or setting up things.

They'd been doing these for so long now that they were finding it harder and harder to always come up with new and original ideas.

"Why don't we just reuse some old stuff?" Nicola suggested. "I mean, not totally, just partially."

"We better not," Peter replied quickly. "You remember what happened that time when we both had the flu."

* * *

Peter was referring to the very scary event from a year and a half ago, in the third week of January. Both he and Nicola had caught the flu, so neither were able to do anything to prepare Zoltan's weekly challenge. But they knew if they prepared nothing, that Zoltan might create some type of storm or other catastrophe. They were both so miserably sick that all they could do was quickly combine together parts of previous challenges, and hope it would be good enough. They were wrong. Very wrong.

Zoltan always arrived to do his puzzle at eight o'clock on Sunday morning. On that particular Sunday, at exactly 8:22, a horrendous hailstorm hammered down on the town. It was relentless. It shattered and cracked windows of homes, cars, and stores, and sent people running like mad for safety. It was Zoltan's way of telling Peter and Nicola to never try something like that again.

* * *

"But we are seriously out of ideas," Nicola said. "I mean, last week, it took us a whole day just to think of where to start."

As much as he hated to admit it, Nicola was right. These days, they were scraping the bottom of the barrel when it came to creativity.

"But it's only Wednesday," Peter replied. "We've still got a few more days. C'mon, let's worry about that later."

They paddled the final ten minutes or so back to shore in silence. They weren't angry or upset at each other, they were just trying to brainstorm ideas for Zoltan's next puzzle.

As they were pulling the canoe back up on the beach, Peter stopped and snapped his fingers. "Got one!" he said excitedly.

As he prepared to launch into an explanation of his ingenious idea, a cold wind started to pick up. They wanted to be back inside before the weather turned ugly, so they quickly finished securing the canoe, and headed for the shelter of the cabin.

But the wind rapidly increased in intensity and as the sky darkened, it suddenly got a lot colder.

"What's going on?" Nicola asked while pulling her hood up over her head to block the wind.

"I don't know," Peter replied.

Before he could say another word, they both watched a huge tornado touch down in the middle of the lake.

"Look!" Nicola yelled. "C'mon, we've gotta get back to the cabin!"

They ran back to the rental cabin, fighting hard to keep their balance. Once safely inside, they watched in amazement from the window. The tornado was enormous. It was fierce. They pleaded for it to stay far from the shore, as it would certainly tear apart their flimsy log cabin if it came too close. Thankfully, it remained over the lake.

Two long and agonizing minutes later, the tornado magically vanished, and the peaceful weather returned.

While everyone else breathed a sigh of relief, Peter and Nicola looked at each other in shock. Peter's stomach started churning, just like it did every time he had to give speeches at school.

"Zoltan knows he has to wait until Sunday for his puzzle," he whispered in Nicola's ear. "What's he doing? Why is he so angry?"

Too many questions and no quick or easy way to find the answers. Well, so much for the relaxing escape from city life...

CHAPTER 2

They arrived back home from their camping trip late Friday afternoon. Peter's dad always booked the cabin from Sunday through Friday, as the weekend rental fee was outrageous.

They spent about thirty minutes unpacking and putting everything where it belonged. Peter's mom was a neat freak, so things always had to be put away as fast as humanly possible. Once they were done, Peter and Nicola went upstairs to his room.

"Okay," he said with an anxious look on his face. "First, we need to contact Zoltan so we can ask him why on Earth he did that."

After the flu incident, Peter and Zoltan had arranged a way to contact each other whenever necessary. If Zoltan wanted to get in touch, he would tape a leaf on the outside of Peter's bedroom window. And if Peter wanted to call Zoltan, he would turn on a light which he had installed in the chimney on the roof. (Peter had told his mom he was putting up Christmas lights, and then secretly installed a bright light inside the chimney.) When turned on, no one could see it unless they were above the house. Peter had only used it twice, and both times he felt like he was calling a superhero to come and save the day. It was very simple to turn on: The cord from the light in the chimney came to just outside Peter's window. All he had to do was attach it to an extension cord (which he kept hidden in his closet) and plug it in.

And regardless of whom called whom, the meeting place and time were both fixed: The bottom of Silverhead Mountain, at nine in the morning, on the nearest Saturday.

They plugged in the light and went back downstairs.

"Nicola, you're welcome to stay for dinner if you want," Peter's mom said. "It's nothing fancy, just spaghetti."

"Thank you for the offer," she replied politely. "But I think I better head home. My parents only agreed to let me go camping if I promised to do a huge pile of chores as soon as I got home."

* * *

Later that night, Peter puttered around in his room well after he should have been asleep. He always needed to reason everything out. He hated unanswered *whys*, and right now there were way, way too many of them.

He unplugged the chimney light, turned off the lights in his room, and picked up his glow-in-the-dark dice, a present he received from Nicola last Christmas. Wow, did that girl ever know how to get to Peter's heart! He tossed the dice back and forth between his hands for a while, and the movement of the colors helped Peter to finally doze off a few minutes past midnight.

CHAPTER 3

The next morning, Saturday, Peter cycled up Nicola's driveway at exactly 8:40. Another one of Peter's quirks was his obsession with preciseness. *Be there by 8:45* meant I'll be there way before 8:45, because I want to make absolutely sure that there is no possibility of being even a second late.

Nicola knew Peter's character well by now, and was already waiting for him on the front steps. They could easily cycle out to Silverhead Mountain in less than fifteen minutes, which would leave them some time to spare while waiting for Zoltan.

Peter still hadn't decided exactly what to say to Zoltan. He knew he shouldn't appear too angry. They were dealing with a supernatural being with unbelievably destructive powers, right? But at the same time, Peter was still upset and wanted Zoltan to know that there were better and far less dangerous ways to get their attention.

Zoltan showed up at exactly nine o'clock, literally coming out of nowhere. He always just *appeared* for their meetings. He never walked or rode in, or arrived by any means that would make him seem somewhat human.

And as always, Zoltan waited for Peter and Nicola to approach first. Peter quickly stormed over, as he was extremely anxious to know what was going on.

"What was with that tornado at the lake on Wednesday?" he asked very loudly and directly.

"Yeah," Nicola quickly followed, also unable to contain her frustration. "You could have hurt someone!"

Zoltan was silent. And since his face was hidden by his hood, neither Peter nor Nicola could gauge his reaction.

"C'mon!" Peter asked again loudly. "What's going on?!"

"This is quite perplexing," Zoltan replied. "I did not make a tornado, at a lake, on Wednesday. I have not made any tornados, anywhere, for ages."

"Gimme a break!" Peter said back sharply. "It was NOT a natural one."

"Whether or not it was natural, I can't say," Zoltan answered. "But what I can tell you for sure is that *I* did not cause it."

A long silence ensued. Someone was lying. Or maybe they weren't. Or, quite possibly, they were all just really confused. Peter shuffled around, impatiently waiting for Zoltan's next comment. He needed a feasible explanation, and he wanted it now.

Zoltan turned around to walk away.

"Where do you think you're going?!" Nicola yelled at him.

Zoltan stopped, but he didn't turn around to face them. "You asked me a question, and I answered it," he said coldly. "I have no idea what caused that tornado."

Peter looked at Nicola, shrugged his shoulders, and started heading toward his bike. There was no point in arguing about something that all three of them didn't understand.

Just as he was about to sit down on the bike seat, someone kicked or jerked his bike hard. Peter lost his balance, and both he and his bike toppled over sideways. He twisted around to scold Nicola for her untimely and immature little prank.

"Nik, what are you...?" he said angrily.

But Nicola was at least four or five meters away. She clearly hadn't done anything.

Before he could say anything, the ground started shaking violently. An earthquake?! Peter couldn't believe his eyes. He turned in the direction he had last seen Zoltan to scream at him. But Zoltan was already facing them, with his hands in his pockets, and his hood off for the first time ever. Peter and Nicola were startled by Zoltan's face: Not because he looked like a monster or zombie, but by the fact that he looked so human. And the expression on Zoltan's face showed that he was just as confused as they were about the earthquake.

Since they were outside, they were relatively safe. It wasn't like something would fall from above and injure them. All they had to do was wait it out. But when a person panics, especially a nervous kid like Peter, logic doesn't always prevail. Peter darted around aimlessly, looking up in fear at the shaking tree branches. It was as if he were riding a surfboard while dancing the tango. Even Zoltan, who never showed any emotion, cracked a smile while watching Peter's performance.

When the shaking finally stopped, Zoltan walked over to Nicola and Peter. "Well, now you know I wasn't lying," he said very matter-of-factly.

"But hold on a sec," Peter said while trying to catch

his breath, his heart still beating insanely fast. "If it wasn't you, then who? Or what? There are no fault lines around here. It's completely impossible for earthquakes to happen in this region. That earthquake was NOT natural."

"Yeah, he's right," Nicola added. "Zoltan, what's going on?"

Zoltan pulled his hood back over his head, and turned to walk away again.

When he was a few meters away from them, he twisted his head back to say something. "As you know," he said seriously, "I am the only weather god assigned to Earth. But it would appear, for a reason I don't know, that we have company. I'll look into it. Meet me back here tomorrow. And you can forget about my weekly challenge. There is no longer any time for games."

CHAPTER 4

Peter's house had been completely undamaged by the earthquake. His family, and all of the neighbors, hadn't even noticed it. If it had been a natural earthquake, it would definitely have been felt throughout the whole town. So that just reinforced Peter's theory that someone had both caused it and focused it on only the area they were in at the time. But the notion that there might be another weather god on Earth made Peter nauseous.

* * *

Unfortunately, Peter had the bad habit of worrying himself sick. He hated his overly active mind, which had to play out every possible negative outcome, as if one of them was guaranteed to happen. Back when he was eight, his parents went to Europe for five days, on a trip they had won from a cereal box sweepstakes competition. While they were gone, Peter's grandparents walked him to the school bus every morning. While waiting for the bus, he'd say, "I feel like I'm gonna barf." Peter was paranoid that an engine failure was going to cause the plane to crash somewhere over the Atlantic Ocean. His grandparents took him home and allowed him to miss school for the day. Shortly after arriving home, he would throw up, sometimes more than once. When you're a worrier, you can never, ever turn it off.

* * *

Peter tossed and turned all night. His stomach was in such a knot the next morning that he could barely even manage a few spoons of cereal. But breakfast or no breakfast, Peter needed to get to Silverhead Mountain again. Hopefully, Zoltan would have some information for them, as there was no way he could possibly get back to normal life until he knew more.

* * *

Zoltan was already waiting for them when they arrived, and he uncharacteristically waved when he saw them coming.

"Since when did he develop a personality?" Peter whispered to Nicola. "He must be even more scared than we are."

"Good to see you both again," Zoltan said as Peter and Nicola sat down. "I managed to find out a few things yesterday."

"A *few* things?" Peter asked. "What do you mean?"

"I don't want to bore you with a long lecture on the history and bloodlines of weather gods," Zoltan began. "But without a brief one, none of this will make any sense. I'll try to keep it as short as I can.

"As you already know, I was sent to Earth about twenty-eight years ago, as a punishment of sorts. You remember why the lead weather gods sent me here, right? Because I tried to cheat my way into being assigned to a small and easy planet. Well, I've always assumed that I was the only weather god to ever receive any type of punishment. There are no courts or judges or prisons where I'm from, and I'd never heard any stories about weather gods causing even the slightest trouble. But was I ever wrong.

"It would appear that I have an older brother. Much older. And I only learned about his existence last night. You know the fairy tale about the girl with the evil stepsisters? I suppose you could say I have an evil brother. And it's my brother, in fact, that's been causing the weather problems here recently."

"Your brother?" Peter said, dumbfounded. "But why would he come to Earth? And why would he start messing with the weather here? It makes zero sense."

"It didn't make any sense to me either," Zoltan replied. "Well, until last night. As outrageous as this may sound, my brother, whose name is Xavier by the way, is here to get revenge."

"Revenge?" Nicola asked. "On whom? For what?"

"On me," Zoltan answered. "I'll fill you in on the rest later, I promise. I must go now. I need to find out as much as I can about Xavier."

Peter and Nicola watched as Zoltan started walking away very quickly.

"Meet me here again on Wednesday morning!" he yelled back at them.

"But school starts this week," Peter said back. "Can't we wait until next weekend?"

Zoltan stopped walking and turned around to face them. "No, we can't wait that long," he said very sternly. "Just skip school on Wednesday. See you then."

CHAPTER 5

Peter had missed a few days of school here and there whenever he was sick, but he had never intentionally played hooky. He had wanted to do so on many occasions, but was terrified of the possible consequences. More specifically, he feared the wrath that would come down from his mother. She had absolutely no patience for kids with a slack attitude. He'd seen Bradley punished for skipping school more times than he could count.

Peter had thought up a very believable lie to get himself and Nicola out of school for the day. It was extremely simple. And, well, simple is always best, right?

On Wednesday morning, he left for school a couple of minutes earlier than usual and rode directly to Nicola's house. Her parents were both nurses, and were currently working the 6 a.m. to 4 p.m. shift, so that meant Nicola would be the only one home.

The *trick* to getting them out of school was going to be implemented by Nicola. She was going to make two calls to the school: one posing as Peter's mom, and one posing as her own mother. She'd wait at least fifteen minutes between calls, to reduce the chance of arousing any suspicion. But they actually weren't too worried about the phone calls raising any red flags. Their high school's one and only receptionist, Miss Perkins, apparently had a reputation for always being buried in fashion magazines. (That was something Bradley had mentioned quite a few times.) The likelihood of her noticing that the two calls had come from the same person or even the same number was virtually zero, especially if Nicola used a deeper voice for one of the calls.

As expected, all went smoothly. Nicola was going to miss the morning, and possibly the whole day, to get a filling at the dentist. And Peter had a nasty case of diarrhea, so he couldn't possibly make it to school today. As long as they both returned to school on Thursday and stuck to their stories, it was highly unlikely that anyone from the school would phone to confirm. Well, unless someone spotted them outside somewhere today...

Thankfully, small towns have plenty of side streets, paths, and parks. They could easily navigate their way to Silverhead Mountain using a route that would put them at very little risk of being seen.

* * *

They got there a couple of minutes later than expected, and Zoltan was already waiting as promised. He waved again today when he saw them approaching, and this time he was holding a bag with some cookies and juice boxes he'd just bought at a convenience store.

After exchanging a few quick pleasantries and happily getting started on their snacks, they all sat down at one of the picnic tables.

"We are going to be here for a while today," Zoltan began. "What's going on is far, far worse than I originally thought.

"I suppose I should start by explaining everything I just learned about my long-lost brother. When he was very young, way before I was even born, people realized his weather altering skills were developing faster than anyone in history. By the age of eight, he was already more powerful than most of the adults. The young Xavier loved all of the attention. People came from far and wide to catch a glimpse of this prodigy. They wanted to see, with their own two eyes, the kid who was destined to become the greatest weather god ever.

"And then when Xavier was fourteen, I was born. You'd think that he would've been happy to get a sibling after being an only child for so long, but his reaction was the complete opposite. He despised that his parents' time was now split between him and a screaming baby. He just couldn't tolerate the fact that he was no longer the center of his parents' world.

"His attitude turned full circle, and he started to rebel. He wouldn't listen to anyone and began doing whatever he wanted. When my parents tried to punish him for any type of inexcusable behavior, he rebelled even more. Then one day, he did the unthinkable; he snuck out after dark and unleashed an enormous storm, centered directly on our home. And since it was the dead of night, no one noticed in time to try to stop him.

"Our house was reduced to rubble, and we were all seriously injured. I was still a baby, but somehow my mom managed to grab me from my crib before the roof collapsed. We were lucky to make it out alive.

"But before Xavier could be caught and punished for his brutal act, he vanished. And no one has heard from him since. Well, until now.

"In his mind, I destroyed his ideal world. Xavier truly

hates me. He despises me. And he wants me to suffer. He believes I ruined his world, so now he wants to ruin mine."

"So how do we stop him?" Peter asked.

"We don't," Zoltan replied. "We can't. He is far too powerful. He could, and I'm not joking, wipe out everyone on Earth in a few weeks if he really wanted to. During all those years since he went into hiding, he must have been honing his destructive powers."

"So what do we do?" Peter asked again.

"There is only one thing I can imagine that might work," Zoltan replied. "We have to trick him or fool him. And then finally, trap him."

"Trap him?" asked Nicola. "But how do we trap someone so powerful?"

"Our trap will have to be something he won't see coming," Zoltan said. "We have to create a trap that he'll never suspect is a trap."

"Uh... I'm a little lost," Peter said. "How do we do that?"

"Oh, I haven't thought of *how* to trap him yet," Zoltan replied. "That's what I need you two for!"

CHAPTER 6

Peter was unbelievably paranoid about being caught skipping school. Right now, he really wished he had an invisibility cloak, as that would guarantee him safe passage home. Too bad he didn't live in a world of magic…

They rode home on the same seldomly used streets and paths, stopping at the end of each one to make sure there was no one was around the next corner. And they timed it so they'd arrive home at roughly the same time as any other school day. They had even taken their backpacks with them, filled with schoolbooks, to ensure everything appeared completely normal.

* * *

Only Sophia was home when Peter got back. He casually walked into the kitchen and grabbed some chocolate chip cookies and a glass of milk, just as he would on a typical day after school. Then he carried them to the family room, placed them down on the coffee table, and grabbed the TV remote. Sophia came and sat down beside him, likely because she was bored and had nothing better to do.

"Guess what happened today?" she said excitedly.

"You remember Mr. Phillips, right? You know, the science teacher. When he turned on the overhead projector, the words 'I am a dork' shone up on the screen! Someone, maybe Keith or Tony, had written it on there between classes. It was like, soooo funny! He went crazy!"

Peter was trying to listen to his sister's story, but everything she said was going in one ear and out the other. He kept thinking about whether he was acting normal or not. He didn't want to do anything to tip Sophia off to the fact he'd played hooky.

"That's cool," he replied, not really knowing what else to say. "Mr. Phillips has been a grump, like, forever. I never saw that guy smile."

"Yeah, no kidding," she said. Then she got up and skipped happily out of the room.

Alone again in the family room, Peter felt like he was in some weird and bizarre trance. He looked down at the empty plate and glass on the coffee table, but he couldn't remember taking a bite of a cookie or a sip of milk. But when a chocolaty, milky burp suddenly came out, he realized that he had indeed finished his snack.

* * *

Right after dinner, Peter went up to his room, locked the door, and sat at his desk. He grabbed a sheet of loose-leaf paper and wrote "How to Trick Xavier" at the top. Peter approached every challenging puzzle the same way: He started by putting all his ideas down on paper. Then he eliminated the bad ones before continuing. This technique helped Peter save tons of time.

CHAPTER 7

A ridiculous dream, which involved dancing babies and giant talking vegetables, startled Peter awake. He had been sleeping face down on his desk for hours, and a small pile of drool had formed on the list he'd spent so much time writing.

Peter checked his wristwatch. It was a quarter past nine. No wonder his neck hurt so much. He pulled a couple of tissues from the box on his desk and wiped the spit off his papers.

The list was so messy and disorganized that 99.999 percent of the population would have no chance of understanding it. First, he had scribbled down every single idea, good or bad, that had popped into his mind. Then when he could come up with no more, the next steps were to eliminate some, link some with circles and lines, and add more detail to the good ones. What he had produced in the end looked like a cross between the brainstorming of Einstein and the doodling of a two-year-old.

Peter knew he wouldn't be able to get back to sleep, so he grabbed a fresh sheet of paper and started on a more organized version of the first list. Once he'd rewritten everything, he leaned back in his chair and smiled. He had managed to come up with a masterful plan to first trick, and then trap, Xavier. It wasn't going to be easy, but if somehow they could pull off everything to perfection, it would work.

Just like two years ago, the innocent people of earth needed to be saved, and Peter was the only person capable of doing it. But why now? It didn't seem fair. He was enjoying life. He had the perfect girlfriend. Everything was just like he had hoped for in his wildest dreams.

Peter thought about what his dad would say when someone started complaining about how hard things were: *Too bad, so sad.* Peter had never understood where his dad got all of the weird expressions. But he kind of felt like he had finally figured out the meaning of this one: *Stop whining and complaining, and get on with it.*

CHAPTER 8

Despite the urgency of getting started on the plan, skipping school again today was not an option. Peter and Nicola had gone undetected yesterday, but another absence would certainly raise some eyebrows. And if they did try and were caught, Peter knew his mom would ground him for at least a week. He wouldn't be allowed to go anywhere other than school. Plus no friends would be allowed to come over. That would end up being counter-productive, as it would mean they wouldn't be able to meet Zoltan on the weekend.

So all he could do was wait. Wait and wait and wait some more, until Saturday morning finally arrived.

* * *

At slightly before nine on Saturday morning, Peter, Nicola, and Zoltan were sitting at a picnic table at Silverhead Mountain again. Peter launched into the explanation of his complicated and confusing plan. He tried to cover everything, leaving out no details at all. Nicola had trouble wrapping her head around a lot of it, and Zoltan had to ask for clarification numerous times.

Just before noon, it seemed as if they were both up to speed on everything. They knew what they had to do, and exactly how they had to do it. It was going to be an extremely challenging and complex process. But if each and every part of the plan could be done to perfection, then a couple of weeks from today, Xavier would be trapped. And once trapped, he could then be banished from Earth forever.

CHAPTER 9

The first part of the ingenious plan would be initiated that very afternoon. But before getting started, they decided to grab a quick sandwich at a small café on the edge of town. Peter had brought a pair of his dad's jeans and a t-shirt for Zoltan to use today, as Zoltan's usual cloak would have attracted way too much attention. Dressed in Peter's dad's clothes, Zoltan managed to blend in just fine.

After lunch, the three of them returned to Silverhead Mountain. What they needed to do first was to get Xavier's attention. They climbed as far up the mountain as they could, until it would have been dangerous to go any further. It was exhausting, but they were able to get within about a hundred meters of the peak.

"This should be high enough," Peter said, huffing and puffing. Although Peter was reasonably good at most of the sports he did in gym class, climbing a steep mountain was another story altogether. "Alright, Zoltan, you know what to do."

Zoltan's face hardened, and he raised his hands in the air. He started chanting something, which Peter knew was his way of commanding the weather. Zoltan easily created a massive storm, which pounded hard against the lower half of the mountain.

"Xavier will definitely see this!" Peter yelled at Nicola through the noise. "I mean, how could he not?"

Zoltan gradually increased the ferocity of the storm. Within less than two minutes, it was so huge that making it any bigger would start to uproot small trees or possibly even initiate a landslide.

"Still no sign of Xavier..." Peter said. "Now what?"

Zoltan, looking somewhat burnt out from his efforts, decided to add some fireworks to the mix. He made loud claps of thunder and bolt after bolt of lightning.

"He's gotta notice soon," Nicola said. "Why isn't he here yet?"

Zoltan's arms were now trembling. Clearly this was taking a huge toll on him. Peter figured that Zoltan would be incapable of maintaining this huge storm much longer.

And then, in an instant, the storm completely vanished.

"Are you okay?" Peter yelled while spinning around to look at Zoltan. He figured that Zoltan had overexerted himself and passed out. But Zoltan was just fine, and by the bewildered look on his face, it was obvious that he was just as confused as they were.

Realizing how strange he looked with his arms high up in the air, Zoltan lowered them and put his hands in his pockets. "This is far worse than I feared," he said. "Xavier's powers are beyond what I could have imagined. Stopping another weather god's storm, or even just reducing its intensity, is extremely difficult. Nearly impossible, actually. He made mine vanish instantaneously. I've never heard of anyone capable of doing that."

"Guys, don't worry about that yet," Nicola said supportively. "I mean, we came here to get his attention, right? And we just did that. Now all we have to do is wait and see when he—"

But before she could finish her sentence, the infamous Xavier appeared behind them. Aside from his golden cloak and somewhat messy hair, he was the spitting image of Zoltan. If it wasn't for the fourteen-year age gap, you'd have thought they were twins.

"You're even weaker than I thought!" Xavier said loudly. "I can't believe they sent you to Earth. You're not capable of controlling the weather here!"

As they had planned, Zoltan began taunting his evil brother. "Gimme a break," he said. "I could've made that storm a hundred, or even a thousand times more powerful if I had wanted to."

"Ha!" Xavier laughed back. "I'd love to see that!"

"Anyway," Zoltan said sharply. "I know why you're here. You came to get revenge, right? Revenge because you think I destroyed your ideal world so many, many years ago. Well, let's just cut to the chase. I want you gone. Now."

"Oh, I see," Xavier replied. "The *good* son, the one mom and dad love the most, wants his bad brother to disappear. You just can't stand to see—"

"Xavier," Zoltan said, interrupting his brother. "This isn't about who's good or who's bad. Earth is *my* planet to manage. I was assigned here by the lead weather gods. And although you may seriously doubt this, I am completely capable of carrying out my duties."

Xavier let out a huge roar. "Stop! Please!" he said while laughing. "I'm going to pee my pants."

"What makes you think you are so special?" Zoltan continued, trying to rile his brother up even more.

"You stupid and naïve brat!" Xavier screamed. He put his palms and fingertips together and raised them up to the sky.

A powerful bolt of lightning came down directly on Zoltan's head, causing him to jerk and quiver, and then fall over sideways. Peter and Nicola ran over, but Zoltan was unconscious.

"Don't worry, he'll be fine in a couple of weeks," Xavier said. "I want to watch him suffer, not die."

As much as he felt like yelling at Xavier, Peter knew he had to keep his mouth shut. Zoltan could recover from a lightning blast, but he and Nicola certainly could not.

"Nik," Peter whispered. "Don't look at Xavier. Just put your hand on Zoltan's head and act really worried. Make yourself cry or something."

She did as Peter had instructed, and less than thirty seconds later, tears were streaming down her cheeks. Peter, though a poorly skilled actor, did his best to squeeze out a few tears as well.

"You stupid kids," Xavier said while shaking his head. "Why do you care about my brother? He's weak! He's useless! He's a complete joke! *I* am the real thing!"

Despite being terrified beyond belief, Peter and Nicola stuck to the original plan. They needed Xavier to think they loved Zoltan as if he were family. This crucial point would become essential later on.

"Look at me!" Xavier yelled. "You heard me, LOOK!!"

They turned to face him, their cheeks red and wet from crying. "Please leave Zoltan alone," Peter begged. "Please. He helps people. He would never, ever hurt anyone."

"I know that," Xavier barked back. "He's not powerful enough to hurt anyone. Anyway, I have better things to do than sit around here and listen to you crybabies."

Xavier created a dust storm, and as more and more dust began swirling, Peter and Nicola couldn't see him clearly anymore. Once the dust storm had dissipated, Xavier was gone.

"How'd I do?" Zoltan asked while sitting up. "He thought I was out cold, didn't he?"

"You were perfect!" Nicola replied, slapping him lightly on the shoulder. "But that lightning bolt must have hurt."

"Not at all," he said. "Look."

Zoltan showed them the thin and nearly invisible wire he had rigged up, which went from the tip of his cloak's hood to the ground behind him.

"You know how lightning works," he said. "It always takes the easiest path. And a wire is a much better conductor than a person's body. Xavier's lightning bolt didn't touch me at all. It only went through the wire."

"Man, science is cool," Peter said with a smile.

CHAPTER 10

The next part of the plan was linked to what had happened at Silverhead Mountain yesterday. What they needed to do next, in a nutshell, was to make Xavier feel jealous. And not just a little jealous, but so jealous that it would consume him.

They decided to change up their meeting spot today, as they figured that Xavier may come looking for them at Silverhead Mountain.

"I don't get it," Nicola said to Peter, as they rode toward Meeks Park to meet up with Zoltan. "If we rattle him too much, he might go berserk and unleash a huge hurricane or something."

"Yeah, I suppose he could," Peter replied. "We are taking a risk. But my gut tells me he won't. Let's hope my gut is right on this one."

* * *

Zoltan was waiting for them at a picnic table by the river. These days, he seemed more like an *odd-ball uncle* than a supernatural being. And his people skills were getting much better too.

"Yo," Zoltan said while waving them over.

Both Peter and Nicola held back their laughter, not

wanting Zoltan to know how ridiculous he sounded when trying to talk like a teenager.

"No aftereffects from that lightning bolt yesterday?" Peter asked as he and Nicola sat down. "Are you sure none of that lightning went through you?"

"I'm totally fine, dudes," Zoltan replied, sounding even more ridiculous than before.

"Quite the group you've got here!" a raspy voice said from behind them.

They all turned to see Mr. Winchester slowly walking their way. He looked way younger than he had two years ago, when he was on the brink of death from pushing himself too hard while training Peter's team. But since he no longer had any responsibilities, he was now able to maintain a fairly healthy lifestyle. He occupied most of his free time playing chess with his newfound friends at the community center. And when he couldn't find anyone to play against, he buried his head into a crossword or Sudoku puzzle.

"Leonardo, you look great," Zoltan said while standing up to shake his former entertainer's hand.

"I figure I got a few good years left in me still," Mr. Winchester replied with a big smile. "And by the sound of what's going on, you'll need all the help you can get."

There was, of course, a reason behind why Mr. Winchester had shown up today. Peter had phoned him last night, and they spent close to an hour discussing what had happened already and what was being planned next. Despite his age, Mr. Winchester felt he could still provide some good suggestions and guidance. And when he offered to help, Peter was ecstatic.

After giving Zoltan and Mr. Winchester a chance to catch up and reminisce about the past for a while, Peter figured it was time to get down to business. "Here's what we do next," he said. "Xavier thinks he almost killed Zoltan yesterday. We are going to use that to our advantage. We are going to milk it for all it's worth."

"Milk it?" Zoltan asked. He knew what milk was, but clearly didn't understand all the colloquial expressions or slang yet.

"Anyway," Peter continued quickly, not wanting to waste time explaining what *milk it* actually meant. "Here's the plan: Mr. Winchester, you will fake a heart attack, or something like that, and get yourself hospitalized."

"Hospitalized?" Mr. Winchester replied. "Why would I—"

"Let me explain," Peter said before the old man had a chance to finish his sentence. He hadn't meant to be rude; he just wanted everyone to listen to the whole explanation and save any questions for the end. "What we need is a bed in a hospital room. Once you've been admitted, Zoltan will show up as a visitor. When no one is watching, you'll quickly swap clothes and he'll replace you in the bed. And then he'll lie there and look like he's on the verge of death."

"Peter," Mr. Winchester said with curiosity. "Why would we want to hospitalize Zoltan? How would that do anything other than just make Xavier smile?"

"Because," Peter continued, "I am going to have a least a hundred people come to visit the *almost dead* Zoltan in that hospital room. We know Xavier will be curious about how badly he harmed his brother, right? That means he'll be hanging around somewhere near the hospital. We are going to show him the last thing he wants to see: Tons and tons of people coming to pray for his brother's recovery."

"Yeah, don't you get it?" Nicola added. "When he sees all these teenagers coming to visit his brother, he'll get soooo jealous. Xavier wants to be the center of attention. He'll go insane with jealousy when he sees how much love and respect people have for Zoltan."

"I have more questions about this plan than you could possibly imagine," Mr. Winchester said. "But you have proven yourself countless times before, and I'm sure you know what you're doing. You just tell me when you want me to fake that heart attack."

"Wednesday morning," Peter replied immediately. "I'll need until then to get things set up."

CHAPTER 11

Peter and Nicola came directly back to his house, and were now eating lunch in the family room while looking over the next part of the plan on Peter's master list. The next thing they had to do was going to be really tough, and they knew they couldn't do it without some more assistance. Peter could think of no one better than Neil, one of his closest friends, to help them out.

Peter and Neil had been hanging out a lot since they teamed up to take on Zoltan two years ago. But in the past six months, they only got together a few times. The tall, skinny, and dorky Neil had put on a lot of muscle during Grade 8, plus he changed his hairstyle and fashion choices before starting Grade 9. In doing so, he had managed to become quite a hunk, and droves of girls became interested in him.

After a few relationships that lasted a few weeks each, or in some cases even less, Neil had finally found someone suitable. Claire, a tall girl with long auburn hair and the captain of the girls' volleyball team, had stolen Neil's heart. They were inseparable. When Peter did manage to get together with Neil, it was almost always for a double date. But Peter was truly happy for his friend. Claire seemed to ignore all of Neil's oddities, and they were always laughing and having fun.

Peter and Nicola knocked on Neil's door a little before three o'clock. They had phoned him after lunch, and he told them that he and Claire were watching a DVD at his house. He said they were welcome to drop by anytime in the afternoon.

"Come on in, your majesties," Neil said, bowing deeply to Peter and Nicola. "Your arrival is a true honor."

"Neil, stop that," Claire said from behind him. "You're embarrassing Pete. His face is all red."

Claire was right, on both counts. Even though Peter was only slightly embarrassed, his face and ears were bright pink. Peter had spent years and years wishing he had a complexion that was a little better at hiding his emotions.

Claire ran over and grabbed Nicola's hand. "Nik, you're coming upstairs with me," she said. "I've got some juicy gossip you've gotta hear. And these boys' ears are not privileged to hear this stuff."

Nicola wasn't really one for gossiping, but she needed to be a polite house guest. Plus it would give Peter the chance to explain everything about Zoltan and Xavier to Neil.

* * *

"Pete, this is seriously bad, man," Neil said after listening intently to the information about Zoltan's evil brother and the basic outline of the near impossible task that lay ahead.

"Yeah, it's pretty dire," Peter replied. "But at least we have a ray of hope. If, and only if, we can pull off everything perfectly."

"Well, I'm in," Neil said supportively. "You know you

can always count on the Neilster."

Peter thought the silly nickname Neil had concocted for himself had gone out of use a couple years ago, but apparently not. The *Neilster* was still alive and kicking.

Peter then went into more detail about what they'd done so far, and how they were currently working on making Xavier jealous. He also explained how he needed Neil's help to get this next part to succeed.

"Petey, my boy," Neil said at the end of the explanation. "I read you loud and clear."

Nicola had heard an earful about how Steve, the captain of the boys' volleyball team, had a massive crush on Courtney. But apparently Courtney preferred Bob over Steve. But Bob was too dumb to notice all the flirting she was doing. Tons of other names and dating rumors were also thrown into the mix, but Nicola had lost track.

"We'll have to do this again soon!" Claire said as Peter and Nicola were tying up their shoes to get ready to head home. "That was so fun!"

"Yeah, let's," Nicola replied, trying to be nice. But she had heard enough gossip in the last thirty minutes to last her a lifetime.

"So will Neil do it? Is he gonna help?" Nicola asked quietly as they got on their bikes.

"You bet," he replied. "The *Neilster* is in, one hundred percent."

"Awesome!" Nicola said. "But is he really still calling himself that??"

CHAPTER 12

On Wednesday afternoon, everything was set up as planned. Mr. Winchester had faked severe chests pains just before noon and had been taken to the hospital in Stoneburg via ambulance. He was currently hospitalized for more careful monitoring and testing.

At three thirty, Zoltan arrived at the hospital and begged the staff to let him go in and see Mr. Winchester. He said they had known each other their whole lives.

While Peter scanned the hallway to make sure no one was coming, the two men quickly changed clothes, and Zoltan hopped into the hospital bed. Mr. Winchester simply snuck down the back stairwell and walked to a coffee shop down the road.

As soon as Mr. Winchester was out of sight, Peter rejoined Neil and Nicola outside the front doors of the hospital. Just as they had hoped, tons of kids from their high school started showing up just before four o'clock, all looking extremely sad and emotional.

Neil and Nicola were in charge of keeping the students lined up in single file, starting a few meters from the doors and running down the sidewalk. Peter was going to take four students up at a time to see

Zoltan. Each student would wish Zoltan a speedy recovery, shed a few tears, and be taken back outside and thanked for coming.

"Look how long the line is," Neil whispered in Nicola's ear. "There's at least, like, a hundred people here."

"Yeah, this is perfect," she replied. "It'll take an hour or so for everyone to get in and out. Xavier will surely notice this."

Neil and Nicola made sure the line didn't get in the way of anyone entering or exiting the hospital. They didn't want someone to complain, as a complaint would likely prompt a visit from unhappy hospital personnel.

Peter quickly took group after group up to see Zoltan, using a staircase that couldn't be seen from the front desk. All went smoothly, and about ninety minutes later, he escorted the final four students back to the front doors and thanked them. Zoltan had had 124 visitors in total. They were hoping that Xavier had been watching from somewhere. Peter and his team were counting on it. Actually, they were depending on it.

"How'd it go?" Mr. Winchester asked as he walked up to the flower garden behind the hospital: the place where they had agreed to meet. The old man had finished three cups of coffee and read through every free newspaper at the coffee shop.

"Perfect," Peter replied. "Well, I think it went perfectly."

"But I still don't understand how you convinced over a hundred high school kids to come here and look so devastated," Mr. Winchester said. "Did you bribe them or something?"

"We did better than that," Neil replied, handing Mr. Winchester one of the light green flyers in his hand.

Open Auditions Today!

Stoneburg Memorial Hospital. Starting at 4:00 pm sharp.

Look as sad as you can while lining up and then wishing a speedy recovery to a very sick man. The best 2 performers will be hired for a video we are making, and paid $50 each.

Peter, Neil, Nicola

"You tricksters," Mr. Winchester said while laughing. "That was clever!" After a brief pause, and a little more thinking, he continued, "But tomorrow morning at school, won't people be asking who won? They'll be expecting to hear the winners' names. And then those winners will be owed fifty dollars each. And you'll—"

"No need to worry, Mr. Winchester," Peter said, interrupting the old man. "We'll pick two kids and pay them tomorrow morning. We've got enough cash between the three of us to cover that. Then we'll just say we're still working on the writing part of the video script. As long as they get their money, I doubt they'll care about actually having to do any acting."

Now all they needed to do was get Mr. Winchester back in his hospital bed before six o'clock, when dinner would arrive. No one would ever discover what had just happened.

CHAPTER 13

On Sunday morning, after four nights in the hospital, Mr. Winchester was released with a clean bill of health. The doctors had run numerous tests on him and had been monitoring his vital signs diligently, and decided he was in good enough shape to return home. This was the obvious outcome of course, as the whole *chest pains* thing was completely fake from the start.

But all their efforts would end up being in vain if Xavier saw Zoltan looking fine again too quickly, so they needed to keep up the façade. Mr. Winchester had set up the guest room in his house for Zoltan to use during this *staged* recovery. Zoltan was currently lying in bed there, awaiting the arrival of his evil brother.

* * *

Since today, Monday, was a professional development day for every teacher in town, there was no school. Peter, Nicola, and Neil arrived at Mr. Winchester's home mid-morning. Now all they could do was wait.

* * *

As expected, Xavier did show up, once again in spectacular fashion. In the early afternoon, he came *spinning* down to the front yard of Mr. Winchester's house in a long, narrow tornado. Yes, a tornado. Thankfully, it didn't cause any damage to the house or anything around it.

"Was that really necessary?" Mr. Winchester said strongly. "Don't you think you've shown off your powers enough already?"

Peter froze. "Shut up, Mr. Winchester," he whispered. "You're going to get us all killed."

"Get out of my way, old man," Xavier said, pushing Mr. Winchester hard to the side as he walked up the front steps. "Just tell me which room he's in."

"Follow me, sir," Peter said timidly, leading Xavier down the hallway to the last room on the left.

Xavier marched into the guest room and stood directly over the bed where Zoltan lay. "Aw, my poor brother," he said sarcastically. "Did that little lightning bolt of mine really hurt that much? You've been bed-ridden for almost a week now. C'mon, are you really that weak?"

"Xavier," Peter said nervously from behind. "All your brother does is sleep. The only reason they released him from the hospital is because he can finally breathe on his own. He can't hear what you're saying. And even if he could, he certainly can't reply."

"What's this got to do with you?" Xavier snapped back. "Why do you, and all those kids I saw at the hospital on Wednesday, care so much about my stupid brother?"

Peter was smiling on the inside, but made sure it didn't show on his face. This was exactly what they were hoping for.

"Zoltan is a legend, sir," Peter replied. "Everyone in Clearville, well, not just Clearville, everyone everywhere more or less worships him. Thanks to his powers, the weather is kept under control. No more floods. No more droughts. No more hurricanes. He keeps us safe. He's like, a, a god."

"A what?!" Xavier yelled. "Him? A god? This weak, useless, pathetic pile of garbage?!"

"Sir," Peter replied cautiously, "you saw for yourself yesterday how much everyone loves him. If people ever find out that it was you who put him in this state, they will band together and come after you."

"Ha!" he laughed. "And what could you humans possibly do to me?"

Peter had carefully planned what to say when it got to this point. "You're right," he said. "Humans would have no hope against you. I mean, the reason we love Zoltan so much is because of his amazing powers. Who wouldn't, who couldn't, love such a powerful and amazing being?"

Xavier had heard enough. His face grew even redder, and he furrowed his brow. In his mind, all the love and respect his brother was getting was completely undeserved.

"They should be worshipping me!" he yelled at his brother. "I'm way more powerful than you! You are nothing compared to me! NOTHING!!"

Xavier then turned around and stormed out without looking at anyone. This was good news for Peter and his team, as it meant the seeds of jealousy had been successfully planted.

Once Xavier was gone, they all went back to the guest room to congratulate Zoltan on his performance.

"Me?" Zoltan said after getting high-fives from everyone. "I didn't do anything. I just lay here with my eyes closed. It was Peter who did all the talking."

"Anyway," Peter said happily. "The important thing is

that we've got Xavier exactly where we want him."

CHAPTER 14

Peter, Neil, and Nicola spent the next few afternoons gathering at Mr. Winchester's home. This gave them the opportunity to carefully discuss and further plan out the next course of action.

Zoltan, as instructed by Peter, was faking a very slow recovery. He began by waking up on Tuesday, a full ten days after Xavier had tried to fry him with the lightning bolt. Then he started sitting up in bed on Wednesday, and attempted to stand up a few times on Thursday.

Their plan for Friday was to have him make a few attempts at walking. And finally, they'd choose a suitable time on Saturday or Sunday to have him try walking out the front door, down the steps, and to the end of the sidewalk. They knew that as soon as Xavier saw his brother up and moving again, he'd quickly show up.

"Pete," Neil said just as everyone was getting set to head home on Thursday before dinner. "After Xavier arrives, then what?"

"As crazy as this sounds," Peter replied. "We are going to make Xavier want to take over for Zoltan."

"Take over for Zoltan?" Neil said as his eyes opened

wide with surprise. "But he would never help people. He'd probably just flood the whole planet or something."

"Don't be silly," Mr. Winchester said, slowly standing up from his rocking chair. "We are going to make Xavier think that being Earth's weather god is the ultimate honor. We want him to imagine himself being worshipped by people all over the globe."

"Okay, I get that part," Neil replied. "But couldn't he just knock off Zoltan and claim himself as the new weather god for Earth?"

"Yes, he certainly could," Peter said. "But I don't think he *would*. He wants to see Zoltan suffer. Really, really suffer. And that won't happen if Zoltan is dead."

"Hmmm..." Neil replied, still appearing a little confused.

"Stick with me, Neil," Peter said supportively. "It'll all make sense in due time."

CHAPTER 15

The team realized that rushing Zoltan's recovery might cause Xavier to become a little suspicious, so they decided to put off the front yard stroll until late on Sunday afternoon.

"Okay, everyone," Mr. Winchester whispered. "It's show time."

With Neil and Peter supporting his arms, Zoltan slowly shuffled across the front porch, from the door toward the steps. They both continued holding onto Zoltan as he began to make his way slowly down the steps. He was doing his best to make it appear extremely difficult, grimacing in pain with each and every movement.

When they reached the bottom of the steps, Peter let go, and Neil helped Zoltan to the end of the sidewalk.

Then Zoltan turned around to face the house, and loudly announced the line Peter had given him, "Let me see if I can do this on my own. Neil, let go of my arm, but stay close. If I start wobbling too much, grab me before I fall."

Nicola and Peter stood on the front porch. Their job was to act as Zoltan's cheerleaders.

"You can do it!" Nicola yelled with a big smile.

"Yeah, one step at a time!" Peter added. "We know how strong you are!"

Zoltan put on quite a performance. He would take a couple of very awkward and shaky steps, and then pause for a few seconds to catch his breath. He also faced the palm of his hand up to Neil twice, as if to say *stop, don't help me.*

On his twelfth step, just as planned, Zoltan started to fall. Neil promptly grabbed his arm and helped him into an upright position again. About two minutes after this near collapse, Zoltan finally managed to get back to the steps and railing. The instant he touched the railing, Peter and Nicola jumped in celebration.

"Awesome!" Peter said happily. "You're on your way to being the Zoltan of old again!"

"You may be right," Zoltan replied, also smiling. "I think I may finally be on the mend."

"We are so, so happy to hear you say that!" Nicola exclaimed, getting ready for the line she had rehearsed. "The world desperately needs you and your powers back!"

They all sat down on the front steps and chatted happily while soaking up the sunshine. A few minutes later, Mr. Winchester came out with lemonade and cookies for everyone.

"You are a true marvel," Mr. Winchester said. "Are you sure you aren't stronger than that silly brother of yours?"

Peter had planned that line too. He knew it would really aggravate Xavier to hear Zoltan being referred to as his superior.

They all felt the ground start to shake. No doubt

another earthquake by Xavier. This guy sure didn't like being number two to anyone.

"Zoltan? Stronger than me?" Xavier yelled from the end of the sidewalk. It startled them all, as no one had noticed him there prior to hearing his voice.

Now it was Mr. Winchester's turn to shine. "My dear Xavier," he said as Xavier approached the stairs. "I'm honored to have you visit my home again." He then bowed as if he were addressing royalty.

"Don't start sucking up to me, old man," Xavier replied coldly.

"Obviously you're here to see your brother's miraculous recovery," Mr. Winchester continued. "Quite something, isn't it? We were worried he would never improve."

"Well, maybe I should've hit him with two lightning bolts instead of one," Xavier laughed.

"If you had done that," Mr. Winchester continued, "then you'd be the most hated person on the planet. Everyone here worships Zoltan. They've never seen anyone with powers like his... Well, at least not until now."

Peter jumped in, according to plan. "Xavier may be a little more powerful than Zoltan," he said. "But he certainly could never match Zoltan's intelligence."

"Intelligence?!" Xavier yelled so loudly that the volume almost pierced their ears. "That's the most ludicrous thing I've ever heard!"

"Don't doubt your younger brother," Mr. Winchester said boldly. "You'd be surprised how clever he is."

"Are you all insane!?" Xavier yelled, even louder than before. "Zoltan's a moron! He couldn't find his glasses if they were on his head!"

"But sir," Nicola said on cue, "of course you don't know this, but Zoltan has been doing extremely challenging puzzles for years and years. Mr. Winchester used to make them all, and then Peter and I took over two years ago. And no matter how hard we make them, he always figures them out."

"Yeah," Neil added. "I'd even go as far as saying Zoltan's a genius."

"I can guarantee you," the red-faced Xavier said while shaking with anger, "that Zoltan's mind is nothing, NOTHING, compared to mine!"

Peter smiled on the inside again. Everything was going as planned.

"Give me one of your stupid riddles or puzzles to solve," Xavier continued. "I promise you I'll solve it in half the time it took Zoltan!"

"Hold on a second, Peter," Mr. Winchester said, exactly as he was supposed to. "We both know that *creating* puzzles is way harder than simply solving them. If he really wants to prove his intelligence, then he should make a puzzle for Zoltan to do."

"With pleasure," Xavier replied quickly. "But he wouldn't even have a hope."

"In my current condition," Zoltan said, "you're probably right. But I'd be happy to have my friends here do it on my behalf."

"These kids?" Xavier laughed. "Are you telling me you'd put your trust in a bunch of teenagers?"

Now Neil was up to bat. "He certainly would," Neil announced proudly. "Two years back, he created eight incredibly difficult puzzles for us. And we solved them all. Every single one!"

"But what's in this for me?" Xavier asked. "Let's say I

make a puzzle or riddle or whatever, and then, just like I expect will happen, you don't solve it. Other than pride, I'd come out of this with nothing. It's a pointless waste of time."

"Then let's put more than just pride on the line," Zoltan said while slowly shuffling toward his older brother. "Here's what I propose. You make a series of difficult challenges for my friends to solve. Let's say, uh... five. Five really difficult ones. If they can't solve all five, then you win, and the following two things will happen: You will replace me as Earth's weather god, in a lavish ceremony that people will come from far and wide to see. And I will become your personal servant, for the rest of my existence."

"Now we're talking!" Xavier replied, almost showing the beginnings of a smile. "My own personal servant... I can already imagine all the things I'd make you do. Oh, but I suppose there's a catch, right? I suppose you're going to say that if they *do* solve all five, that I leave Earth and never come back?"

"Yes, something like that," Mr. Winchester said. "Look, if you don't like these terms, then I suppose you could just kill your brother here and now, and declare yourself as Earth's new weather god... But if you do that, you'll have no big welcome ceremony. And no servant. Plus, everyone on Earth will despise you."

"Hmmm..." Xavier said while nodding his head, clearly weighing the pros and cons of their proposal. "Maybe you caught me on a good day. Fine. I agree to your terms." Then he started chuckling as he prepared to walk away. "But you don't actually think these babies have a chance of solving puzzles created by *my* mind, do you? Zoltan, you must be a lot dumber than I thought."

Zoltan had to bite his tongue. An argument right now would be beneficial to absolutely no one. "And I suggest," he said to Xavier, "that we use the same location I used when I created puzzles for them two years ago: the ancient ruins at Silverhead Mountain."

"Fine," his brother replied. "I could really care less about where we do this. But I do care about *when*. I'm not prepared to wait forever so you guys can train and practice. I can get everything set up within a week. So the day for these challenges will be this coming Saturday, the twenty-eighth. Until then, adios!"

Then Xavier conjured up a dust storm to take himself away.

Once Xavier was completely out of sight, Mr. Winchester put up his hand. He looked like an elementary school student who needed to ask his teacher for permission to go to the washroom.

"What? No high-fives for old guys?" he said with a big smile.

They all high-fived him, then each other. Xavier had fallen for their trick hook, line, and sinker.

CHAPTER 16

In order to increase their odds of successfully completing Xavier's challenges, Peter needed to convince Bradley to join their team again. Bradley didn't excel academically, but Peter knew he had a number of other traits that would be hugely beneficial. Bradley's strength, speed, and most of all his courage, would no doubt prove necessary.

Peter was pretty confident that Bradley would immediately jump at the opportunity to help. He figured that the *new* Bradley, the one who was more focused and serious about life now, would love the feeling of being a kid in a game again.

* * *

When Peter got home from school shortly past three o'clock on Monday, Bradley was in the garage, fussing around with his mountain bike. Bradley loved tinkering with stuff, especially his bike. He was in a constant struggle to make his already perfect bike even a little more perfect. Maybe smoother. Or lighter. Or more shock absorbent.

"Petey boy!" Bradley said loudly as he noticed his little brother walking up the driveway. "Isn't this the most aerodynamic bike you've ever seen?"

"I have no clue about its aerodynamics," Peter said with a smile. "But if you let me take it out for a spin around the block, I'll tell you what I think."

"Nice try," Bradley replied. "But you know I never lend this bike to anyone. Not even you."

When Peter didn't head toward the house, which would be the natural thing to do when arriving home, Bradley noticed he was acting weird.

"What's up, dude?" he asked. "You need to borrow some money or something?"

"No," Peter replied, sitting down on one of the big storage boxes. He knew the explanation he was about to start was going to take a while. "Brad, Zoltan has a brother. An evil brother."

"Oh, c'mon," Bradley laughed. "Today is not April Fools' Day."

"Brad," Peter said with a serious look. "I know it sounds crazy, but it's true."

Peter spent the next fifteen minutes or so giving Bradley a condensed version of everything that had happened over the past two weeks. The more Peter spoke, the more Bradley became immersed in the tale.

"So I really need you on the team this Saturday," Peter said at the end of his explanation. "That way we'll have a chance against Xavier."

"Dude," Bradley replied right away. "Why didn't you tell me all this stuff earlier? Of course I'm in!"

Peter smiled and gave Bradley a high-five. Although he was relieved to have Bradley's help, there was no way he could mask how afraid he really was of being able to successfully complete every part of the plan...

CHAPTER 17

Peter, Nicola, Neil, and Bradley decided to gather at Mr. Winchester's home every afternoon for the rest of the week. Zoltan was still staying in the guest room and acting as if he weren't well enough to be on his own.

Shortly after the reunited team of four arrived on Tuesday, they expressed their reservations about being able to talk and plan without being spied on by Xavier.

"Xavier is a weather god, and nothing more," Mr. Winchester explained. "He can't see through walls or hear conversations from great distances."

"But he could," Bradley said, "sneak up and hide outside one of the windows, right? He'd be able to at least hear, or maybe even see what we're planning."

"Good point," Zoltan said. "He certainly could."

"I think I've got us mostly covered against that happening," Mr. Winchester explained. "My home has motion sensors outside, which would pick up someone approaching from any side of the house."

"And just to be safe," Peter (the excessive worrier) added, "we should make sure all doors and windows are closed and locked, and always keep the curtains shut."

"Smart ideas, Peter," Mr. Winchester replied. "And I

would also suggest that we never, ever discuss these plans outside the confines of my home. Xavier could, in theory, be hiding behind any tree or sitting on any bench."

* * *

They knew their time was limited, so they went through as much as they could each afternoon. Today, which was Wednesday, Bradley couldn't come, as he had track and field practice until six.

Together with Mr. Winchester and Zoltan, they were slowly and tediously mapping out their plan. Peter liked to refer to this as the "dot the i's and cross the t's" stage.

* * *

About two hours later, which meant it was getting close to six o'clock, they figured it was time to call it a day and head home for dinner. Everyone, but most of all Peter, was exhausted. Preparing to save the world was much harder than it sounded.

"Tell you what," Peter said to Neil and Nicola as they walked to their bikes. "I'll buy you guys dinner tonight. My parents are going out for their anniversary and Sophia has ballet from five till seven, so I'm on my own for dinner anyway."

"Sure, how about pizza?" Nicola suggested.

"Good call, Nik," Neil replied immediately. "I've been cravin' some good 'za!"

* * *

They went to the small pizza shop on Third Avenue, the same one they'd been to so many times that the owner knew them all by name.

"Neil," Nicola said as they sat down at the open table in the far corner, "this sure feels like old times, doesn't it? I mean, hanging out with you when Claire isn't clinging to your arm."

"Yeah, it does feel a little weird," Neil admitted. "But as soon as we get through all of this trapping Xavier stuff and things go back to normal, I'll be hanging out with her as much as I can again."

"Speaking of Claire," Peter said, pointing at the door.

"Neil?" Claire said to him in shock. "What are you doing here?" Her face quickly began to turn red with rage. "You said you were going to Pete's house to do homework. But you're here! Having pizza? And Nik was invited, but not me?" Tears were beginning to form in her eyes.

"Hold up, baby," Neil said casually, hoping to quickly diffuse the situation. "It's not what you think..."

"Shut up!" she yelled at him. "You've been acting weird for the last week or so. You never answer my calls. And when we do meet, you seem preoccupied with something. It's like you've always got somewhere else you'd rather be."

"Claire, baby," Neil said, a little more timidly than before. "It's just a misunderstanding."

"A misunderstanding!?" she yelled back, looking like she was about to hit him. I think I now know why you always get *Cs* in English. Think about it. You don't even know what the word *misunderstanding* means. This is not a misunderstanding. This is called *lying*. L-Y-I-N-G!"

She slammed the pizza shop door as she stormed out. The young clerk holding the two boxes of take-out pizza which her family had ordered by phone had no clue what to do or say.

Neil was shaken. Peter and Nicola quickly stood up to go over and console him, but he was in no mood to listen to any advice. In a bizarre trance, he opened the door and slowly started toward his bike.

CHAPTER 18

Neil looked like a zombie the next day at school. Peter knew what it felt like to stay up all night worrying, and gauging by the black bags under Neil's eyes, he had just had one of those nights. His poor friend was currently staring blankly at his open locker. With the first bell of the day set to ring in a few minutes, Peter figured now was his best chance to ask Neil how bad things were.

"She won't talk to me," Neil replied, still looking straight ahead. "She won't even look at me. And look at this note I just found in my locker."

He handed Peter the crushed piece of paper in his hand. There were only three words written on it:

We are over.

"I've been dumped, man," Neil said. "Plain and simple. Dumped."

Since Nicola was Peter's first girlfriend, and they were still together, he didn't know what it felt like to be dumped. But right now, he needed to think of something to say to his friend, and he needed to think of it quickly. Unfortunately for Peter, the only thing he came up with was something that he wished he hadn't.

"You shouldn't have lied to her," Peter said. "What were you thinking?"

Neil slammed his locker door hard and glared at Peter. "I lied to her," he said sharply, "to protect you and your little secret about the weather god stuff."

Peter didn't want this to escalate into an argument. But at the same time, he also wasn't prepared to take the blame for everything.

"I told you it was okay to tell Claire the truth," he said back to Neil. "It was you that decided not to. You said she'd never believe it, and that she would think you're a weirdo."

"Whatever," Neil said while walking away.

Peter noticed the all too familiar *butterflies in the stomach* feeling coming on.

"Pete, you dummy," he said to himself. "Why did you just say that?"

The bell had already started to ring, so Peter jogged toward his English class. On the inside, he knew he was going to spend the entire day playing through countless scenarios of how to smooth things over with Neil.

CHAPTER 19

Peter lay down on the sofa the instant he got home from school. He was emotionally exhausted. He had spent the entire day trying to figure out when and how to approach Neil, but ended up doing nothing. Now it was a quarter past three, and his worrying was only set to continue.

"Should've talked to him after P.E." Peter mumbled to himself. "There was no one close by in the change room. That was my best chance."

Peter's cycle of worrying always went something like this: Make a mistake. Regret it. Think endlessly about how to undo it. Do nothing. Worry more.

His mom had told him numerous times that he would give himself an ulcer by the age of eighteen if he didn't learn how to relax more and stop obsessing.

"Catch!" Bradley said as he came around the corner into the room, passing a basketball that Peter wasn't expecting.

"Ouch!" Peter yelped as the ball smacked him hard in the chest.

"You still suck at b-ball," Bradley laughed. "C'mon, let's play a game of twenty-one or something."

Back when Bradley was fourteen, he had decided that

becoming a rich and famous basketball player was in the cards for his future. He had somehow managed to convince their parents to spend a few hundred bucks on a regulation height hoop for their driveway. Up until last year, Bradley and his buddies used to use it all the time. They would crank up the volume of whatever cheesy rock song was popular, and take turns trying to show off their moves to each other. They put even more effort into displaying their skills whenever a girl their age happened to be walking by. But now that Bradley was at college, and actually taking his education seriously for the first time ever, the hoop rarely got used.

"I'll give you a ten-point lead," Bradley begged, desperately needing an opponent to play against. "And if you beat me, I'll do all your chores this weekend."

Everyone knew Bradley was a great athlete, as his name often appeared in the local paper for winning this or setting a new record in that. But few people knew that Bradley also had an amazing ability to read peoples' emotions. Peter's current expression tipped off Bradley to the fact that something was wrong.

"Something happen with Nik?" he asked Peter while picking up the basketball and sitting down beside him.

"No, actually it's about Neil," Peter replied. "Claire dumped him."

"Ouch, that sucks," Bradley said. "Why? What did he do?"

Peter spent the next ten minutes explaining everything to Bradley. At first, he thought it was a *funny and cute* little tale of teenage love. But once he realized that Neil might be so upset that he wouldn't want to help them defeat Xavier, his expression quickly changed.

"Petey," Bradley said to him. "You may be smart, but

you've got no tact."

"Tact?" Peter asked.

"Hey," Bradley went on. "Neil still got that part-time job at the veggie shop on Fifth Avenue?"

"Yeah," Peter answered. "Wait. You're not gonna go there by yourself and try talking to him, are you?"

Bradley paused for a few seconds, thinking carefully about what Peter had just asked. "No, I'm not," he replied. Then he got up and quickly left the room. A minute or two later, Peter heard the car engine start, and watched through the window as Bradley backed out of the driveway.

CHAPTER 20

The plan was for everyone to meet up at Mr. Winchester's house on Friday afternoon to review (for the umpteenth time) all the fine details for the big day tomorrow. Peter and Nicola arrived by bike first, and Bradley drove in shortly after. Considering all that Neil had been through in the last two days, Peter thought the chances of him coming today were extremely slim, or more likely, zero.

"Don't worry, Petey," Bradley said with confidence. "He'll show."

"What did you do?" Peter asked, sounding quite concerned. "You didn't threaten to beat him up if he didn't come, did you?"

"Threaten him?" Bradley laughed. "No, I did much better than that."

"Yo!" Neil yelled loudly while riding up. "Sorry I'm late. I dropped by Claire's house on my way here."

"Really?" Nicola asked. "You mean she's not angry at you anymore?"

Bradley walked up to Neil and gave him a big high-five.

"Thanks again, Brad," Neil said. "I owe you big time."

"Can someone please explain what's going on here?" Nicola asked with a smile.

"I'd love to," Bradley said, as if he'd been waiting for someone to ask him that exact question. "Yesterday, after promising Petey that I wouldn't go to see Neil *by myself,* I set out on a mission to get Claire and Neil back together."

"You what?" Nicola asked. "But how did you know it would work?"

"Well, if there's one thing I learned from living with Petey all these years," Bradley continued, "it's that an *organized* plan almost always succeeds. So anyway, after Pete filled me in on what happened at the pizza shop, I drove straight to Claire's house. I used to be friends with her brother Chris, like way back in Grade 5 or 6, so I know where she lives. I rang the doorbell, and when she answered I gave her that DVD of Zoltan demonstrating his powers and begged her to watch it. You know, the one we all watched two years ago. Then I waited outside on the front steps while she reluctantly watched it."

"You mean she didn't invite you inside?" Peter asked.

"She was home alone," Bradley replied. "So that would've been weird. After she watched it, she came back outside. But she had that deer in the headlights look on her face. I explained everything to her, you know, all about the weather gods and stuff. I told her what we did two years ago, and about what's going on now."

"And?" Nicola jumped in, eager for Bradley to get to the good part.

"And she felt so bad after hearing the whole story," Bradley went on, "that she wanted to see Neil and forgive him as soon as possible. I drove her over to the veggie shop where Neil works, and left her in the car while I went in and bought two boxes of apples. I asked Neil to help carry one back to my car, and when he got there, voila! There was Claire, waiting for him with open arms! I didn't feel like watching all the lovey-dovey stuff, so I went for a jog in the park behind the shopping mall. And when I came back fifteen minutes later, Claire said all was good!"

"You cupid!" Nicola remarked, lightly punching Bradley on the shoulder. "You got them back together!"

"And Claire even offered to help us out," Neil added.

"Cool," Peter said while nodding. "I mean, cool about both things. About you guys getting back together, and that she's happy to help."

CHAPTER 21

After allowing everyone a little more time for chitchat, plus some time to joke around with Zoltan, Mr. Winchester suggested they all congregate in the living room to go through everything one final time.

He looked over at Peter, Neil, Nicola, and Bradley in utter amazement. Wow, they sure had grown up a lot in two years. He wasn't focusing on the increase in their height, but more on how mature they all had become. He could still recall the first time he met Peter, the geeky puzzle-loving kid who was teased at school and had very few friends. But the Peter standing in front of him now was beaming with pride and looked more than ready for what lay ahead tomorrow.

"Peter," Mr. Winchester said, slowly standing up. "I'm not going to pretend that I'm in charge this time. I may be the eldest, but you are the leader. Thanks to all your hard work, and the help of your talented and dedicated friends, I can say, with complete confidence, this plan will work."

"I'll second that!" Bradley said, turning to give Neil another high-five.

"Any last words of wisdom, then?" Mr. Winchester

asked Peter. "Or any final changes we need to know about?"

Peter's emotions could turn on a dime, and he could feel his throat growing tighter. He didn't want to start fumbling his words or crying in front of everyone right now, but it looked as if that was going to be unavoidable. He turned around to gather his composure, and then spun back to look at his team.

"To quote one of the cheesiest phrases I've ever heard," Peter said. "A chain is only as strong as its weakest link."

"Well, that's definitely me!" Bradley joked. "At least as far as brains go."

"No," Peter replied, his voice a little shaky. "We have no weak links. None. Zero. Zilch. This plan WILL work. I am certain of it." Peter started to choke up, to the point that he could hardly get the right words out. "We'll meet some smags, oops, I mean some *snags* along the way. But we are all capable of figuring out how to deal with them."

Peter then reached into his backpack and pulled out three small boxes. "Here you go, guys," he said while passing them out. "Remember when you three pitched in to buy me that watch two years back? Well, I went out and bought all three of you digital watches. Wait, that sounds like I spent a lot of money, which I didn't. I found them at one of those shops where they sell used clothes and stuff, so they cost like next to nothing. Anyway, they are all synchronized, to the second."

"Petey the perfectionist!" Bradley said while putting the watch on his left wrist. "You've thought of everything, haven't you?"

"My first ever watch!" Neil said excitedly. "But I guess I'll have no excuse for being late for school anymore."

Peter smiled. Only Neil could make a group of people laugh without having had the slightest intention of doing so.

CHAPTER 22

The next day, September 28, the day which Xavier had set for the challenges, Peter and his team arrived at Silverhead Mountain about fifteen minutes earlier than Xavier had told them to be there.

They now stood staring down the path which led to the ruins, the exact same place they'd been standing at two years ago to start Zoltan's challenges.

"So what's the drill?" Bradley asked, since he hadn't been there for the start of the challenges two years ago.

"Last time we just walked to the end of this path, and a note was waiting on a tree for us," Peter replied.

Peter and Nicola were leading the way, hand in hand. Bradley and Neil followed behind them, making childish comments about the lovebirds in front of them.

After putting up with their remarks for a minute or so, Nicola spun around. "Would you guys grow up?" she joked. "Especially you, Neil. You and Claire are stuck to each other like white on rice!"

When she turned to face forward again, they were now close enough to see the end of the path. But instead of a note on a tree, Xavier was waiting for them in person.

"I've never been one for pleasantries," Xavier said in a low and monotone voice. "And since we all know why you are here, let's just get on with it."

No one replied. There wasn't really anything that needed to be said.

"But at least make it interesting for me to watch," Xavier continued, with a cruel grin on his face. "Don't go and fail on the first one. Then I would have wasted so much time preparing puzzles two through five!" He turned around quickly. "This way, KIDS!"

Peter and Nicola looked back to face Neil and Bradley. All four of them shrugged their shoulders, and then began to follow Xavier.

Peter's anxiety was somewhere up in the stratosphere right now. But a teeny tiny part of him was actually excited. There was still that little kid inside him that LOVED the challenge of a new puzzle.

CHAPTER 23

Xavier led them into an open chamber, which was roughly half the size of a school gymnasium. The only thing in the room was a cage, which was on the floor right in the middle. It looked like something that would be used to transport a tiger or lion from one zoo to another. There was a thick chain attached to the top of the cage, and as their eyes followed the chain up, they saw where it disappeared into a hole in the ceiling.

"You've gotta be kidding me," Peter said. "We are going to have to lock ourselves in there, aren't we?"

Neil took the note taped to the open cage door and went to hand it to Peter. No one really needed to read it, as they were pretty sure about what it would say.

"May I do the honors?" Bradley asked, snatching the note from Neil before it got to Peter's hand. He unfolded it and read its short contents aloud.

> *Go in the cage and close the door behind you.*
> *You'll hear the click when it locks.*

"Pretty pointless note," Bradley said while crushing it into a ball. "We could've figured out that much on our own."

They cautiously stepped into the cage, which easily had enough room for all of them. But the top of the cage only came up to Peter's shoulders, so they had to crouch once inside.

"First time in a cell, Petey?" Bradley joked.

* * *

Bradley had stayed in jail, very briefly, a few months back. He and his friends were held there under suspicion of drunk and disorderly conduct after a night out. But Bradley and his friends hadn't been drinking, nor had they been looking for trouble. They actually had just been trying to be good Samaritans. While walking back to their car after watching a movie, they had spotted a group of drunk losers hassling a couple of girls outside a convenience store. The drunks took offence when Bradley told them to *leave the girls alone and go home*, and their group quickly jumped Bradley and his friends. Luckily, drunks are easy to outrun, so no one was hurt too badly. But the cops were called and they decided to hold everyone involved overnight while they investigated the incident. The next morning, after the police had spoken to several witnesses, they apologized to Bradley's group and released them.

* * *

They heard the sound of metal on metal, and then watched as the chain began to move. The cage was slowly being raised off the ground. Peter and his team had to grab hold of the bars to keep themselves from falling over.

About thirty seconds later, when it looked like they were about a meter off the ground, the cage stopped.

A digital timer on the wall, which they hadn't noticed

before, was set to countdown from five minutes. But for some reason, it hadn't started yet.

"Guess Xavier is a little slow on the ball, eh?" Bradley said softly. "He forgot to start the timer."

Just as Bradley finished his comment, the entrance door opened again and in walked Xavier.

"You didn't think I'd lock you in there without the key, did you?" he laughed.

Xavier dropped the key, which was attached to a large key ring, on the ground in front of his feet. Then he turned around and walked back out the same door. As soon as the door closed behind him, the timer started.

"But how are we supposed to reach the key?" Nicola asked. "It's way too far away. And there's nothing in here that can help us."

"Yeah," Neil added. "It's gotta be at least, like, two or three meters away."

Peter had played the crane game at the arcade many, many times. What they were dealing with now was more or less the same, in principle. Or one could compare it to fishing off a pier: something Peter did every year when he visited his grandparents.

"What we need to do is fashion together something that can reach that far," Peter said. "And put some kind of hook on the end."

"Well, we all brought our jackets," Nicola suggested. "Why don't we tie them all together?"

"Roger that," Bradley said, saluting Nicola. Bradley much preferred the manual labor to the thinking. "And while I do that, someone come up with a way to make a hook."

"That's a cinch!" Peter said right away, reaching into his backpack.

He pulled out the cutlery case from the bottom. Peter always took his knife, fork, and spoon everywhere he went. One reason was that he didn't like the environmental impact of using disposable ones at fast food shops. But even more than that, he absolutely hated it when he picked up a utensil at a restaurant with food caked on it.

"Sorry, Mr. Fork," Peter said to his utensil. "It's been nice knowing you."

He bent the fork into a U-shape. Bradley and Neil had just finished tying the jackets together, so Peter attached his "hook" to the end of the last sleeve using some string he had brought with him.

"Time to go fishin'!" Neil announced like a hillbilly.

They should have been more concerned about the timer on the wall, but they all seemed very calm and cool. It was as if they knew their plan was going to succeed.

"Let me give it a go," Bradley said, ready to show how his years of sports made him the ideal candidate to do this.

He held one end of the *rope made of jackets* in his left hand, and tossed the hooked end in the direction of the key. Unfortunately, it didn't land even remotely close. This task was apparently going to be much harder than they all thought. He quickly reeled it back in and made a second attempt. A little closer than the first, but nowhere near close enough.

"You've gotta aim past the key," Peter advised, "and then try to hook the ring as you pull it back."

"I know. I know," Bradley said impatiently, already getting frustrated with himself.

His third throw was perfect. The fork bounced once and then came to a stop just beyond the key. He carefully pulled it back, trying to make sure the fork was lined up to slide into and grab the key ring. But the fork was upside down, so even though it slid over the right spot, it didn't hook the ring.

"This isn't working, guys," Nicola said. "If we had hours, we'd probably get it, but—"

"But we don't," Neil said, finishing her sentence for her. "In fact, we've only got two minutes and eighteen seconds to go."

Peter felt the initial stage of panic start to set in. He knew these sensations all too well: sweaty palms, racing heart, slight dizziness, shortness of breath.

"Deep breaths," he said softly to himself. He couldn't afford to have a full-fledged panic attack right now.

Bradley was getting angrier and angrier. He dropped the jacket pile and began kicking at the cage bars. He looked like a three-year-old having a temper tantrum. Needless to say, this caused the cage to shake, which in turn distracted the rest of them from thinking.

"Stop that!" Nicola yelled sharply at him. "You don't think you're strong enough to kick your way out of here, do you?!"

Neil spun around. From the expression on his face, he had just had a stroke of genius. "When the odds are stacked against you," he said with a smirk on his face, "you call the Neilster."

"Dude, if you have an idea," Bradley said sharply, still unable to shake off his own frustration, "spit it out."

Neil put his hands on the bar closest to where he was standing.

"Let me guess," Bradley said sarcastically. "The *Neilster* is going to bend the bars with his bare hands?"

"Ignore Brad," Peter said to Neil supportively. "C'mon,

let's hear your idea."

"Well, what I'm thinking," Neil continued, speaking quickly, "is that maybe the cage was built with a couple of bars that were intentionally not welded in place."

"Huh?" Bradley said rudely.

"You know how cages are built," Neil continued, ignoring Bradley. "The bars are inserted into the holes in the thick frame, and then welded."

"So maybe a couple of the bars can be lifted up and slid out!" Nicola said excitedly.

They each took a side, hoping to find a loose bar or two that could be removed.

"No dice," Peter said. "Anyone?"

The other three had the same result. The timer had just reached fifty-nine seconds. They were almost out of time.

"Hold on," Neil said. "I've got another idea. Righty tighty. Lefty loosey!"

"Righty what?" Bradley asked.

"Quickly Neil!" Nicola said in a panic. "We've only got forty seconds left."

"Twisting screws or lids to the left loosens them," Neil explained. "Maybe a couple of the bars can be unscrewed and removed from the frame."

With no time to spare, and no other suggestions, they all began quickly checking the bars.

"Bingo!" Bradley yelled about ten seconds later.

The two bars in front of him could be twisted. Neil came over to help, and he and Bradley twisted like crazy until the bars came loose.

"Only eighteen seconds to go!" Nicola announced. "C'mon! Let's go!"

One by one, they squeezed through the gap and

jumped to the floor. The last one out, Peter, hit the ground when the timer read 0:04.

Before they could start celebrating, Xavier walked through the door.

With no expression on his face, he looked directly into Peter's eyes. "You can consider that first challenge an easy warm-up for you and your team," he said coldly. "Now the real tests begin."

CHAPTER 24

Xavier led them through a long, winding, seemingly endless corridor to get to their next challenge. "Don't tell me," he said, looking back at Peter and his team, "that you are expecting the rest to be so easy?"

Peter had strictly instructed his team to never speak to Xavier during their challenges today, even if they were being asked a direct question.

"Cat got your tongues?" Xavier said loudly, unimpressed by the silent treatment he was getting. "Here are the instructions for your second challenge. Read them carefully."

Xavier handed the note to Peter, but he decided not to look at it until Xavier had left the room.

Just like their first challenge, they were in another chamber of roughly the same size, and there was nothing inside it other than what was going to be used for the challenge.

At the far end of the room, there an empty wooden barrel. Well, it wasn't a complete barrel, it was only the bottom half of one. Xavier must have cut it in half in order to set up the challenge. Beside the barrel was a garden hose, hooked up to a faucet. Just behind the barrel and hose, there was a staircase, which looked like it rose to roughly the same height as a basketball net. The staircase led up to some sort of loft or platform.

With Xavier no longer in sight, Peter unfolded the note.

Fill the barrel with water up to the red line, which as you can see, is about a finger length below the rim. The challenge is to carry the barrel to the top of the stairs. Sure, it'll be heavy, but the four of you can certainly manage it. But here's the catch: If you accidently spill any of the water, even one drop, then you fail. And for this challenge, you may make four attempts.

"Where does he come up with this stuff?" Neil asked, shaking his head.

Bradley had already turned on the hose and was filling up the barrel. As the water slowly rose, Peter got down on his hands and knees to get a closer look.

The first thing he saw was the *110 Liter* black stamp. Since that was the stamp for a full barrel, a half barrel would hold 55 liters. And the red line being about ten centimeters below the rim meant they'd probably only have to put in about 45 liters. That converted to roughly 45 kilograms, plus he had to add the weight of the barrel itself. Once he'd finished his calculations, he figured the combined weight of water and barrel would be pretty close to his own body weight.

Due to the reddish stains covering the entire inside of the barrel, Peter guessed that it had contained red wine at some point in the past. But kegs like this were typically moved around using trollies, so there were no handles or grip holds. The only way to lift it was going to be by getting their fingers under the bottom.

"There we go," said Bradley. "Got the water up to the red line."

"This is going to be pretty awkward to lift," Peter said. "But I think as long as we move in sync, we should be able to do it without spilling any water."

They took their places around the barrel.

"On the count of three," Peter said. "One, two, three!"

The water-filled barrel was heavier than they thought. They groaned and grunted while slowly lifting it off the ground. Just before they had it high enough to be able to straighten their knees, it wobbled a bit and some water splashed over the side.

"Lower it down slowly," Peter instructed.

"Guys, I think that was my fault," Nicola said. "My wrist started hurting and I tried to adjust my grip."

Bradley grabbed the hose and topped up the water. "It wasn't your fault, Nik," he said supportively.

"What we need," Neil suggested, "is something flat, like a board, to put underneath it. Xavier never said we couldn't use stuff like that."

It was almost as if a magician had been listening to Neil, because suddenly they spotted a wooden board, which was about the size of the top of a coffee table, leaning against the far wall of the room. Since they all knew the chamber had been empty, except for the barrel, when they entered the room, they had no explanation for the board's appearance now.

They carefully managed to slide the board under the barrel without spilling any water. This was going to make it way easier to lift and carry.

Once again, on the count of three, they lifted. It was still heavy, but they were able to get their legs straight without too much trouble. Next, they shuffled to the bottom of the stairs. Peter and Nicola climbed up backward, so that Neil and Bradley, the two strongest, could support the bulk of the weight while facing toward the steps.

"Man, this thing gets heavier by the second," Neil said, face purple from straining so hard.

"Don't wimp out now," Bradley said, in a half-sincere and half-sarcastic tone.

They were almost halfway up when Neil's shaking caused a bit of water to splash out.

"No!" Bradley yelled. "We were so close!"

They tipped the barrel and dumped the rest of the water out over the side of the stairs. There was no sense in wasting valuable energy carrying a full barrel back down.

"I think the problem was that we tried to do it all in one go," Nicola said.

"You're right, Nik," Peter added. "Xavier never said we couldn't put it down to rest while climbing the steps. Why don't we put the end Nik and I are carrying down every couple of steps? Then we take your places and support it for a while so you guys can rest your arms. When you're ready, we all go back to our original spots, and we do a couple more steps."

It took close to five minutes to fill up the barrel for their third attempt. Neil was lying on his back, arms aching from the last try. Bradley was swinging his arms in big circles, hoping to improve his circulation as much as possible.

Once everyone was sufficiently rested, they began

their third attempt. They decided to take breaks every two steps, and by doing so, everyone seemed to be managing just fine. It was going magnificently.

"Only two more to go," Nicola said happily. "We're almost there."

"Shhh," said Neil. "Don't jinx it."

But it was too late. It had just been jinxed. Peter wobbled a little, and that jolt was just enough to make some water slosh and then spill over.

"You've gotta be kidding me!" Bradley yelled in frustration. "We only had two steps left!"

They dumped out the rest of the water, and descended the stairs in silence. They would all need a fair amount of rest before their final attempt.

Angry with himself for screwing up at such an inopportune time, Peter turned on the hose to refill the barrel, and then quietly walked a few meters away from everyone. He kept his back facing them in order to avoid making any eye contact.

Bradley and Neil were both lying on their backs, breathing heavily. Meanwhile, Nicola was sitting on the bottom step wishing she hadn't unintentionally jinxed Peter.

"Alright, Petey. Let's do this," Bradley said, walking over and patting Peter on the back. "No point in sulking. It's not going to make this last attempt any easier."

They got into position again. And they all looked very, very serious. They were all business.

"On the count of three," Bradley said. "We got this, guys. One, two—"

"Hold on, hold on," Peter said suddenly. Thankfully, no one had started to lift yet.

Peter took a couple of steps back and removed the

note from his pocket. From the expression on his face, it was clear that Peter was having some sort of brainwave. The other three quietly sat down and faced away from him, to give him space to think.

"When we started this challenge," Peter said quietly to himself, "Xavier told us to read the note carefully. Carefully. He wouldn't have specifically said *carefully* if there wasn't something in the note we needed to spot."

Peter read the note over and over, mumbling away the whole time.

Nicola watched her boyfriend in awe. No matter how complicated or confusing a problem was, Peter would never, ever consider throwing in the towel. The world needed more *Peters*.

"Let me take a look at it," Nicola said after walking over and putting her arm around him. Peter, happy for the help and support, passed the note to Nicola and then kept pacing around.

"No hidden message?" Neil asked him.

"Not that I could see," he answered.

Nicola was awful at math and science, but she always got As in English. Apparently, it depends on which side of one's brain is dominant. If there was something hidden in the words of this note, Nicola was by far the most qualified to find it.

Nicola and Peter certainly had different ways of concentrating. Nicola stood in one spot and silently looked at the note. Peter, on the other hand, paced around endlessly. He was currently doing a weird figure eight pattern, where he'd keep going around the barrel and then step over the hose. When he tried to spin around too quickly, he tripped over the hose and fell.

"You okay, Pete?" Bradley asked, although it was

obvious that the only thing Peter had hurt was his pride.

"I'm fine," he replied. "I accidentally tripped over that stupid hose."

Nicola's face lit up. "Xavier, you tricky little..." she said. "And you thought we'd never notice."

"Notice what?" Bradley asked.

HI READER! (^_^)
NICOLA JUST FIGURED IT OUT! CAN YOU?

"Listen again to the note," she continued. "*But if you accidentally spill any of the water...* Accidentally. Accidentally."

"Not following you," Neil said, clearly needing a more accurate explanation.

"That word is the trick, or hidden message, or whatever you want to call it," she explained. "Think about it. On our first three attempts, we accidentally spilled some water, right? But what if we spill it *intentionally?* All of it. You know, just tip it over and pour it all out. Then all we'd have to do is carry the empty barrel up the stairs."

"But that would be too easy," said Neil, thinking she was trying to create a solution out of nothing.

"Yeah, that sounds sketchy to me too," Bradley added. "But it's your call Petey. You're in charge here."

"No, it's Nik's call," Peter said right away. "She's the one who spotted it. If she thinks it's worth going for, then I'm with her. One hundred percent."

"Well, I can't say I'm one hundred percent sure," she said, sounding slightly less confident than before. "But I'm pretty sure it'll work."

Bradley and Neil pushed the barrel over. Once all the

water was out, Peter took a towel from his backpack and wiped it until it was bone dry.

Satisfied that every last drop was gone, Peter gave Bradley and Neil the okay to carry the barrel up the stairs. It was light enough now that this task was a breeze. When they reached the top, they slammed it down hard.

The entrance door opened and Xavier walked in. He looked a little flustered. It was obvious from his expression that he certainly hadn't expected them to find the word trick he'd hidden in the note.

"Follow me," he mumbled. "And wipe off those smug grins. The next one is way harder."

CHAPTER 25

Their third challenge looked similar to a place at the big mall in Stoneburg where Peter had spent countless hours playing while his parents shopped. Their family called it the *ball room* or the *ball pool* or the *ball pit*. Just like at the mall in Stoneburg, they were now standing in front of a large square pit, about half the size of a swimming pool, filled with thousands and thousands of baseball-sized, hollow plastic balls.

"Petey," Bradley said. "I used to love going to the ball pit. Man, this takes me back." He looked like he was getting ready to dive in.

"Wait," Nicola said, sounding a bit concerned. "You don't wanna hurt yourself."

"Hurt myself?" Bradley laughed. "By landing on a pile of light plastic balls? C'mon, you know what these things are like. When you land on them, it's like falling down on a mattress."

Bradley jumped high in the air, spread his arms and legs, and did a belly flop into the colorful balls.

"Can someone remind me how old he is?" Peter asked while watching this childish display.

Less than a second after Bradley landed, numerous

holes opened up in the ceiling, and more balls started to fall into the pit.

"Brad, get out of there! Quick!" Peter yelled.

Bradley was already pretty close to the ledge, so it only took him a few seconds to get there. The instant his hand touched the ledge, the holes in the ceiling closed, putting an end to the falling balls.

They heard some footsteps. They looked up, and as they had expected, Xavier was standing on the ledge on the opposite side of the ball pit.

"Allow me to explain," he announced loudly. "The rules are fairly simple. All four of you have to get over here, to this ledge where I am standing, in twenty-five seconds or less. And that doesn't mean twenty-five seconds per person. The timer starts the instant someone enters the pit. And then all four of you have to get to this ledge before the twenty-five seconds elapse. And as you just saw, balls will fall from above while you're moving through the pit. I figured it would make it a little more, I don't know, let's say... fun to watch?"

"Twenty-five seconds?" Bradley asked. "That's way too short."

"Stop whining," Xavier barked back. "It's more than ample. And before I forget, for this challenge, you get only three attempts."

Since he was in no mood to field any more questions, Xavier turned around and walked out the door behind him.

"He can't be serious about the time limit," Bradley said. "I mean, I might have a chance, if I take a big runup first. But, and no offense, the rest of you aren't really big athletes or anything."

They took a few minutes to scan both the ball pit and

the ledge that led up to the start of the pit. It was just under three meters from the wall to the ledge. That would be enough space to get some pretty good momentum before leaping in. But making forward progress through the balls was going to be the hard part. It was probably so deep that their feet wouldn't reach the bottom. That meant they were going to have to *swim* through the balls to get across. Not an easy thing to do.

"Pete," Nicola said nervously, squeezing his hand hard. "This looks really tough."

"Yeah, it does," he replied, trying to mask how scared he really was. *Scared* was a drastic understatement. Peter was absolutely, utterly terrified.

* * *

Back when Peter was five and a half, which meant he was old enough to enter the mall's ball pit as long as a parent or responsible sibling was with him, he had one of the most traumatic events of his life. While his parents were shopping with Sophia, he and Bradley were allowed to play in the ball pit. Bradley had promised to stay close by and keep an eye on his younger brother the entire time.

When his parents finished shopping and came back to fetch the two boys, Peter was nowhere to be found. Bradley had been enjoying himself so much that he had long since forgotten his duty to be watching his little brother.

Everyone just figured that Peter probably became bored, got out, and went to one of the two hobby shops in the mall. He loved looking at the puzzles and games in both shops, and could do so for hours on end. But a search of those two shops, followed by the rest of the mall, yielded nothing. A few announcements were then made, but Peter still couldn't be found.

Peter was actually stuck at the bottom of the ball pit. Physically, he was completely fine. He could breathe, and he had no injuries. But as soon as he realized that he was stuck, he got scared and peed his pants. And he was so embarrassed about people seeing him that he decided not to call for help.

By this point, everyone was getting quite concerned, as of course they should be when a child suddenly vanishes. The ball pit staff, who were just a couple of lazy high school kids, ordered everyone out. Then his parents and Bradley started calling out to him, asking if he could hear them. Peter knew he didn't want to spend the rest of his life soaked in pee at the bottom of the Stoneburg Mall ball pit, so he decided to respond. The staff then carefully followed his voice until they located him and pulled him out safely.

Finally out, Peter lied about what had happened. He said he had fallen asleep, and had no idea how long he'd been down there. That way no one would ever know how much of a chicken he really was.

* * *

But like it or not, Peter needed to push that awful memory aside.

"Well, how's this for starters?" Neil suggested. "If we all take a big runup and leap at the same time, then we'll all have the full twenty-five seconds to use."

"That might work," Peter replied, still half stuck in his flashback. "But moving forward in those balls is harder than you think."

"Why don't we use our first attempt," Nicola suggested, "to gauge how hard it's gonna be?"

They spent a couple minutes figuring out the ideal

place and position to start running from. It was time to give it a go.

"Ladies and gentlemen," Bradley said in a deep voice. "Start your engines."

"You know the drill," Neil said next. "On three. One, two, three!"

They all simultaneously sprinted toward the ball pit, and jumped at more or less the same time. Bradley, of course, launched himself way further than anyone else. Once in the ball pit, while balls rained down from above, they flailed and scrambled to get across as quickly as possible. Bradley was making good time and Neil was doing fairly well. But Peter and Nicola were pretty much going nowhere, almost like cars spinning their wheels on ice.

Bradley could see the end. He spun around and yelled to Neil. "Neil! We gotta help them across! Grab whoever is closest to you and pull them along!"

But the hailstorm of balls falling from the ceiling made it difficult to see Peter and Nicola clearly.

Neil finally managed to spot Peter, and Bradley found Nicola. They did their best to try to get them moving forward, but it wasn't helping enough.

A loud buzzer sounded, and the holes in the ceiling closed, stopping any more balls from falling.

Xavier was standing on the ledge they had been trying to reach.

"You weren't even close!" he laughed. "You guys are pathetic."

Bradley got ready to throw a couple balls at Xavier, but Peter quickly grabbed his wrist before he had a chance to do so.

"Save your energy," he said softly to Bradley.

They slowly made their way back to the start, hopped out, and sat down on the ledge. After at least two or three minutes of silence, Neil offered up a suggestion.

"How about this?" he said. "Brad and I launch Nik as far as we can. You know, like we throw her in. Then we quickly jump in after."

"And what about Pete?" Nicola asked.

"Pete can make it across fine on his own," Bradley said, hoping to insert some confidence into his little brother. "You got this, Pete. Right?"

"Suppose I don't really have a choice," Peter mumbled. "But yeah, I'll go for it."

"But timing is everything if we do it this way," Neil continued. "We will swing Nik back and forth. Then Pete starts his run up. And just as he leaps in, we launch Nik."

"I think it'll work," Bradley said. "But you and I have gotta move like lightning the second we let go of Nik. By the time we go back to get a runup and then jump in, we'll be at least five or six seconds behind them."

Everyone got into position. Peter was crouched down at the wall, like a sprinter at the start line. Nicola lay down by the ledge of the ball pit. Neil took her wrists, and Bradley her ankles. They lifted her up and started swinging her back and forth.

"Okay, Pete," Neil said loudly. "You start running on two. One, two."

Peter bolted for the ball pit.

"Three!" Neil yelled. He and Bradley sent Nicola soaring just as Peter was leaving the ground.

Peter had never had such a perfect jump in his life. It was most certainly one for the record books. Neil and Bradley scrambled to the wall and then ran and jumped.

But the balls were raining down hard from above, so it was tough for them to see how far they'd actually gone.

"I made it!" Nicola yelled as she touched the far ledge.

"I think I'm almost there too," Peter said a few seconds later. "Yeah. I can see it!"

But when Peter was within the last meter of the wall, the bell sounded and the balls stopped falling again. Peter and Bradley were both very close to the end, but Neil still had at least two body lengths to go.

Exhausted, they all lay down on top of the balls. They knew Xavier was standing on the ledge looking at them, but they chose to avoid making any eye contact with him.

"Sorry, guys," Neil said. "I slipped during take-off. That's why I only got this far. But don't worry, I'll be fine next time."

Bradley looked flustered. He wasn't angry at Neil, but at himself. He had been the top athlete in school for all of his junior high and high school years, but he had just failed to complete what seemed like an easy challenge. He hated losing. Really, really hated it.

"I don't know, guys," Bradley said. "I had a perfect jump, and I was moving along pretty fast. But I still didn't make it. I might be able to go a little quicker, but not much."

They went back to the start again and lay on the ledge to catch their breath. They only had one more shot at this, so they couldn't waste it.

"Don't look so down," Nicola said to the boys. "We were super close. I'm sure with a little luck, we'll get there on our next try."

"But to quote my little brother," Bradley said. "When the odds are extremely against you, you have to find a way to improve them."

"I just wish there was a way to shut off the balls raining down from above," Neil said.

"No kidding," Peter added. "Then at least we could make sure we are moving in a straight line."

A fairly long period of silence ensued. With no new ideas about how to do anything differently, it looked like all they could do was hope for a whole lot of luck on try number three."

"I wonder how many balls are in there in total?" Neil asked absent-mindedly. "I mean, you think eventually the stock in the ceiling would run out. He can't have an endless supply."

Peter looked at Neil. But nothing needed to be said. By the expression on Peter's face it was obvious he was on to something.

"How could I have overlooked that?" Peter said while beginning to stand up. "Look at the ball pit. Notice how the balls have never overflowed? But they should be overflowing. He's dumped thousands of balls from above."

"So?" Bradley said.

"Well there's only one possibility then," Peter continued. "When the balls start dropping from the ceiling, some sort of hole must open up in the bottom of the ball pit. That's why the level always stays the same."

"And you want us to find that hole, right?" Nicola asked.

"Actually, I think I already know where it is," Peter replied quickly. "Look right out there. About a body length in front of me. See where the balls are a little lower than the rest?"

"Yeah, the shape kind of looks like a mini-whirlpool,"

Neil said.

"The hole that the balls are exiting through is right below it," Peter said. "I'm willing to bet it's big enough for a person to fit through. And I also think once we drop through it, there will be a path to some stairs that lead directly to the opposite ledge."

"Sounds a little over the top to me," Bradley said. "I think our best chance is to do the same thing as last time, but just do it flawlessly."

"But you just said," Peter reminded his brother, "that we need a new way."

"I'm with Pete on this one," Nicola said in support of Peter. "I mean, like, how many times has he been wrong?"

"Well, not that many, I suppose," Bradley answered. "Okay, I'm cool with it. Pete, let's hear how we play this."

Peter outlined what to do for their final attempt. He would jump in feet first, and land exactly where he believed the hole to be. As soon as he felt himself getting sucked out along with the balls, he'd yell for the next person to jump.

He got them to stand behind him in single file, and stressed how important is was for them to remember the exact spot they were aiming for. Peter knew that once he jumped in, the falling balls would make it extremely difficult for the other three to see where they were jumping.

All things considered, Peter was remarkably calm. He had enormous faith in math and physics, and he was sure this plan would work. Peter recalled watching the sand pass through the narrow part of the egg timer his mom used while boiling eggs. They were about to do more or less the same thing with their bodies right now.

Peter took a short runup, jumped high, and his feet hit the exact spot he was aiming for. A couple seconds later, he felt himself being pulled down along with the balls. "Nik, now!" he yelled.

Nicola did the same as Peter. Neil and Bradley were both ready and waiting for their turns.

Peter felt his speed accelerate as he dropped through the hole onto the landing area below. The staircase to the opposite ledge, the exact thing he had been hoping for, was right in front of him.

"I was right!" he yelled, even though he knew no one could hear him.

He bolted for the stairs. He didn't want to be in the way when then rest of his team started dropping out of the hole.

Nicola, followed by Neil, and finally Bradley, dropped through in rapid succession. They too saw the staircase, plus they could hear Peter screaming for them to hurry.

When Bradley reached the top of the stairs, meaning all four were now on the ledge they had been heading for, the bell still hadn't sounded. They had made it in time.

"YES!" Bradley yelled as if he'd just hit the jackpot. "Take that, Xavier!"

Peter quickly hushed Bradley, as he knew what Xavier could do to them if he wanted to.

"Take what?" Xavier said, taking a few steps closer to Bradley.

"Sorry, sir," Peter said in a desperate attempt to keep Xavier calm. "Brad's just excited. He didn't mean any disrespect to you."

To their relief, Xavier decided to forget Bradley's cocky comment. "Anyway, kids, I am almost impressed," he said. "Almost. But you still have two more to go.

C'mon, this way."

CHAPTER 26

Xavier impatiently led them into a huge, empty chamber. It was by far the largest room they had entered here at the ruins, and was likely used to host big ceremonies and events in ancient times. Xavier was visibly irked by how clever and capable this group of kids had turned out to be. "Like most of your other challenges," he said in a powerful yet monotone voice, "your goal is simple: get over there, to the exit."

"We could've figured out that much by ourselves," Bradley blurted out rudely without thinking.

"Brad!" Peter said quickly, nudging him with his elbow. The last thing they wanted to do right now was irritate Xavier even more. What was Bradley thinking? Peter had just finished apologizing for Bradley's last inappropriate comment, and he doubted this one would be forgiven so easily.

"Oh, so you're all geniuses now?" Xavier asked, refusing to let Bradley's comment go unnoticed. "I suppose I should start getting worried then, right?" He paused, and looked at the other three kids, waiting to see if anyone else had something to add. When he was met with nothing but silence, he continued, "Well, now that Bradley here seems to be finished interrupting me, I will continue. There are six blocks on this table. As you can see, each one is a different shape. On the wall behind you, there are six holes. The six holes match the shape of the six blocks."

"This is just like that game we did as little kids," Neil said excitedly. "Where you put the different shapes through the matching holes in the plastic lid on the box. My mom said I loved that game."

Since the game Neil was referring to was only played by two-year-olds, no one, Peter included, could actually remember how good or bad they were at it. But Peter had heard one story countless times about how Bradley used to play that game.

"We better not let Brad touch the blocks today," Peter said to everyone. "Apparently when he was two, he slammed and smashed the square block into the hole for the triangle until he actually broke the lid."

"Whatever," Bradley mumbled, having also heard the same story many times. "Maybe I was just trying to be original. You know, do things my own way."

"Excuse me, AGAIN!" Xavier announced loudly, angry about being interrupted yet again. "Be quiet and let me finish. Once placed in the matching hole, each block initiates some sort of natural force, like wind, or rain, or something else. You may test all six, one by one, in order to find out exactly what each one causes. After you've tried them all, then you must choose which TWO shapes you will use. Put those two blocks in the holes, and then all four of you have to place one hand on the entrance wall. Then the timer will begin, and you will have exactly twenty seconds to run to the opposite wall. If all four of you touch it in time, you succeed.

"Wait a minute," Bradley said. "You mean, if we choose the wind one and the rain one, then we'd have to run through a wind and rain storm? In only twenty seconds?"

"The next Einstein!" Xavier answered sarcastically. "I will be waiting by the far wall. That way I can start the timer once you've chosen your blocks and are ready to start."

"How many attempts do we get?" Peter asked, just as Xavier was turning to walk across the chamber.

"How many attempts?" Xavier replied without turning back to face them. "Weren't you listening? Only one! But since you are a group of *self-proclaimed* scholars, one attempt should be all you need!"

Peter despised the *you only get one try* type of games. He knew even the easiest games and puzzles often involved making a couple of mistakes and then correcting them.

"Don't worry," Nicola said, hoping to raise everyone's spirits a little. "Let's start testing them out. I'm sure we'll be able to figure out what to do once we've seen all six."

"Let's start with this bad boy," Bradley said while picking up the star-shaped block.

The instant he slid it into the star-shaped hole, the ground started shaking violently. They all lost their balance and fell over.

"Take it out, Brad!" Peter yelled.

It took a good ten seconds for Bradley to get up to pull the block out. The shaking was so intense that standing up had been next to impossible. When he finally pulled it out, they all breathed a sigh of relief.

"We certainly won't be using that one," Neil said.

"We'd have to crawl across on our hands and knees, and we'd never make it in time."

"Next they tried the triangle. Right after Neil pushed it in, hundreds of holes opened up on the walls, and torrents of water gushed into the room. Within seconds, the water was up to their knees, and was quickly approaching their waists. It was coming in with such force that it knocked them off their feet again.

Neil did what he could to haphazardly swim back and yank the block out. Once removed, gates opened in the floor and the water quickly drained away.

"This sucks," Neil said while wringing the water from his shirt. "It's like having to choose how you're going to die."

"No one is going to die," Nicola said to reassure Neil. "C'mon, let's try the next one."

They went with the round block next. This one produced an extremely loud high-pitched noise. They all covered their ears in agony. It was impossible for anyone to remove the block, as that would mean exposing a bare eardrum to the piercing noise again.

Before anyone got any permanent hearing damage, Bradley somehow managed to knock the block out with his elbow.

"Well, we can scratch that one off the list, too," Neil announced.

The fourth block, shaped like a diamond, caused a powerful wind. It was so strong that it blew them all back against the entrance wall. It felt like they were glued to it. It reminded Peter of a school trip he'd taken in Grade 7, where his class was allowed into a wind tunnel used for testing airplane wings.

The only way to make any forward progress was to

crawl on their hands and knees. But they would never be able to crawl across the giant hall in twenty seconds.

Bradley pulled the block out. Exhausted, all four of them lay on the ground.

"Let's catch our breath before trying the next one," Peter suggested.

A couple of minutes later, they all sat up and leaned against the entrance wall. If the final two blocks were anywhere as severe as the first four, then they were in big trouble.

"Okay, Brad," Peter said once he thought everyone looked ready. "Give the square a shot."

Bradley looked a lot more nervous than he had fifteen minutes earlier. He slowly picked up the square and slid it in. The room started shaking violently again.

"Another earthquake one?" Neil yelled while trying to prevent himself from falling down.

Peter got knocked over right away, and hit his elbow hard when he fell.

"Hurry, Brad! Yank it out!" Nicola yelled, hoping to spare the rest of them from being hurt.

Bradley had an awful time getting up to pull out the block. When he finally got his hand on it, he lost his balance, and smashed his head on the wall. He removed the block while fighting off the pain.

Nicola ran over to check out Bradley's injury. She lightly touched the spot he pointed to, which was already starting to swell up.

"I'm going to have a goose egg here tomorrow," Bradley said while testing to see if any blood was coming out.

"I doubt it," Nicola said while giggling. "Your head is pretty thick."

"Very funny," Bradley said with a smile. But Nicola's silly comment had come at just at the right time, as it had prevented Bradley from getting too angry about what had just happened.

Neil picked up the final block, which was shaped like a hexagon. "May I do the honors?" he asked.

"Be my guest," Bradley replied while bowing to him.

Once the hexagon was completely in, the room darkened, and then bolts of lightning shot down randomly in front of them,

"Hey, this one might have some promise," Neil said. "If we just watch carefully to see where the bolts are hitting, maybe we can map out a path across so that they don't strike us."

"Nice idea," Peter said. "But unfortunately, that's not how it works. Lightning always follows the easiest path. If we go out there, it'll use us as conductors. We'd get fried."

"Oh," Neil said sheepishly, "guess I slept through science class one too many times."

Neil removed the hexagon, and they all sat cross-legged facing each other. They had a very big decision to make, and they wanted to ensure that everyone was free to voice their opinions.

But instead of sharing and comparing various ideas, everyone just sat in silence. It looked as if Nicola was getting ready to speak, but she stopped before saying anything. In all likelihood, she had an idea of how to beat *one*. But *two*? There was no chance.

HI READER! (^_^)
WHICH TWO BLOCKS DO YOU THINK THEY SHOULD CHOOSE?

Peter noticed that the rest of his team was now looking his way, like they were waiting for him to make the final decision. The pressure began to make him feel a little uneasy.

"I'm open to suggestions," he said, making eye contact with all three of them while waiting for a response. "Just throw your ideas out there. One might lead to the next."

"Here's mine," Bradley said, catching them a little by surprise. "Wind plus water."

"Wind and water?" Neil asked. "How would that work?"

"You remember when we used to have swim practice at the outdoor pool?" Bradley continued. "When we were swimming, the wind pretty much made no difference."

Bradley had a good point.

"That makes sense," Nicola added. "Plus we are all pretty good swimmers."

Bradley's suggestion did deserve some merit, but Peter needed to run it through the *calculator in his mind* first. He knew that most people swam about four or five times slower than they ran. Gauging the distance they had to cover and the time limit imposed, swimming would be too slow. But he needed to explain this to Bradley in a way that wouldn't sound like he was talking down to him.

"Brad, what's your fastest fifty-meter freestyle time?" he asked.

"Just under twenty-six seconds," Bradley answered proudly. "Third fastest in the entire district."

"Okay," Peter continued. "Well, you know none of us are even close to being as fast as you, right? And we have to get across this whole room, which looks to be about the same length as a 25-meter pool, in twenty seconds. Plus we are wearing clothes, and swimming with backpacks on. You might be able to make it, but the rest of certainly won't."

"Oh," Bradley said, not knowing what else to say.

"I think I might have an idea about how to beat the wind one," Neil said. "One of my cousins is really into cycling, and when they go as a group, they ride in a line to reduce the wind. I think he called it drifting, or maybe drafting, or something like that. If we went across in single file, very close to each other, then only the front person would get the strong wind. We could use our arms to push each other forward. What do you think?"

"If it was only wind, that might work," Bradley said. "But we have to combine it with one more."

Peter started to get a little irritated with himself. This happened quite regularly when he found others were coming up with more ideas than he was. He needed a new perspective. He also wanted to relieve the pressure he was feeling from the rest of his team. He got up and walked a few meters away from everyone, then started pacing around in circles and talking to himself.

Bradley looked like he was about to say something sarcastic to Peter, but Nicola quickly put her hand on his mouth before he had a chance. "Shhh," she whispered to Bradley. "Just let him think. You know that's how he does things."

Bradley then suddenly stood up. It was almost as if a light bulb, indicating that he'd just figured it out, was right above his head. "Believe it or not, I actually remember a couple of things from high school physics," he announced. "And the thing that just popped into my head is this: For each and every action, there is an equal and opposite reaction!"

"Sounds more like poetry than physics," Neil remarked. "And didn't Pete have to help you with all your physics homework?"

Neil was right. Even though Bradley was three years older than Peter, he was way behind him as far as understanding both math and science. If it hadn't been for Peter's assistance, Bradley never would've passed those subjects in junior high and high school.

"Allow me to demonstrate," Bradley said boldly. "Neil, stand up, face me, put up your hands, and lock fingers with me."

"I don't wanna hold hands with you!" Neil said back quickly.

"Fine," Bradley replied, unimpressed by Neil's reaction. "Pete and Nik, you'll do this, right? Face each other and lock hands."

They quickly stood up and did as instructed.

"Okay, Nik," Bradley continued. "Start pushing Pete backward."

As she pushed, Peter took steps backward to prevent himself from falling.

"Nik, now stop pushing," Bradley said. "Pete, now it's your turn to push."

Nicola began shuffling her feet backward to maintain her balance.

"What's this," Neil asked while laughing, "the waltz of the geeks?"

"Ignore him," Bradley said without even looking Neil's way. "Okay, now I want you to both push at the same time. Ready, set, go."

Being the weakling he was, Peter had no hope of pushing Nicola over. But Nicola wasn't so big or strong either. Neither was losing any ground.

"A dead heat!" Neil laughed. "The wimps are deadlocked!"

"Okay, you can both stop pushing now," Bradley continued, ignoring Neil's remark completely. "Please tell me at least one of you can see where I'm going with this?"

Peter jumped with excitement. "You're a genius!" he yelled. "It's almost too simple, isn't it? Brad, I'm so glad you're here. I totally overlooked this one."

"Overlooked what?" Neil asked, needing to hear the rest of the explanation.

"Don't you see?" Peter said, speaking rapidly because he couldn't contain his excitement. "It's the two earthquake ones we need. I'm willing to bet that if we insert them at exactly the same time, they will cancel each other out!"

"Ladies and gentlemen, it's been a pleasure," Bradley gloated in jest, taking a deep bow in front of his team.

"Are you sure?" Nicola asked.

"99.9 percent," Peter replied. "But that's good enough odds for me. Brad, you take the star. Neil, the square. I'm guessing that one starts shaking to the left, and the other one to the right. If you put them in at exactly the same time, the ground should remain still."

Bradley and Neil got ready.

"On three, guys," Peter said. "One, two, three!"

They slid their blocks in and everyone immediately got into a stance that would help them remain standing when the shaking started.

But nothing happened. No shaking. Not even the slightest tremor.

"Brad," Nicola said loudly, "you rock! And I always

thought you were just the dumb jock."

"Well," Bradley replied, looking a little embarrassed. "I suppose I—"

"C'mon guys, let's win this!" Peter yelled, impatient to complete the challenge. "Line up and put one hand on the wall. Remember, we still gotta run across in twenty seconds or less. And don't do anything stupid, like skip or do cartwheels. If you trip or fall, then you might not make it across in time."

They lined up along the entrance wall, and everyone put one hand on it. On the count of three, they all started sprinting. Getting across to the opposite wall was a breeze. When the slowest of the four, Nicola, touched the wall, only twelve seconds had elapsed.

Xavier pointed toward the exit door without saying a word.

Peter surreptitiously looked at his watch while walking through the door. It was a little past two. They still needed to give Zoltan and Mr. Winchester another hour or so to finish setting everything up...

CHAPTER 27

Xavier led them into the next room, the location for their fifth, and final, challenge. Directly in front of them, there was a steep staircase. At first glance, there looked to be about twenty or twenty-five steps in total, and the riser part of each step had a large yellow *1*, *2*, or *3* on it. The order of the numbers was random.

There were no railings on either side, but they could see the holes where the railing posts had been at some point in the past. Peter's first guess was that Xavier had removed them for today's challenge. Without railings, the staircase looked extremely intimidating. If anyone were to fall over either side while climbing up, especially closer to the top, they'd sustain a serious injury.

Peter knew most staircases were constructed to rise at a thirty-two-degree angle, but this one was clearly not made to follow modern building standards. Instead of the normal thirty-two degrees, this one looked to be closer to forty-five.

"Talk about deja vu!" Nicola said. "This reminds me of that checkerboard one we did against Zoltan two years ago."

"No kidding," Neil added. "I remember we had to roll

dice for that one, and then—"

"And then," Peter jumped in, "step on only those squares matching the number we rolled."

"Dice?" Bradley asked, not really following the conversation. He had only shown up after they had completed seven of the eight challenges two years ago, so he hadn't seen this checkerboard challenge they were talking about now.

"Well, there's no such thing as a three-sided dice, is there?" Xavier said coldly. He then turned to walk toward the door they had all just come through. "The instructions are simple. At least three of you must get to the top of these stairs." He paused for a few seconds, waiting for any questions. "And don't start whining about the time. You have one full hour, and may make as many attempts as you want."

Peter pressed the button on his wristwatch to start the clock.

Bradley looked at the steps, and started saying the numbers aloud, beginning from the first step. "1, 3, 2, 1, 1, 3, 2, 2, 1, 3, 2, 3, 1, 2," he said. "Pete, maybe there's a code or something hidden in there."

Peter had already begun running the numbers through the *code-cracker* in his mind. He loved number puzzles, no matter the type, and prided himself in being able to crack even the most difficult codes.

"But you guys also see what you can make of it," Peter said. "You've solved just as many puzzles, or even more, than I have today."

Peter wasn't lying about that comment. Although he had the most academic brain, Neil, Nicola, and Bradley provided the creative thinking and ideas that Peter could not.

"For starters," Bradley said. "Why don't I just walk up? I'll go one step at a time, and see what happens."

"Can't hurt," Peter replied nervously, knowing this was just Bradley's impatience speaking. "But don't go too fast."

Bradley started up the steps, going at such a snail's pace that it looked like he was moving in slow motion. Nothing odd or dangerous happened at first, but when he put his foot on the tenth step, which was a *three*, they all heard a loud grinding noise. In less than a second, the steps rotated until they became flush with each other. The stairs had just turned into a flat slide! Gravity quickly pulled Bradley off his feet and he slid down to the floor where he had started. The instant he finished sliding down, the grinding noise occurred again, and the slide rotated back into stairs.

"Wow! That was cool!" Neil said without thinking.

In order to make the amount of pain any one person would suffer after sliding down and crashing to the floor no worse than the other three, they decided to take turns.

"I'll go next," Peter announced. "On the *ones*".

He was doing fine until he stepped on the fifth *one*, which was three steps above the spot that had caused the stairs to rotate for Bradley. The grinding noise began and the exact same thing happened to Peter.

Nicola and Neil ended up suffering the same fate when attempting the *twos* and *threes*, respectively. It appeared that any step beyond the ninth one would cause the stairs to transform into a slide.

"From the tenth step on," Peter said, "every step seems to activate a switch that turns the stairs into a slide."

"What if I climb up to the ninth step," Bradley suggested, "and then jump as far up as I can? I can clear at least five or six. Maybe that's all we need to do. You know, maybe only steps ten through thirteen or fourteen activate the switch."

Although they decided to let Bradley give his idea a shot, Peter had serious doubts about its chances of succeeding.

Bradley leapt high from the ninth step and landed on the fifteenth one. He hoped he was in the clear this time, but just like every other attempt, the stairs changed into a slide again.

"It must have something to do with the order then," Peter commented as Bradley slid down fast and hard.

They took turns trying all sorts of number orders and combinations: going up in numerical order *(1,2,3,1,2,3)*, or reverse numerical order *(3,2,1,3,2,1)*, using *ones* and *threes* only, or *ones* and *twos* only, and anything else they could think of.

But no matter what they tried, their fate was always the same. They could never get past that ninth step. Plus everyone's bottoms were now sore and bruised from the multiple impacts taken from hitting the floor.

Peter looked at his watch. It was ten minutes to three, so Zoltan and Mr. Winchester should be almost finished setting everything up…

"Wait a second," Neil said out of the blue. "I think I might have an idea."

"Sure," Peter replied.

"Maybe someone always has to be standing on one of each of the numbers?" Neil explained. "You know, like there's always gotta be someone on a *one*, a *two*, and a *three*. Since there are four of us, we can easily do this.

We move up as a team, making sure all three numbers are always covered. The last person would just have to go ahead and stand on the same number as the second last person. And then we could continue up like that.

"I think I get it," Nicola said. "If we do that, we can move our way up while keeping all three covered."

Peter stood on the first *one*, Neil on the *three*, and Nicola on the *two*. Then Bradley walked past them up to the fourth step, which was a *one*. Step five was also a *one*, so Peter stepped off his *one* and walked up to it.

They carefully proceeded like this, but when Peter got to the tenth step, a *three*, the stairs began to rotate again. They slid down in a big pile and thumped hard on the ground on top of each other.

"Ouch!" Nicola said from the bottom of the pile. Neil's shoulder had accidentally rammed her right in the nose. It was already starting to bleed.

"I'm so sorry. I'm so sorry," Neil apologized, thinking his clumsiness had broken her nose.

"Don't worry," she answered. "I don't think it's broken. Or at least I hope it's not."

Peter had already fished another towel out of his backpack and was trying to stop the bleeding.

Bradley looked down at his watch. "Only seven minutes left guys," he said. "What now?"

When it looked like the bleeding had stopped and Nicola was back up on her feet, they got ready to focus on the task again.

Peter put his hands in his pockets and looked up at the stairs. It was now or never.

"Petey," Bradley said from behind him. "You've got a hole in your jeans, dude. I can see your underwear."

"Yeah," Neil added. "They're purple!"

Peter twisted his head back and spotted the hole. "They're not purple, losers," he said, obviously embarrassed. "They're navy. The color has just faded because they're old. I guess my jeans got caught on something and ripped on the way down."

Nicola tenderly touched her nose a few times. It seemed to be in one piece.

Neil, Bradley, and Nicola noticed the exact moment that Peter got *that look* on his face. He must have just figured something out!

Peter got his team to lean in close, like athletes do in the huddle at football or basketball games.

"Guys, I think I solved it. But you remember what we talked about, right?" he said quietly. "We have to lose this last one. Intentionally. That's always been the plan. That way, Xavier will get the ceremony he wants, which is what Zoltan and Mr. Winchester have been setting up for all day. By now, they should be finished all the preparations."

"Are you sure?" Nicola whispered.

"A hundred and ten percent," Peter whispered back. "Now let's just make a few feeble attempts at the staircase until time runs out."

They tried a few disorganized and haphazard attempts up the stairs, trying to make them look as real as possible. During the final minute or two, Peter did his best to appear to be in outright panic mode. And when the buzzer finally sounded, indicating they had lost, he even forced out some fake tears.

CHAPTER 28

Xavier walked up to them with a sinister grin, like a joker in a horror movie, plastered on his face. He also clapped loudly while approaching them, which was his way of rubbing salt in their wounds.

"Well," Xavier began, "I will admit that you put up quite a fight today. I figured you would get through the first one or two, but never imagined you could solve four."

Peter and his team knew they had to keep the act going. Nicola was forcing out tears and Peter was pacing around in frustration. Neil and Bradley were standing, motionless, staring at the ground in front of them.

"So," Xavier said while rubbing his hands together in excitement, "just like we agreed, you guys now owe me an extravagant welcoming ceremony."

"Yes, sir. We do," Peter replied softly. "Everything has already been set up: the stage, the microphones, the speakers, and everything else. The location is the large hill behind Clearville High School. We chose that spot because with the stage at the bottom and people sitting on the hill, everyone will get a clear view of you."

"You guys certainly seem to know how to do the most

important things right, don't you?" Xavier said with a smile. "Shall we all head there now?"

"The ceremony is scheduled to start at four o'clock." Peter replied. "It's about a quarter past three right now, and it'll take us at least twenty minutes to ride our bikes over there. Once we arrive, we'll need a little time to test the electronics and stuff to make sure there are no glitches."

"You really are a precise young man, aren't you?" Xavier said in a mocking tone.

"So we'll start riding our bikes, and see you there just before four. But meet us by the big trees to the right of the stage. That way the audience won't notice you before we make the official announcement."

"I suppose I can handle waiting forty-five minutes," Xavier replied, nodding his head. "Off you go to your bikes, and I will see you there shortly before four. Toodle loo!"

"Pete," Bradley said once Xavier was gone. "You know I drove here, right? I can drive us all to Clearville High."

"Actually," Peter replied, "I knew you drove. But Xavier didn't. I wanted to buy a little more time for Mr. Winchester and Zoltan, just in case they aren't completely finished all the prep yet."

CHAPTER 29

When they rode up to the field it was exactly 3:42, and it looked like at least a few hundred people had already arrived. The hillside was quickly filling up, and more and more people were still pouring in.

They needed to keep up the facade of being upset and defeated, so they hung their heads as they walked toward Mr. Winchester and Zoltan.

Zoltan was holding a handful of colorful pamphlets. It was this flyer, in fact, that had led to the amazing turnout today.

One Day Only! Free Entertainment!
Come and See the Most Amazing Show Ever!
Witness the Best of the Best!
The one. The only – XAVIER!

Show starts at 4pm on September 28.
Be there or be square!

"Pretty impressive ad, don't you think?" Mr. Winchester bragged. "I wrote it in a way that even if Xavier saw one, it wouldn't arouse any suspicion."

Claire, who had been waiting anxiously for Neil to arrive, completely refused to let go of him. It appeared that she planned to continue hugging him until the end of time.

Although Neil was getting a little short of breath from the strength of her hug, he was ecstatic to see her again. "I missed you so much today, babe," Neil said affectionately. "And I am so glad you are now a member of our elite team. Think about it babe, with your help, we are gonna save the world."

Peter was close enough that he caught the last part of that comment, and felt the immediate need to laugh. Before the snicker came out, he quickly walked away. But then after thinking about it a little, he realized what Neil had said was true: They were about to save the world.

Xavier walked up to them just before four o'clock. "It's almost time," he said in an arrogant tone. "Who will be introducing me to my audience of new worshippers?"

"As your servant," Zoltan replied, "that honor will be mine. But we really want to make a bang here, so let me outline the plan for your introduction."

"A little fireworks?" Xavier said with some excitement in his voice. "I like the sound of this."

"Once everyone has found a place to sit," explained Zoltan, "I will warm up the crowd a little. You know, make them really, really, really want to see you. Then when they are screaming for you, I will raise both my arms in the air and loudly announce, 'Allow me to present the powerful, the amazing, the talented, XAVIER!'"

"Not a bad plan so far," Xavier replied smugly.

"Then you arrive from above," Zoltan continued, "in

some sort of tornado or something like that. Land yourself beside me on the stage, just behind the second microphone. I taped a yellow *X* on the floor so it will be easy to spot from above."

"Zoltan, you are going to make a wonderful servant," Xavier said, slapping him hard on the back. "I'll be watching and listening for your cue from a place where the audience will be unable to see me."

"Understood, sir," Zoltan replied. "Your entrance is going to be fantastic, and people will be telling their grandchildren and great-grandchildren about it."

Once Xavier had disappeared from sight, Mr. Winchester quietly whispered for everyone to huddle together. "Okay, you all know what to do. Just do everything as planned and practiced. Good luck everyone."

They quickly split up to their respective stations. The time had come to implement the final part of their masterful, yet highly risky plan.

CHAPTER 30

At about ten past four, it looked like everyone, including the last-minute arrivals, had found a place to sit on the hill. Mr. Winchester slowly limped up the stairs to the stage and began to make his way toward one of the microphones. The closer he got to the microphone, the quieter the crowd became.

He cleared his throat a couple of times, and then began loudly, "Ladies and Gentlemen! Children of all ages! I know why you have all come here today. You have come from far and wide to witness something truly magnificent. To see someone more amazing than anyone else in the entire world."

The crowd started to perk up, just as he had anticipated. "But before I introduce the one you are really here to see," he continued, "how about we give Zoltan one last chance to show off his stuff?"

Of course, the audience had no clue who "Zoltan" was, but that didn't seem to matter. They had come for a show, and couldn't wait for it to start. The crowd began cheering. Mr. Winchester, following the advice Peter had given him, began chanting, "ZOLTAN! ZOLTAN! ZOLTAN!" Before he knew it, the whole crowd had joined in.

Zoltan, with his face hidden almost completely by his hood, walked to center stage.

"Bear with me, everyone," Zoltan said into the microphone in a deep voice. "I know you are here to see Xavier. And I really appreciate you giving me this opportunity to be the opening act for such a fantastic show."

Zoltan slowly raised one arm high in the air. That was a cue for Neil, who was hiding high up in a tree at the top of the hill, a fair distance back from the audience. In one hand, Neil was holding a huge bag filled with multicolored confetti.

"The best way to start off any show is with some glitter and sparkle, isn't it?" Zoltan asked the crowd.

Neil opened the bag and emptied its contents. The instant Zoltan spotted the confetti falling, he used his powers to make it spiral high above the entire audience. He guided the confetti to form long, wavy lines, which soon were moving in a pattern similar to the Northern Lights. And finally, he changed the lines into a few big balls, which he sent high up in the sky. The balls exploded like fireworks, and the sparkling confetti twinkled down slowly to the audience.

"My friends," Zoltan said loudly. "Now we are REALLY ready for the show, aren't we?!"

The audience, mesmerized by what they had assumed was some kind of magic trick, ooed and aahed. Claire, who was in charge of the sound system, turned on some mysterious background music to intensify the effect.

With the crowd so pumped up, Mr. Winchester yelled as loud as he could into the microphone, "You think that's impressive? That is nothing, my friends,

NOTHING compared to what you will see next!!"

The crowd roared. It was deafening. They couldn't wait a second longer for the main act.

Zoltan cleared his throat and raised both arms high in the air. "Then without any further delay," he announced. "Allow me to present to you the powerful, the amazing, the unbelievably talented... XAVIER!!"

The crowd erupted. They were jumping up and down, begging for Xavier to take the stage as soon as possible.

On cue, Xavier made his spectacular entrance. He had created a long, narrow, transparent tornado, and he was currently spinning inside it. The tornado then moved closer and closer to the stage, and Xavier dropped himself right on the yellow *X*. For added effect, he quickly sucked the massive tornado into the palm of his left hand. Then he slowly looked up and raised his arms in the air.

The already erupting crowd increased the decibel level even higher. Xavier kept his arms raised high, revelling in the moment.

It was at least a full minute before the volume of cheering started to taper off. Once the majority of the crowd had quieted down, Zoltan figured it was time to continue. Mr. Winchester had just walked off the stage and was watching everything from behind a tree.

"You just saw the sudden, dramatic, and magical appearance of Xavier with your own two eyes." Zoltan announced. "Wasn't that something??"

They started cheering and clapping instantly. They had all loved it.

"So what could possibly top such an incredible appearance?" Zoltan asked the eager fans. He paused a few seconds for dramatic effect. "How about an equally, or even more spectacular, vanishing act?!"

The crowd screamed even louder. They desperately wanted this show to go on.

Zoltan leaned over and whispered in Xavier's ear, "Create some fog or smoke, and engulf yourself. When it's thick enough so no one can see you through it, walk off the back of the stage. Once you're gone, I'll slowly make the smoke dissipate. While I'm doing that, slip through the row of trees and go up the back of the hill. Then casually start walking through the audience from behind the last row. They'll eat it up."

"I think I'm already liking this new fame," Xavier quietly replied. "The more drama, the better."

Xavier then leaned into the microphone and said, "Ladies and Gentlemen..."

The crowd instantly became silent.

"Prepare yourselves to witness something BEYOND spectacular!" Xavier exclaimed.

He looked up to the sky, and spoke softly in a language that no one other than Zoltan was familiar with. He slowly raised his arms until they were at a ninety-degree angle from his body. Then he began slowly waving them around in a fancy and beautiful pattern. At first, a light fog began to appear over the stage. The fog then began to expand and become thicker. It would only take another fifteen or twenty seconds before the fog would completely hide Xavier from the audience.

Zoltan gave the thumbs up sign behind his back. That was the cue for Peter and Bradley to start crawling to the middle of the stage from behind Xavier. As soon as Nicola saw them crawling, she pulled the lever, just as planned. This caused the trap door, which was directly under the yellow X, to open under Xavier's feet. Peter and Bradley had just arrived at the edge of the opening as Xavier was falling through the trap door.

Xavier was caught completely off guard. The floor below him disappeared so suddenly and quickly that he didn't know exactly what had just happened. All he could tell was that he had fallen feet first into a large box.

Before Xavier had a chance to do anything, Peter and Bradley closed the lid of the box and locked it. The crowd, of course, couldn't see any of this, as the thick fog was completely blocking their view. Nicola pushed the lever back and the trap door closed flush with the stage. Zoltan waited for some of the fog to start clearing on its own, and then used his powers to get rid of the rest. When the crowd saw that Xavier was gone, they burst into applause. But what they were really waiting for was whatever would happen next. The crowd craned their necks in every direction, trying to see where Xavier would reappear.

Xavier, meanwhile, was trapped in the box. He tried to stand up, but smashed his head on the top while doing so. Next he tried kneeling, but the box was still too low to straighten his back completely.

"They think they've trapped me," he said to himself. "The fools. How could they be so stupid? The instant I get out, I am going to show Zoltan and those kids what happens to those who defy me!"

Xavier sat cross-legged, raised one hand until it touched the roof of the box, and got ready to speak. The box he was trapped in was pitch black, but he knew the door was directly above him. All he needed to do was conjure up a strong gust of wind to blow the lid open. But for some weird reason, something wasn't working right. The big gust of wind he tried to conjure up didn't materialize.

"What's going on?" he said, with a slight tinge of panic setting in. "Well, I guess I'll just burn a hole through one of the walls instead."

He began chanting something, holding his wrists and fingertips together and straightening both arms as far as possible. But the bolt of lightning that was supposed to build up and then shoot from his hands didn't appear. It was baffling. In exasperation, he started yelling, louder and louder. But he had no clue that they had completely soundproofed the box. No one could hear his screams.

Bradley leaned over to Peter, the two of them now kneeling down just behind the stage. "Petey," he said. "I think it worked. I mean, if he could have busted out, he would have done so already, right?"

"Let's hope you're right," Peter replied nervously. "Keep your fingers crossed that we didn't miss anything."

Back inside the specially designed box, Xavier was now kicking, punching, flailing and screaming. He also tried using any and all of his supernatural powers in an effort to escape. But no matter what he tried, it didn't work. There was no way out for him.

"Zoltan!!" Xavier screamed. "This is all your doing, isn't it!? The moment I get out of here, I will make you regret the day you were born!"

The crowd wouldn't be satisfied until the disappearing trick was complete. Xavier needed to resurface, somewhere far away from where he had vanished mere moments earlier.

Neil, the second tallest of the team, had already put on a replica of the hooded golden cloak that Xavier was wearing. Peter's team had noticed that Xavier always wore the same cloak, so they had purchased some golden fabric, and asked Peter's mom to sew a cloak. (When she asked what the cloak was for, Peter *fibbed* and said he wanted to wear it to make himself stand out at the District Science Fair.) In addition to the cloak, Nicola's friend's older sister, who was training to be a make-up artist, made up Neil's face so he looked much older. The chance of the hood being blown back and revealing Neil's face was very low, but not zero. And they wanted to be prepared for everything.

Neil started walking from the top of the hill toward the back row of the audience. He walked very slowly and purposefully. Once he got close enough to be noticed, murmuring began in the crowd as a few people started looking his way.

"Look, there he is!" said one man.

"How did he get back there?" another asked loudly.

The rest of the crowd quickly turned around to have a look. Once they'd all spotted "Xavier," the roars and claps began to grow and grow. However, if anyone were to approach him and get close enough to his face, they might notice it wasn't Xavier. So it was imperative for Zoltan to assist, which is exactly what he set about to do.

While hiding behind a few trees to the right of the stage, Zoltan conjured up a dust storm, which looked like a short and stubby tornado, right in front of Neil. Neil jumped into this dust storm, and Zoltan used his powers to lift Neil above the crowd and carry him all the way back to the stage.

Neil stood at the microphone, but he didn't say anything. He raised his arms and started spinning them around above his head, giving the impression he was about to create some new type of magic. As he did this,

Zoltan started creating a storm. First came the dark clouds. Then a powerful wind. Then intense rain. And finally, hail. As the hail stones grew larger in size, the crowd got both scared and angry.

"Stop it!" someone close to the stage yelled.

"Yeah, there are kids here!" another screamed. "What are you trying to prove?"

The crowd quickly grew more outraged, and more terrified.

"What kind of magic show is this?" a man said while standing up to leave.

Some people covered their heads with their jackets. Others started booing loudly. Mr. Winchester limped as fast as he could to Neil. He whispered something in Neil's ear, and Neil brought his hands down. And at that exact instant, Zoltan stopped the storm.

The storm had stopped, but the crowd's anger certainly had not. Zoltan went up the stairs, ran to center stage, and grabbed a microphone.

"We are so sorry, everyone," he pleaded to the angry crowd. "We are terribly, terribly sorry. I think we must have had, well, some technical difficulties. This last illusion went... umm... well... horribly wrong. This is so embarrassing, but... we will have to, um, end the show now. For your safety, of course."

The heckling escalated even further. A few people near the stage even threw some half-filled soft drink cups and cans towards the stage.

Zoltan quickly ushered Neil off the back of the stage. The last thing they needed now was an angry mob chasing after them. Their whole team ran and jumped into the two rental vans they had prepared as their *getaway vehicles*. The box with Xavier in it was hooked up to one of the two vans. They had built the box on a proper trailer with wheels, and even had an official license plate on the back of it. They'd had it hooked up to the van for the entire show, so they could make their escape without any delay.

They sped away through a series of rarely used back roads, in an attempt to make following them extremely difficult. And since the audience's parking lot was fairly far from the hill, they were quite sure no one would track them down.

CHAPTER 31

After about forty-five minutes of winding through a confusing series of old country roads, they arrived at the plot of land with Mr. Winchester's shed on it. Although the land and shed were officially in the old man's name, they had been used by no one other than Peter and Nicola for the last two years.

"Peter, we followed your instructions to a T when building that box," Zoltan said as he stepped out of the van. "You were right. Inside it, he is completely powerless."

Peter had been very carefully watching Zoltan for the past two years, trying to learn about any weaknesses he might have. He wanted to be prepared if Zoltan ever turned on the people of Earth. Those two years of close observation led him to the conclusion that a weather god's powers can be severely inhibited, or possibly even nullified, by two things: darkness and mirrors. Peter's guess was that the combination of both had the greatest possibility of success. Therefore, all the inside surfaces of Xavier's box were covered in shatter-proof mirrors, and it was sealed to be one hundred percent pitch black.

"Yeah," Peter said. "I just thought about how the

strongest of superheroes, you know, the ones you see on TV and the movies or read about in comics, always have some sort of weakness. I figured weather gods might have weaknesses, too."

"Looks like your love for comic books finally paid off!" Nicola said, pulling Peter in for a huge hug. "We did it, Pete!"

"Once again," Bradley announced, "we've proven ourselves invincible!"

They sat around outside as night fell. They ate. They laughed. They told silly stories. This oddball group of Mr. Winchester, Zoltan, Peter, Nicola, Bradley, Neil, and Claire had officially bonded. They were like family now. And no one would ever know how this group of seven had just saved millions, or possibly even billions of lives.

"But what do we do with him now?" Peter asked while pointing at Xavier's box. "I mean, we can't just leave him in there. He'll die of hunger and dehydration."

"That's being taken care of, Peter," Zoltan replied. "The lead weather gods, all twelve of them, will be here at midnight to cart away Xavier. They'll take him back to our planet inside that box."

"Are you sure you guys can keep him in there?" Neil asked, sounding a little concerned. "I mean, what if he figures out a way to escape?"

"Our planet has both advanced technology and highly skilled engineers," Zoltan replied. "And our experts are already building a big replica of this box to serve as Xavier's prison. Don't worry, he will never be able to escape. I can promise you that."

CHAPTER 32

Three weeks had passed since the successful trapping and banishment of Xavier, and life was more or less back to normal. It was a beautiful sunny Saturday morning at Meeks Park, where Peter, Neil, Nicola, Bradley, and Claire were digging into a box of freshly baked chocolate chip cookies.

"Pete, your mom's cookies rock!" Neil said, stuffing a fifth cookie into his mouth. "I could eat a hundred of these!"

"Dude," Peter replied, "if you tell her that, she'll make a truckload for you."

They all chatted away until the box was empty, pausing occasionally to drink some milk. Not only had Peter brought cookies, but he also came with a small carton of milk and five plastic cups.

"Okay, Mr. Smarty pants, and his clan of geniuses," Claire said after standing up, "give this challenge a shot."

It turned out that Claire was both interested in and very good at puzzles and riddles. She was actually almost as good as Peter himself.

Since Peter and his friends had helped save the world,

Zoltan no longer demanded that Peter and Nicola create weekly puzzles for him. But they all seemed to enjoy doing challenges so much that they agreed to keep making new ones for each other from time to time.

Claire, realizing how much fun this could be, made a suggestion: She thought it would be fun to form an unofficial "club," consisting of Peter, Nicola, Neil, Bradley, and herself. Plus Mr. Winchester and Zoltan were welcome to participate whenever they felt like it. She suggested they take turns creating the puzzles. And today, it was her turn to be the puzzle-maker.

Peter, Neil, Nicola and Bradley now were standing next to the river at Meeks Park, in the exact place Claire had instructed them to go. Claire passed Bradley a small cardboard box, and then handed Peter an envelope.

"You don't really think you made something too tough for *us*, do you?" Neil said while laughing.

Claire walked over to Neil and playfully punched him in the arm. "Don't underestimate your girlfriend," she said. "And you can save that big macho attitude of yours until you have actually *solved* the puzzle."

Bradley put the box down and opened up the flaps to see what was inside. Meanwhile, Peter removed the note from the envelope, and looked at its contents.

"Come on, man," Bradley said impatiently, "What does it say?"

Peter smiled at Claire, "Wow, you really have made this hard," he said.

"Just hurry up and read it," Bradley repeated.

"I'd love to, but I can't," Peter replied quickly. "It's written in code. We can't even start the challenge until we decipher the coded message."

"I'll be back in a few hours," Claire said while

skipping toward her bike. "I'm gonna go home and get my weekend chores out of the way. It looks like you four will be busy for quite some time."

"Ride carefully, babe!" Neil said back to her.

While Peter was trying to decipher the code, Bradley, Nicola, and Neil walked up to him. Really, really close to him.

"What's going on, guys?" Peter asked, twisting his head back and forth to look at all three.

"Petey," Bradley said, putting his hand on Peter's shoulder. "It's been three weeks since we banished Xavier."

"I know," Peter replied.

"Of course you do," Bradley continued. "But, there's still one thing the three of us don't know."

"Something I know that you guys don't?" Peter asked innocently.

"Okay," Bradley replied. "I'll get right to the point. Remember puzzle number five? The one you said you had figured out the solution to, but we had to intentionally lose? Well, we've asked you a few times to tell us the solution, but you always dance around the question or change the subject."

"Yeah," added Neil. "We are almost starting to think you really didn't solve it at all."

"Either that," added Nicola, "or there is some reason why you won't tell us."

Peter paused and turned away from his friends for a few seconds. The real reason he hadn't told them was that he had been planning to adapt the solution into the puzzle he was scheduled to make next weekend.

Peter felt his anxiety rising quickly, so he chose to set the record straight. "Okay, here it is," he began. "I'll tell you, but as soon as you hear the solution, you are all going to be shocked that you missed it."

"Was it that simple?" asked Bradley.

"Too simple," Peter replied. "The fact that it was so simple was actually what made it so hard."

"Come on, enough mumbo jumbo," Bradley said impatiently. "Just spit it out."

"Remember when you guys spotted that hole in my jeans?" Peter asked them.

"Sure do!" replied Neil. "I also recall seeing your lovely purple underwear through the hole."

"Neil!" Nicola said sharply, putting her hand over Neil's mouth to stop him from saying anymore.

"That hole is what got me on track to solve it," Peter said excitedly. "I knew sliding down a flat surface wouldn't rip a hole, so I looked for something sticking out of the ground. I couldn't find anything at first, but after closer inspection, I spotted six small circular stone tiles. They were flush with the floor and exactly the same colour as the stone used on the floor. All six of them were in a line, less than a millimeter away from the riser part of the first step. That's when it just, like, dawned on me: They couldn't have been part of the original stone floor. So that meant they had to be part of the challenge. The only logical thing I could come up with was that they were buttons."

"Buttons?" asked Nicola.

"You got it. Buttons," continued Peter. "I was so sure that I watched them carefully during the final few minutes, while you guys were making those fake attempts to get up to the top. I noticed that the instant the stairs changed into the slide, all six buttons rose out of the ground, but only very slightly. Maybe by a couple of millimeters. So when Brad was sliding down once, and was getting close to the floor, I stepped on a button. It, along with the other five, went flush with the floor again. And at that instant, the slide shifted back into stairs."

"Oh, man!" Bradley yelled. "You mean that for the first fifty-something minutes, it was our own butts hitting those buttons on the floor that caused the slide to rotate back into stairs?"

"Bingo," Peter answered, smiling.

"So the numbers meant nothing?" Neil asked.

"Yup. Absolutely nothing." Peter answered.

"So that's why he said only three of us needed to reach the top," Nicola added. "Because one person needed to stay at the bottom, keeping their foot on a button. All six buttons rose or fell as if they were one, right? So if one button was held down by someone's foot, then none of them could pop up!"

"I think I get it," Bradley said. "As long as the buttons couldn't pop up, the stairs couldn't rotate, right?"

"Bingo again," Peter replied. "Brilliant trick, wasn't it?" He paused, waiting to see if anyone wanted to comment on the solution they had missed. When no one spoke up right away, he quickly changed the subject. "But enough about that. Let's get going on Claire's puzzle. Any of you think we can solve it before lunch?"

"Dunno," Neil replied. "But we will certainly give it our best shot."

Peter loved this stuff: He was hanging out with his girlfriend, best friend, and brother. A confusing and complex riddle was waiting to be tackled. What could possibly make him any happier?

EXTREMELY PUZZLED

THE PUZZLED MYSTERY ADVENTURE SERIES: BOOK 3

CHAPTER 1

Peter was home alone on a chilly Friday evening in early November. His girlfriend of two and a half years, Nicola, had started a new part-time job at a restaurant a few weeks ago, and they always gave her the busy Friday night shift. He wouldn't dare mention it to Nicola, but he really missed hanging out with her on Fridays. For over two years, they had been going to movies almost every Friday afternoon or evening, so this new routine—and Peter hated new routines—was going to take some time to get used to.

The clock on the wall read 7:47, which meant Peter had been pointlessly channel surfing for well over an hour. Most Grade 10 kids would have been watching one of the latest primetime dramas, or maybe a hockey game, but not Peter. He was flipping around trying to catch any *breaking news* stories. Not about celebrities showing up in restaurants or politicians caught going back on their word, but ones about where the most recent natural disaster or severe weather was occurring.

Zoltan was still Earth's weather god and had another twenty-two years until he would be replaced. But despite his best efforts, the weather was wreaking havoc all over the globe. And it wasn't because Zoltan was just sitting around and twiddling his thumbs. It was due to Earth's immense size, and the fact that there were so many things happening simultaneously. How could Zoltan reduce the intensity of an earthquake in Brazil if he was over in Australia trying to provide some rain to drought-stricken areas? The answer, of course, was that he couldn't.

Peter had spent a month or so researching how much damage—in terms of both dollars and human lives—had happened over the past year. The results of his investigation led him to the only plausible resolution: the carnage being caused by the weather could only be controlled if Zoltan had help. To put it simply, Earth needed at least a few more weather gods.

Peter turned off the TV and went up to his room. He had decided two weeks ago *how* he was going to try to get Zoltan some desperately-needed help, but kept putting off *actually doing it*. Peter wished he hadn't been born with procrastination in his DNA. But his mother refused to let Peter use genes as an excuse; she just called it straight-up laziness.

He sat down at his desk and prepared a few sheets of loose-leaf. He needed to draft a letter that was clear, concise, and direct. But he also wanted to make sure it wouldn't come across as being disrespectful in any way.

* * *

About half an hour later, he had completed a draft that he was reasonably satisfied with. Now all he needed to do was type it up and print it. For the majority of kids his age, typing was as easy as riding a bike. Unfortunately, Peter didn't fall into that category; he typed with two fingers and had to look at the keyboard to search for each and every key. Well, he didn't have to search for the *backspace* key, as he used that one far more than the rest.

Dear Lead Weather Gods,

My name is Peter, the teen who helped trap Xavier a few months back. I am writing to you today with an important request: I would like you to seriously consider assigning more weather gods to Earth. In my opinion, Earth needs at least another 6. Zoltan works around the clock, but Earth is huge, and he simply can't do it on his own. I have attached a spreadsheet to this letter which contains statistics of how much damage the weather is causing here. I totaled up the number of deaths linked to severe weather and natural disasters for each continent. And I also calculated the amount of money spent or lost due to those weather events. The numbers are terrifying. There must be something you can do.

Sincerely,

Peter

Peter checked his wristwatch. It was shortly past nine, and he could hear people stirring around downstairs. His parents and sister were obviously home now, but they hadn't come up to check on Peter yet. Either that or they saw his bedroom door was closed and figured he didn't want to be disturbed.

"Oops, I forgot to plug in the light," Peter said to himself. He was referring to the light hidden in the chimney: the one he turned on whenever he needed to contact Zoltan.

He took the extension cord from its hiding place in the closet, plugged it in, and opened his bedroom window. The cord from the light came to just outside his window, so he plugged it into the extension cord and voila, the light came on. Since it was cold outside, he closed the window as much as he could without pinching the cord.

He wanted to leave the light on for at least an hour, so he decided to head back downstairs. Sophia was already in bed, and his parents were sitting at the kitchen table having some chamomile tea.

"Hey, Pete," his dad said. "You want some tea?"

"No, I'm good," Peter replied.

"Are you sure?" his mom asked. "It's a very effective way to help people relax and calm down before bed."

Peter's parents must have thought his visit to the kitchen was because he couldn't fall asleep.

"No, I'm fine, really," he said. "But thanks for the tip. I know where you keep the teabags, so maybe I'll give it a go the next time I find myself tossing and turning at midnight."

Peter went into the living room and continued where he'd left off: flipping through channels to see if any new weather problems were being reported. When Peter's mind got locked onto something, he became obsessed with it. Even if he had wanted to do something else tonight, his brain would never let him.

CHAPTER 2

He woke up way too early the next morning, but this was nothing neither new nor rare for the overly anxious Peter. If he had received a dollar for every minute he had spent awake staring at the ceiling, he would already have enough to buy himself a car.

He knew flopping around in bed was nothing more than a useless waste of time, so he decided to get up and go downstairs to eat. But since Peter's mom turned the furnace down before she went to bed every night, this task was going to be much easier said than done. The chilly air in his room was very uninviting compared to the warmth of his blanket.

He quietly walked downstairs, turned on the kitchen light, and pushed the lever on the thermostat a couple centimeters to the right. Then he let out a yawn and opened up the fridge.

Although Peter was an amazingly creative kid, his breakfasts certainly didn't demonstrate it. He prepared his bowl of cornflakes with milk and a tall glass of orange juice—the same breakfast he had been eating since he was about five. It wasn't that he didn't want to eat something different; he was just worried his stomach might get upset if he did. Basically, he ate the same thing every morning to give him one less thing to worry about.

He knew his mom's razor-sharp ears would hear him moving about at such an early hour, so he chose to use a plastic bowl, spoon, and cup.

Peter took little or no pleasure in his morning breakfast ritual, and he was finished eating in less than six minutes. He left his empty bowl, spoon, and cup on the table—another bad habit he was regularly scolded for—and went back to his bedroom.

With too much on his mind and no way to speed up the clock, Peter started pacing around in circles. He read and reread the note for the lead weather gods so many times that he'd quickly memorized the whole thing without even having tried.

After what felt like an eternity, eight o'clock finally arrived, so Peter got changed, brushed his teeth, and got ready to go. He needed to tell a *little white lie* about where he was going, as he certainly couldn't tell his mom and dad he was off to meet up with a weather god! So he started writing a note saying that he and Neil were going to the mall. But just as he was finishing the note, his mom came into the kitchen to turn on the coffee maker.

"*You* are going to the mall?" his mom asked. "But you hate the mall."

"Well, Neil needs help choosing a Christmas present for Claire," Peter replied, digging himself deeper into his lie. "And I couldn't say no."

"Yo, Pete," Bradley yelled from the family room. Peter was a little startled, as he didn't know Bradley was already up. "I'm heading there, too. Well, not this instant, but pretty soon. Wanna lift?"

"Nah," Peter answered nervously. "I'll ride there. I need the exercise."

"You sound like Dad, man," Bradley laughed. "Don't tell me you're gonna start counting calories, too?"

"I heard that!" Peter's dad said loudly while walking down the stairs.

"Anyway," Peter said before Bradley had a chance to reply. "It's fine. I'll ride. That way Neil and I can come home whenever we want."

"Suit yourself," Bradley replied. "But you can't say I didn't offer."

Peter went back upstairs and put on a few layers of clothes to get ready for his chilly ride. Luckily snow hadn't fallen yet this year, but it was bound to one day very soon.

* * *

Peter arrived at Silverhead Mountain shortly after nine o'clock. It was a rarity for Peter to ever be late, but today he had to stop a couple times to take off layers when he got too sweaty. He ended up arriving three minutes and fifteen seconds past the designated time.

Zoltan was sitting at one of the picnic tables and turned to wave to Peter as he rode up.

Peter was shocked at the drastic change in Zoltan's appearance since the last time they had met, which was only about five weeks ago. Zoltan looked like he had aged a few years, or perhaps hadn't slept a wink in days.

"Zoltan," Peter said in a tone that clearly conveyed how worried he was. "Are you okay? Are you sick or something?"

"No," he replied. "But thanks for asking. I'm just burnt out. Totally burnt out. Earth's weather is a nightmare to control. Well, I guess I technically should've known that all along, but I never took my responsibilities seriously until a few months ago." Zoltan paused. "But I didn't come here to complain. I came because you asked me to. So, what's up?"

Although Peter was slowly improving his communication skills, he always found it difficult to choose the right words to start with. "I, uh," he said, "uh, I wrote a letter."

"A letter?" Zoltan asked.

"Yeah," Peter replied, suddenly feeling anxious for no reason at all. "It's for the lead weather gods."

"You wrote those guys a letter?" Zoltan asked, looking very surprised.

"Well," Peter said. "You are welcome to read it first if you want. It's a request that they send more weather gods here to help you out. You know, like, maybe half a dozen or so."

"Half a dozen?" Zoltan said with a smile. "Peter, I have been requesting backup for over two months. And every time I make a request, I always get the same reply: *We don't have anyone available to spare.*"

"But don't they know how many people are dying because Earth is too big to manage on your own?" Peter asked.

"They do," he replied. "And they sincerely care. The fact of the matter is that there are no fully-trained weather gods available who aren't already assigned somewhere else."

"What do you mean," Peter asked, "by fully-trained?"

"To become a weather god," Zoltan began, "you have to attend a special school for your education, training, and practice. I suppose one could compare it to what you call a *university* here on Earth. But from start to finish, it takes ten years to complete."

"Ten years?!" Peter reacted in disbelief. "Why so long?"

"There's a lot more to controlling the weather than meets the eye," Zoltan answered with a wink. "The techniques we use are extremely difficult to master. Over eighty percent of the students who enter the school drop out because it's too hard. And if you don't graduate, then you are not qualified to be a weather god."

"But still," Peter said with a befuddled look on his face, "there are plenty of graduates every year, right? So why can't they just send a bunch of them here to help?"

"Unfortunately, it doesn't work that way," Zoltan replied while shaking his head. "Things are pretty archaic as far as the system goes. All planet assignments are done once every fifty years, which means everyone switches planets on the exact same day. And right now we are twenty-eight years into the current cycle."

"So what do all the new graduates do?" Peter asked. "Don't tell me they just sit around and wait for the next fifty-year cycle to start. That's ridiculous!"

"You're completely right," Zoltan agreed. "It is ridiculous. But that's just how they do it."

"What do all the graduates do while they wait all those years?" Peter asked, feeling more agitated by the minute.

"Various things," Zoltan explained. "Some take on part-time teaching positions at the school. Some do at-home tutoring for students. A few have even opened up a prep school: you know, to help kids who want to enter the training school get the skills they need to pass the entrance exam. And there are others who decide to get into the research side of things. Instead of becoming weather gods, they try to discover new and more effective ways of controlling the weather."

There was a long and uncomfortable pause in the conversation. Peter wanted to ask something, but he knew it would just sound like another complaint about their bizarre system.

"However," Zoltan said, breaking the silence, "I will take your letter and spreadsheets back to planet Sevlar, which some people refer to as the planet of the weather gods, and deliver them in person. I'm not sure it will initiate any sort of drastic change, but it certainly can't hurt. After all, you are extremely respected on Sevlar, as it was *your* ingenious plan that led to the capture of Xavier."

"Really?" Peter said with a bit of a grin. "You mean, they actually talk about me there?"

"They do more than just talk about you," Zoltan answered. "The history textbook used for twelve-year-olds is currently being rewritten to include a new chapter, dedicated specifically to explaining what you did and how important it was."

"You mean," Peter said, feeling proud and embarrassed at the same time, "kids on Sevlar will be taught about me?"

"You've already become a household name," Zoltan replied while holding up his hand for a high-five. "And after the textbook gets republished, the younger generation will know everything about you."

"Cool!" Peter said, high-fiving Zoltan's hand hard.

"I promise I'll deliver what you've just given me to the lead weather gods today," Zoltan said. "And return tomorrow to tell you how it went. Meet me back here at ten o'clock again."

"How do you get there and back so fast?" Peter asked.

"Let's save that explanation for another day," Zoltan replied.

"Okay," Peter said. "Anyway, good luck. I'll keep my fingers crossed."

"Keep your fingers crossed?" Zoltan asked, awkwardly trying to cross his fingers on both hands. "Why would you do that? How would you write? Or how would you ride your bike? Or—"

"Let's save that explanation for another day," Peter said with a big grin. "Off you go."

CHAPTER 3

Peter ended up having a power nap on the sofa mid-afternoon, which helped him feel somewhat refreshed. He found it amazing how thirty minutes of sleep on the sofa seemed to make up for three or four hours of missed sleep the previous night. He was really looking forward to tonight, as he and Nicola were going out for an early dinner, followed by a movie. Nicola had miraculously managed to convince her boss to give her the lunch shift today, so she was off at three o'clock. She had told Peter that she needed time to shower after work, plus she wanted to take a quick nap before heading out, so they had set five o'clock as the meet-up time.

One of the most awkward things about "date night" for two young people without driver's licenses was the transportation issue. You either had to get dropped off and picked up by a nosey parent or older sibling, or you had to take the bus. Unfortunately, bus service in Clearville was abysmal. The closest bus stop to Peter's home was a twelve-minute walk, and there was only one bus an hour on weekends.

The last time they'd gone out, Nicola's mom had been their "chauffeur," so today it was Peter's turn to sort out how they'd get to the movie. He couldn't ask his older brother Bradley, as he was away for the entire weekend at a big indoor track and field competition. So that left his mom and dad as his only two options, both of which had their pros and cons.

His mom was the "queen of punctuality," so she would definitely get them to where they wanted to go, and back, at exactly the times requested. But along with her punctuality came her fairly irritating habit of dominating the conversation for the full journey both ways.

His dad was also reliable as far as time was concerned, but having him as the driver included the risk that he'd fire off an array of outrageous questions to Nicola. Peter's dad had unintentionally embarrassed him more times than he cared to recall.

* * *

When Peter and Nicola were still a fairly new couple back in Grade 8, his dad had happily agreed to drop them off, and then later pick them up, from a concert they had tickets to in the neighboring city of Stoneburg. The drive there was thankfully free of any ridiculous comments, but the ride back was another story. When they hopped in the car after what had been an awesome concert, instead of asking how the concert was—the most natural thing anyone would ask—Peter's dad turned around and directly asked Nicola, "If I offered you fifty dollars to cut off your long hair, would you do it?"

She was so stunned by the obscurity of the question that she had to ask for clarification. "My hair? For fifty bucks? Why?" she asked back.

"Don't answer a question with a question," his dad said in what almost sounded like a condescending tone.

"Fifty bucks. Yes or no?"

* * *

The thing Peter seemed to have forgotten today was that he may not be able to choose who to ask. Just because his parents were in their late forties didn't necessarily mean that they both always stayed home all weekend.

He went to the backyard where they were both busy raking up the autumn leaves. Their house was a bit old, but it came with a huge yard and garden. When the leaves changed colors in fall, the backyard was absolutely stunning.

"Pete, come here," his dad said. "I want to show you something."

Peter knew that whenever his dad *wanted to show him something*, that it meant whatever was about to occur would involve little "showing." Peter was ninety-nine percent sure that his dad was about to hand him the rake and then go inside to catch the end of a golf tournament on TV.

"Stephen, don't make Peter do your work," his mom said sternly. "You know he's got a date with Nicola tonight. He probably came out to ask if one of us can drive them."

Peter hadn't mentioned anything about tonight's date to either of his parents, or Bradley, or even his younger sister Sophia. "How do you know Nik and I are going out tonight?" he asked with curiosity.

"I heard you talking on the phone with her last night," his mom answered. "If you want your conversations to be private, you'll need to speak a LOT more quietly."

Peter had indeed spoken to Nicola on the phone the previous night, but had done so in his room with the door shut. Either his mom has superhuman hearing, or the thin wall separating his bedroom from theirs lacked sufficient sound insulation.

"Your father will be happy to drive you," she said without even conferring with Stephen first. "Right?"

Peter's dad knew the consequences of putting up even the slightest resistance in this type of situation, so he immediately nodded and then responded, "No sweat." But Peter knew his dad didn't really mind. He'd probably stop by the driving range and hit a couple hundred balls after dropping them off.

CHAPTER 4

Nicola's house wasn't even a five-minute drive from their place, which meant leaving by 4:55 would get them there on time. But for some strange reason, Peter's dad kept hassling him to hurry up and get ready.

"Dad," Peter explained. "There's no point in leaving so early. We'll just end up sitting in her driveway waiting."

"And by the way," his dad responded, tossing the keys to Peter unexpectedly. "*You* are driving us there. You're old enough to drive as long as I am in the car with you, right?"

Peter had obtained his learner's permit shortly after turning fourteen, so he was technically allowed to drive as long as he was with an adult. He was actually signed up for driving lessons this coming January, so there was no reason for his dad to put him behind the wheel today.

But before Peter had a chance to plead his case, his dad was already sitting in the passenger seat, seatbelt done up snugly.

"Dad, you know I've never driven anywhere other than an empty parking lot," Peter mentioned. "And I've only done that twice."

"Life in the fast lane," Peter's dad replied, an answer

which made absolutely no sense. But Peter was long since used to the way his dad used proverbs and other sayings completely out of context.

"You're only driving until we get to Nicola's place," his dad answered. "And the streets to get there are all residential. You won't see another moving car, I promise."

"But we still don't have to leave yet," Peter said. "We can—"

"Things to do, people to see, places to go," his dad said, interrupting him.

Peter realized, like it or not, that he was going to have to start driving immediately. He slowly backed out of the driveway and started to head toward Nicola's home.

"Turn left here," his dad said suddenly.

"But Nik's house is straight, not—"

"Just turn left," his dad repeated. "There's something you have got to see."

"Oh, here we go again," Peter whispered to himself so that his dad wouldn't hear him over the radio. He knew he was about to be led "somewhere" to see "something" he'd have no interest in.

"Now go right," his dad instructed. "And park up at the end of that cul-de-sac."

Peter did as he was told, and the second he put the car into park, his dad opened the door and hopped out. "Come on, we don't have much time," his dad said as he shut the door.

Peter reluctantly got out, carefully checked that he'd locked the doors—something completely unnecessary considering where they were—and jogged to catch up to his dad. He followed him through the walkway between two of the houses at the end of the cul-de-sac.

"Check it out," his dad proudly announced, pointing at the big, yellow piece of construction equipment in front of them. "They brought in that excavator last Sunday, but it hasn't done any work yet. I wonder what they are going to do or build here?" He paused as if waiting for Peter to enthusiastically jump into the conversation. All Peter did was look at his watch.

"Dad, we gotta head back to the car," Peter said, tossing the keys to his dad. "If we don't go soon, we'll end up being late getting to Nik's. And you know how much I hate being late."

* * *

Peter and Nicola decided to try something different for a change, so they went to a new Greek restaurant that had just opened in October. It was within walking distance of the movie theater, so it seemed like a logical choice—and Peter, above all things, always chose logical.

The food was great, the waiter was funny, and the atmosphere of the restaurant was perfect. But despite all of those positives, it was clear to Nicola that a big chunk of Peter's mind was somewhere else.

"Okay, Pete," she said right after they ordered dessert. "I'll be blunt. You've barely said anything tonight, other than meaningless one-word comments about the food. And even those sounded more or less robotic. Don't get me wrong here. I'm not trying to tell you I'm bored. I'm just, well, confused."

Peter felt his throat tighten. He knew he'd been acting a little odd, but it certainly wasn't intentional. He was just preoccupied with the upcoming meeting with Zoltan. And he figured blabbering on about that meeting would be selfish and rude, which could potentially ruin the evening.

"Pete," she said, taking his hand. "I'm your girlfriend. I'm not going to get angry or anything like that. Just tell me what's going on inside that busy mind of yours."

With the open invitation to speak freely, Peter rapidly went through everything that had happened earlier that day. Nicola remained silent as she listened intently, nodding every so often to indicate that she was following along.

As soon as he finished, she playfully punched him in the shoulder and said, "That's what's been eating at you? Oh, man... I thought you were going to tell me something serious like you were thinking of breaking up."

Peter got goose bumps from just hearing that phrase. Nicola was the perfect girlfriend.

"Break up with you?" he said timidly. "I'd never do that. You're, like, too perfect."

Nicola stood up from her seat and walked to the other side of the table. She leaned down and hugged Peter from behind.

"Aw, aren't you just the sweetest," she whispered in his ear. "You're pretty perfect yourself, too. But PLEASE be more honest the next time something is bugging you. I don't want to have to drag it out of you like I did today."

"I promise, I promise," he answered quickly, feeling embarrassed that quite a few people sitting nearby were now looking their way.

"And if you think I'm going to end this hug just because you're embarrassed everyone is looking at us," Nicola continued, obviously reading Peter's mind, "then you are wrong with a capital *W*. You'll just sit there and let me hug you for as long as I want."

* * *

Since they both knew Peter wouldn't be capable of focusing on a movie tonight, they decided to go to a coffee shop near the theater instead. They chose a table in the far corner so they could talk about the whole Zoltan situation without being overheard.

Nicola agreed that Peter's letter was a good idea, but figured it would probably amount to nothing. And she also informed him that she was coming along to meet Zoltan tomorrow.

"But don't you have to do a history paper that's due on, like, Tuesday?" Peter asked.

"Of course I do," she replied, drinking the last of her cafe latte. "But I'm sure my *too perfect* boyfriend would be happy to come to the library to help out with the research after we finish talking with Zoltan, wouldn't he?"

CHAPTER 5

Rain hammered down on Peter's bedroom window that night. It, along with the gusting wind, seemed unrelenting. His room overlooked their big backyard, and the branches of the huge trees were blowing so hard that Peter figured it was only a matter of time before one would snap off and come smashing through his window.

It sounded like the storm just kept growing in power. That being said, Peter was so overly focused on each and every sound it was making that he couldn't be a reliable judge. He really needed to get his mind off the storm, or else he'd drive himself crazy. He tiptoed downstairs, poured himself a glass of milk, and then walked back toward his room.

When he opened his bedroom door, he immediately felt the powerful wind blowing in through the broken window. He spotted the branch on his bed, the one that was obviously responsible for smashing the window. There was also lots of shattered glass both on and around his bed.

One side of Peter's bed was right against the wall with the window in it, so he didn't dare get up on his bed to try to *do something* about the window. Instead, he just stood there, like a statue. After a minute of doing nothing, he decided it was time to go get his parents. But when he spun around to walk out, he stepped on a piece of broken glass, which pierced the soft skin in the arch of his foot. He sat down and looked at the glass shard wedged in his foot and the blood that was dripping out. It hurt, but not nearly as much as it should have. Maybe the psychology professor who had given a guest lecture at their school last month was not joking about the "mind over matter" concept.

* * *

Peter jolted himself awake. That whole crazy storm, broken glass, bleeding foot thing had been nothing more than another one of his wonky dreams.

He was drenched in sweat. Even though it was a dream, his sympathetic nervous system had been fooled into thinking it was completely real. And it wasn't just his clothes that were wet, his sheets and pillowcase were damp as well. Peter technically suffered from a condition his doctor called hyperhidrosis, which in laymen's terms means excessive sweating. But since there was no medicine for this condition, he had to, well, just sweat... a lot...

His heart still racing from the nightmare, Peter peeled off his drenched pajamas and put on a dry pair. Then he threw an extra blanket from his closet on top of the wet sheets, as he was too lazy to bother changing them. Plus he flipped his pillow over to rest his head on the dry side. And then he did the same thing he always did after every one of his silly nightmares: stared at the ceiling, trying to see if he could get the stucco to form any shapes he hadn't spotted previously. He did this, of course, because he knew he wouldn't be getting back to sleep.

CHAPTER 6

Considering the time of year, and the fact it had been so cold yesterday, today was refreshingly warm. This was great news for Peter and Nicola, as they wouldn't have to freeze their butts off riding out to meet Zoltan.

They were in pretty good spirits as they rode to Silverhead Mountain. Although Peter was far too shy to admit it, having Nicola with him today actually meant a lot to him.

* * *

When they turned the corner to head to the picnic tables, what they saw was both fantastic and shocking... Zoltan was not alone! Three other people, whom Peter immediately guessed were weather gods, were sitting at one of the picnic tables.

"Pete! Nicola!" Zoltan said loudly, with a big, welcoming smile. He grabbed Peter's hand and shook it fast and hard, and then gave Nicola a big hug.

But something didn't seem right. Zoltan was acting weird. Or maybe he was just excited?

"Guys," Zoltan continued, "you ARE NOT going to believe this! After I delivered Peter's letter, the lead weather gods called an emergency meeting. Meetings like that are almost NEVER called. Then twenty minutes later, they called me in to see them."

"Twenty minutes? Wow, that was fast," Peter replied. "And I am assuming these three people are the results of that meeting?"

"You got it," Zoltan answered proudly. "Pete and Nicola, everyone on my planet owes you two, Neil, and Bradley a huge debt of gratitude. The ten lead weather gods voted unanimously to send some students to help."

"What do you mean by... help?" Nicola asked.

"Yeah," Peter followed. "You told me yesterday that they never break with tradition. You said they were not permitted to use their abilities outside of school until they'd graduated."

"They made an exception," Zoltan replied, "for the first time in history. These three are all set to graduate in six months' time. And they are the top three in their class. Guys, they sent me the three *best!* Isn't this fantastic?"

"Uh... yeah," Peter said softly, fumbling to find a suitable way to react.

"It's awesome!" Nicola said loudly and clearly, bailing out her tongue-tied boyfriend.

"Come on guys," Zoltan said while starting to head to the picnic table. "I can't wait to introduce you to them."

They followed Zoltan over to the picnic table to meet these three young—and apparently very talented—assistants.

Zoltan was almost uncontrollably excited to do the introductions. As they got closer, it became clear that the group consisted of one man and two women. When they were within a couple of meters, the two women politely stood up, but the man remained seated and didn't even glance their way.

"Allow me to introduce," Zoltan said proudly, "going clockwise: Cynthia, Aurora, and Maximilian. Everyone, this is Peter and Nicola, who you of course already know a lot about."

Peter and Nicola shook hands with Aurora and Cynthia. Maximilian remained seated and completely ignored them.

"Now, come on Maximilian," Zoltan said, hoping that calling him out would encourage him to talk. "Don't be so rude. The least you could do is say hello to these two wonderful teenagers. You know how much we owe them for—"

"Fine," Maximilian blurted out. "Peter, hello. Nicola, hello," he said coldly. Then he turned and stared at Zoltan. "There, satisfied?"

You didn't need to have a degree in psychology or communication to figure out how awkward this was going to be.

"Don't worry about Maximilian," Zoltan laughed, trying to artificially lighten the mood. "He's just tired from the long trip here."

"Peter!" Cynthia jumped in before Maximilian had a chance to debate or argue that point. "My niece and nephew absolutely adore you. They are soooo jealous that I get to meet you in person."

"No way," Peter said, face reddening. "You're exaggerating."

"Not at all," Cynthia replied, pulling out two sheets of fancy-looking paper and a special pen. "I promised them I'd get your autograph if I had the chance."

Peter's face grew even redder.

"Oh, so now you're Mr. Popularity?" Nicola joked,

nudging him with her elbow. "Suppose you'll have to start up a fan club and charge a membership fee to join, eh?"

Peter and Zoltan got a good laugh out of that, but obviously "fan clubs" didn't exist on planet Sevlar, as all three students looked confused.

Peter politely accepted the papers and pen, and placed them safely in a folder in his backpack. "I'll sign them later," he said. "After I have a chance to think about what to write."

"Great!" Cynthia replied. "I wrote their names in pencil on the back, as I figured you'd never be able to get the spelling right."

Aurora had been watching the whole exchange but was politely waiting for her turn, as she didn't want to interrupt. "Peter," she said, "I actually only told my parents about being sent here. If I had told everyone where I grew up, I would have needed a few suitcases to carry all the things they'd have wanted you to sign."

"You're going to need a security team if you ever go to Sevlar," Nicola laughed, almost in stitches from imagining Peter being a rock star or idol.

"Zoltan," Maximilian barked rudely. "We were sent here to help you manage Earth's weather, not to make pointless chit-chat with a bunch of kids. Hurry up and assign me to a continent. I want to get started."

"Settle down, Maximilian," Zoltan replied, with a bit of irritation showing in his voice. Then he turned to Peter and Nicola. "Although Aurora and Cynthia are extremely pleased to spend their final six months of school here, Maximilian DID NOT want to come."

"Yeah," Cynthia added. "You see, Maximilian comes from a family of *very powerful* weather gods, many whom have gone on to become lead weather gods. He thinks he's too good for this."

"I *am* too good for this," Maximilian said loudly, crossing his arms and staring right at Cynthia.

"Look, we know you're way more skillful than Cynthia and me," Aurora said, hoping to reverse the downward spiral of the conversation. "That's why we are so lucky to have you here with us."

"Good on you," Peter whispered to himself. "He certainly can't refute that comment."

"Whatever," Maximilian replied. "But Zoltan, can you please explain why I have to waste my time talking to these kids when I could be practicing?"

"Maximilian!" Cynthia yelled right in his face. "Show Peter and Nicola some respect!"

"It's fine, it's fine," Peter said nervously.

"No, it's NOT fine," Zoltan said. "Maximilian, if you insist on knowing, there are two reasons I am introducing you to these *young adults:* First of all, Peter has a huge amount of data and statistics about where the worst of the weather damage is occurring. Discussing these things will help us in our efforts to get the weather under control. And secondly, and this is more for Aurora and Cynthia since you seem set on being antisocial, Peter here is one of the best puzzle-makers alive. And you know how much everyone on Sevlar loves puzzles and riddles. He and Nicola said they would be happy to come up with a couple of riddles a month to give you some entertainment while you are here."

Before Maximilian had a chance to open his mouth and inject something negative, Zoltan kept talking. "Peter and Nicola," he said. "Please take a seat with my three trainees. There is so much they need to hear from you. Spare no details. They need to know everything. Give them all the info you can about the current state of things here on Earth."

"Um... okay," Peter replied timidly. "But I don't really know where to start."

"Let's go one continent at a time," Nicola suggested.

"Sure," Peter agreed. "Which one first?"

"Europe," Maximilian said loudly and coldly. "That's where I'm going. And I could care less whether or not the rest of you approve."

* * *

After spending a good forty-five minutes running through the details of Europe, South America, and Africa, Zoltan decided it was time to call it a day. All three trainees were visibly tired, and there was no way they would be able to stay focused enough to take in everything they needed to know about the remaining continents. On top of that, Zoltan couldn't expect Peter and Nicola to spend their entire day here. He instructed his trainees to take a short walk along the river, and be back at the picnic table in twenty minutes.

"Peter, Nicola," Zoltan said once Maximilian, Aurora and Cynthia were out of sight. "Thanks a million."

"No problem," Peter replied.

"And before you head home, I have a big favor to ask," Zoltan continued. "I'm really, really hoping you can come up with a puzzle for them to do next Sunday. You know, it would give them something to look forward to."

"Sure," Peter replied happily.

"And it might even get Maximilian to stop being such a selfish jerk," Nicola said.

"I doubt it," Zoltan laughed, "but it just may help a little."

* * *

Shortly after arriving home, Peter talked to Bradley, phoned Neil, and asked Neil to call Claire. Everyone agreed to try to help come up with an idea to use for the challenge. They all promised to call Peter when they thought of something suitable. Although the obsessive part of Peter's mind wanted to start brainstorming ideas right away, he needed to put that aside for the rest of the afternoon. He had promised Nicola he would join her at the library and help her with research for her history report. Besides, seeing as he had destroyed their date last night, he wanted to "give it his all" this afternoon.

CHAPTER 7

Peter didn't even have to wait twenty-four hours before someone on his "team" came up with a great idea. He was eating lunch with Nicola at school on Monday when Claire and Neil came over and sat down with them. Claire told them her idea, making sure to speak quietly so the group near them wouldn't overhear and wonder what they were talking about. Peter immediately gave her the thumbs up. Not only was it an awesome idea, but it also involved very little preparation. Now that the pressure of thinking up a puzzle was off, Peter felt like he was going to be able to enjoy the rest of the week a lot more.

* * *

All five of them—Peter, Nicola, Neil, Claire, and Bradley—wanted to be there on Sunday morning. Neil, Claire, and Bradley were especially excited, as it was their first time to meet the three trainees. Bradley kindly offered to drive everyone. His car could comfortably fit five, which meant no one would have to cycle there in what was forecast to be a very cold Sunday.

Bradley was a very slow and cautious driver these days. Actually, he had changed his somewhat reckless driving habits a few years back, right after causing an accident. The accident was one hundred percent his fault, but thankfully didn't cause any injuries to anyone in either car.

* * *

The accident had happened when he was seventeen, less than two weeks after he had finally saved up enough money to buy himself an old clunker. As most high school boys do, he and a buddy were cruising around town, tunes cranked, trying to impress any girls their age that happened to be walking beside the road. What they didn't realize back then—and most likely still don't understand now—is that this type of behavior repels more girls than it attracts. (But anyway, that's beside the point...)

Bradley and his friend Thomas had been driving back and forth on the town's main drag for over an hour in the early afternoon. On their sixth or seventh pass of the swimming pool, they spotted two Grade 12 girls walking to the outdoor pool. Of course, heading to the pool meant they were wearing their bikinis and flip flops, which gave Bradley and Thomas something to really focus on. Unfortunately, this *focusing* lasted a few seconds too long, and when Bradley's eyes finally went back to the road, there was a car stopped right in front of him, waiting to make a left turn into the parking lot.

He slammed on the brakes as hard as he could, but there wasn't enough distance between him and the other car. His tires locked, and there was a second or two of rubber screeching on asphalt before the *bang* when his car hit the stationary car.

Luckily for everyone involved, both Bradley and Thomas, and the woman driving the other car, all had

had their seat belts on. And the impact had not been all that hard. The two boys quickly hopped out of their car and went to see if the woman, who had no passengers with her, was okay. She said it had scared the living daylights out of her, but that she wasn't hurt in any way.

Then she also got out so they could all survey the damage to the cars. Bradley's front fender looked as if nothing had happened, but the woman's rear bumper and license plate had been dented. As is customary after any car accident, they exchanged insurance and license information. In addition, an eyewitness came up and gave them his name and phone number.

The increase in insurance fees was more than enough to convince Bradley to smarten up when it came to paying attention while behind the wheel. His "fender bender" was going to cost him a total of about two thousand dollars in extra insurance fees over the next three years.

* * *

Just as they had expected, Aurora and Cynthia were eagerly awaiting their arrival, but Maximilian was being completely anti-social again. The two women stood up and started walking over to meet the new arrivals.

"So how'd the first week go?" Peter asked as he got out of Bradley's car. "Must have been a real eye-opener, eh?"

Aurora and Cynthia looked at each other and shrugged their shoulders. Bradley quickly picked up on their body language as an indicator that Peter's choice of words had not been ideal.

"What my little brother was trying to ask," Bradley said, "was if you were surprised by the huge number of weather disasters that are happening all over this planet?"

"It's crazy here on Earth," Aurora answered. "I can't believe they've always just assigned a single weather god here. There should be at least five or six, or maybe even a dozen."

Even though her reply was nothing more than just a simple, honest, and clear one, Bradley hadn't been listening to a single word of it. This had occurred because, in classic Bradley style, he had noticed how incredibly beautiful Aurora was.

Nicola immediately noticed Bradley's expression, which clearly showed he was thinking *wow, this chick is hot!* She couldn't resist the chance to embarrass him a bit. Plus this gave her a fun way to start the official introductions.

"I apologize for Brad's staring, and for Peter's absentmindedness," she said. "Allow me to introduce everyone. Brad, Neil, Claire: meet Aurora, Cynthia, and Maximilian."

Aurora and Cynthia shook hands with Bradley, Neil, and Claire. Bradley's handshake with Aurora appeared to last far longer than was necessary.

When they walked over to Maximilian—whom they'd been warned about in advance—he stuck up his palm and coldly said, "I'm not going to pretend to be friendly and chatty with everyone. I now know your names, and you know mine."

Feeling like he was the unofficial coordinator of today's little event, Zoltan jumped in to get things moving. "These five talented friends of mine have done exactly what I promised they would," he said. "They made a challenge for you to try today."

"An easy one?" Cynthia asked, clearly excited to get started.

"No way," Aurora said to her, "I bet it's super hard. You've heard all the stories about how clever this group is."

"Actually, I know nothing about its difficulty level," Zoltan replied honestly, putting his hands into his pockets and taking a few steps back. "I have absolutely no idea what today's challenge is."

"Don't expect me to take part in this!" Maximilian announced from his seat.

Zoltan elected to pretend he hadn't heard that. But his slightly furrowed brow indicated the stress that Maximilian was causing him.

"The floor is yours," Zoltan said to Peter.

"Not this time," Peter replied. "It's Claire's. She's the one who came up with today's challenge."

Claire was carrying a shoebox with a small envelope taped to the lid. She walked over to the picnic table that Maximilian was sitting at and placed it down very hard right in front of him. It was a no-brainer that she was doing this to make Maximilian understand that, like it or not, he *would* be participating. Her tenure as the volleyball team captain in junior high school had given her enough confidence to challenge people with bad attitudes without worrying about the possible consequences.

"Your instructions are on the note in the envelope," she explained. "And everything you need is in the box. You have one hour to complete this challenge, starting now."

Peter pressed the start button on his wristwatch.

CHAPTER 8

Despite having the shoebox placed right in front of him, Maximilian was acting as if it didn't even exist. Aurora and Cynthia, on the other hand, darted over to the picnic table to see what creative and innovative puzzle lay in store for them.

"Aurora," Cynthia said to her, "why don't you read the note, and I'll check out what's inside the box?"

Aurora quickly pulled the note from the envelope and read it aloud.

> *First of all, we'd like to take this opportunity to welcome you to Earth. We were so glad when we found out that Zoltan had finally been given some talented people to help him!*
>
> *Inside the box, you'll find one golf ball (don't worry, you do not need to know what golf is to do this challenge), and a whole bunch of feathers. The feathers were collected yesterday afternoon from the farm of a close friend.*

Your task is as follows: You must hold the golf ball and a feather (or a few feathers) at waist level, and let go of both at exactly the same time. The feather(s) must hit the ground before the golf ball does.

The rules: You may bend, twist, contort or combine the feathers in any way you wish, but you may not attach anything to them. Additionally, you are not allowed to wet the feathers. And finally, you can't use things like glue or tape to stick them together.

And that's all! Let's call it the "changing the law of gravity" challenge. Ha, aren't we funny?

Good Luck!

"Can't be done," Maximilian said immediately, despite the fact he had announced just moments ago that he would only be watching.

"Come on, Maximilian," Cynthia said. "You remember what Zoltan told us, right? How these kids can both solve and make really, really challenging riddles?"

"Yeah," Aurora added. "She wouldn't give us one if it were impossible to solve. That's not how this game works."

Maximilian elected to keep his mouth shut. Even though he had said that he didn't want to take part in this game, something instinctive inside him was compelling him to participate. Just like everyone else from planet Sevlar, he couldn't turn down a challenging riddle.

Aurora picked up the golf ball and one of the feathers. "We all know gravity is gravity," she said. "But the air here may be very different from the air on Sevlar."

She held both at waist level and let go of them simultaneously. The feather started fluttering down very slowly and the golf ball dropped like a rock. (Well, a golf ball pretty much is a rock, isn't it?)

"Eeeps!" she said as the golf ball landed on her toe.

"Eeeps?" Bradley asked, since he was still close enough to hear what they were saying. He was supposed to be sitting with Peter and the rest of the group at a picnic table far away from Maximilian, Aurora, and Cynthia, but had stuck around to get a chance to ogle Aurora a little longer.

She looked at Bradley and smiled, "You mean you don't say *eeeps* when you hurt yourself?"

"Nah," Bradley replied, doing his best to look as cool as he could. "We usually say *ouch*."

"Do you realize your senseless exchange with that boy is doing nothing but wasting part of our precious sixty minutes?" Maximilian asked coldly. It looked like he was going to get involved with this puzzle after all.

"Brad, stop flirting!" Nicola yelled from the picnic table they were at. "Or at least hold off until their hour is up!"

Bradley came over and joined them at the picnic table, desperately hoping that Aurora wasn't familiar with the word "flirting."

"Nice one, Nik," Peter said, giving her a high-five. For once, Bradley was the one with the red face.

"Well, why don't we start by examining the feathers more closely?" Cynthia suggested.

"For what?" Maximilian asked, but a little more

rudely than he should have.

"I can't answer that," Cynthia replied harshly, looking Maximilian right in the eyes. "But I'd love to hear YOU tell me what to examine."

His cockiness seemed to temporarily vanish, and he stood up to look more closely at the feathers. "Hmm..." he said quite softly. "I wonder how we can significantly reduce the wind resistance?"

"Wind what?" Aurora asked.

"Oh, give me a break, please," Maximilian said, his rude attitude front and center again. "We are talking rudimentary science here."

"Don't speak like that to her!" Cynthia yelled, slamming both hands hard on the picnic table. "Even though you may be a big *know-it-all,* it does not give you the right to talk rudely to others."

Although Maximilian didn't apologize, he did seem to show a shift in attitude after that comment. "The reason a feather falls so slowly," he explained, "is due to, uh... resistance. Air resistance. Which means, uh... basically that, uh..."

"Well, at least you're trying," Cynthia commented. "Allow me to help. Aurora, air looks clear, right? But it's actually composed of countless tiny particles. A feather can't push through those as easily as a golf ball can. Feathers are supposed to be like that. That's why, well, birds are able to fly."

"Umm..." Aurora said. "So how do we change this?"

"We have to find a way," Cynthia explained, "to make the feathers have very, very little air resistance."

"And do we know how?" Aurora asked back.

"By figuring out the best way to bend or twist one, or maybe even putting a few together, or something like that," Maximilian answered.

"How long do we have left!?" Cynthia yelled toward Peter's group.

"You've still got fifty-two minutes! Plenty of time!" Peter replied. "Here, I'll bring you my watch! That way you'll be able to keep track of the time on your own!"

He jogged over and gave his watch to Cynthia. As soon as he got back to the picnic table, he told Neil to start his stopwatch.

"Why?" Neil asked.

"Because we need a way to count down from fifty-two, or, uh, about fifty-one minutes," Peter answered. "And I just lent them mine."

"Here's what I propose," Maximilian said in a logical-sounding tone. "We each grab a third of the feathers and try different ways of bending and twisting them. I figure it might be possible to bend a feather into one of those bizarre things humans have created, which I believe they call rockets? Or are they torpedoes? Anyway, if we can find a way to do that, it should fall quite straight and fast."

"Now that's more like it," Cynthia said, liking the fact that Maximilian was finally being a team player. "And as soon as anyone makes one that looks viable, say something and we will test it out."

Nicola, Neil, Claire, and Zoltan were having a great time chatting away. Bradley and Peter, on the other hand, were both pre-occupied. But their pre-occupations were about two very different things: Peter had asked Neil, "How many minutes left?" so many times now that Neil had just given his watch to Peter. And Bradley was, no doubt, contemplating his *next move* on how to impress Aurora.

Maximilian, Aurora, and Cynthia were really getting into this challenge. Only twenty minutes had elapsed, and they'd come up with some very inventive and creative ways to contort the feathers. Some of their creations even fell quite quickly. Cynthia had produced the best one so far. She had folded one feather exactly in half and then twisted it incredibly tight.

Their fingers were starting to get a little sore, so Aurora proposed that they take a short break and discuss some other options.

"What we haven't tried yet," Cynthia suggested, "is twisting two or three together."

"Interesting idea," Maximilian pondered. "That would make it a little heavier. And if we could twist them tightly enough, that should cut down on the air resistance a lot."

"And it might be best," Aurora suggested, "if we use two short ones and one long one. That way you could use the extra part of the long one to tie knots on both ends. That would hold them together for sure."

Once they decided on which three feathers to use, Cynthia—the one with the strongest fingers of the three—wound them together so tightly that you heard the shafts of the feathers snap and pop as she did so.

"Looks great!" Maximilian said. "Let's call it our *feather rocket*. Go ahead and give it a try."

Cynthia held the feather rocket and the golf ball at waist level and let go of them at the same time. It was actually a pretty close "race," but unfortunately the golf ball hit the ground first.

"I think we just have to roll it even tighter," Aurora suggested.

"I agree," Maximilian added. He placed it on the

picnic table, put a rock on top of it, and rolled the rock back and forth a few times. This caused some of the barbs of the feathers to break off from the shafts. It had become quite a bit tighter, which should equate to a quicker drop.

When they tested it this time, their "finely tuned" feather rocket landed just a split second after the golf ball.

"Close, but no cigar," Peter said under his breath as he watched from a nearby tree which he was hiding behind.

Time was running out for the trio. They only had about ten minutes to go, but no matter how tightly they wound it, they just could not get it to beat the ball to the ground.

"How about a hint!?" Aurora yelled toward Peter, fully aware of where he was hiding.

"A hint?" Peter replied, caught off guard by this unexpected request.

"Peter," Zoltan said loudly from the picnic table. "Come here for a second."

Peter ran back to where Zoltan and the rest of them were sitting.

"We want this to build their camaraderie," Zoltan explained. "I think a hint would be a good thing."

Peter got up and ran back to Maximilian, Aurora, and Cynthia. "Okay," Peter said. "Here's your hint: think location."

"Location?" Maximilian replied. "Location of what?"

"Of you!" Peter replied with a smile. He couldn't say anything more without spelling out the solution for them.

Maximilian, Aurora, and Cynthia sat back down at

their picnic table to contemplate the meaning of Peter's hint. They only had about seven minutes left, so they needed to decipher his clue quickly.

"Our location?" Maximilian said. "Is he implying that this task could be completed if we were in a different spot?"

"But where could we go that would make any difference?" Cynthia asked aloud. "I mean, gravity doesn't change based on where you are standing."

"You've got to be kidding me!" Aurora blurted out with a huge smile on her face. "Follow me! Quick!" She grabbed the golf ball and the feather rocket and started running.

"Where are we going?" Maximilian asked, struggling to catch up to the sprinting Aurora.

"Over there," she said while pointing at the steep hill just beyond the tree line.

Peter and Bradley decided to follow the group, as they wanted to officially witness whether or not they were able to complete the challenge successfully.

"You think they're onto it?" Bradley asked Peter. "You think your clue gave up too much info?"

Claire came running over to join Bradley and Peter, as it was she who had come up with this brilliant puzzle in the first place.

"Five minutes to go!" Peter yelled.

Aurora climbed to the steepest part of the hill. "Watch and learn!" she announced loudly.

She then turned and faced sideways. Since the hill was so steep, this meant her right leg was straight and her left one was bent. Her left foot was at about the same level as her right knee. It looked like she was going to lose her balance.

"I'll do the dropping," she said in a silly voice, "and you all do the watching!"

She held the golf ball in her right hand on her right side and the feather rocket in her left hand on her left side. Both were at waist level.

"I get it!" Maximilian suddenly blurted out.

"Me too!" Cynthia yelled.

Aurora let go of both. Since she was standing sideways on the steep slope of the hill, the golf ball had much further to fall than the feather rocket. They all watched as the feather rocket hit the ground first.

"Well done!" Claire said happily. "I had a feeling one of you'd figure it out eventually."

Peter walked over with his right hand up in the air. Maximilian, Aurora, and Cynthia had no idea what he was trying to communicate to them. Bradley, realizing the trainees were not yet familiar with high-fives, came over and gave a big one to Peter.

Now aware of this new way of celebrating, they all gave numerous high-fives to each other, smiling and laughing the whole time.

"That was so fun!" Cynthia said. "Got any more?"

"Not today," Peter replied. "But we certainly can do something like this again, uh... maybe next Sunday... or possibly the Sunday after that?"

CHAPTER 9

They began walking back toward where Neil, Zoltan, and Nicola were waiting. Peter was smiling on the inside. He had always been fascinated by how strangers or acquaintances could turn into friends so quickly by simply playing some sort of game together.

Since there were six of them in total on the hill, they naturally split up into smaller groups during the walk back to the picnic table. At first, no one noticed that Bradley and Aurora were lagging a fair distance behind, but Claire realized it after a couple minutes. Peter shushed her just as she was about to say something.

"He's in the zone," Peter told her. "Let's leave them alone. I mean, how often do you get the chance to pick up a hot weather god? Can't hurt to let him try, can it?"

"Suppose not," Claire replied.

Bradley had a history of relationships that ended either abruptly, disastrously, or unexpectedly. And another pattern that seemed to be the same was that all of his ex's were attractive, well-dressed, and very concerned about their image. And although Peter had never—and would never—mention this next part to Bradley: all of Bradley's ex-girlfriends were also fairly "dumb and ditzy," to put it politely.

So Peter felt pleased and content that Bradley was currently interested in a highly intelligent woman. But what would a sexy weather god find attractive about a simple human? Anyway, enough with that train of thought...

* * *

"We've heard so many stories about Peter back on Sevlar," Aurora said to Bradley, "but so few about you."

"Well, Petey is the brains behind our team," Bradley replied, sensing that complimenting his younger brother was going to benefit him in his goal to get Aurora to like him more. "I mean, he's one of the smartest people his age in the whole country!"

"That is so cool," Aurora replied. "But I want to know more about *you*, Brad. Or is it Bradley? You know, what makes you tick?"

Bradley carefully contemplated his next move. He knew not only *what* he said next, but also *how* he chose to say it was going to significantly impact his chances with this beautiful young woman.

"As silly as this may sound," he replied, "my answer to that question has changed dramatically over the last three or four months."

"What do you mean?" she asked, eager to hear more.

"Well, and I hope this doesn't make me sound like a *stupid typical* male," he continued. "Back in high school, I only cared about two things: how well I was doing at sports, and how hot my girlfriend was."

"How hot?" she asked, obviously not familiar with the slang.

"*Hot* means beautiful... or sexy, or attractive," he replied nervously. "But then when I started college, which was only about three months ago, it was as if someone switched on my brain for the first time ever. I chose to major in sports science, you know, just because I like sports and I'm good at them. But as soon as I started learning the science behind sports, I just fell in love with the science part of athletics."

"That is so amazing," Aurora said with a twinkle in her eyes.

* * *

Peter, Claire, Maximilian, and Cynthia had rejoined the others and had just finished telling them how Aurora had solved the riddle. Bradley and Aurora were extremely far back now, and they had even stopped walking. No one could hear what they were talking about. But maybe that was for the best...

Bradley noticed everyone was looking their way, so he decided it was time to start moving again.

Once they were within a few meters of the group, Zoltan made an announcement, "Guess what, everyone? We are all heading to Mr. Winchester's now for a big lunch!"

"Mr. Winchester's!?" Peter asked. "But he—"

"No need to worry," Zoltan said confidently. "I visited him last night, and he said he would be happy to host us for lunch today."

"But he's, like, really old," Nicola said, sounding concerned. "That's a lot of people to cook for."

"No need to worry about that either," Zoltan replied. "The arrangement with him is that we will bring all of the food and drinks with us."

"Cool," Bradley said. "But what are we going to buy? And where?"

"Pizza! Pizza! Pizza!" Neil chanted while jumping up

and down like an immature boy.

"Would you five mind doing the shopping?" Zoltan asked, handing Bradley an envelope with cash in it.

"Not at all," Bradley replied while glancing down briefly at the money. "But where did you get this from?"

"Let's just say," Maximilian answered quickly, "that the lead weather gods gave us all a lot of money to bring back for Zoltan. You know, kind of like, uh, what do you call it on Earth... an, uh, expense account? You know, to cover any costs involved during our training."

"But how did they get *cash*?" Peter asked.

"Oh, Peter," Maximilian said, laughing off the question. "Always the inquisitor. I think I'm beginning to really like you."

Bradley handed Peter the cash and started walking to his car. "You know my track record with losing things," he laughed. "You're in charge of the money, Petey."

Peter could tell by the thickness of the envelope that there was way, way more than would be needed for a bunch of pizzas and a few bottles of soft drinks.

CHAPTER 10

On the drive to the pizza shop, Peter started counting through the money in the envelope. Every bill was a ten, and he counted forty in total. His second count reconfirmed his first: they had just been given the sum of four hundred dollars. This was at least three times more than they actually required.

When Peter told everyone how much they had received, they didn't believe him at first. But one glance at Peter's face, which had that "I'm not making this up" look on it, immediately convinced them.

"Let's go to that place on Third Avenue. You know, Antonio's," Neil suggested.

"Of course that's where we're headed!" Bradley replied. "I mean we are definitely NOT going to one of those cheap pizza shops where they barely put any toppings on, and then either overcook or undercook them."

"And while we are waiting for them to make the pizzas," Claire added, "why don't some of us go to the supermarket across the street and get the snacks and drinks?"

"I love it when a plan comes together," Bradley said in

a deep voice, imitating a phrase he must have gotten from some TV show. "But while you guys are doing that, I have to make a quick pit stop somewhere."

Everyone in the car suddenly went silent. Something about the tone of Bradley's voice was odd and eerie.

"What are you guys acting so weird about?" Bradley asked. "All I need to do is go and get gas!"

The other four looked instantly relieved. They were expecting to hear Bradley say something a lot more serious or bizarre.

"And Petey," he continued, "score me some of that money for gas. Because technically, I *need* the gas to drive us to Mr. Winchester's, right?"

Peter passed Bradley one of the ten-dollar bills.

"Come on, give me at least twenty bucks," Bradley pleaded.

"No way, Brad," Peter replied. "We are not going to take advantage of this. You get ten for gas and not a penny more."

"Cheapskate," Bradley joked while pulling into the pizza shop parking lot. "Alright, jump out here everyone; I'll be back as soon as I can."

"And please ask the gas station attendant for a receipt," Peter said before getting out. "I want proof that you spent the entire ten on fuel."

"Aren't you lucky?" Claire said to Bradley. "It's like you have two moms!"

* * *

Twenty-five minutes later, with five fresh pizzas, half a dozen big bottles of pop, and four bags of chips, they started the drive to Mr. Winchester's home. Bradley told Neil, who was now sitting in the passenger seat, to open up the glove compartment and pick a CD.

"Dude," Neil replied. "You just leave the tune selection to the Neilster!"

"Stop! New rule, effectively immediately!" Bradley announced with a big smile. "The next person who says the word *Neilster* is walking the rest of the way."

"I second that idea!" Nicola said right away.

"Me too!" Claire agreed.

"Me three!" Peter said, putting up his hand for some high-fives.

Neil turned around to look at everyone in the back seat. "Are you guys trying to tell me," he asked, "that I've grown out of that nickname?"

"That would be impossible," Peter replied, "as you never grew into it in the first place!"

Everyone, Neil included, burst into laughter.

"Dudes," Neil said with a grin, "I'm hurt. But man, why didn't someone tell me this, like, years ago? I thought my nickname was cool!"

Everyone was still laughing too hard to reply.

"Well then," Neil continued, "I will *temporarily* retire that nickname."

"Temporarily?" Bradley asked. "Why not permanently?"

"Never put all your eggs in one basket," Neil replied.

Peter was laughing so hard now that his stomach muscles were starting to hurt and his face was beet red. Neil had just done what Peter's dad did all too frequently: completely misuse a saying, without having a clue that he'd done so.

The drive to Mr. Winchester's was turning out to be so much more entertaining than they ever could have imagined.

CHAPTER 11

When they pulled into Mr. Winchester's driveway, he was sitting on the front porch soaking up the sunshine. He did have a coat on, but it was a very thin-looking one, and definitely too light for such a cold day.

"You must be freezing?" Nicola asked as she ran up the front stairs and gave him a big hug.

"Suppose I might be," he answered with a giggle, "but I'm so old now I wouldn't even notice."

Claire also gave him a hug, but the boys decided to use high-fives instead. For some reason, boys this age weren't comfortable with the man hugging man thing.

"So when is this weather god crew due to arrive?" Mr. Winchester asked. "I can't wait to meet them."

"Dunno," Neil answered. "We figured they'd be here by now."

"Yeah," Bradley added. "It's not like they have to use cars to get from *A* to *B*."

"Hmm..." Mr. Winchester said while rubbing his chin. "Anyway, I'm sure they'll arrive soon."

"Alright everyone," Claire announced loudly. "You're all more than welcome to continue chatting in the cold, but I'm heading inside. My fingers are freezing."

"I'm with you!" Nicola said quickly.

The boys and Mr. Winchester agreed as well, and quickly followed suit.

It looked as if Mr. Winchester had prepared his home for a huge holiday feast. He had even somehow managed to get the kitchen table into the dining room. With the two tables together, they easily had enough space for ten. He had also put out the placemats, plates, napkins, cutlery, and salt and pepper shakers. Plus he had added a few candles—which weren't lit yet—to give his plain and simple home a little more ambiance.

"Mr. Winchester," Peter asked, "how did you manage to haul that heavy kitchen table in here?"

"Yeah," Bradley added. "Have you been pumping iron behind our backs?"

"Afraid not, Bradley," Mr. Winchester said while slowly sitting down in his rocking chair. "My weight-lifting days, or whatever you young folks call it now, stopped long before you were even in grade school." He rocked back and forth a couple times, and then continued, "Actually, when Zoltan came over to ask me to host this gathering, he used a little bit of his supernatural powers to move the table."

"I see," Peter replied, relieved to have his inquiry answered. (Peter despised the part of his brain that always latched onto unanswered questions and obsessed over them endlessly.)

"So how do we decide who sits where?" Claire asked. "I mean, it would be best if we mixed everyone up, right? That way we'd be talking to them instead of just to each other."

Claire was, once again, using her experience as the former volleyball team captain when making that suggestion. She obviously knew what was required to help people break the ice.

"I'm going to make little name cards," she continued, "and put them on the plates."

"Assigned seating, eh?" Mr. Winchester laughed from his rocking chair. "Quite the organized operation!"

"You bet!" Claire answered.

"There's plenty of paper and pens in the third drawer of that desk in the corner," Mr. Winchester said. "Knock yourself out!"

"Awesome," she replied. "I'll get on it."

* * *

"Wonder what's taking them so long?" Peter asked, looking first at his watch, and then out the window again.

"No kidding, eh?" Neil added. "They could have easily *tornadoed* their way here in an instant!"

"Think they got lost?" Bradley asked. "Want me to drive around and—"

"There's no need to do anything like that," Mr. Winchester said. "Let them take their sweet time. The pizzas are in the oven, so they'll still taste like they're fresh. And in case you all forgot, there's an old man in a rocking chair who'd love to hear how you are all doing."

The sofa wasn't big enough to seat five, so Bradley effortlessly hauled over two chairs from the dining room table. Everyone sat down and started watching Mr. Winchester rock slowly back and forth.

"This isn't grade school," the old man laughed. "There is no rule about who has to speak first. Just fill me in on what's new."

Although the ensuing conversation felt a little unnatural at first, within a few minutes, everyone was chatting and laughing away. And before they knew it, they had diverged from current up-dates to reminiscing about the past. The more they talked, the more the volume of laughter increased.

Ding-dong

Everyone kind of froze right after hearing the doorbell. They had been so relaxed for the last little while that they had almost forgotten about the actual purpose of today's get-together.

"You're not waiting for me to struggle out of this rocking chair to get the door, are you?" Mr. Winchester asked his young friends.

"Sorry," Peter said, quickly walking over to open the door for the special guests.

While he did that, Bradley helped Mr. Winchester out of his chair, so that he would be standing when the three young weather-gods-to-be came to shake his hand.

As soon as Zoltan had removed his boots, he walked directly to Mr. Winchester and gave the old man a long hug.

"Don't squeeze too hard," Mr. Winchester joked. "Old guys like me break pretty easily!"

This joke seemed to make the atmosphere a little less tense for Maximilian, Aurora, and Cynthia to come up to shake hands with him.

* * *

The meal and all of the various conversations going on were great. Zoltan had had pizza a few times, but Maximilian, Aurora, and Cynthia had never even heard of it. And when they said that they'd never eaten anything with their hands before, it was quite an entertaining task to watch.

Once everyone was stuffed to the gills, Neil stood up and announced that he and Claire would do all the clean-up.

Mr. Winchester then suggested they retire to the living room.

"So, Leonardo," Aurora said. "Oh, I'm sorry, is it okay if I call you that?"

Mr. Winchester chuckled. "It's completely alright," he replied. "I can't even remember the last time someone so pretty called me by my name."

"We are so keen to hear," Aurora continued, "how you managed to create all those puzzles for Zoltan for so long. He told us how hard, complicated, and confusing they were. But he also said that despite the high level of difficulty, he managed to solve every single one."

"Did he now??" Mr. Winchester replied, looking over at Zoltan.

"Sure," Cynthia added. "Or at least that's what he told us."

"Hold on," Zoltan said, pausing and clearing his throat. "I didn't tell you I solved *every single one*."

"Yes, you did," Maximilian said. "I specifically remember you saying that he never outsmarted you."

Mr. Winchester's grin grew. "A little too embarrassed to admit I got you that one time, eh?" he said to Zoltan. "Come on now, don't you want them to hear about the one that stumped you?"

Sensing Zoltan's discomfort, Bradley quickly changed the subject. He wanted to divert the conversation away from Zoltan's "one and only" incomplete challenge.

"What *we* don't get," Bradley said, "is why everyone on Sevlar is so obsessed with puzzles and riddles. What's with that?"

"No kidding," Neil added. "Sevlar sounds like a world full of Peters!"

That got everyone laughing.

"Please, not that!" Nicola said mid-laugh. "One Peter is all we can handle!"

When the laughter had finally subsided, the six earthlings were waiting to hear the answer to Bradley's question. They had all assumed that Zoltan would be the one to answer, but it was actually Maximilian who spoke up.

"The reason is quite simple," Maximilian began. "On Sevlar, we begin doing puzzles and riddles from a young age. Very young. Think of it this way: Little Earth kids go to the park. Little Sevlar kids do riddles. And then when we are being schooled, the whole focus is on developing our problem-solving skills."

"You mean," Bradley asked, "you don't study math or science or stuff like that?"

"Of course we study those as well," Maximilian replied. "But education is geared at giving us minds capable of analyzing and solving problems." He paused and looked at his audience. "Well, I can see this is getting boring already, but—"

"Boring?" Peter said, interrupting Maximilian. "No way! A world full of people who all love puzzles? An education system based around problem-solving?"

"That would be your dream world, eh Petey?" Bradley commented.

Peter recognized that he now had a rare opportunity that would score him some points with his girlfriend. "If they'd let me take Nik there," he proudly announced. "Then it would be perfect!"

"You little Casanova!" Claire laughed, elbowing Peter. "Don't tell me you've already made plans to get married?"

* * *

The luncheon had been a huge success. Both groups had learned a lot about each other, and everyone felt much more comfortable being in the same room.

Mr. Winchester had originally estimated the whole affair would last no longer than ninety minutes, but his four weather god guests had spent almost three hours in his home. Very soon, it would start getting dark outside. Mr. Winchester was thanked graciously as they departed, and all four told the old man they couldn't wait to see him again.

The five teenagers were in a giddy mood as they also put their coats and shoes on. Bradley went outside first, so he could start the car and give it a chance to warm up.

Mr. Winchester, on the other hand, looked as if he was worried about something. He rocked slowly back and forth, staring at, well, nothing...

"Everything okay?" Nicola asked him. "You must be exhausted. We should've ended things earlier today."

"Oh, it's nothing like that," he replied. "It's just, I, uh... I can't really put my finger on it."

"What do you mean?" Peter asked, realizing Mr. Winchester had something he needed to get off his chest.

"I've always been quite a worrier, so I'm sure it's all just in my head," he went on. "But a few times today while we were eating, and even a couple of times while seated in the living room, I noticed the three trainees occasionally making eye contact with each other."

"What's weird about that?" Bradley asked. "I thought eye contact was considered a good thing."

"Well, it is…" he replied awkwardly. "I mean, it _usually_ is. But something just didn't seem a hundred percent natural about theirs… it was, and as I said before, I'm sure I am just being paranoid, it was like they were coordinating their answers."

"Mr. Winchester," the concerned Peter said. "You know I take the gold medal when it comes to worrying. I didn't notice anything."

"Thanks, Peter," he said softly. "Just hearing that will help me sleep a little better tonight."

CHAPTER 12

After finishing the last of his final exams at three o'clock on Friday, Bradley felt like shouting "Yes!" at the top of his lungs as he walked toward his car in the college parking lot. He had studied very hard for all seven classes this term and was confident that his exam grades would reflect his efforts. He had an 80% or higher in all of his classes going into the finals, so his odds of getting straight A's in his first term at college were quite good.

"Hi, Brad," a soft voice said from behind him as he was preparing to unlock the car door.

Bradley was sure he had heard that voice somewhere before, but couldn't pinpoint who it was without twisting his head around to look. He was blown away to see Aurora standing by the back bumper of his car.

"H... hi," he replied, in what seemed to be a very uncharacteristic display of nervousness. "Wh... what are you doing here? Sorry, that came out wrong. Aren't you supposed to be busy, you know, dealing with weather stuff?"

"Actually," she replied with a smile, "Zoltan gave us the afternoon off today. I think he could see that we were all pretty drained."

"Oh," Bradley replied.

"Well," she continued quickly, "we weren't really that drained. We were just getting a little tired. Actually, *bored* would be a better word to describe it." She started blushing a bit. "Anyway, I figured I would come and find you, and see if you'd be able to, I don't know, show me around a little?"

Bradley had asked out or been asked out by tons of girls over the past six and a half years. His well-trained instincts were telling him this girl liked him.

"Let me think," he said very nonchalantly, preparing a little lie he expected would impress her. "I was planning to work out this afternoon, and then drop by Thomas' party tonight. But..." He paused to add some drama. "I can skip the gym once in a while, right? Plus the party will probably be lame anyway."

"Hold on," she giggled. "Does that mean you *can* or *can't* take me somewhere?"

"What I am saying, young lady," Bradley said while opening the passenger door for her, "is that I will be your personal chauffeur. Oops, I guess you've probably never heard that word." He laughed. "That just means your driver and guide, I guess. And I'll be taking you to all of the coolest places I know."

"Really?" she said as Bradley got ready to close the door for her. "Wow!"

Bradley smugly grinned to himself as he walked behind the car to go back to the driver's side. He knew the next few hours would decide whether or not this would turn into a relationship. Based on her positive reactions so far, he had already convinced himself that things with this beautiful lady were indeed heading in the right direction.

* * *

They started off with coffees at a funky little cafe that let the patrons make requests about which songs were played. There wasn't a DJ or anything like that, just shelves upon shelves of CDs. All you had to do was take one down, hand it to the owner, and tell her which song or songs you wanted to hear.

Shortly after being introduced to her first-ever cup of coffee, and music like nothing she had ever heard back on Sevlar, they got back into Bradley's car and headed toward the five-pin bowling alley in Stoneburg. Stoneburg also had a fancy new bowling alley, with only ten-pin lanes. But the older five-pin place was popular enough with the regulars that it somehow managed to stay open. This bowling alley was Bradley's *go-to spot* for every first date. There was never anyone their age there, plus the bowling itself always led to laughs, high-fives, and occasionally a few celebratory hugs. No one knew how to pull off a first date as well as Bradley.

Once they'd finished their game and a milkshake, they drove back to Clearville, to a little Mexican place on Fourth Avenue. The owner knew Bradley quite well since his son and Bradley had played basketball together in high school. The food was delicious and cheap, and even more importantly, they had two semi-private tables. Bradley, thinking ahead, had phoned before they started bowling and reserved one of those tables for tonight.

They hadn't even been at the restaurant for twenty minutes when Aurora reached across the table and took Bradley's hand. "Brad," she said with a sparkle in her eyes. "You're so different from the men where I am from. It's like you know what I'm thinking."

"Know what you're thinking?" Bradley smiled. "Afraid

I'm not a mind reader. Wish I were, but—"

"Brad," she said, cutting him off and squeezing his hand even tighter. "Maximilian, Cynthia, and Zoltan can never know about us going out today. Never. They'd send me back to Sevlar instantly."

"Why?" he asked. "They have no right to tell you who you can and can't hang out with."

"No, technically they don't," she answered. "And there are no guidelines regarding what's considered *acceptable* while we are here. But the lead weather gods gave Zoltan the authority to send home anyone who does anything he deems inappropriate."

"Your secret's safe with me," he said with a wink.

They finished up their evening at another one of Bradley's favorite date spots. Before driving there, he stopped by a convenience store and picked up two large hot chocolates. Then they made the short drive to the area before the landing strip of the tiny Clearville Airport, which was a town park with a few picnic tables and park benches. No planes took off or landed after six, so this place was always empty in the evenings. That meant they would have complete privacy.

As soon as they were out of the car and heading toward one of the benches, Aurora wrapped her arm around Bradley's. This girl certainly wasn't shy.

They sipped their hot chocolates in the cold, sitting so close to each other that there was no air space between them. His years of dating experience, plus his talent for reading people, told Bradley that the opportunity for a first kiss was presenting itself. He leaned in and gave her a soft, quick kiss, and then pulled back to see her reaction. The expression on her face told Bradley that the little peck had been exactly the right thing to do.

"I don't have a curfew," Bradley said, "but I should be getting home soon. School is out for the Christmas holiday, but track and field practice doesn't take a break between terms. I've gotta be there at seven o'clock sharp tomorrow morning."

She patted him lightly several times on the chest. "No problem, off you go, big guy," she said. "We don't want you to do anything that could raise suspicions about us. Oh… and unless you've already got plans for tomorrow, do you think we could continue this date once your practice is done?"

That question caught Bradley off-guard, but he made sure to respond in a positive (but not excessively eager) way. "Yeah, sounds good to me," he said cool and collectively. "So where should I drop you off tonight?"

She leaned in close to his left ear. "I'm a weather god, in case you forgot," she whispered. "I can go where I need to go on my own. But I think I'll just sit here by myself for a little while. This bench has just become a spot with special meaning for me."

"You sure?" he asked again.

"Positive," she replied. "But before you go, I have a little favor to ask."

"A favor?" Bradley inquired.

She leaned in close again and whispered in his ear.

Bradley turned to look at her. "That's it?" he asked.

"Yes," she replied.

"Should be no problem at all," he said while starting to walk to his car.

"You're the best!" she said just as Bradley closed the car door. "See you tomorrow!"

"I wonder if all girls from Sevlar are like this?" Bradley asked himself while driving back toward the highway. "If they are, I've gotta find a way to visit there some day!"

CHAPTER 13

With Bradley gone to track and field practice, and Sophia off at a ballet recital with his mom, that left only Peter and his dad home on Saturday morning.

"Hey, Pete," his dad announced in a loud voice as he walked into the kitchen where Peter was eating breakfast. "Your mother has given you and me a job to do today. And you know that when she gives someone a job to do, it better get done."

"Great," Peter answered sarcastically. "What is it?"

"We have been placed in charge of putting up the outdoor Christmas lights," his dad said.

"Really?" Peter replied. "I thought she had decided against putting them up this year. And isn't it a little late? I mean, other homes have had them up for weeks."

"What we think about this is completely irrelevant," his dad explained. "If *Her Highness* orders them to go up today, then that's what has to happen."

Peter laughed at the way his dad would make these silly comments about his mom when she wasn't around, but wouldn't dare do such a thing if she were at home.

His dad had already hauled in the two boxes from the garage which contained the outdoor Christmas light sets.

Each set was basically just a long electrical cord with a colored light every twenty-five centimeters or so. Their first task was to plug in each set—of which there were four in total—in order to spot the bulbs that were burnt out and needed replacing.

"But dad, we haven't bought any replacement bulbs," Peter said.

"Pete," his dad smiled, pointing at the dining room table. "You know your mother. She bought eight packs of replacement bulbs yesterday. Two of each color."

"Does she ever forget anything?" Peter asked.

"Forget stuff?" his dad replied. "Nope. That's my job."

The bulb replacing was the easiest of part today's operation, as it could be done in the comfort of their warm living room.

* * *

When all four sets were ready to go, they put on their heavy winter clothes, got the folding ladder and extension ladder from the garage, and headed outside to get their task over and done with.

Neither Peter nor his dad had to ask about which set went where, as they had been well-labeled by his mom. One had "outdoor tree" on it, one had "garage," one had "living room window and front door," and the last one had "upper gutter."

They decided to start with the easy ones first and leave the worst one—the upper gutter one—until the end.

When the first three were all up nicely, Peter's dad set up the extension ladder in just the right position to get started on the final set of lights. He figured he could put the cord into three or four clips at a time before he'd have to climb down and move the ladder over a little.

"Hold it tight, boy," his dad instructed, getting ready to head up the ladder for the first time. "Not just with your hands."

"Wait," Peter said suddenly. "Uh... I'll go up."

"Nah, I'll be fine," his dad said back.

Peter hadn't made the offer because he was worried about his dad's safety, it had been for a completely different, and quite selfish reason: he had just remembered about the light he had rigged up in the chimney—the one he used when he needed to call Zoltan. If he let his dad go up the ladder, his dad would surely spot the cord that came from the chimney to just outside Peter's bedroom window. And then a full "investigation" was bound to happen.

"No dad, I got this," he said. "You've done most of the hard stuff today. It's only fair that I do this part. Plus, I've got way better balance than you."

His dad was obviously not really that concerned about who was in charge of each task. His only real concern was that it got done, and done properly. (They both knew the tongue-lashing they would get if they did a sloppy job.)

Luckily for the both of them, the plastic clips which Peter's dad had attached to gutter a few years back were all still intact. That meant all they had to do was simply clip the cable in. Peter was using Bradley's hi-tech cross-country ski gloves, which were really thin but also warm. And his multiple trips up and down the ladder had gotten his blood pumping enough to prevent his hands from feeling cold.

* * *

Job now complete to a level that would definitely satisfy *the boss*, Peter's dad said, "Alright, let's hope there isn't a message waiting for us on the answering machine with another chore."

"No kidding," Peter agreed, as they both started peeling off the multiple layers of clothing they'd needed while outside.

"You want a tea?" his dad asked as they hung up their jackets and put their gloves and winter caps back into the plastic box labeled "gloves and hats."

"I hate tea," Peter replied. "You know that."

"How about a coffee, then?" his dad asked.

"Coffee?" Peter laughed. "That stuff tastes like tar."

"Try telling your mother that," his dad said. "She drinks five or six cups of that stuff a day."

Peter went up to his room. Unlike his dad, he didn't need a hot drink to warm himself up. Well, he wanted one, but he still remembered that awful wintery day when he had scalded his tongue on hot chocolate at age nine. And the *paranoid little boy inside him* couldn't convince the logical fifteen-year-old to forget about it.

He lay down on his bed and kind of zoned out. He didn't even start staring at the stucco ceiling; instead, he just moved his eyes around the room, without really stopping to focus on anything. It took him ages to notice something he should have spotted straight away: there was a leaf and a note taped to the outside of his window.

"What the...?" Peter said, feeling his anxiety start to ramp up. He began to take deep breaths in an effort to calm his nerves and settle down. This seemed to help a little, especially when he forecast that the note was likely just a request from Zoltan to make another puzzle for tomorrow.

"Yeah, that's probably all he wants," Peter told himself. "It's just a puzzle request."

He slid the cold window open, reached his arm outside and took off the leaf and the note. He chucked the leaf in the garbage can beside his desk and then lay back down on his bed. He got ready to check the message, already guessing about its contents.

Peter started reading the note and then suddenly gulped. Twice. "Okay, this is weird," he said to himself. "Really, really weird."

He folded the note, put it in his back pocket, and started heading for the front door. This was the first time Zoltan had ever used phrases like *of great urgency* or *as soon as you see this* in a note. The last part of the note told Peter where Zoltan was currently waiting for him. Their usual rendezvous point was too far away to get to in this cold weather, so Zoltan had picked a spot in a small park less than two hundred meters from Peter's front door.

Peter's arms couldn't manage to put on his outdoor gear as fast as his mind was ordering them to. He almost fell over twice while bending down to tie up his boots. As much as he hated to admit it, he was panicking. But this time, maybe his panic was warranted.

"Dad!" he yelled as he was about to open the door. "I'm going to Neil's!"

"Gotcha," his dad replied. "Tell the Neilster that I said hi!"

CHAPTER 14

Peter wanted to get to the park as quickly as he could, but knew the fresh snow on the sidewalk—which had been falling since yesterday afternoon—combined with his poor co-ordination skills, was likely a recipe for disaster if he were to run. So he elected to compromise and did a very awkward-looking version of speed walking instead.

When he got to the park, he saw Zoltan sitting quite peacefully on one of the benches, reading a thick, hardcover book.

"Zoltan!" Peter said loudly as he got closer. "Sorry I didn't spot your note earlier. I wasn't in my room this morning at all. I was outside helping my dad put up the Christmas lights."

"You have nothing to apologize for, Peter," Zoltan said calmly. "And since I visited that big library on Leeds Street a few days ago, where I borrowed this fascinating book, I've had plenty to occupy my mind."

"How did you do that?" Peter asked. "You can't get a library card without having an address."

"True," he answered. "Actually, I went with Leonardo, and he technically borrowed the book for me. Now, sorry to change subjects so abruptly, but there is something we need to discuss."

"I gathered that much from the language in your note," Peter replied. "What's going on?"

"First, please have a seat," Zoltan said, motioning for Peter to sit down beside him. "And before I start, I think I should point out to you that I occasionally catastrophize. So everything I am about to say may simply be my mind creating negative outcomes."

"Gotcha," Peter said. "I can certainly relate to that. No judging here."

"Then allow me to begin," Zoltan continued. "The specific thing concerning me is related to yesterday afternoon and evening. On Fridays, I have all three trainees come back from their respective continents. That way I can check in with them on how things went over the past week and then we can work on a new technique or two. But something was off yesterday. They all showed up a little early, something which had never happened before. Okay... I guess *that* part wasn't too strange. Anyway, they were talking away as I approached them, but the instant they noticed me, they completely hushed up. When I casually asked what their conversation was about, they just laughed it off and changed the subject. Once the weekly check-in was complete and we had finished lunch, I noticed all three were very reluctant to put any effort into practicing the new technique I had just demonstrated. I decided to give them the benefit of the doubt, and just put their lackluster effort down to tiredness."

"I know I shouldn't interrupt," Peter said. "But in all likelihood, they were just tired. I mean, they just spent four consecutive days, in separate parts of the globe, battling weather troubles."

"True," Zoltan continued. "I also considered that possibility myself. Now, where was I? Oh… so I elected to give them the afternoon off. Not only that, but I also told them to take Saturday off, too. Plus, I said I would talk with you about creating a Sunday puzzle for them. That news, or at least the possibility of it, did appear to raise their spirits somewhat."

"Sorry again, Zoltan," Peter interjected. "But so far nothing seems weird or out of place to me."

"It's what occurred next that's troubling me the most," Zoltan went on. "I was a little worried about them, so at about half past seven yesterday evening, I went by to see how they were doing. And get this, no one was there. I waited for a good hour or so, but not even one of them returned."

"If you gave them Friday night and all day Saturday off," Peter said, "then they probably decided to go out and party. Or at least go out and explore the town. I mean, they haven't been on Earth for long."

"Also true," Zoltan nodded. "But there's more. I knew I wouldn't be able to sleep with all this worry, so I went to Mr. Winchester's house. Basically, I wanted to tell him the exact same thing I just told you."

"And did he react any differently than me?" Peter asked.

"No, not at all," Zoltan replied. "Just like you are doing now, he listened and then told me I was worrying about nothing. It was when I was *leaving* that I got the real shock."

"Shock?" Peter asked.

"Yes," Zoltan answered. "You know there was a light snowfall on Friday afternoon. Not heavy, maybe two centimeters or so. After I had thanked Leonardo, closed the front door, and went to head down the steps, I noticed there were two fresh pairs of footprints that went up the steps and toward the living room window. But there were no footprints leading away from the window."

"So you think that two of the three came here, spied on you from outside the window, and then used their supernatural powers to depart, don't you?" Peter asked.

"Yes, that's exactly what I'm thinking," he replied.

"I'd be lying if I said nothing sounds odd," Peter admitted, "but I wouldn't say it warrants too much worrying yet. For all we know, they could have been trying to plan some kind of surprise for you."

"Hmm..." Zoltan mumbled. "I suppose it's theoretically possible, but..."

"Tell you what," Peter suggested. "I will make a Sunday puzzle for them to do, and bring Nik along with me. She, if anyone, knows how to coax information out of people without them knowing. If something is up, she'll be able to find out."

"Excellent plan," Zoltan replied happily. "Thank you, Peter."

"Hey man," Peter said, putting his hand up for a high-five. "We are on the same team now. And that's what friends are for!"

CHAPTER 15

Peter and Zoltan's high five then somehow morphed into a handshake that seemed to go on for an eternity. When Zoltan finally released his hand, Peter smiled at him and turned around to start heading back home.

"And Peter," he said after Peter was already about five meters away, "it doesn't need to be something too complex. I don't want you to waste an entire Saturday afternoon because of me and my worries."

"Okay!" Peter said back. Today's rendezvous with Zoltan made Peter realize that even weather gods could be excessive worriers, and something about that fact actually comforted him a little.

* * *

Peter was planning to ask Bradley to drive him and Nicola tomorrow, but Bradley was gone when Peter returned home.

"Bradley out of the house before noon on a Saturday?" he said to himself. "That's gotta be a first. He must have a special track practice or something. Anyway, guess I'll check *option B* then."

By option B, Peter was referring to Neil. Neil was his only friend who had already completed the driver training course and successfully passed the driver's test. Hopefully, Neil would be able to borrow his mom's car tomorrow to drive them. And by *them*, of course, he meant Claire would be included too.

"Neil, it's me," Peter said into the phone when Neil finally picked it up after six rings.

"Yo, the Petester! What's up, dude?" Neil asked. "It's not like you to phone me up out of the blue. Well, unless you need help with something…"

"C'mon, that's not completely true," Peter said hesitantly. Although it wasn't completely true, it was pretty close. It wasn't that Peter *used* Neil or anything like that, it was just that Peter had always been a very solitary kid. He was completely happy and content to think up, create, and do puzzles and games on his own. So he rarely ever felt the desire to phone up friends.

Peter explained his situation and asked about the possibility of Neil borrowing his mom's car to drive them. Neil told Peter to hold on a second while he went downstairs to ask his mom. Less than a minute later, he was back on the line.

"You have yourselves a driver!" Neil proudly announced.

"Awesome," Peter replied. "I owe you one."

"No, you don't," Neil replied while giggling a little. "You owe *my mom* one. And what you owe has already been decided: as soon as we get back tomorrow, you and I are going to be putting up the outdoor Christmas lights at our house."

Peter forced out a happy-sounding reply. "Cool," he said. "I suppose I'm becoming somewhat of an expert *Christmas light putter-upper.* My dad and I just did ours this morning."

He regretted that comment the instant it came out. Not the "expert" part, but the "dad" part. Neil's dad, who Peter had met a couple of times when he was younger, had divorced Neil's mom and run off with his secretary a couple of years ago. And not only had he left his wife for a younger woman, but he had also chosen to have nothing to do with Neil anymore. Neil hadn't heard from his dad since that unforgettable day two and a half years ago when his mom had to tell him that his dad had left.

"Sorry," Peter said nervously into the phone. "I... uh... didn't mean to..."

"Petey," Neil interrupted in a happy tone. "It is what it is, man. I've got the best mom in the entire world. The entire universe, actually! I consider myself lucky."

After hanging up, Peter quickly called Nicola and said he really needed her help getting a puzzle ready for tomorrow. Nicola offered to help, but only until about four or so, as she had the five to ten o'clock shift tonight. But hey, a few hours of help was certainly better than none at all!

CHAPTER 16

Peter was planning on getting his older brother up to speed on everything that afternoon or evening, but Bradley still hadn't come home by the time Peter went up to his room at ten thirty. Bradley didn't have a curfew, but there was an unwritten agreement with his parents that he would never stay out past midnight. Any later than that was considered "far too late" by his mom. Bradley had broken his curfew a ridiculous number of times back in high school, but since starting college a few months ago, he rarely ever stayed out late.

But after thinking it through a bit more, Peter figured that Bradley really didn't need to know what was going on right away. He'd just tell him the next time an opportunity presented itself.

* * *

The next morning, as Peter walked by Bradley's bedroom door, he put his ear up against it to make sure Bradley had actually come home. Sure enough, Bradley was snoring away, at a volume that would certainly hurt your ears if you were in the same room as him.

* * *

Bradley's snoring took Peter's mind quickly back to

the days when their family lived in a small bungalow, which had been big enough (and cheap enough) until his younger sister Sophia was born. After she arrived into the world, Peter and Bradley were put in a room together in bunk beds and baby Sophia got her own room.

Peter was relegated to the top bunk, as his parents decided that the elder of the two had "first choice." This seemed to make sense, since Peter's bedtime was earlier than Bradley's. (If Bradley had chosen the top, then he would have unintentionally woken Peter up every time he climbed into bed...)

Peter was too young to remember things vividly, but the one thing he would never forget was the awful snoring that emanated from his older brother in the bottom bunk. According to both Bradley and their parents, Peter originally thought Bradley was wide awake and "fake snoring" just to bother his little brother. But when he climbed down to check things out, it was one hundred percent clear that Bradley was sound asleep.

When Peter had asked his parents about it, they said Bradley had been a big snorer, even as a baby. Apparently, when his mom consulted their family doctor about this, the doctor had told her that babies couldn't snore. Peter's mom hated it when people doubted her, so she rocked baby Bradley in her arms until he fell asleep in the doctor's waiting room. And once the loud snoring began, the receptionist went and asked the doctor to come and hear for himself. The middle-aged doctor was nothing less than astonished. "How can such a cute little guy make such a huge and horrible noise?" the doctor had joked.

After being referred to an ear, nose and throat specialist in Stoneburg, who was equally shocked by Bradley's snoring, a full examination revealed that there was absolutely nothing wrong with Bradley's throat or airways.

So poor Peter tried everything: earplugs, covering his head with pillows, sleeping under his covers, and various other methods. But no matter what he did, Bradley's snoring was always overpowering enough that it kept Peter from sleeping.

Then (and this is what he was told, as he doesn't actually remember any of this) Peter decided to take matters into his own hands. Every time Bradley's snoring got too loud to bear, Peter leaned over the edge of the top bunk, pillow in hand, and whacked Bradley in the face until the snoring ceased. It was effective in that it quickly put a stop to the noise, but the snoring always started up again, sometimes within minutes.

* * *

Peter giggled as he tiptoed down to the kitchen, imagining what life was going to be like for Bradley's future wife. He continued smugly laughing while eating breakfast. He kept creating images of Bradley's *darling* whacking him over and over with a pillow.

Peter checked his watch and realized he was ready way too early again: a habit his doctor referred to as "obsessive-compulsive." But official diagnosis aside, Peter was a worrier, and worriers never want to be late.

Neil said he'd roll by to pick up Peter at eight thirty, and it was currently 7:14. He knew his mom would be up soon and wanting her morning coffee fix, so he pushed the "ON" button on the coffee maker. This simple task, which was always appreciated, was something that his dad just never seemed to figure out how to do. His dad was a genius in so many respects, but a moron in others. He'd heard his mom say, so many times, "Stephen, all you have to do is push this button when you come into the kitchen to make your breakfast."

It wasn't that Peter's dad didn't feel like turning on the coffee maker. It was just that despite being the most social and likable person in the whole town, he was notoriously forgetful. Or at least that was the excuse he used...

With over seventy minutes to kill, Peter decided to make good use of his time and started reading the novel which he needed to finish before writing a book report due on Wednesday.

* * *

The book was not as boring as Peter had expected, so he managed to get a reasonable amount of enjoyment out of the hundred-odd pages he read through. This made time fly by, and before he knew it, it was time to put on his outdoor gear and wait just inside the front door for Neil to arrive.

CHAPTER 17

Neil leaned on the horn as he approached Peter's driveway, which was completely unnecessary—and also a little rude and inconsiderate, considering the time of day—since Peter had promised to be waiting and watching through the window next to the front door.

"Yo, the Petester!" Neil said loudly when Peter hopped in the back seat. That was now the second time in two days he'd been called that by Neil. He didn't like this new nickname at all. But since he was extremely grateful that Neil was driving them today, he chose not to complain.

"Hi, Pete," said Claire. "Sorry about the horn. I tried to pull his hand off it as soon as he started. He probably woke up a few of your neighbors."

Peter pointed at his living room window, where his mom, still in her nightgown, was staring at Neil and wagging her finger back and forth. "No biggie," Peter replied. "But don't pull a repeat performance of that when we get to Nik's."

After picking up Nicola, the foursome started the short drive to Meeks Park. It was a chilly morning, and there was not a cloud in the sky. They'd want to find a picnic table in the sun to sit at while Maximilian, Aurora, and Cynthia tackled their puzzle.

"Where's Brad?" Claire asked. "I figured he'd want to come today for sure."

"No kidding," Nicola added. "He's obviously got the hots for Aurora."

"Actually," Peter said, "I was trying to invite him along, but he was out from before I woke up yesterday until after I went to bed last night. Currently he's snoring away in his room. I just figured it was best to leave him be."

"You didn't ask Mr. Winchester to come?" Claire then asked. "He would have loved an invite. You know how much he likes hanging out with us."

The thought of inviting Mr. Winchester hadn't even crossed Peter's mind. Since he didn't want to admit that fact, he quickly came up with a silly excuse. "Well," he said, "I did think about it. But considering how cold it is, and how old he is, I thought it would be better to just go visit him at his house after their challenge is done."

"You're right, that's probably better," Nicola said. "But someone needs to let him know we're coming over, right?"

* * *

They pulled into the main Meeks parking lot at 8:52, eight minutes before the arranged meeting time. They couldn't spot Zoltan or any of his three trainees, so they randomly picked a picnic table in the sunshine and sat down.

"Should've brought some coffee and cookies," Neil said.

"Coffee?" Peter asked. "Don't tell me you are drinking that junk already?"

"I sure am!" Neil replied. "Well, as long as it's got three creams and at least four packs of sugar in it."

"That's not coffee," Claire laughed. "That's *sugar cream.*"

* * *

Peter checked his watch. 9:04.

"Oh Pete, always obsessed with punctuality," Nicola said, lightly punching him in the arm. "Who cares if they're a little late?"

"Tell you what," Peter said, half-ignoring Nicola's comment. "Since we usually meet up at the picnic tables closer to the river, I'm going to walk over there and take a look. For all we know, they're already sitting over there waiting for us."

"I doubt it," Nicola commented. "But I can see from the expression on your face that you've already made up your mind."

"I'm comin' with you, Petey," Neil announced, standing up quickly. "For moral support."

They all laughed as Peter and Neil started walking away. Peter, of course, was not in need of any moral support. Neil just wanted to talk to him away from Claire, as he needed some advice about what to buy her for Christmas this year.

"What are you getting Nik?" Neil asked bluntly. "Jewelry or something?"

"I haven't decided yet," Peter replied. "And you know Nik, she's not exactly a materialistic person."

"Ah..." Neil answered. "Whatever that means... hey, do you think you could, like, ask Nik to casually inquire about what Claire wants, and then report back to you? And then you tell me?"

"Sure," Peter replied. "Nik would be cool with that."

392

"Awesome," Neil said, giving Peter a high-five. "Thanks."

They were now only a few meters away from the picnic tables by the river. No one was at the tables, or anywhere else in sight.

"This is a little weird," Peter said, looking at his watch again. "It's almost a quarter past nine now. They should be here."

"Hey, what's that?" Neil said, pointing at something on one of the picnic tables.

As they got closer, they saw that the "white thing" was an envelope, which was taped to a picnic table. On the front of the envelope, one word was written:

Peter

"Must be a note to say they couldn't show up for some reason," Neil remarked. "Let's take a look."

Peter picked up the envelope and removed the note. As he was taking out the note, something else fell out of the envelope: a key. Attached to the keyring was also a small plate with a number on it.

Neil wasn't looking at the note or the key, but instead at Peter. The color slowly drained completely from Peter's face as he read the long note.

"What's going on?" Neil asked.

Peter couldn't speak. He sat down on the picnic table bench and handed the note to Neil. When Neil saw the first couple of lines of the note, he understood exactly why Peter was terrified.

CHAPTER 18

Greetings Peter! Or perhaps we should refer to you as the naive, stupid, easy to fool Peter! We (Maximilian, Aurora, Cynthia) really only came to Earth with one goal in mind: to kidnap Zoltan. And that, we have successfully done.

The one who sent us here on this mission also gave us a secondary mission, which was to silence you, your friends, your brother, and Mr. Winchester. And by "silence" we were told to use any means necessary. But none of us are killers. (Or at least we don't want to be...) Nor do we have anything personal against any of you.

As you already know, there is nothing weather gods enjoy more than creating or solving a good puzzle, so we have prepared a series of puzzles and challenges for you and your friends. Solving them will give you a chance to find and rescue both Bradley and Mr.

Winchester. Oops! I suppose we forgot to mention that we kidnapped them as well... And we've "hidden them away" somewhere. In order to get to them, you'll have to navigate your way through all of the challenges and figure out clues that will take you all over the place.

Good Luck! (We don't really mean that, as we could care less if you find them or not...)

However, if you cheat (and we'll know if you are cheating because we have installed video cameras at all of the locations of the puzzles) then we will "permanently silence" your brother and the old man, if you know what we mean...

This envelope contains the key to a room at the big, new Stoneburg Royal Hotel. We've hung the "Do Not Disturb" sign on the doorknob, so the cleaners will not have been in the room.

Go there, and you'll find the instructions for the first of your challenges.

And don't forget, we'll be watching! The whole time!

Maximilian, Aurora, Cynthia

With a somewhat blank look on his face, Peter sat

down, took a few deep breaths, and prepared to collect his thoughts. The psychologist he'd been seeing for a few years, Dr. Stanley, had spent countless sessions helping Peter build an array of simple and effective techniques to use whenever he felt an "emotional volcano" coming on.

Neil had known Peter for a very long time, and vividly remembered how often Peter used to panic, run away, or cry whenever something overwhelmed him. But the changes in Peter over the last three or four years were astounding. Neil was so happy that his best friend was now quite capable of not letting his emotions affect his behavior.

But Neil did feel a little awkward by the silence, so he chose to say something simple, supportive, and true. "Pete," he told his friend. "This wasn't your fault. Don't even entertain the thought that you did something wrong."

"Thanks, man," Peter replied while looking up at Neil.

Neil casually walked a few steps away from Peter, as he was a little confused about what he should or shouldn't do next.

But Peter knew exactly what to do: He needed to, right here and now, utilize one of the techniques Dr. Stanley had taught him to make sure he stayed in charge of his emotions.

"Okay, Pete," he said softly to himself. "You know what to do: State the facts, man. Say them out loud and believe them." He paused and took a few more deep breaths. "One: As Neil just pointed out, this is NOT your fault. Two: Mr. Winchester and Brad have been kidnapped. Kidnapped. Not hurt or killed or anything like that. Three: There is a way to save them. Four: The way to save them is to solve puzzles, and you are the master of doing that." He paused again and looked over at Neil. "Neil, take the note over to Nik and Claire. I'll catch up with you in a minute."

"Roger," Neil replied, happy to see that Peter was running the show again.

"Okay, Pete," Peter said to himself at a normal volume now that Neil was far enough away that he wouldn't hear anything. "You know what's next: Decide and act."

Before he had even realized it, Peter was pacing in circles. He wasn't doing this because he was worried or nervous, but because it helped him think more clearly.

"The *decide* part is easy," he said to himself. "I mean, there really isn't even an option, is there? Obviously, we take on the challenges."

Peter started walking back, knowing exactly what the *act* part was going to be. "You are going to lead this team," he told himself with fire in his voice. "And the best way to do that is to instill confidence in them the instant you see them. You tell them there's nothing to worry about, and you say it with confidence. Confidence, Pete. *Contagious* confidence."

Peter smiled and started jogging instead of walking. "Thanks, Dr. Stanley," he said, doing the thumbs-up sign with both hands.

As soon as he rounded the corner and his friends were in view, the two girls' body language made it clear that they had had time to read the note.

Nicola ran up and hugged Peter. "I'm sorry, Pete. I'm so sorry," she said, voice a little shaky.

Peter hugged her back. Just because he wanted to be a confident leader didn't mean he wasn't allowed to be compassionate toward his girlfriend.

"Guys," Peter announced after Nicola had gone from hugging to standing beside him with her arm around his waist. "Let's go do what we do best. My brother and our mentor are counting on us. And I am NOT planning on letting them down."

CHAPTER 19

They quickly jogged back to Neil's car and hopped in. Peter was holding the note tightly in one hand and the room key in the other.

"You know how to get there, right?" Claire asked Neil.

"Not exactly," Neil replied. "But isn't this new hotel, like, one of the tallest buildings in Stoneburg? It's somewhere near the city center, right? It shouldn't be that hard to find."

Although all four wanted to get to the hotel as quickly as possible, Neil made sure to obey every single traffic law while driving there, even going as far as keeping his speed a few kilometers under the posted speed limit. (Their parents would always speed, especially on the big highway between Clearville and Stoneburg.) But the last thing a sixteen-year-old new driver needed was a speeding ticket.

* * *

"There it is!" Nicola said, pointing at the tall, shiny and very modern hotel. "Just keep heading down this road. It should take us right there."

A few minutes later, Neil pulled into the hotel parking garage. "Do you guys want to run in first while I find a place to park?"

Nicola and Claire both turned to face Peter. They clearly wanted him to be in charge of making that decision.

"No," he replied quite quickly. "We are all going in together. We have absolutely no idea what's waiting for us, or what could happen if we split up."

The first available parking spot was on the third floor. Once parked, they all got out and ran to the closest stairwell they could find, and quickly went down to the ground level. Then they walked up to the front entrance of the hotel, and took a few seconds to marvel at the massive revolving door that would let them in.

Peter looked at the key in his hand. It had the number 1124 on the attached tag. They certainly weren't going to be using the stairs to get up there.

This fancy hotel actually had four elevators, so they barely even had to wait after pushing the *up* button. They got in and Peter quickly pushed the *11* and then the *door close* button. When the doors didn't close right away—which is a standard safety feature in all elevators—he started pushing it over and over. (Even though Dr. Stanley had helped Peter in many ways, the impatient part of Peter's personality still took over occasionally.)

When they finally reached the eleventh floor, he began banging on the *door open* button over and over. "What's taking so long?" he said in frustration. Before his three friends had a chance to tell him to chill out, the doors started to open. Peter jumped out and the rest quickly followed him.

The wall right in front of them had a plate on it, which showed that rooms 1101–1120 were to the left, and 1121–1140 were to the right. Peter took big strides to get to 1124 as quickly as he could.

Nicola, Neil, and Claire jogged to catch up to Peter as he put the key in the lock and twisted it. He pushed the door open and went inside. He was so eager to see what was inside the room that he accidentally forgot to hold the door for Nicola, who was right behind him.

The lights in the room were all on, and just as promised, a single envelope lay on the small table between the two double beds.

"Look, there's the camera they mentioned," Nicola said, pointing at what looked like the kind of security camera you would see in a jewelry shop or convenience store. It was on top of the TV, with the lens facing toward the bedside table. The little red light was on, indicating the camera was indeed working. And since it was wireless, that meant it was somehow hooked up remotely to the location where Maximilian, Aurora, and Cynthia were watching them from.

Claire lightly touched the side of the camera. It didn't slide or twist. "Look," she said. "I think they used double-sided tape or something to stick it to the top of the TV."

"Best we just leave it as is," Nicola advised her. "Tampering with it in any way might make them think we are trying to cheat. And we don't want that."

They sat down on the beds and Peter frantically removed the note from its envelope. He took a deep breath, closed his eyes, and then let the air out. He began reading aloud.

CHAPTER 20

Welcome!

Just in case you are wondering if we are really watching you, the answer is a resounding YES! We can see you and your friends clearly. We've installed cameras like this one at all of the locations for today's wild goose chase. (We found that term in a dictionary, and it seemed quite appropriate...)

Well, enough small talk. (We found that one in a dictionary, too.)

Your first task: Find the next key.

Your instructions: Go up four floors, and then decipher this rhyming clue to locate the key.

Clue: Your search for a key, so easy to hide,
We've made not too difficult, as time's not on your side.
And speaking of time, all people here certainly

save a bit,
By using this, something so simple, but obviously a big hit!

"A rhyming hint?" Claire said while shaking her head. "That's a first."

"I'm brutal at these things," Neil said. "I always get Ds in poetry."

"The fact that it rhymes," Peter advised, "means nothing. Zero. This clue is no different than any other clue."

"Ah," Neil nodded. "Okay, thanks Pete."

"Why don't we go up there before we start thinking too hard," Nicola suggested. "It might be easier to decipher once we're up there."

"Good call, Nik," Peter replied. He folded the note in half and slid it into his back pocket, and picked up the 1124 room key and put it in his backpack. His sixth sense told him he just might have to get back into this room again sometime today; And just like every other decision Peter faced, "better safe than sorry" always played a huge role...

They left room 1124 and went back to the elevators. It didn't take long before one arrived, and when it opened, thankfully no one else was inside. They all hopped in, Peter leading the way, and he immediately pushed the *15.* Then just like he had done last time, he started rapidly pushing the *door close* button again.

When they got up to the fifteenth floor, they exited the elevator in a rush. But after that, no one really knew what to do next. Before Nicola, Neil or Claire had a chance to ask Peter if he had any idea where to start looking, Peter had taken the note out of his pocket, and was reading it aloud again.

"How about this," Nicola suggested as soon as Peter finished the rhyme. "What if we, I don't know, start walking around or something? Maybe we'll see something that helps?"

"Sounds good to me, Nik," Neil said. "How about Claire and I check the hallway on the right, and you and Pete do the same on the left? The hallways aren't that long, so if anyone sees something, just shout and the other two can run over."

"Awesome plan, Neil," Peter said. "Let's do it."

Peter and Nicola walked to the left hallway, which was for rooms 1501–1520. The hallway was quite fancy, as least as far as hotels go. The carpet looked very expensive, and paintings lined the walls on both sides. And there were large, elaborate vases at both ends of the hallway.

"I bet the riddle has to do with something in one of the paintings," Nicola said.

"I was thinking the same thing," Peter replied. "I'm pretty sure that the rhyme is telling us to look for something... uh... simple or convenient. Let's look through each painting and see which one or ones show convenient items or things like that."

"Sounds good, Pete," Nicola replied. "I'll do this side and you do that one."

"Neil! Claire!" Nicola shouted. "We think the answer is going to be hidden in one of the paintings!"

"Uh... okay," Neil *kind of* replied. "But what are we looking for?"

"Something convenient!" she said back loudly. "You know, like something that would, I don't know, save you time!"

"Gotcha," Neil answered.

As Peter moved from painting to painting, there seemed to be no rhyme or reason to them. Some were of animals, some of old homes, some of nature, and some were just abstract obscurities.

* * *

"Anything Nik?" Peter asked after checking the last painting on his side, the one just beside room 1520.

"Not yet," she replied. She had been spending more time than Peter on each one, so there were still four or five on her side that she hadn't looked at.

"Okay," Peter said, a little impatiently. "I'll help look at the last few on your side."

* * *

Neil and Claire had adopted a slightly different approach for their scanning of the paintings. They stayed together while looking at each one: Claire stood very close and Neil stood a few steps back.

On their sixth painting, Claire spotted something promising. "Neil, come closer," she said. "Look at this." She was pointing at the shirt pocket on one of the men in the painting. More specifically, at the mechanical pencil in that man's shirt pocket.

"A mechanical pencil," Neil said. "Those things certainly are convenient. And they save time, right? No more using pencil sharpeners! And when they were first invented, I bet they were a big hit. I mean, like, EVERYONE uses them now!"

"Pete! Nik!" Claire shouted. "Come over here. We've found something!"

Peter and Nicola ran as fast as they could to get there. Upon closer inspection, they both agreed that Claire had found what might be the right painting.

"So if this is the right one," Claire asked. "Then where would the key be?"

"Not sure," Peter answered. "But in all likelihood, it's probably taped to the top of the frame. Or maybe on the back. Those would be the only places where it would be completely out of sight."

Neil jumped high to get a look at the top of the frame. "Not on the top," he said.

Claire then carefully pulled the bottom part of the painting away from the wall by about twenty centimeters. Peter stuck his face in behind it to look for the key.

"Guys," he said with obvious disappointment in his voice, "it's not here."

"Are you sure?" Neil asked, joining Peter behind the painting.

Convinced that they were looking at the wrong painting, Claire slowly lowered it back to its original position.

"There are still a few more to check in this hallway," Claire said. "One of them has got to be hiding that key."

With the four of them working together now, they finished their scans of the remaining paintings in no time. But none of them contained anything that could be considered even remotely convenient.

"Man," Peter said in frustration, after looking at the final painting.

"Hold up, Pete," Neil said. "We haven't looked at the vases yet."

"True," Peter replied. "But vases aren't exactly new, convenient items."

"And they don't save people time, either," Claire added. But she was careful to say it in a way that made it clear she wasn't making fun of Neil's suggestion.

Peter started walking back down the hallway. "Guys, I'm going to sit down on those chairs near the elevators," he said. "I wanna reread the rhyme a few more times. I need to think it through a little more carefully.

They followed their *fearless leader*—who was beginning to appear a little agitated—back to the chairs. Then they listened to the rhyming hint again, three times in total, a little slower each time.

"Why can't we figure this out, guys?" Peter said after the third reading. "The answer is probably staring us right in the face."

Claire's eyes lit up. Really, really lit up.

"What is it?" Neil said to her. "You've got an idea, don't you?"

Claire, smiling, pointed at the sign on the wall. The one right above Peter's head, that showed which rooms were to the left and which were to the right.

"That sign," Claire explained, "is certainly convenient. It tells guests whether to go left or right after they get off the elevator."

Peter jumped up from his seat to look at the sign. He could barely contain his excitement. "Which saves time," Peter said, "for EVERYONE who stays here! Claire, you're brilliant!"

Peter felt around the frame of the sign to see where the key might be taped. Unlike the painting, this sign wasn't hanging from the wall, it was screwed to it. So the only place the key could be hidden was somewhere on the frame.

He slid his fingers along all four sides. On the top, he collected a lot of dust on his finger while doing so. (The cleaning staff at this hotel was obviously not as meticulous as his mother when it came to dusting...)

"It's not here," he said, sounding both surprised and upset.

"Don't give up so quickly," Neil said supportively. "They probably couldn't tape it to the sign. It would have been too obvious to the hotel staff. It's probably hidden under one of the chairs here. Or maybe under this little table."

A very close inspection of the table and chairs revealed their worst fears: no key.

"I bet those three are watching us right now and laughing their heads off," Claire said, looking around to see where the camera had been placed.

"I don't see a camera anywhere," Neil said. "Looks like that *we'll be watching you* threat was just a bunch of balderdash."

"Balder what?" Nicola asked.

"Oh," Neil giggled, "that's a word my mom encourages me to use instead of swearing."

"So what do we do then?" Claire asked loudly. "I mean, is this actually even a puzzle? Or are they just running us around and taking us for fools?"

Peter was already a few meters away from his team, pacing around in a discombobulated pattern. He wasn't prepared to accept that this could be a trick. Nor was he ready to say that this puzzle was too hard.

But something certainly was amiss. There should be a camera watching them, but there wasn't. And the key should be taped to the sign directing people to their rooms, but it wasn't.

Peter did what he often did when stuck, he took the note out again and began rereading it ad nauseum to himself. Nicola, Neil, and Claire remained silent, knowing this was not the time to disturb him.

This carried on for quite some time. Claire, who was the least familiar with Peter's quirky habits, eventually broke the silence. A little louder than she should have, she said, "Maybe today just isn't our lucky day."

Neil tried to shush her, but it was too late. Peter hated (actually despised) and completely disagreed with the concept of luck. He had caught Claire's comment. He stopped pacing and glared at her.

"Sorry, Pete," she said softly. "I was, just, like, uh…"

Peter looked at the note again. His face began to change. It wasn't one of frustration, but one of amazement. "Claire, thank you!" he said loudly. Then he crushed the note into a ball and hit the elevator button.

"Are we going back to 1124?" Neil asked.

"No sir," Peter smiled. "As you can see, I pushed the *up* button, not the *down* one."

"Up? Why?" Claire asked.

"Because, Claire, my dear," Peter replied with a silly smirk. "You just reminded me of something when you said the word *lucky*."

"Really?" she asked.

"I don't get it," Neil added.

The elevator came and they all stepped inside. "Look at the buttons," Peter said. "Notice anything?"

"Uh…" Neil answered. "Nope… why?"

"Okay," Peter continued. "Then follow my fingers."

Peter pointed at the 11, then the 12, and then… the next button was the 14.

"Wait! I get it!" Claire yelled. "Hotels don't have a thirteenth floor! People think it's unlucky!"

"Nicely done," Peter said.

"So that means," Nicola added, "that we actually only

went up three floors, not four like the note instructed."

"You got it!" Peter replied.

Claire hit the *16* and they all waited. Time seemed to slow to a snail's pace before the elevator took off.

When they stepped off on the 16th floor, Neil looked around in search of the camera. He spotted it, concealed very well, in the corner above one of the elevator entrances. Just like the one that had been taped on top of the TV in room 1124, this one also had a red light on.

Peter strode over to the room direction sign and felt around it with his fingers. As he slid them across the top, he felt something, which he knew without looking was the key. It had been taped to the top, in a way that no one could ever have seen unless they had been looking for it.

"Awesome job!" Nicola said loudly, giving him a big hug.

Peter hugged her back, and then walked over to Claire and gave her a powerful high-five. "Without you," he said to her, "we would never have figured this one out."

Once they'd done enough celebrating, Peter looked more closely at the key. It was a key to a home. It looked like one for a doorknob, or possibly a deadbolt. On one side the key, a very small piece of paper had been glued. The paper only had two words on it, which were written in very tiny letters:

Winchester's house

So now they knew where this wild goose chase was going to take them next.

CHAPTER 21

Once they were back in Neil's car and "ready to roll," a strange silence seemed to fall over everyone.

It was Nicola who decided to speak up first. "This is getting really weird, guys," she said. "First, starting us off at a hotel in Stoneburg? And now sending us to Mr. Winchester's?"

"I'd call it mega-super weird," Neil added. "Why didn't he just set up the next challenge in the hotel room?"

"Unfortunately," Peter interjected, not meaning to be rude. "We have to try our best not to think about those things. All we can do is solve the puzzles and follow where the clues lead us. If we do that, eventually we WILL get to Mr. Winchester and Brad."

"Okay," Neil replied. "I'll do what I can to keep the *Neilster* part of my brain focused."

"Anyone hungry or thirsty?" Peter asked while reaching into his backpack. "I brought a couple boxes of granola bars, and, like, nine juice boxes. I was planning on us having these at a picnic table back at Meek's Park while *they* did *our* puzzle."

"Sure," Neil said, happy that the conversation was on the topic of food. "What have you got?"

"Let's see," Peter replied, looking at the two boxes. "Chocolate chip... or honey and oats."

"Score me one of each, if you don't mind," Neil said. "I skipped breakfast... And what are my juice choices?"

"This isn't a restaurant," Claire jokingly scolded him.

"Certainly isn't," Nicola followed. "Because Peter would make the worst waiter ever."

"What are you talking about?" Peter laughed. "I'd be a great waiter!"

"No, you wouldn't," she said back. "You'd get too nervous. You'd fumble your words and leave all the customers super confused."

"Settle down, boys and girls," Neil joked. "Let's get back to what's important here... what drinks have you got?"

"Apple, orange, or mixed fruit," Peter replied. "The apple and orange are one hundred percent fruit juice, but the mixed fruit one has added sugar. So even though it may taste better, it—"

"See!" Nicola jumped in. "What kind of waiter would launch into that explanation when—"

"Mixed fruit!" Neil announced. "I need the extra sugar to help me concentrate."

Peter took a mixed fruit box, removed the little plastic drinking straw attached to its side, and stuck it through the hole.

"I'll hold it for you," he said to Neil. "And just let me know every time you wanna take a sip."

"You guys are so weird," Claire said.

"Thanks, baby!" Neil replied sarcastically, winking so she could see it in the rear-view mirror.

CHAPTER 22

When they got to Mr. Winchester's home, Peter suggested that they be very cautious before approaching the front door. He had a feeling that this would be an easy place for Maximilian, Aurora, and Cynthia to have set up some kind of trap. And if they had, he didn't plan on falling for it.

"Better safe than sorry, right?" he said as they got out of the car.

"You're the boss," Neil replied.

Before getting anywhere near the front door, they walked around the entire house once, making sure to keep a reasonable distance between them and the house the whole time. Nothing looked suspicious or out of place.

Confident that there weren't any traps, they began to walk up the sidewalk and then the front steps. When they were safely up on the front porch, Peter walked to the front door and put the key in the deadbolt. He nervously twisted the key and then took the cold doorknob in his right hand and turned it.

After pushing the heavy door open, he saw a single white envelope on the floor, just beyond the inside floor mat. He knelt down and picked it up.

"Pete, you okay?" Nicola asked.

"Yeah," he answered hesitantly. "But I'm really worried about Mr. Winchester. I mean he's not exactly in perfect health, and if they've duct-taped him to a chair, and—"

"Oh, Pete," Neil said, slapping him on the shoulder. "You're letting that crazy imagination of yours run wild again. Think about it: they aren't from Earth. There's no way they'd ever even consider doing something like that."

"He's right," Claire said. "You've gotta get that mind of yours out of worry mode."

"Easier said than done," Peter whispered to himself. His mind spent more time in worry mode than it did in any other mode.

Neil took the envelope from Peter and removed the note. He read it aloud slowly and clearly.

Such a big and lovely house for an old and clever man! So many possible places for us to hide your next clue! But we didn't make this one too hard either.

Here's your hint:

knobs
levers
switches

What are you waiting for? Don't just stand there! Get running!

"Dudes," Neil said. "That trio would get an *F* in

poetry."

"No kidding," Peter added. "It's like they wanted to make a rhyming clue again, but then when they couldn't, they just wrote down three words."

"Let's go sit down together at the kitchen table," Nicola suggested. "I'm willing to bet that there is a hidden clue within those three words.

"I like your thinking, Nik," Claire said. "That's better than just running around the house senselessly."

Since Claire knew where Mr. Winchester kept his papers and pencils, she got enough for everyone.

"Now I'm not saying this is the right thing to do," Nicola said with slightly less confidence than a minute ago, "but here's my, uh… advice: write those three words down somewhere on your paper. Then just keep looking at them. Look for… I don't know… for… I don't want to say too much, 'cause if I do, then we'll all end up looking for the same thing."

"Uh… okay," Peter replied. "And how about we do this in silence?"

"Sure, cool," Neil replied.

"Alright," Peter said. "Let's see what we can come up with in five minutes, starting now."

Peter pressed the start button on his wristwatch.

The silence was very awkward at first, but in no time at all, all four were immersed in their own thoughts. Not knowing what the others were thinking of made it that much more intriguing to Peter.

When Peter looked down at his watch and saw that about three minutes had passed, he couldn't help but take a peek at Nicola's and Claire's papers. He immediately realized they were doing more or less the same thing; they were trying to rearrange the letters to spell other words. Peter had a feeling they were on the right track. But just in case they weren't, he wanted to take his own mind down a different one. The more options the better, right?

"Time's up," Peter announced the instant the timer on his watch hit five minutes. "So what d'ya got?"

"Actually, I got a little overwhelmed there," Nicola said. "I mean, considering the number of letters, there are just way too many words that can be spelled." She showed them her list:

shelves
rest
is
it
with
vest
see
his
know
best
hiss
bee
rose

"Hey, my list looks pretty similar to yours," Claire said. "We have lots of the same words written down. But how do we know which ones actually mean something?"

"Well, the nouns on your list at least give us somewhere to start," Peter explained. "You know, like shelves. We can go to his bookshelves and look there."

"I don't mean to tell you that you're barking up the wrong tree," Neil said apprehensively, "but I looked at this puzzle completely differently. I tried to think of a place in a house that has knobs, levers, and switches. And I think the clue is telling us to go to a washroom. More specifically, the ensuite one that has a shower in it."

"A washroom?" Claire asked. "Why?"

"Well, uh…" Neil said. "There are knobs on all the cabinets, levers for the sink and shower, and the main fuse box—you know, that big yellow thing that controls the electricity for the whole house—is mounted above the door in the ensuite bathroom. And that sucker is loaded with switches."

"Can't do us any harm to check it out," Peter agreed.

They all went through the master bedroom into the ensuite bathroom and started looking around for the next clue. They checked everywhere they could think of: under the mat, in each and every drawer, and in the medicine cabinet. They even took off the top of the toilet tank and looked in there.

"Guys!" Neil said suddenly. "Check it out! I found it!"

Mr. Winchester's bathroom had been renovated a year and a half ago. They had removed the big old bathtub and replaced it with a shower unit. He had the contractors install bars along the walls both inside and outside the shower, to reduce his chance of having a bad fall. They had also bolted a sturdy plastic seat in the shower which was set in a fairly high position. That way he could sit down while showering and stand up quite easily when finished.

Neil opened the clear glass door of the shower stall and pointed at the message that had been written in blue crayon on the light beige shower seat.

Just as he got ready to read what it said, he looked up

and spotted the camera, which was taped to the ceiling and pointing straight down at his face. They had definitely found the right room.

Well done! You are quite a team! Peter, you must be running things very well. Or, is someone else running this group? Or is no one running anything?

"Guys," Neil said, baffled by the meaning of the new clue. "This doesn't make any sense at all."

"Certainly doesn't," Claire added. "The messages keep getting more and more cryptic."

"Something's not right," Peter said. "I have no idea what, but something just isn't right."

"Pete," Nicola said. "Pass me the note."

She read it quietly to herself while the other three waited for her to say something.

Peter, impatient to hear what was going on in her mind, couldn't help but ask, "What is it Nik? You got—"

"Shh..." Claire said, covering Peter's mouth with her hand. "Give her some time. Just like you, she probably thinks more clearly when left undisturbed."

"Sorry," Peter whispered to Claire.

But being silent didn't mean the same as doing nothing. For his entire life, Peter had clearly been unable to "sit still."

* * *

When Peter was in Grade 3, his teacher had pointed out Peter's "excessive restlessness" to his parents, and recommended they consult a specialist.

Peter, although only eight at the time, still remembers being told he may have a mild form of ADHD.

He also recalls how the specialist thought that he shouldn't be in the room while she explained to his parents exactly what ADHD was. So during that fifteen-minute span, he sat in the waiting room, sucking on a lollipop the receptionist had given him. On the drive home, his parents seemed no different than usual, so Peter figured that was a good sign.

But once home, curiosity got the better of him and he asked his mom if she could take him to the library the next morning, which was a Saturday. He said he wanted to borrow some books on the solar system, since they had just started learning the basics of it in science, and he thought it was really cool. Peter's "second" favorite place in the world was the library. (His "first" was the games/hobby shop at the mall.) And he never needed any help finding the books he was looking for, as he had long since mastered the library's shelving system.

So that Saturday, while his mom flipped through sewing magazines and sipped coffee, Peter found a book on ADHD and read through a couple of chapters while sitting on a step stool between aisles. He chose that odd location to read so his mom wouldn't know where he was.

Having read enough, he put the book back and went quickly to the science section. He grabbed the first two solar system books he saw. Then he went to his mom and said, "Thanks mom, I found two good ones."

"And don't you forget, young man," his mom responded, "that you promised to polish the silverware if I brought you here today." Peter's mom never ever forgot anything...

* * *

So Peter just attributed his overactive mind and body

to ADHD. He walked out of the washroom and went back to the living room, where he paced around in a loop thinking and rethinking the message Neil had just read.

"Pete!" Neil yelled. "Get back here! Nik's got something!"

"Yessss!" Peter said, pumping his fist. He knew Nicola was great at cracking these kinds of codes.

"Okay, here's what I'm thinking," she said once Peter was back in the washroom. "The word *running* was used in the first note, and then again three more times in the message on the shower seat. That can't be a coincidence."

"You wouldn't think so," Claire said.

"So, *we* certainly can't be running in here," Nicola said. "But... the water can."

"The water?" Peter asked.

"Yeah," she went on. "Let's turn on the hot water for the sink and the shower and—"

"Why?" Peter said, interrupting her.

"Pete," Nicola said softly, taking his hand, "C'mon, just trust me here."

Peter always wanted to know the answers to all the *whys* before acting, but apparently was not going to have that luxury this time. He managed to hold his questions back, and cranked on the hot water for both the sink and shower.

Nothing happened at first, but as steam built up in the bathroom, they could see a message had been written for them on the mirror above the sink, and a second one on the inside of the shower door. And these only became visible because the surfaces were now covered in condensation.

Above the sink, were three words:

Go back to

And on the inside of the shower was a number:

1124

"Awesome, Nik," Peter exclaimed, hugging her.

"Those three are pretty good at making tough puzzles, eh?" Neil said.

"Well, somewhat true," Peter answered. "But they haven't been able to fool us yet!"

"Pete, you've still got the key, right?" Neil asked as they ran out of Mr. Winchester's house and back to his car.

"Think about who you are talking to," Peter answered his friend with a smile. "You know I'm *mister overly prepared and excessively paranoid*. Of course I kept it! It's in my backpack! But now that you've said that, let me double-check..."

CHAPTER 23

Neil took the exact same route they had used to drive to
Mr. Winchester's house to get them back to the big hotel
in Stoneburg. And once again, he made absolutely sure
not to break any traffic laws. (Even though everyone else
on the highway kept whizzing past them.)

Once they had parked, entered the hotel, and were in
the elevator heading up to floor eleven, Claire
commented on something which Peter had actually been
pondering himself.

"If they're sending us back here again," she said, "that
means they must be fairly close by."

"I bet they are in this hotel somewhere," Neil said. "I
mean, we know Zoltan was provided with a huge amount
of money, right? If they've trapped him, and taken it all,
they certainly could have booked more than one room.
Wait… maybe they are even holding Mr. Winchester and
Brad here, too!?"

"The tough thing," Peter said, "is figuring out which
room they're in."

"First things first, everyone," Nicola said as the
elevator doors opened and they started their walk back
to 1124. "Let's see what they've left for us. We can think

about *playing detective* later."

"Peter unlocked the door and they all went back inside the room they had been in only a couple of hours ago. Only one thing was different. And it wasn't only different, but it was also obviously part of the next puzzle.

On the table between the two beds, where the phone and alarm clock had previously been, there were now four digital timers. They were quite small, maybe half the size of an alarm clock. They were lined up neatly in a row. They reminded Peter of the timers that were used at the finish line of the 100-meter dash to display the winner's time. Each timer was set to a different time, and none of them were counting either up or down. The four timers, in order, were set to:

$$2{:}06 \qquad 6{:}18 \qquad 46{:}14 \qquad 30{:}45$$

They looked around the room for an envelope, but there clearly wasn't one for them this time. So this weird combination of numbers contained the clue about where to go or what to do next.

Neil decided to say each time aloud, if for no other reason than to convey how confused he was. "Two minutes and six seconds, six eighteen, forty-six fourteen, and thirty forty-five," he announced, trying to mimic the voice a sports caster would use when calling names as athletes cross a finish line.

Then Neil did something very out of character. He walked up and put his face right in front of the camera and said, "We don't need to see you to know that you're all laughing like crazy right now!" He paused, took a few steps back, pointed at the timers, and continued, "But I guarantee, unequi..." He paused, as the word he wanted to say had suddenly vanished.

"Unequivocally," Peter said, helping Neil out.

"Unequivocally," Neil continued, "that we will figure this one out. So laugh away now, while you still can!"

As Neil sat back down on one of the beds, Peter turned toward the timers and glared at them, as if it was *Peter vs. the timers* in a gladiator pit. Peter considered himself the king of number puzzles, and Neil's comments to the camera twenty seconds earlier had only made him even more eager to break this code as fast as he could. He closed his eyes for a few seconds and took a couple of deep breaths.

With his eyes still shut, he began to speak, "Guys, I'll try my absolute best to figure this out. But the more help you give me, the better."

Nicola had already taken Peter's hand before he opened his eyes back up, "Pete," she said. "Of course we are going to help you. We would never make you tackle one of these on your own."

"No kidding, dude," Neil laughed. "Don't go all mushy on us!"

Claire laughed at that, followed immediately by Nicola and Peter too. The contagious laughter went on for a good thirty seconds, and all of their faces were red before they settled back down.

All four looked toward the timers again, with their "thinking caps" on now. Peter reached into his backpack and took out pencils and papers for everyone. (He'd "borrowed" a bunch from Mr. Winchester's house, just in case they needed to use them again). Just like they'd done at Mr. Winchester's, they decided to start by thinking separately.

Peter tried his best to keep his eyes off their papers, but couldn't resist a quick peek at Neil's.

Neil was calculating the time difference between each of the timers. He had written those three numbers down, but the baffled expression on Neil's face indicated he had no clue what to do with them next.

Since he'd already looked at Neil's paper—and considering his own was completely blank—Peter decided to walk over to the small circular table in the corner where Nicola and Claire were sitting and working together at it.

As Peter approached, Claire told him what they were up to. "Nik and I," Claire said, "are both thinking the same thing. We think each number represents a letter. So if we can figure out which letter corresponds to each number, we should be able to spell out the answer."

"Ahh... I see," Peter replied. "That's good thinking."

"We haven't produced any words yet, but here's what we are on to," Claire explained. "Notice how each timer has either a zero or a one, and that those are always one of the middle digits of each timer. Never the first or the last number. That must mean that these are both vowels. Since 'u' is the least used vowel, that means we only have four others to choose from. So we are currently experimenting with different combinations."

"If we can figure out the third timer," Nicola added, "which has a *4* at both the start and the end, then we should be able to get the rest of them."

"Neil," Peter said. "Come and give us a hand. Claire and Nik have figured out what to do. If all of us work on it, we'll surely decipher it a lot quicker.

"Well, let's brainstorm ideas for what words forty-six fourteen can spell," Nicola suggested. "And just say anything you come up with."

Everyone started playing around with letters in their mind and on paper, to see what words they could create.

Neil was the first to say something. "I've got two," he said, "but they're both pretty weird. B-L-O-B, blob. And P-R-O-P, prop."

"Awesome," Nicola said, not wanting to say what she was actually thinking: *only tell us words that could be useful!*

"How about P-R-E-P?" Claire suggested. "Prep is short for preparation, right?"

"The only one I've come up with," Peter said, "is way too morbid. D-I-E-D. Hope it's not that..."

"Could it be that?" Nicola said.

"No way," Peter replied.

"Not died, that, T-H-A-T!" she exclaimed.

"T-H-A-T, eh?" Neil said. "Definitely a common word."

"And it fits nicely into the middle of a short phrase," Nicola added.

"Okay, so let's assume we are right," Peter said. "Then the second word starts with H-A."

"H-A-Y is a word, isn't it?" Neil asked. "You know, hay, the stuff horses eat."

"I can think of quite a few others," Claire added. "There's *had*, *has*, um... and *ham*."

"I think you're onto something," Peter said. "I doubt it's *ham*, though. It's gotta be either *has* or *had*."

"So the clue would be," Nicola said. "*Something* has that *something*. Or *something* had that *something*."

"And since *had* is just the past tense of *has*," Claire said right away, "then it shouldn't really matter which one we use."

"Plus, we already know the number *4*, which is the

third letter in the last word, is a *T*," Peter added.

"Cool," Neil said. "Let's see what we can come up with for the fourth word."

There was a minute or two where no one spoke as they mentally ran through the alphabet, trying to find words that both worked and made sense.

Neil broke the silence. "*Has that fits?*" he said awkwardly.

"*Has that duty*," Nicola said right after him.

"Both usable," Peter nodded. "Any others?"

"I've got two, actually," Claire said excitedly. "*Has that cuts*. Or *has that bite*."

"Those are good, too," Peter said happily. "But figuring out which one is correct is going to be tough."

"Yeah," Neil followed. "Like, all four of those phrases point at totally different things."

"Then maybe," Peter suggested, "we need to crack word one first."

"Sounds good, Pete," Claire agreed. "Let's give it a shot."

"Hold on a sec, everyone," Neil said suddenly, but in a tone that sounded not at all promising or positive. "I think we are, and pardon me for using this cheesy expression again, barking up the wrong tree."

"What do you mean?" Peter asked.

"Well, the *6* is an *H*, right?" Neil explained. "So the first word ends in an *H?* I don't know any words, or at least any three-letter English words, that end in an *H*..."

"You're right," Nicola said.

"Aaargh," Claire said loudly. "This is so frustrating!"

"Don't let it get to you," Nicola said while patting Claire on the back. "We've all felt the same way before, overwhelmed by puzzles like this."

"I feel like my brain is going to blow up!" Claire blurted out.

"Tell you what everyone," Peter suggested. "Let's take five. Do whatever you want for five or ten minutes, but DO NOT think about this puzzle. You'd be amazed how big a difference a little breather can make."

Claire and Nicola leaned back in their chairs, and Peter went and sat on the edge of one of the beds. Unable to just sit there and do nothing, he picked up the remote. He knew he needed some alternate stimulation to truly get his mind out of the puzzle.

While Peter started channel surfing, Neil lay down on his back across one of the beds. Since Peter had ended up choosing a news channel which was talking about some money laundering scandal—something that Neil had zero interest in listening to—Neil turned his head away from the TV. Of course, this meant he was now looking right at the four timers again. His head was hanging off the edge of the bed a little, so it was almost as if he was looking at them upside down.

"You guys aren't going to believe this until you see it!" Neil announced loudly and proudly.

Peter hit the mute button on the TV, and Nicola and Claire stood up and came closer.

Neil was sitting up on the bed now, waiting for his audience.

Neil picked the timers up, turned them upside down, and then placed the upside-down timers back in their original spots on the table.

"Man," he said loudly. "What a group of tricksters!"

He got no reaction, at all, from his team.

"Oh, please," he said with a huge grin. "Someone tell me you can see it too."

Still silence.

"Okay, but this will make it way too obvious," Neil continued. "You must remember when we were in, like, Grade 4 or so, and we would enter numbers in a calculator, flip it upside down, and show everyone whatever rude or inappropriate words the upside-down numbers looked like?"

"Neil!" Peter said, giving him a huge high-five. "You're a genius, man!"

"The second, third and fourth ones are easy, BIG HIGH SHOE," Nicola said. "But the first one doesn't make any sense. What is G-O-Z? I've never heard of the word goz."

"It's not goz," Neil explained. "The 2 is to, you know T-O. So the first timer says: *GO TO.*"

"Go to big high shoe?" Claire asked. "What's that supposed to mean?"

"I know exactly what it means," Neil said while standing up and darting for the door. "Let's go, I'll explain in the elevator. No time to waste!"

Unfortunately, there was a family of three in the same elevator, so Neil had to wait until they were outside and heading for the car before he could explain anything.

"They want us to go to that big statue of the soccer ball and soccer shoe," he said.

"I know that one," Claire added. "That really ugly bronze statue behind Livingston Stadium!"

"I do agree it's ugly," Peter said, "but I can't speak badly about it. The funds for building the stadium, along with all the practice grounds around the stadium, were all donated by Alfred Livingston. He had played semi-pro soccer sometime in the past."

"Wait a second," Neil added. "Is that the local guy who

won big in the lottery?"

"That's him," Peter answered. "And he thought, for some reason we'll never understand, that putting a statue there would look cool."

"Ah," Nicola said, "and since he was covering the bill, no one could tell him *no*."

"Exactly," Peter answered.

They were now back at the car. Neil quickly unlocked the doors and they all got in.

"To the statue Mr. Chauffeur!" Peter said in a silly accent.

"With pleasure, sir," Neil replied, copying Peter's ridiculous accent. "But not till you all fasten your seat belts!"

CHAPTER 24

About fifteen minutes later, they arrived at the beautiful Livingston Stadium. Since it was not soccer season, the parking lot was virtually empty. They parked in the corner nearest the statue and quickly jogged over to it.

Before anyone spotted the note, Neil pointed to the camera that had been taped high up on the *ball* part of the big statue. The lens was aiming down, giving whoever was watching a clear view of everyone at or near the statue.

"That camera wouldn't be up there if this was the wrong place," Neil said.

They started scanning every part of the shoe for the note. Claire found it, taped in a crevice under one part of the shoelace. A typical passer-by would never have seen it by accident. (But the statue was so ugly that most people did what they could to avoid it anyway...)

"What's it say?" Neil asked impatiently. "What are we supposed to do?"

"Hold your horses," Peter said to Neil. Right after he said that expression—which he had never heard anyone other than his mother use—he added, "Just give her a second. She hasn't even opened the envelope yet."

Claire hopped down from the statue, pulled out the note, and began reading aloud.

Well done! You certainly are better at these puzzles than we expected.

So now what?

We certainly can't make you do one here in public, can we? So we could think of no better place than Silverhead Mountain for the rest of your challenges.

Everything has been set up. Just drive out there, park in the small parking lot where the three hiking trails begin, and follow the map on the back of this note.

"This really does feel like a wild goose chase, doesn't it?" Neil commented.

"Yeah," Peter gulped. "Unfortunately, we all know whatever's waiting for us at Silverhead Mountain is going to be harder than anything we have done so far. Waaay harder."

"Petey boy," Neil said, puffing his chest up.

"Neil," Claire said, interrupting him. "Don't even think about using that ridiculous nickname for yourself right now. We all know you're about to tell us *we can count on the Neilster*, right?"

Peter and Nicola started laughing, as Claire had just hit the nail on the head.

Ignoring Claire's comment, Neil smirked. "Never underestimate the power of the Neilster," he said in a deep, mysterious tone, as if he were imitating the evil character in a spy movie.

"Okay, fine, *Mr. Neilster*," Claire said in between laughs. "But for now, can't you just... uh, drive?"

"As you command, your highness of all highnesses," he replied in a low voice again, doing an awful rendition of a sinister grin.

CHAPTER 25

They began the drive out to Silverhead Mountain, a location that everyone other than Claire knew all too well. There wasn't too much conversation going on, as everyone's level of fear began to rise as they got closer to their destination.

Since she'd never been there before, Claire was extremely curious as to what to expect. "Can someone tell me why Silverhead Mountain is always the spot that is chosen for the challenges?" she asked.

"It's because of the structures, buildings, and ruins left over from whatever ancient civilization lived there," Peter explained.

"Yeah," Nicola added. "It's like Machu Pichu meets the Pyramids, with some ancient Rome and medieval castles thrown into the mix. It's too bad we are going there to do these challenges, as it's totally fascinating as a sightseeing spot."

"Oh…" Claire replied, in what seemed like a combination of confusion, amazement, and terror.

* * *

After what felt like an eternity, but was actually only a fourteen-minute drive, they pulled into the parking lot.

Peter had already examined the map very carefully during the drive, so he was pretty confident they'd be able to follow it successfully. The map was quite detailed and had arrows indicating exactly where they had to trek.

"Am I the only one who's thinking this is some kind of trap?" Claire asked. "I mean, according to Pete, we start by walking down a very narrow path, then turn right where there's a huge boulder to climb over."

"Technically speaking," Peter replied, "anything's possible. And considering who we are dealing with, trust is definitely not a word I would feel comfortable using. But like I said earlier, we really don't have any other choice."

"I guess you're right," Claire said back. "But is it okay if I walk in the middle of the group?"

"Of course, babe," Neil said. "Pete'll lead, Nik behind him, then you, and I'll take up the rear."

"Makes sense," Peter said. "Just don't forget to look behind you every so often. You know, to make sure no one is following us."

Peter wished he hadn't said that, as all it did was make an already scared Claire even more terrified. He quickly followed his comment with one to try to undo the damage. "But I HIGHLY doubt that's going to happen," he told her.

The map was quite simple to follow, but the route it was taking them on was nowhere near easy to traverse. They had to push through huge bushes, scramble over numerous boulders, climb up a couple of fairly steep rock faces, and even walk through a stream at one point. But they were, slowly but surely, approaching what was shown as an arched brick area on the map, labeled

"ENTRANCE."

"Look, there it is!" Nicola announced. After over twenty minutes of trekking along a path they would never be able to retrace without the map, they'd arrived at the eerie-looking entrance.

"And look, there's another camera," Neil pointed out. The camera had been attached to the top of the arch, its lens facing outward. A white envelope was wedged tightly in between two of the bricks. No doubt it contained the instructions to the first of the challenges that lay beyond the arch. Peter took the envelope and handed it to Nicola.

"I'm too nervous right now to read it aloud," he said, hands trembling quite a bit. "Would you mind?"

"Of course not," she said as she opened it. Once she'd unfolded the note, she tightly gripped Peter's hand, and then began reading.

CHAPTER 26

Peter, Neil, Nicola, Claire,

After you walk through the entrance and down the tunnel (Don't worry, we have lit the torches on the tunnel walls so you won't be in the dark…) you will come to a room that then branches off into 4 separate tunnels. Above each one of those 4 tunnels, there will be a sign. The sign has the name of the person who is to use that tunnel. All four of you are to enter your respective tunnels at the same time. Once you've reached the end of your individual tunnels, you'll each end up in separate small rooms. Each of those rooms will have four doors, and those doors will be numbered.

There will be a clue, in an envelope on the floor, waiting for each of you in your rooms. You must figure out, ON YOUR OWN, which of the four doors to open by solving a riddle. And by the way, all four of you will have different riddles.

If you choose the correct door, it will open to a new tunnel. That tunnel will take you to an area where you will reunite with anyone else on your team who also chose the correct door. The other three doors in each room, the incorrect ones, spell doom for you all! (Don't worry, it doesn't trigger a bomb or anything like that...)

If anyone twists the knob of a wrong door, it triggers a mechanism that locks all sixteen doors. And since all of you must get through this challenge for it to be considered complete, that means no one can make even a single mistake!

Nicola looked at her three teammates, wondering who was going to react first. It appeared as if everyone was still in a state of shock.

After a fairly long silence, Claire said, "Guys, this is not good. I mean, you three have done plenty of these kinds of challenges. But I've only done, like, a few."

"That's not true," Nicola said quickly, hoping to quash Claire's fear and negativity. "You haven't faced so many challenges *under these circumstances*, but you have been doing lots of the ones that we have been creating for each other over the past few months."

"She's right," Peter added. "And not only are you really good at puzzles, you are also exceptionally smart. There's no way that trio's riddle will fool you."

Claire's face reddened a little. It was pretty embarrassing to hear how highly they thought of her.

"I had a feeling that one of the challenges was going to be an individual one," Peter continued. "Well, it was probably more like a *fear* than a feeling."

"Anyway, guys," Neil said quite loudly. "Whether all together or all apart, a puzzle is a puzzle."

"That doesn't make much sense," Claire said while giggling.

"Uh... I suppose it doesn't," Neil admitted, giggling a little himself. "But how much of what I say usually does?"

"Well, I've known you a long time," Peter said to Neil. "And I've become pretty good at translating what you say into what you mean. I think what he means is, well, uh..."

"You said you understood him!" Nicola said with a laugh.

Now everyone was laughing. But it didn't sound like genuine "that was funny" laughter. Part of it, or possibly even most of it, could easily be interpreted as nervous laughter.

"Guys," Peter suggested. "Let's sit down for a while before we do this."

Since they were not looking forward to the pressure of what lay ahead, no one objected to Peter's idea. They all sat cross-legged in a circle, so close that their knees were touching.

"I won't pretend I am the superstar coach who is going to give you a pep talk about how to hit the game-winning shot," he began. "All I want to say is this: Take. Your. Time... Read the riddle. Reread it. And then reread it again and again. There's no need to rush. Take as long as you need. And DON'T put your hand on a doorknob until you are a hundred and ten percent sure it's the correct one."

"Got it," Neil replied, somewhat unaware that he really didn't need to reply. Claire and Nicola also nodded, indicating they had caught the gist of what Peter had just said.

Peter stood up. "Okay, team," he said. "Let's do this."

Peter first, followed by Claire and Nicola (who were holding hands because they were so scared) and then finally Neil entered the long tunnel. It twisted and weaved a few times. And in a couple of spots, parts of the walls and ceiling had crumbled off, so they had to walk very cautiously.

Less than two minutes later, they arrived at the chamber that had been described in the note. There were two torches, one on each of the side walls, providing sufficient light. On the far side of this small chamber, were the entrances to the four individual tunnels. And just like the note had said, each of their names, written on wooden boards, were nailed above the four tunnels.

Neil's name was above the tunnel on the far left. Nicola's was beside his. Then Claire's and finally Peter's.

Some light was emanating from each tunnel, so at least they weren't going to have to trek through them in darkness.

"Okay, now I am officially scared," Neil said, gulping.

"If you're scared," Claire said softly. "Then I am way, way scared." She held her hands out to show how badly they were shaking.

Neil took both of her hands: they were ice cold. That was partially due to the fact that it was cold down in these chambers, but also due to human physiology. (He vaguely remembered hearing somewhere that it is was part of each human's "fight or flight" response.)

"The longer we wait, the more scared we'll get," Nicola said.

"Yup," Peter remarked, agreeing with her completely. "Let's go and get this over with."

Peter walked and stood at his tunnel's entrance. Each member of his team, despite how unbelievably terrified they were, went to their tunnels as well.

"I know this is not the correct thing to say," Peter said with a smile, "but see you all on the other side." He giggled at his poor choice of phrase. "Anyway, you know what I mean."

CHAPTER 27

Neil's teeth chattered as he nervously walked down his tunnel. He wasn't consciously attempting to measure its length, but made a ballpark estimate that it was between twenty and thirty meters long. It gently curved to the left the entire time, which made it that much harder to guess how long it was. As he got further and further along, he finally spotted the "room" at the end. It was a lot smaller than he had expected. It was only a meter deep, and a meter and a half wide. The four doors, which had large yellow numbers painted on them, were significantly narrower than typical doors. And there was only a five-centimeter gap between each one: just enough space for the door jams.

"Yikes," Neil said to himself, feeling somewhat claustrophobic. He bent down to pick up the single white envelope which contained his unique riddle: the one which he now had to solve... by himself... with no help... double yikes.

Neil,

The 1,2,3,4 on the doors represent January 1st,

2nd, 3rd, and 4th. Imagine that today is January 4th. What day was the day before yesterday's tomorrow?

HI READER! (^_^)
BEFORE READING ON, SEE IF YOU CAN FIGURE OUT NEIL'S RIDDLE!
GOOD LUCK!

Neil paused. He had just read through the entire note without taking in a single word of it. "C'mon, man," he said to himself, slapping his cheeks a couple times. "Pull yourself together."

He reread the note, a lot slower this time. He enunciated every word carefully, even pausing when he got to the commas and period.

He now fully understood what the riddle was asking, but Neil felt it was going to require some math skills to solve, and math was not one of Neil's strengths. And his confidence in solving math word problems was almost non-existent.

"I've got no hope unless I write this down," he mumbled to himself.

Following Peter's advice, (well, it was actually Peter's *order*) Neil had kept the paper and pencil that he had used at Mr. Winchester's home. He sat down, leaned against the wall, and wrote "*1, 2, 3, 4*," from left to right on the page. Then he put his pencil on the *4*.

"Yesterday's tomorrow," he said slowly, "would be today." As soon as he finished saying that, he moved his pencil to the *3* and then returned it to the *4*. "So we are still on January 4th. And the day before that," he said while moving the pencil one number to the left, "is the 3rd."

Neil looked up at the door with the *3* on it.

"Pete told me to make sure I was TOTALLY sure before touching a knob," he said aloud. "I better to this again."

Neil went through the same thing one more time, and once again ended up with his pencil on the *3*.

"Alright," he said. "Now comes the moment of truth." He walked up, grabbed the cold doorknob of door 3 and twisted it. It opened, revealing a tunnel behind it.

"Yessss!" he said loudly while pumping his fist. "The Neilster is the man!"

* * *

Nicola's nerves were fairly under control as she walked down her tunnel. Her tunnel was a little longer than Neil's (but she had no way of knowing that...) and was straight for the first half, and then gently curved to the left for the second half.

"What a tiny room," she said as she entered the little chamber with the four doors in it.

"Ah, Mr. Note," she said to the envelope as she picked it up off the ground. "What bizarre riddle do you have in store for me?"

With a reasonable amount of confidence, she took out the note and read it to herself, slowly and silently:

Nicola,

The 1,2,3,4, on the doors represent 1st place, 2nd place, 3rd place, and 4th place in a 100-meter dash. The four participants in this race are Christopher, Anthony, Jason, and Robert.

Christopher, who is usually the fastest by far, couldn't pull off the win this time.

Anthony got off to a spectacular start, but ran out of gas toward the end.

Jason had a great race, and even though he beat Christopher by a nose, he didn't win.

Robert ran, quite possibly, the best race of his entire life. But he saw Christopher pass him just before he crossed the finish line.

What place was Robert?

HI AGAIN READER! (^_^)
IF YOU ENJOYED TRYING TO FIGURE OUT NEIL'S RIDDLE, WHY DON'T YOU GIVE NICOLA'S RIDDLE A SHOT, TOO?

"Talk about a long riddle," she muttered to herself, after reading the whole thing. "It's more like an essay. I'm going to have to re-enact this one in order to figure it out."

Since Nicola was not a six-year-old girl anymore, she did not carry around a bunch of dolls in her bag which she could have used as the "racers." But she did, of course, have some paper that she could tear into pieces, fold in half, and then place on the ground so they "stood up." She also took out her pencil and wrote "C, A, J, R" on the folded papers. Then she placed her bag on the ground a meter or so away, to use as a makeshift finish line.

Nicola lined the four boys up along the wall, imagining it as their start line.

"What I need to do is begin with the clues that contain at least two names," she said.

She began with the Jason clue, and picked up the two people it referred to, *Jason* and *Christopher*. "Well, all I know for sure is that Jason finished ahead of Christopher," she said. She put *Jason* about five centimeters away from the finish line, and *Christopher* five centimeters behind him.

Then she moved onto the Robert clue, as it also contained two names. "It says Christopher passed Robert before the finish line," she said softly. "That's just another way of saying Robert finished after Christopher." She placed *Robert* about five centimeters behind *Christopher*.

She looked at the position of the three "sprinters." Currently, Jason was in first, Christopher in second, and Robert in third. Now she had to deal with Anthony.

"I need to go through the other two clues," she said, "really, really carefully."

Just then, she felt a cold and sudden burst of wind.

"Oh?" she said with surprise. "Maybe someone just figured out their clue and opened the right door. That would've caused a little gust of wind due to a slight change in air pressure."

She turned back to her racers. "The first clue says Christopher didn't win," she said, wanting to double-check that she hadn't made any mistakes. "And I have him in second place right now, so that works."

Then she picked up Anthony. "Sounds like Anthony was leading at the start," she continued, "but ran out of juice. So that means he finished either second or third or fourth."

She reread the Anthony clue. "But how do I figure out which of those he was?" she asked herself. "I mean, it doesn't say."

Nicola held onto *Anthony*, and calmly read all four clues again. "I'm missing something here," she said. "And probably something, like, crazily obvious."

She sat down and leaned against the wall, reading the clues "ridiculously slowly" this time. (This was a technique that Peter had taught her ages ago...) Then she spotted it. "Got it!" she yelled. "The Jason clue says that he DID NOT win. And I currently have him in first. That can mean only one thing, then. Anthony won! Or did he... yeah, he must have! Bingo!!"

She placed *Anthony* down so he was against the edge of her bag. Then in a silly, deep, "broadcaster" voice, held up her pencil to her mouth like a microphone and announced, "What a final! But we'll have to wait for the photo replay to confirm the outcome. Hold on, everyone..." She paused a bit, giggled at herself, and then continued, "The results are now in! Anthony takes the gold! Jason the silver! Christopher the bronze! And Robert comes in an unfortunate fourth."

She kept giggling after finishing this announcement, since this type of silly behavior was very "un-Nicola" like. Her giggle then escalated into an all-out roaring laugh.

When her laughing fit finally ended, she stood up and picked up her bag. She strode confidently over to door four. "Sorry, Bob. Oops, I mean, Robert," she said. "But every race has to have its loser." She grabbed the doorknob of door 4 and twisted it... a tunnel! She'd done it!

* * *

Claire was terrified beyond words as she slowly shuffled her way down her tunnel. Hers began the same as Nicola's, going straight for the first half. Then it veered to the right just past the halfway point.

By the time she reached the tiny room with the four doors, her heart was pounding so hard that it hurt. She felt faint and dizzy, almost like she was about to pass out. This feeling was a first for her, as she was always overflowing with confidence when she captained the volleyball team in Grade 9.

She sat down on the cold stone floor, crossed her legs and closed her eyes. She knew she needed to calm herself down before even picking up the envelope.

It took over three minutes, but after a series of deep breaths, she'd managed to get her pulse rate back under eighty. (She knew it was eighty because she measured it by counting the number of beats in fifteen seconds with a couple fingers from her left hand on the inside of her right wrist, and then multiplying that number by four.) Her usual resting pulse rate was under sixty—which she knew from being an athlete—but eighty was low enough for now, all things considered.

The envelope which lay on the floor just to her right threatened to drive her heart rate up again, but she mentally refused to let it do so.

"Not this time," she said to herself strongly. "You've got this, Claire. You're in charge."

She removed the note and read the message aloud:

Claire,

The 1,2,3,4 on the doors represent the time span of 1 hour, 2 hours, 3 hours, and 4 hours.

You went to bed at 11:00 p.m. and you set your alarm for 5:00 a.m. the next morning. After an hour of staring at the ceiling, wide awake, you decided to change your alarm to go off an hour later. Then you slept like a baby for a while, but woke up three hours before your alarm was going to ring. You tossed and turned and tossed and turned and didn't get back to sleep until the time you had originally set your clock to go off. The next time you woke up was when your alarm starting ringing.

How many hours, in total, did you sleep for that night?

HI AGAIN READER! (^_^)
IF YOU ENJOYED TRYING TO SOLVE THE PREVIOUS TWO RIDDLES, WHY DON'T YOU TRY TO SOLVE CLAIRE'S AS WELL?

Claire rolled her eyes. "Why," she asked herself, "did my riddle have to be a novel instead of just a sentence or two? This is like one of those bonus questions that Mr. Zalasky puts at the end of his math tests. The ones that no one; well, no one other than Pete, ever manages to get right."

Claire put the note in her back pocket and then began stretching. Yes, stretching. Claire was both an athletic and academically talented young woman. She was also a strong believer in the mind-body connection. So Claire knew when her body felt good and relaxed, that her mind was more efficient. And vice versa. By getting her shoulders, back, legs, and neck a little more limber, she was expecting her mind to get super-charged to solve this riddle.

While stretching, she heard something. Soon after the noise, she felt a short, cold burst of air. "That must mean either Nik, Neil or Pete just opened the right door in their room," she said. Her comment threatened to drive her pulse up again, but she nipped it in the bud. "No way, brain," she ordered herself. "I'm the boss right now."

Claire took out her pencil and paper and leaned against one of the walls in the most comfortable way possible. First, she drew a long straight line on her page. Then she put little ticks on the lines every few centimeters, which were each going to represent a specific time. She wrote *11:00* at the far left of the line, *12:00* above the first tick to the right, *1:00* above the next tick, and continued until the end of the line, where she wrote *6:00*.

All I've gotta do," she said to herself, "is read it slowly. I'll draw wavy lines for awake hours and zigzag ones for asleep hours. It can't be that hard."

Claire tediously read each sentence three times, which was another technique Peter had taught her. (Peter had told her that careful people double-check, but perfectionists triple-check).

Once she was done all the reading and line drawing,

she ended up with:

A wavy line from 11:00 to 12:00.
A zigzag line from 12:00 to 3:00.
A wavy line from 3:00 to 5:00.
A zigzag line from 5:00 to 6:00.

"Three hours here plus one hour there," she said to herself, "totals four." She looked up at door 4, back down at her paper, and then at the door again. "Sorry Petey, but I ain't triple checking my triple-checked answer." She giggled at that comment. "If I had needed to check each and every math problem this many times, I never would have had enough time to finish the easy math tests we did back in Grade 2!"

But then, she started rethinking what to do... Did it need to be looked at one more time??

"Claire, you know you're right," she said loudly, like she was being her own coach. She whistled while walking up to door 4, heart racing again. But this time it was from excitement rather than nervousness. She opened the door and looked at the tunnel on the other side.

"Yeah!" she said in a deep, loud voice, just like she always did after hitting a blistering spike in a volleyball match.

CHAPTER 28

Peter's tunnel slowly curved to the right from start to finish. Of course, Peter couldn't *just walk*—as that would be way too boring—so he began counting his steps, a habit that seemed to happen for him as unconsciously as blinking or breathing.

When he reached the room at the end, he paused for a few seconds before actually entering it.

"Wow," he said softly. "This certainly wasn't what I was expecting."

Peter had figured that since the majority of the rooms and chambers of the old ruins here at Silverhead Mountain had always been quite large and grand, that his "room with four doors" was going to be big as well.

"This place is tiny," he said.

The tininess was surprising, but the most bizarre thing was that it looked as if a kindergartener had been given a piece of yellow chalk and told to write the alphabet on the walls. The letters, each of which were written numerous times, were all jumbled up and in various sizes and locations. (Of course, a kid hadn't written them, but whoever did must have been half asleep, as very few were straight.) Many were written sideways or on angles, and some were even upside-down. It reminded Peter of the "pasta in a can" his dad used to serve them when his mom went out for dinner with friends. There was no easier way of "cooking" than just dumping two cans of that alphabet pasta stuff in a bowl, setting the microwave for two and a half minutes, and pressing start. But hey, kids would never complain, they loved the stuff.

He slapped his cheeks twice. "Pete, stay focused," he said to himself. Peter's overly active mind could be flipped on a dime. This was apparently another common symptom of ADHD.

"Pete, the puzzle," he said to himself. "Right now, it's all about the puzzle."

He picked up the envelope, taking deep breaths while doing so, and then closed his eyes as he removed the note.

"They are all counting on you," he said, eyes still shut. "You are NOT going to let them down."

He opened his eyes and looked at the very short note.

$$A \rightarrow A = 2$$
$$I \rightarrow I = 4$$
$$Y \rightarrow Y = ?$$

HI READER! (^_^)
WELL, PETER'S RIDDLE IS DEFINITELY HARDER TO FIGURE OUT THAN THE OTHER THREE, BUT EVERYONE LOVES A GOOD CHALLENGE, DON'T THEY? HAVE A GO AT THIS ONE, IF YOU DARE!

"What the...?" he said loudly, flabbergasted at what he was looking at.

"They've obviously given me the most confusing one to solve," he grumbled. "The losers... well, I'll show them who's the boss."

"First things first," he said to himself. "Clearly the answer has something to do with the letters *A*, *I*, and *Y*. So I might as well start by counting how many of each has been written on the walls."

"Four *A's*, nine *I's*, and six *Y's*," he said after counting. He tried to conjure up a way to apply some math here. "Hold on," he said, "There are 4 *A's*. If I divide 4 by 2, I get 2. Let me think... so what if I try dividing the number of *I's* by 2 as well? 9 I's, divided by 2, would equal 4.5, right?

He paused before continuing. "But in theory, if I ignore the digit to the right of the decimal point, then I'd have 4, exactly like it says in the clue. And then for the Y's, of which there are 6, if I divide that by 2, I get 3."

Peter looked at door 3. "Hey, door three!" he said loudly to it. "Are you the real thing?"

But Peter was not satisfied with his first attempt at a solution.

"Maybe I counted wrong," he said to himself. "Maybe there are only 8 *I's*, in which case my theory would be more solid."

Peter did a recount. Not only did he double-check the number of *I's*, but he did the same for the other two letters as well. And to ensure he didn't count each one more than once, he took out a chocolate bar from his backpack, and drew a "chocolate slash" through each one as he counted them.

"Nope," he said when he was done. "Same as the first count. Well, when Plan A doesn't work, go to Plan B."

Peter was referring to a saying Mr. Jacobson, his Grade 8 science teacher, used to say all the time. In other words, if your first idea is wrong, just try something else!

Peter paced around the room, even though there was very, very little space to actually "pace" in. He kept reciting the contents of the short note, substituting in the word "something" for the arrows.

"Think it through, Pete," he said to himself. *A* something *A* equals 2. *I* something *I* equals 4. *Y* something *Y* equals..."

When this led to nothing, without even breaking stride, he switched to reciting, "Four *A's*, nine *I's*, six *Y's*. Four *A's*, nine *I's*, six *Y's*."

His legs and mouth stopped almost simultaneously. "Hold on," he said very suddenly, as if he was finally onto something. "This might have to do with how each letter sounds. *I's* sounds like *eyes*, right? And *Y's* sound like *whys*... But wait, the number of *whys* can't be counted, can they?"

Peter's frustration level was on the rise. His first idea had been "okay," but not solid enough. And his second one was worthless. If there had been anything on the floor to kick, like a box or something, he would have taken his frustration out on it. He took a couple of breaths and tried to talk himself down.

"C'mon Pete, you know what to do. Option C," he said, thinking about Mr. Jacobson again.

But before contemplating what to do next, he needed to get those first two ideas completely out of his mind. He lay down flat on the ground and spread his arms and legs out. He closed his eyes and pictured "a smiling Mr. Winchester who had just been rescued by Peter and his team." He was thoroughly enjoying this image and wanted to continue thinking about it, but a brick floor in winter was not the ideal place for rest.

He opened his eyes and looked up at the ceiling. Then he twisted his neck sideways and looked over at the messy letters on the walls again.

Peter then jumped up. (Well, as fast as an inflexible kid with poor coordination skills can...) He closed his eyes again, as keeping them closed made it much easier to create better mental pictures.

"Yes," he said softly once. "Yes... YES!!" he yelled. "Option C! You are the one!"

Peter had just completed the triple-check in his mind, so he didn't need to wait another second. He grabbed the doorknob which he knew was going to open to the tunnel, and twisted it with zero doubt.

"Hello, Mr. Dark Tunnel," he said proudly while entering it. "Yes. Yes! Yes!!" he yelled again, jumping excitedly as he headed to reunite with his team.

CHAPTER 29

"Hey, listen to that," Neil said to Claire and Nicola, "I can hear Pete coming!"

"Pete, we all made it!" Nicola yelled well before Peter was within sight.

"I'm coming, ya'll," Peter yelled back with a hillbilly accent. "I don't wanna trip me-self, so I'm just takin' it slow!"

As soon as Peter got there, all four pulled each other in close for a long, strong group hug.

"We totally have to tell each other what our riddles were," Peter began. "I mean, I gotta hear about the ones you guys just figured out. But not right now. First, we gotta get this last challenge done and dusted, and rescue Bradley and Mr. Winchester. Then we can compare away until our hearts are content!"

Although he hadn't planned it that way, Peter's speech had been just what was needed: both a display of respect and admiration for his teammates, and a reminder that they weren't quite finished yet.

"Well," Neil said, pointing at the yellow arrow on the floor. "At least we don't have to guess how to get to the final challenge, do we?"

The arrow pointed to the entrance of another tunnel, one that looked much older and narrower than the ones they had just come through. Plus this tunnel appeared to be in very, very bad shape.

They could only see a couple of dimly burning torches along the walls, which meant they'd barely be able to see anything while walking through it.

"Let's take the two torches from this room with us," Claire suggested. "You know, it would be like carrying medieval flashlights."

"Nice thinking," Nicola said, giving her a high-five.

"Okay, how about this?" Neil added. "Pete and I will hold the torches. I'll go first, and we walk in single file, very slowly. Pete takes the rear."

"Perfect," Peter said. "That way you can pick the safest route, and I'll be able to light it up well enough for Claire, Nik, and I to see where we are stepping."

The two torches in the chamber weren't fixed to the walls: they were just resting in some type of holder. Removing them was pretty easy.

"Dudes," Neil said, holding his torch up high. "Don't you think what we are about to do would look cool in a movie?"

Everyone laughed.

"Not just *what we are about to do*," Nicola remarked. "I'd say the last few years, you know, all the crazy stuff going on with Zoltan and Xavier and the challenges would turn into a massively successful movie series!"

"You bet it would!" Peter exclaimed.

"I wonder which Hollywood hunk would play me?" Neil asked, trying to keep a straight face.

Everyone burst into laughter again.

"Okay, sorry to rain on your parade," Peter said,

bringing everyone back to reality. "But let's go rescue my brother and Mr. Winchester. We can talk more about movie rights and being famous later."

"Roger, captain," Neil said, saluting Peter.

"Neil," Claire said, shaking her head. "You are the WEIRDEST person I've ever met."

"Or will ever meet," Neil replied quickly, giving her a kiss on the cheek.

Mood now lightened again, it was time to start moving. Neil took his first step into what looked like was going to be a very difficult tunnel to navigate.

CHAPTER 30

The tunnel was way longer and in much worse shape than they ever could have imagined. When they got to a spot about halfway along, they noticed that so much of the ceiling and walls had collapsed that they actually had to climb up and over the rubble. They needed to wriggle through a gap that was no more than sixty centimeters wide.

* * *

When they finally made it to the end of the tunnel, everyone other than Peter—who was already worrying about what was next—breathed a sigh of relief.

"That tunnel was brutal, man," Neil said. "Look at my left hand, and my knees."

Since Neil had been leading the way and holding a torch with one hand, he had slipped, tripped, fallen over, and skidded several times. The palm of his left hand had a few scrapes on it that were bleeding. And the knees of his jeans were ripped on both legs, and some blood was visible there too.

"We'd better disinfect those," Peter said, reaching into his backpack.

"Don't tell me you brought your entire medicine

cabinet with you?" Neil joked. "Pete and his bottomless backpack!"

"Just sit still," Peter instructed him. "And close your eyes."

First, he took out his water bottle, which was still eighty percent full, and poured some water over Neil's hand and knees.

"That wasn't too bad," Neil said, opening his eyes and preparing to stand up.

"Sit down, dude," Peter said to him with a grin. "I'm just getting started."

"Looks like your future husband may be interested in becoming a physician," Claire whispered to Nicola while nudging her a couple of times. She had said it quietly enough that only Nicola had heard her, and the reddening of Nicola's face indicated that perhaps she'd already pictured herself married to Peter one day.

Peter then took out a small hand towel, and dabbed Neil's hand and knees a few times to soak up the excess water.

"Okay, now comes the disinfecting part," Peter explained. "This might sting. A lot. But if I don't do it, your scratches might get infected. Nik and Claire, hold his shoulders so he doesn't try to squirm away."

Neil shut his eyes. That was lucky for him, as it meant he didn't see Peter remove the bottle of iodine and box of cotton swabs from his backpack. He took a swab, turned the bottle upside-down and waited until the iodine had soaked it sufficiently, and got ready to start. He held Neil's left wrist very firmly and began dabbing the scratches with the iodine-soaked swab.

"Weeouch!" Neil yelped in a high-pitched voice, trying his best to yank his hand away.

Peter said nothing in response. He just tightened his grip and got back to work. Once he was confident that he had disinfected Neil's hand sufficiently, he prepared a fresh swab and got started on the right knee first, and then the left.

Neil yelped, squirmed, wriggled, and even begged for Peter to, "Please just stop!" But Peter was focused. Totally focused.

"There you go, sir," Peter said once his work was done. "No need to worry about those scratches anymore."

Neil jumped up and walked a few steps away. It sounded like he was saying some four-letter words, but even if he was; no one could make them out. (But Peter also did the same thing every time his mom used iodine on his cuts.) Having a cut disinfected was no fun, but was necessary.

Pride somewhat damaged, but hand and knees now safe from infection, Neil walked back over to join his friends. As he was approaching them, a series of torches "magically" lit up all over the room they had recently entered. The light revealed what could be described as no less than magnificent. Unfortunately, magnificent in a bad way...

CHAPTER 31

What they were looking at was so fascinating and mysterious that all four of them were speechless.

They were standing on some sort of ledge, which was about three meters long and a meter and a half wide. The ledge dropped off into a huge dark pit. When they peered over the ledge to see how far it went down, there was no bottom in sight.

The ledge on the opposite side of the pit looked to be at least five or six meters away.

The opposite ledge itself had only two things of importance on it. The first was an archway, which likely led to a tunnel, and ultimately to where Bradley and Mr. Winchester were being held. And the second was what appeared to be a drawbridge, like the kind you'd find at medieval castles. (Back in those times, the only way to gain entrance to a castle was to have the drawbridge lowered over the moat.) The drawbridge they were looking at now was connected firmly to the opposite ledge, and was being held in a near-vertical position by thick chains which disappeared into holes in the stone ceiling.

But it was what was on their side that was the most

bizarre. There were numerous stone blocks, each about half the size of a shoebox. Each block was hanging on the end of a long chain. And similar to the drawbridge, these chains also disappeared into the ceiling above. Plus, each dangling block had a yellow number or symbol on it.

"Dudes," Neil said nervously. "This is, like, really, uh…"

The other three didn't know how to help Neil finish his sentence, as they all felt the same way as he did. Peter walked closer to the hanging blocks. While he did that, Neil and Claire went up to the walls, where numerous incomplete mathematical equations had been written in yellow on both sides.

"We've got all the numbers, zero through nine," Peter said while checking out the blocks. "A decimal point. A plus sign. A minus sign. A multiplication sign. A division sign. And an equals sign."

"What is this place?" Neil asked jokingly. "A mathematician's paradise? Or a torture chamber for people who suck at arithmetic?"

"And what do you make of all these equations on the walls?" Nicola asked. "Like, this one says $8x4=$, and that one says $3.2+8=$, but none of them have the answers written."

"No kidding, eh," Claire remarked. "It looks like a Grade 4 math test!"

They had been so preoccupied with the drawbridge, hanging blocks, and wall equations, that none of them had noticed the envelope on the floor. It wasn't until Neil stepped on it accidentally that they became aware of its existence.

"Oh," he said, sounding a little surprised. "So there is

a note this time." He pulled the note out of the envelope and read it aloud.

Your final challenge! You're almost there! (But as we all know, in this game, ALMOST means nothing...)

Allow us to explain your final challenge:

You must pull on ten of these hanging blocks, in the correct order, to trigger the drawbridge to lower.

You have 3 attempts. For each attempt, you can pull on each block only once. (Just in case you weren't reading slowly enough, if you pull the same block twice during an attempt, you automatically fail that attempt.)

You will know if you have made a mistake because a loud buzzer will sound. After it sounds, the blocks that you pulled down will shift back up to their original positions. Then you may start your next attempt.

Now I suppose you want a hint as to how to figure this out...

Well, you are a pretty clever group. Or at least that's what you'd like to think, right?

So you don't need any more hints, do you? Just look around!

"Yikes," Neil said without thinking. "This is N-O-T going to be easy."

"Certainly isn't," Peter said. "But think about how many times we have felt like this before." He paused, as a way to prepare to ram home his point. "And out of all those times, how many did we end up failing?"

"Zero!" Nicola said loudly.

"You got it!" Neil yelled. "A big, fat, gross, stinky zero!"

"Neil," Claire said, a little shocked by Neil's crudeness, "I don't think zeroes can be big, or fat, or gross, or—"

"Neilster!" Peter said, catching everyone by surprise. "You may use any and all adjectives you please to describe that Z-E-R-O!"

"I bet I know what you're planning to say next," Nicola said, looking at Peter.

"Be my guest, beautiful," he said, encouraging her to finish his speech for him.

"You're gonna say something like *if we've always done it before, then we're gonna do it again.*"

"Well, something like that," Peter admitted. "But I was also going to add one thing to that."

"Which is?" Claire asked.

Peter took a deep breath, exhaled it, and then got a very serious expression on his face. "Bradley and Mr. Winchester are depending on us," he said. "We can't let them down. I cannot, I will not, allow that to happen."

"Then let's do this!" Neil said confidently, putting his hands out for everyone to receive high-fives.

"Yeah," Peter said with vigor. "Game on!"

CHAPTER 32

"Pete," Nicola said, "I don't mean to put any pressure on you, but... uh... where, or, uh... how do we start?"

"Yeah, you're the math man, dude," Neil said, slapping Peter on the back.

Peter smiled and took a few seconds to look at each member of his team. They all respected and admired him, and even more importantly, they were also kind people and genuine friends.

"I do indeed like math," he said, feeling his voice starting to get shaky. "But not even a *fraction* as much as I like you three." His lips were now quivering, an unintentional display of how emotional he was. "I will... do... whatever I can to solve this. I've got to. But I need you three to have my back. Wait, that sounded a little weird, didn't it?"

Peter's word choice was not the best, but he had effectively made his point.

"Your request is our command," Neil said. "Wait, that's not right... Your wish is our... C'mon, what's that expression again?"

Comical Neil, though completely by accident, had once again managed to lighten the mood. Good on him.

"I'm currently only in the brainstorming stage of this puzzle," Peter replied. "But seeing as how there is a *times*, *divided by*, *plus*, *minus*, *equals*, and *decimal point*, I think we can be safe in assuming that we need to make a math equation. And in all likelihood, one that is mathematically sound."

"Oh," Nicola said. "You mean, like 1+2×3=9, right? Oh wait, that only uses seven blocks, so that wouldn't work. But you know what I mean."

"Umm..." Peter said, eyes looking upward and to the left: something that not only Peter did, but most humans do while thinking. "Well, both yes and no. Yes to the fact that we have to use ten blocks. But no to the fact that your example was mathematically wrong."

"Wrong?" Nicola asked. "1+2 is 3, right? And 3×3 is 9."

"Ah, I think I get what he's after," Neil commented. "Don't you all remember when Mrs. Baird taught us *P.E.M.D.A.S.* in Grade 7?"

"Good old pemdas," Peter smiled, "is exactly what I'm referring to. You know, the order of operations: Parenthesis, exponents, multiplication, division, addition, subtraction. Remember that when doing a calculation, multiplication and division must be done before addition and subtraction."

"Oh, I remember that now," Nicola said. "So I should have done 2×3 first, which is 6. Then added 1, for a total of 7."

"Yup," Peter answered.

"It's going to be confusing to create one that will work, don't you think?" Neil asked.

"Without any clues, it would be," Peter answered. "But look at the walls. That's where the hints are. We just have to, well... find them, I guess. I can't tell you where to start looking, as I don't really know."

"That's what we are here for, Petey," Neil said. "We'll look at numbers on the wall on your behalf."

Another senseless comment from Neil, but they all laughed a little. Good on him, again.

Thankfully, they all still had their papers and pencils with them. Plus, Peter reached in his backpack and handed them all erasers.

"Is there anything you didn't bring?" Neil joked. "I'd love for you to whip out four calculators next!"

"I wish," Peter smiled. "I only wish." But Peter had the absolute worst poker face in the world, so everyone knew instantly that he was hiding something.

"You do have a calculator in there, don't you?" Nicola said playfully, pinching the back of Peter's neck.

Now quite red-faced, Peter reached into his backpack again and triumphantly pulled out his calculator.

"Petey," Neil remarked. "You are a true mystery. I can't even imagine why anyone would carry a calculator around with them."

"Good," Peter replied, "'Cause I wasn't planning on telling you anyway."

More laughter.

He placed the calculator on the ground near the entrance. "Since I only brought one," he said, "I'll leave it here. And anyone can use it whenever they want."

"And I suppose *you* will be doing all the math in your head, right?" Claire asked Peter.

"*All* the math, no," he answered. Then he winked once. "But most of it, yes."

They each set out to look more closely at the walls, pencils and papers in hand. There were so many equations to look at that they literally could start anywhere.

Basically, they were all doing the same type of thing: calculating the answers of any two of the incomplete equations, and then seeing how (or if) they could add or subtract those two numbers to produce an answer that didn't use any digit more than once.

* * *

About ten minutes after beginning—which was way too much math for anyone other than Peter—they noticed Claire walk over and pick up the calculator again. Since it wasn't the first time she had done so, neither Peter nor anyone else reacted. They just kept thinking through their own ideas.

"Guys!" she yelled. "I think I've got it! Look! 3×9=27. And 84÷7=12. I just confirmed that one on Pete's calculator. So if we take 27, and subtract 12 from it, we get 15. Look, the math works. And no digit is used more than once."

Peter looked quickly over her math.

$$3 \times 9 - 84 \div 7 = 15$$

"You got it, babe!" Peter yelled excitedly.

"Excuse me, fine sir," Neil said, bumping Peter lightly in the hip. "Please leave the referring to Claire as *babe* to me, her boyfriend."

That comment sure got all of them laughing.

"Claire," Peter said, "Awesome job! Please do the honors, and pull the blocks in that order."

She handed her paper to Peter and walked up to the *3*. She pulled it and noticed it came down about ten centimeters. Then they heard a loud click from somewhere in the ceiling. She let go of the block, and it remained in its new lower position.

"No buzzer!" Neil said happily. "We are golden!"

"Next, the multiplication sign," Peter told Claire.

She walked over and pulled the "×" block. It came down just like the *3* had, and was followed by another click from above. But right after the click, a loud buzzer went off, startling all of them. Then both of the blocks she had pulled down returned to their original positions.

"What?" Neil said in confusion. "Why?

Peter looked down at the paper again. The math was right. It should be working.

Nicola politely asked Peter if she could take a look at Claire's notes, without saying exactly why. A few seconds later, she looked up at the other three. "I'm afraid," she explained, "we overlooked, or maybe I should say *missed*, a little error in Claire's solution. Hers requires eleven blocks to be pulled, not ten. I just counted carefully. Twice. Look."

Peter quickly snatched the paper back and counted for himself. "Oops," he announced. "My bad. I should have spotted that."

"No, Pete," Claire said, "I made the mistake, not you."

"It wasn't a mistake," Peter said, patting a deflated Claire on the back. "And think of it this way, we now know the first block in the solution is the *3*, right?"

CHAPTER 33

"You're just trying to make me feel better, even though I screwed up," Claire remarked. "But for what it's worth, thanks."

"I was being totally serious," Peter replied quickly. "It's awesome that we now know the first block to pull. Knowing that eliminates so many possibilities."

"Oh, so... that did help?" Claire asked, perking up a little.

"Totally," Peter answered. "Alright guys, figure out an equation that starts with a 3. And remember that the *times* does not come right after the *3*."

They split up again and continued where they'd left off, but with a much narrower range of focus now. Surely someone would come up with the answer eventually. Another big plus they had on their side was the fact that no time limit was being imposed.

"Pete," Neil said, walking up beside him. "I know I'm the worst at math by far, but... well..."

"Let's hear it," Peter said supportively. "And you don't suck at math. You just never do your homework. That's why you make so many careless mistakes on your tests."

"Never thought of it that way," Neil replied, a tad

more energized than before that compliment. "Okay, it seems like we are all trying to create a long equation where the equals sign is near the end. You know, like A+B×C÷D=. But when I look at all the stuff written on the walls, everything is something like A+B= or C×D=. So that got me thinking. What if we try to find two equations on the walls that produce the same answer? Then all we have to do is put the *equals sign* in the middle of the equation."

During Neil's long and academic-sounding speech, both Claire and Nicola had gravitated a little closer, out of curiosity.

"That certainly could work," Peter replied. "I like your thinking. Let's give it a go. Not only is your plan very feasible, it's also much easier than what we've been doing up till now."

They split up for a third time, writing down every equation and the answer to each one. Peter had given each person on his team a specific section of the wall to do, so he knew they wouldn't miss any. The plan was to compare papers and search for any matches as soon as they were ready.

* * *

About fifteen minutes later, they all sat down and put their papers side by side. Claire, drawing on her leadership skills, doled out some instructions. "Okay, Nik," she announced. "You take the calculator. Neil, you read the equations to her. This is how we are going to double-check that our answers are all correct. If any answer is wrong, say stop, and we'll change it."

Peter took advantage of this opportunity to calm himself down a little. His bad habit of catastrophizing was trying to come to the forefront of his mind, and he needed to push it away.

* * *

Of all the equations, of which there were around a hundred in total, only two had been calculated incorrectly. (And both of those were on Neil's page.)

"Okay, guys," Claire said. "Now all we have to do is scan until we find the same answer for two."

There was probably a more efficient way of doing this, but since they didn't feel like thinking up one, they just began randomly picking an answer, and then looking up and down the other pages for a match.

"I found one!" Nicola shouted. "Look! This one on Pete's page and this one on Claire's. The answer for both is 15.5!"

They all leaned in close. "She's right," Claire said. "Now we just gotta make sure it uses ten, you know, ten blocks."

Peter wrote it down.

$$62 \div 4 = 3.1 \times 5$$

"Mathematically speaking," he said he a professor-like voice, "it works! And it requires exactly ten blocks!

"But wait," Nicola commented before anyone stood up to start pulling on the blocks. "It has to start with a 3, doesn't it?"

"Whew, thanks for reminding me," Peter said. He erased what he had just written and then wrote:

$$3.1 \times 5 = 62 \div 4$$

"Neil," Peter instructed, "since you were the one who

got us started on the right track, you can be in charge of pulling the blocks this time. I'll read them out one by one."

"Roger that," Neil said, standing up and saluting Peter.

"Go, Neilster, go!" Claire called out.

The whole group smiled and laughed again.

"Okay, let's do this," Peter began. "Three."

Neil pulled the *3*, and they all heard the click.

"Decimal point," Peter said next.

Neil pulled that block, heard the click... No buzzer.

"One!" Peter said loudly.

Neil pulled the *1*. Just like the previous two blocks, it was correct.

"Multiplication sign!" Peter said loudly, unable to contain his excitement.

Neil remained calm, not wanting to screw this up. He walked over to the "×" block, double-checked to make sure it wasn't the "+" block, and pulled it. Another click. But then a loud buzzer! And then those four blocks moved back up to their original positions.

"What?!" Claire yelled. "Not again!"

"I pulled the right one!" Neil said, wanting to confirm he hadn't done anything wrong.

Peter, now visibly shaken up, started pacing around in a figure eight. His friends knew by now that pacing in a circle meant thinking, but a figure eight meant Peter was in a more panicked state. They also were worried that interrupting him with a comment, or even something as simple as a hug, could do more harm than good.

Nicola, Neil, and Claire sat down and leaned against the wall. They remained completely silent. They also avoided all eye contact with Peter. They simply listened to the repetitive sound of his footsteps on the stone floor.

Now what??

CHAPTER 34

Peter was not intentionally avoiding his team, but he was completely in a world of his own. He just kept retracing his figure eight over and over, occasionally looking at the four papers or at the walls, and mumbling away indecipherably the whole time.

"How long does he usually do this?" Claire whispered to Neil at a volume that Peter definitely couldn't hear.

"For as long as he wants," Neil whispered back. "Could be a few minutes. Could be an hour."

"Yeah," Nicola added, also at a whisper. "And we've all learned by now that the best, well, the only thing to do when he gets like this is just wait it out. He'll either come up with the solution, or come back over here and ask for more help."

* * *

Peter looked at his watch. He had been pacing, non-stop, for twenty-seven minutes now. "What have I missed?" he said to himself for the umpteenth time. "Aargh... the ceiling?" He looked up at the ceiling, knowing it would probably yield nothing. "Nothing up there." And he also knew there was nothing on the floor. He had studied and studied the equations on the walls, but could find nothing new that would help.

And he had scanned through the four papers so thoroughly by now that he'd almost memorized everything on them. There were only two equations that produced the same answer.

He suddenly stopped pacing, which caused Neil, Nicola, and Claire to look up. Peter crushed the papers into a ball and angrily threw them toward the opposite ledge. It didn't even get close to reaching the target. It ended up falling down into the dark pit.

"Why did you do that, Pete?" Nicola asked, even though she wasn't sure if speaking now was advisable or not. "You figure something out?"

"NO!" Peter replied sharply. He paused for a few seconds before continuing. He reminded himself not to take his anger out on his team. "I'm sorry. I'm just angry. Not at you guys, at myself."

Peter's emotions could—and often did—change very quickly, and Nicola guessed that his anger was about to turn to despair. She jumped up and ran over to him.

"Pete," she said, forcing out a fake smile. "Don't worry."

"Don't worry" was probably the phrase that had been said to Peter more times than any other phrase in his entire life, especially when he was in elementary school. But Peter was NOT going let worry take over right now. Absolutely not.

"Don't worry, Nik," he replied. "'Cause I'm not worried at all. Sure, our first ideas haven't panned out. But we have not exhausted every single possibility. We'll figure this out, as a team."

"You bet!" Nicola said supportively, proud of the conviction in Peter's voice.

"Well, I'm glad we are all smiles again," Claire commented. "But, uh…what do we try next?"

"Should we read the note again?" Neil asked.

Peter's photographic memory didn't need to hear the note again. He knew EXACTLY what it said. But just because he had memorized its contents didn't mean the rest of his team had.

"Sure, sounds good," Peter said. "But before you start reading, remember this: We CAN figure this thing out. I promise you that. I, well, I guarantee it. As a team, we are invincible."

"Yeah," Nicola quickly followed. "So let's, like, imagine that we just walked in to start this challenge. You know, so someone reads the clue, and then we all start thinking, from scratch again. C'mon, with our talents, solving this puzzle will be as easy as pie!"

Peter put his hands on Nicola's shoulders and planted a big kiss right on her lips.

"Woohoo!" Neil shouted, having never seen Peter kiss Nicola before.

"You're, uh… welcome," Nicola said shyly, wiping the excess spit off her face, as Peter's kiss had inaccurately landed on part of her nose as well.

But upon closer inspection of his expression, it was clear that this wasn't just a "thank you for the encouragement" kiss.

"Pete," Nicola asked. "You've just figured it out, haven't you?"

"Maximilian, Aurora, Cynthia!" he yelled loudly. "You almost had us! But almost is NOT good enough!"

"Okay, so what did you just figure out?" Neil asked excitedly.

"Me?" Peter smiled. "Nothing, actually. Nik just

figured it out for us."

"Neil, you've still got the note, right?" Peter asked.

"Yup," Neil replied, pulling it out of his back pocket.

"Then could you, kind sir," Peter said with a smile, "please read us the final two sentences?"

"Uh, okay," he said. "The last two are, uh... *So you don't need any more hints, do you? Just look around!*"

"Look around. AROUND. That's the clue!" Peter explained.

But his audience had no idea where this was going. "Okay, sorry guys," he said. "I'm not very good at explaining what's going on in my brain sometimes. The solution hit me when Nik was trying to console me. She said not to worry, and that we could start this challenge all over again, or something like that. And then she said, it would be as easy as pie. Pie! Or, well, what I should say is *Pi*. The equations on the walls were red herrings to try and fool us."

Since they had no idea that he was referring to the mathematical Pi, Peter had to continue his explanation.

"The answer is the numerical value of Pi," he went on. "You know, the number used when calculating anything to do with circles."

"Pi?" Nicola asked. "But isn't that just 3.14?"

"That's the truncated version they teach for the sake of simplicity at school," Claire said, helping Peter out. "You know, so we can get fairly accurate answers without using a calculator. But Pi actually continues infinitely." She paused. "But does anyone know the first ten digits? I think I remember a few more, but not that many."

"Sure," Neil said, very unexpectedly. "3.14159265."

"Wow!" Claire said to him. "Why do you know that?"

"Never underestimate the—" Neil began saying.

"Don't say Neilster!" Claire said loudly, cutting him off.

The laughter was back in their group again.

"Never underestimate the Neilster!" Peter yelled. "As the Neilster, the awesomely cool Neilster, is completely correct!"

Peter wrote Pi on a page and got ready to begin.

"Since this is our final attempt, we can't afford to accidentally pull the wrong one," he explained. "So here's how we'll do this: I will say the number. Nik will walk up to it. Then Claire and Neil will both say 'okay' before she pulls the block. No mistakes."

"Wait guys, wait," Claire said, looking over Peter's shoulder at the paper, with a concerned expression. "The numbers 1 and 5 are each used twice."

"Oh," Peter said, "you're right." His mood began to fall instantly.

"Not to worry," Neil announced before Peter got too deflated. "Look, there are actually two *1* blocks, one right here and one other there. And there are two *5* blocks as well!"

Peter looked up. "You're right, there are! How did I not notice that when we first came in here?" Peter smiled from ear to ear. "Pi is definitely the solution," he announced. "Man, what a tricky puzzle!"

Peter began to say each number, and after an "okay" from Neil and Claire, Nicola pulled each block. As expected, the clicks were heard but the buzzer never went off.

When she pulled the tenth block, a *5*, the click was followed by a loud grinding noise. They watched in awe as the drawbridge slowly began to come down.

About a minute later, the top of the drawbridge

clanked down on their side. They now had a bridge to walk across toward victory!

Peter gingerly put one foot on the bridge. It was very strong and sturdy.

"It's safe," he announced. "But go slowly, and don't look down."

With Peter leading the way, they all walked cautiously in single file. When all four were on the opposite ledge, high-fives and hugs began.

"There's the exit," Neil said, pointing at the archway they were heading toward. He paused. "But I bet Mr. Winchester and Bradley are probably locked in cells or something. And we'll likely have to find a way to break them out."

"Let's hope you're wrong," Peter said. "But even if you are right about that, we can deal with it. C'mon, guys. Let's finish up this rescue. I'm getting hungry!"

CHAPTER 35

As soon as they entered the archway, which was the entrance to another long tunnel, they immediately spotted a white envelope on the ground.

"Not another one!" Neil said with a great deal of irritation in his voice. "That challenge we just did was supposed to be the last one."

Peter, who was running on fumes now, didn't really know how to reply. He quickly picked up the envelope and took out the note. "Nik, please," he said.

Nicola knew that this meant, once again, Peter wanted her to read the note. Having no reason not to, she unfolded the note and began reading aloud.

Well done! You are quite the group!

We hope that was a lot of fun for you four, as it was certainly interesting for us to set up.

At the end of this long tunnel is an unlocked door, which opens to the room where Bradley and Mr. Winchester are awaiting your arrival. (And no, there are no tricks or traps between here and there.)

Congratulations! (We hope you can pick up the sarcasm in that comment, ha ha ha!)

And we shall likely be seeing all six of you (you four plus Bradley and Mr. Winchester) again sometime soon. Possibly a lot sooner than you are expecting!

Maximilian, Aurora, Cynthia

"What are they talking about?" Neil asked. "They'll see us again? Why?"

"No clue," Claire said.

"Hey Pete," Nicola commented. "Even though this note says there are no more tricks or traps, I am guessing that you are not going to take their word for it."

"Definitely not," Peter said. "Corridor technique, team. We take no chances."

"The what technique?" Claire asked. She hadn't been part of the original team two and a half years ago when they learned the corridor technique from Mr. Winchester. Nicola quickly explained how it worked, and that it was the only way to guarantee safe passage down long tunnels or paths like this.

"Okay, I think I get it," she said after hearing the explanation. "So I do Bradley's old role. I go last, facing backward, arms locked with Nik and Neil. And I look for anything behind us that seems out of place. If I don't see anything weird, I say 'clear,' and then we all take another step."

"You're a quick learner, babe," Neil remarked.

Although Claire guessed that Neil's comment was intended as a compliment, another part of her interpreted it as being somewhat sarcastic. She gave Neil the evil eye, something that he hadn't seen from her in at least a couple of months.

Peter noticed it and jumped in to do some damage control. "She's a very quick learner," Peter said. "Without her, we'd never have made it this far."

Neil winked at Peter. Nice save!

The corridor technique was painstakingly slow and tedious, but it made sure they got where they were headed without any surprises.

* * *

It took them a good fifteen minutes before they finally reached the door at the end of the tunnel. There had been no traps along the way, just as promised in the note. So at least they knew the last part of the note was truthful. But they had serious doubts about whether the rest of it was true...

Peter's heart was racing so fast now that he felt faint and dizzy. His imagination was running through so many ridiculous possibilities about what could be lying on the other side of the door. He even pictured Mr. Winchester and Bradley hooked up to some evil contraption, being slowly lowered into a vat of molten metal.

A racing heart, which was making his breaths short and rapid, didn't mix well with the huge amount of dust down here. This caused Peter to start wheezing a little. He quickly reached into his backpack and pulled out his inhaler. He used it twice, the maximum allowable for an acute asthma attack.

Crisis averted?

Peter's friends were all aware of his occasional asthma attacks and knew that usually, with the help of his inhaler, he'd be fine.

* * *

"Okay, thanks guys," Peter said once his wheezing was relieved and his breathing was back to normal. "I'm good to go."

CHAPTER 36

All four of them were blown away (figuratively, not literally!) when they opened the door to the room holding Mr. Winchester and Bradley. The room they had just entered couldn't have been any more different from what they'd imagined the "holding cell" to look like.

They were pleasantly surprised when Bradley and Mr. Winchester, who both looked perfectly healthy, were waiting for them with open arms as soon as they walked in. This, of course, led to a round of happy hugs and big cheers. Peter was extremely relieved that they had finally achieved what they had set out to do, but also suspicious about what was going on.

This "cell" had a large power generator in it, with a big mess of cables heading in two directions. One pile went to a series of six or seven televisions, which were lined up on three big folding tables. The other set of cables went to a fridge, microwave, and heater. Mr. Winchester's rocking chair (the actual one from his house) and a very comfy-looking sofa were set up so that the two "detainees" could comfortably watch TV.

Peter walked over to look at what each TV was showing, since they certainly weren't television shows. It didn't take long for him to put two and two together.

"These monitors," Peter said, "are showing all the locations from the cameras that Maximilian, Aurora, and Cynthia set up. The ones they put at all the spots we just did our challenges at."

"You are correct," Mr. Winchester said.

"B-b-but..." Peter mumbled, thinking (or at least trying to think) about what this all meant. He paused as his mind rapidly ran through possibilities. "Oh, I get it! They brought in the rocking chair and sofa so you could have front row seats to watch us struggle with the puzzles." He paused again. "And then they could watch your reactions first-hand, right? Which I assume was amazingly entertaining for them... well, until right before we came in here. 'Cause that's when they must have bolted, right?"

Mr. Winchester came over, put his arm around Peter's shoulder, and took him over to the sofa.

"Oh, Peter," he said. "That mind of yours really does go into overdrive sometimes, doesn't it?"

He urged Peter to take a seat, and then went and slowly sat down in his rocking chair.

Bradley remained standing, but Neil, Nicola, and Claire came over quickly and squished together on the sofa. They didn't want to miss a single word of this.

"After kidnapping myself and Bradley," Mr. Winchester began, "they brought us here, to, well, be spectators to today's challenges. But shortly after they put us in here, they took Zoltan, who they had trapped in a container similar to the one we had used on Xavier, and left."

"They what?" Neil asked. "You mean they weren't even watching?"

"Well, if they were," Mr. Winchester replied, "they weren't doing so from in here."

"But why?" Nicola asked. "I mean, I thought that people from Sevlar loved everything about puzzles. Wouldn't they want to... uh... look, sorry to change topics so quickly, but weren't those three sent to Earth to *help* Zoltan?"

"Supposedly, yes," Mr. Winchester responded. "But if they came to help Zoltan, then why would they trap him? And more importantly, why did they know *how* to trap him?"

"Hold on," Peter said. "Are you saying that they somehow secretly planned this from the start? I mean, it said so in a note they wrote for us, but I figured they were just trying to scare us or something."

"Peter," Mr. Winchester replied. "The more I think about it, the more confident I've become that there is only one logical explanation."

"Which is ??" Peter asked.

"Those three must be working for Xavier," Mr. Winchester said.

"Xavier!?" Peter blurted out. "But he's jailed back on Sevlar! He couldn't have communicated or coordinated such a scheme from there."

"Unfortunately," Mr. Winchester continued, "when Xavier returned to Sevlar trapped in that box, a lot of people, especially the younger generation, strongly objected to him being held as a criminal."

"How did you find all this out?" Claire asked.

Mr. Winchester hesitated. He looked either unsure of himself, or concerned whether his young friends were ready to hear what he was about to say.

"A couple days ago," he began, "I dropped a tiny

recording device in the pocket of Maximilian's coat, as their suspicious behavior had been causing me many sleepless nights. I wish I had done so earlier, though. That way I might have had a chance to do something before it came to this. I heard them discussing everything: things like how many of the guards in charge of keeping Xavier captive are corrupt, and that Xavier now has more than six thousand followers and supporters."

"Hold up," Peter said. "The lead weather gods specifically chose those three to come to Earth, right? There's no way he could have corrupted the leaders!"

"Directly, no. But indirectly, it's definitely possible," Mr. Winchester replied. "I suspect that his followers threatened the lead weather gods. They could've said things like they would harm their families if they didn't select Maximilian, Aurora, and Cynthia."

"This is ludicrous," Peter said in a panic, standing up and walking around the room. "Okay, let's just assume, for now, that you're right. So they've got Zoltan. So that's that. They've taken him back to Sevlar, where Xavier gets to torture him or torment him or whatever. We, and by *we*, I mean the people of Earth, are really the ones who lose. We no longer have someone to control the weather."

"All true," Mr. Winchester replied.

"So it's over then," Peter said, sitting down. "I mean, we are no longer part of this. They don't need us anymore."

"But then why did that final note say that they would see us again soon?" Nicola asked.

"Unfortunately," Mr. Winchester said, slowly standing up. "I also had a feeling this wasn't over yet."

"I don't get it!" Peter said loudly. "Don't tell me they are planning to kidnap *us* next, take us to Sevlar, and force us to make puzzles for their entertainment?"

"That would be like being their slaves," Claire said.

"No, nothing like that," Mr. Winchester replied. "Look, I'll explain it on the way. There is somewhere we have to go. But first, I need to talk to Peter in private."

"Why?" Bradley asked, looking at Mr. Winchester like he didn't trust him anymore.

"Settle down, Bradley," the old man said. "Okay, if that makes you uncomfortable, I will speak to Peter in the back seat of the car as we drive there. Neil, you will drive Peter and I. Bradley, you take the two girls."

"Where are we going?" Neil asked.

"To my shed," Mr. Winchester replied.

"Why?" Neil asked again.

"As I just said, I'll explain it to Peter on the way," Mr. Winchester answered. "Bradley, follow us closely. And just to prove you can trust me, I'll give you this to hold on to."

Mr. Winchester handed Bradley a small bag with a zipper on it, which was about the size of a wallet. "That's my December supply of medications," he told Bradley. "Without those, my risk of having a heart attack or stroke goes sky high."

Bradley felt a little guilty, but a little guilt now was better than a ton of regret later. He accepted the box.

"Hold on a sec," Claire said. "You just said Bradley's car, right? You mean that when they kidnapped you, they made you drive yourselves out here?"

"Yup," Bradley replied.

"But it wasn't in the parking lot," Nicola said. "You can't just, like, hide a car."

"I can't," Mr. Winchester said. "But weather gods sure can."

* * *

They retraced the path they had taken to get to the entrance to the ruins.

"Mr. Winchester," Nicola said, looking concerned. "How did you get all the way up here? You never could have climbed up this dangerous route."

"I didn't walk up here," he replied. "Maximilian used a little tornado to carry me."

"But how are we going to get you back to the parking lot?" Claire asked.

"Carefully," he replied with a grin. "Very carefully. I'm old, but as long as someone's always supporting me, I'll be fine."

* * *

It took quite some time, and there were plenty of iffy and scary moments, but twenty-five minutes later, they were back at the parking lot safely.

"Over there, guys," Bradley said, pointing to the far end of the parking lot. "Gimme a hand."

Bradley's car was hidden behind a bunch of bushes. The bushes looked so natural that they didn't notice until getting closer that his car was actually even there. The weather gods had uprooted and dropped bushes on and around his car.

"We don't have to move them all," Bradley instructed. "Just enough of them to get my car out."

It didn't take very long to move the ones in front of his car, plus the few blocking the driver's door.

Bradley started the car, revved the engine loudly a few times, and then pulled the car out of its hiding spot. Peter and Neil then pulled branches off the roof and hood.

"Okay, Nik and Claire," Bradley said. "Looks like you two beautiful young ladies are with me."

* * *

"I'll explain the route as we go," Peter said to Neil from the backseat, where he and Mr. Winchester were sitting in order to make a private conversation possible. "Unless you remember?"

"Nah, I don't," Neil replied. "I mean, I was only there that one time, which was, like, four months ago. And I wasn't driving, so I wasn't really paying much attention."

Peter gave Neil the first half of the instructions, which were pretty straight-forward.

"Neil, please put these on," Mr. Winchester said, passing Neil a pair of heavy-duty safety headphones.

"You're joking, right?" Neil said. "You don't trust me?"

"I completely trust you, Neil," he replied. "But for all our safety, it's best that you not hear this now. It might make you too uncomfortable to drive."

"Alright," Neil replied, getting ready to put the headphones on. "But hold on a sec. Where did you get these from?"

"I carry them everywhere I go," Mr. Winchester replied. "Doctor's orders. I have bad tinnitus, and loud noises quickly make it worse."

"Ah," Neil said, nodding while he adjusted them to fit snugly. He gave them the thumbs up, which meant they could begin their conversation.

"Okay, Peter," Mr. Winchester said softly "What I'm about to tell you is, well, of utmost importance."

"I gathered that," Peter replied quickly and inquisitively.

"It's about the reason why I know we'll be seeing them again," Mr. Winchester whispered. "I have something they want."

Peter knew Mr. Winchester would continue, so he remained silent.

"But first I need to quickly explain," said Mr. Winchester, "about Zoltan and Xavier's great-grandfather. He was, at one time, the most powerful weather god ever. He also served as a lead weather god for sixty years. But he wasn't powerful due to luck, or due to diligent training. He was powerful because he possessed an amulet. This one-of-a-kind amulet, when worn, increases a weather god's powers at least 100-fold, or possibly even a thousand. No one knows how he came to own the amulet in the first place. And his family has always kept its existence a secret."

"Hold on a sec," Peter said, interrupting Mr. Winchester. He leaned forward, took the headphones off Neil's ears and said, "Turn left at the next intersection, and then right just before the cornfield."

"Roger," Neil replied.

Peter then let go of the headphones, in order to block Neil's ears from hearing the rest of the conversation.

"Ouch!" Neil yelped.

"Sorry," Peter apologized. "Guess I released those a little too quickly."

"But when people got too suspicious about why he was so unbelievably powerful," Mr. Winchester continued, "he decided it was time to hide the amulet. He should've thrown the stupid thing off into outer space, but he just couldn't. He wanted it to be accessible, just in case a planet was in peril, and then the amulet could be used to help save billions of lives."

"Don't tell me he gave the amulet to *you!?*" Peter asked.

"Gosh, no," Mr. Winchester replied. "He hid it in a place back on Sevlar, and—"

"Is that the shed!?" Neil said very loudly, something people often did when wearing headphones, as they couldn't accurately assess how loud their voices were.

Peter gave Neil the thumbs up, which Neil caught by looking in the rear-view mirror. He parked beside the shed, took off the headphones, and all three of them got out of the car.

It didn't require the presence of a professional C.S.I. to realize that the shed had been broken into. The door, which should have been locked, was wide open.

"Oh my," Mr. Winchester said as he quickly entered the shed.

Bradley's car had just arrived and parked, and they were opening the doors to get out.

"What's going on?" Bradley asked.

"The shed door was open," Peter said to Bradley. "Someone must have busted in. Wait here guys, I'll go in and check on Mr. Winchester."

The inside of the shed looked like it had been turned upside down. Everything that was always neatly lined up on the shelves was in a massive heap on the floor. Mr. Winchester was now on his hands and knees frantically pulling things out of the mess.

"This doesn't make sense," Peter said to him. "I mean, the only people who know how to get to this shed are you, me, and Nik, right? Well, I suppose Claire, Brad, and Neil were all here that one time, too. But no one out of our circle even knows this place exists. Plus, the lock on the door is not one that could be picked or broken easily."

"Maximilian, Aurora, and Cynthia have definitely been here," Mr. Winchester said.

Bradley's curiosity had gotten the better of him, and despite Peter's instructions to wait outside, he went in. "Whoa," Bradley said. "Looks like a hurricane came through here."

"Mr. Winchester thinks Maximilian, Aurora, and Cynthia broke in," Peter explained. "But that doesn't make any sense. How would they have known about the shed?"

"Umm..." Bradley said, looking very uncomfortable.

"Brad!?" Peter said strongly to him. "What happened? Did they threaten you or something? Did they force you to tell them about the shed and show them where it was?"

"Uh..." Bradley mumbled. "Well... not exactly."

Mr. Winchester sensed the hesitation in Bradley's voice, and quickly stood up and faced him. "Bradley," he said quite loudly. "If you have an explanation for this, then tell us. Now."

"Well, you see," he said, fumbling for the right words. "And you probably didn't know this, but Aurora and I kind of started, like, hanging out, and she—"

"Brad!" Peter said, cutting him off. "I don't care about you and your dating history."

"Okay, okay," Bradley replied, sweat forming on his brow. "When I was out with her once, she asked me if I knew anything about the puzzles and stuff you and Nik used for Zoltan."

"So you brought her here?" Peter yelled.

"Yeah," Bradley gulped. "But all we did was walk inside the shed, and then just look at the stuff in here for a while."

"But how did you get in?" Peter inquired angrily. "It was locked, and I have the only key."

"Petey," Bradley said in a somewhat sarcastic tone. "You've always hidden all your money, hockey cards, or anything else you don't want discovered in the same place: in the back corner of your sock drawer."

"So are you saying," Peter said angrily, "that you stole the key, drove her down here, and let her inside the shed?"

"This is not good," Mr. Winchester said, still digging through the pile. "Not good at all."

Feeling really uncomfortable, Bradley decided to leave the shed. He had screwed up. Plain and simple. And it was too late to undo it.

"What are you looking for?" Peter asked.

Mr. Winchester stood up and had a look of extreme concern on his face. "Peter," he said. "There is something extremely important I kept in here. It was a small box that said—"

Peter interrupted him. "That said *open after I pass away* on it, right?" he asked.

"Yes," Mr. Winchester replied. "That's the one. Inside that box, there was—"

"A map!" Peter said, interrupting him again.

"How do you know that?" Mr. Winchester asked. "I'm not dead yet. Did you already look inside it?"

Peter smiled. "Of course I did," he replied. "You know me. I can't leave any mysteries hanging."

"Well," the old man continued. "The map shows how to get to the entrance of where the amulet is hidden on Sevlar. And the clues written on the map are necessary to solve a series of puzzles and riddles between the entrance and the exact spot where the amulet itself is hidden. But now that they've got the map, it'll only be a matter of time before Xavier gets that amulet, and—"

"Nah," Peter said, cutting off Mr. Winchester for a third consecutive time. "They won't find the amulet. At least not with the map they've got."

"Sorry?" Mr. Winchester asked, very confused. "What do you mean?"

"When I took that box home and opened it for the first time," Peter explained, "it was clear that the map was something of great importance. Something that obviously shouldn't be kept in a shed in the middle of nowhere. So I took it out and—"

"Took it out?!" Mr. Winchester asked in shock. "Well then they'll come back here as soon as they see the box is empty."

Peter smiled again. "It's not empty," he said. "I drew a map that bore a smashing resemblance to the original one, and also wrote various hints and clues on the map."

"You mean," Mr. Winchester said, looking quite surprised. "You made a fake map? With fake clues? And put it back in the box? And then brought it back here?"

"Yup," Peter answered.

"Ingenious," Mr. Winchester said.

"But why were you given the map in the first place?" Peter questioned him.

"Their greatgrandfather decided to pass the map down to his eldest offspring," Mr. Winchester explained. "And he also instructed that the map always be given to the first-born son or daughter, from one generation to the next, but never until that person reached the age of eighteen. Xavier and Zoltan's father received it on his eighteenth birthday, in fact. But let's fast forward a little. Xavier ran off at fourteen, so his father was conflicted about what to do. He finally decided that he would give it to Zoltan, but considering Zoltan's behavior and attitude, he felt Zoltan wasn't ready for it at age eighteen. So instead, he asked me to hold on to the map, and instructed me to only tell Zoltan about it when he had matured enough."

"Okay, I see..." Peter said. "Anyway, Xavier and his cronies will be searching for years before they realize they have the wrong map."

Mr. Winchester's expression changed. "Years?" he said. "We could only wish. Your little map trick will fool them for a while, but not for long. At some point, Peter, they will come back to Earth. Back for us. And they'll use whatever means necessary to get the real map."

"So why don't I just burn it?" Peter suggested. "Then the amulet will be lost forever."

Mr. Winchester pondered Peter's idea.

"Everything okay in there!?" Nicola asked, standing a few paces away from the shed door.

"Yeah, we're fine!" Peter replied. "We'll be out soon!"

"Does Nicola, or anyone else, know about the map?" Mr. Winchester asked.

"Nope," Peter replied.

"Then let's keep it that way," the old man said.

"So do you want me to burn it?" Peter asked, referring back to his question again.

"Absolutely not," Mr. Winchester answered. "Like it or not, we are now involved in this. If you burn that map, Xavier's henchmen will burn your home, the whole town, and possibly the whole country out of revenge."

"Sounds like a catch-22 to me," Peter said.

"A what?" Mr. Winchester queried.

"Oops," Peter said, guessing Mr. Winchester wasn't

familiar with that phrase.

"What I'm saying," Peter continued, "is that either way, we lose. If Xavier gets the amulet, he'll have his way with everyone and everything. He'll destroy whatever and whoever he pleases. If we burn the map, he'll kill us out of anger, so we still die."

"There is one other option, Peter," Mr. Winchester said. "Well, it's the only feasible one I can think of right now. And we'll have to do two things to make it succeed. First, we'll need to rescue Zoltan. And second, we'll need to get the amulet. If Zoltan has the amulet, he will be powerful enough to defeat Xavier."

"Hold on," Peter replied. "Both of those things are entirely impossible. We are on Earth and they are on Sevlar. Obviously, we can't get to Sevlar."

"We can get there," Mr. Winchester said with a wink. "But I'll save that explanation for another day. Your friends are already getting suspicious about what we are talking about. I need to plan this out more carefully before we make any moves."

Mr. Winchester and Peter were temporarily blinded by the sunshine as they walked out of the shed. "Nothing of importance missing," Mr. Winchester announced to Bradley, Nicola, and Claire.

"Whew!" Nicola replied. "We were getting worried."

She looked over at Peter—he was hiding something—as he had that "I'm not being one hundred percent honest" look on his face. Poor guy just couldn't lie at all... but she would find out the truth later.

CHAPTER 37

Peter woke up early on Christmas morning, long before the rest of his family would even consider getting out of bed. He went downstairs and looked at the array of presents surrounding their beautifully decorated "fake" Christmas tree.

He walked into the kitchen and turned on the coffee maker. His mom's nose was almost as good as a police dog's, so as soon as the scent drifted upstairs, she'd wake up, have a two-and-a-half-minute shower, and then order everyone to come downstairs for present opening.

Meanwhile, Peter poured himself a glass of pulp-free orange juice, turned up the thermostat, and sat down on the big living room sofa. He looked out the large window at the thick, fresh snow that had fallen last night.

Then he smiled. "Oh, Pete, sometimes you surprise even yourself, don't you?" he said. He was imagining how Neil, Claire, and Nicola would react when they opened up their "gifts" from him this morning.

* * *

Since Nicola was an only child, and her parents weren't even a fraction as strict as Peter's, she was free to wake up and open her presents whenever she wanted.

But it was such a cold day, and she was so comfortable in her warm bed, that it wasn't until her mom knocked on her bedroom door at 9:45 that she finally decided to get up.

For some odd reason she wasn't hungry, so she decided to open up her presents before having breakfast. Most were things she wanted and/or needed, plus a few were envelopes containing cash. The present from Peter, which was the size of a shoebox, she saved for last.

"Mom, Dad," she said. "No offense, but do you mind if I open this one in my room? It's from Pete."

"Not at all, dear," her mom replied, even though she was unbelievably curious about what was inside.

Nicola went back up to her room, sat down on her bed, and ripped off the wrapping paper. It was a shoebox, but gauging from its lightness, she knew there were no shoes inside. She opened it up to find that what it contained was... well... not what one would normally consider a "present." There were three letters of the alphabet, cut from pieces of cardboard: an "A," an "I," and a "Y." Plus there was a small note, folded in fours. She smiled while unfolding it, and then read it silently.

> *Well, I couldn't leave you hanging forever, now could I? You three told me about your riddles from that challenge when we were split up. And I told you about mine. But I never told you the answer, did I? (But it sure was fun to hear all your ideas for the answer!!)*
>
> *But now that it's Christmas and your guesses (and Neil's and Claire's) have all been so brutally wrong, I thought I'd tell you the*

solution.

Just in case you forgot the riddle, it was:

$A \rightarrow A = 2$
$I \rightarrow I = 4$
$Y \rightarrow Y = ?$

And don't forget that there were four A's, nine I's, and six Y's written on the walls.

(Nik, are you sure you really want to read this? If not, just close the note, and keep guessing!)

Well, if you are still reading, then that means that curiosity got the better of you! But not to worry, it happens even to the best of us!

The trick here is that the arrow does NOT represent a mathematical sign.

The number on the right side of the equals sign indicates: <u>the number of ways you can flip the letter so that it will still look exactly the same</u>!

Grab the cardboard letters and follow my instructions. That'll make it way clearer.

First, put the "A" down. Now lift it and flip it to the right. It still looks like an "A," right? Now put it back where it started. Next, flip it to the left. Still looks like an "A" again, right? Put it back where it started again. Now flip it upwards. Now it's upside-down! Put it back a final time. Flip it downwards. Upside-down "A" again!" So the number of ways the "A" can be flipped in order to keep it as an "A" is two.

Now try the "I." Tell me how many of the four flips makes it stay the same? All four, right?

Now grab the "Y" and try it... Just like the "A" – it only looks the same when flipped left or right, so two ways! So there you go! The answer was door 2!

Merry Christmas, Nik!!

She shook her head in disbelief. Only the girlfriend of Peter would be happy to receive a present like this...

Thank you for reading the first 3 books of *The Puzzled Series*. I hope you liked the stories, the characters, and (most importantly) the puzzles! If you enjoyed these books, then I'd like to ask you for a favor: would you be kind enough to leave a review on Amazon or Goodreads? It would be enormously helpful for me. Thank you so much!

Sincerely,

P.J. Nichols

What's next in The Puzzled Series?

Great news, everyone!

As of October 2021, Books 4-6 are now available as one thick (approx. 500-page) volume! That single volume includes:

> Incredibly Puzzled (Book 4)
> Enormously Puzzled (Book 5)
> Colossally Puzzled (Book 6)

And not to worry, The Puzzled Series will continue beyond Book 6! (I still have so many puzzles and riddles that I can't wait to include in the upcoming books.)

I don't have a definite timeline for publication dates, but hopefully Book 7 will be ready by spring. And as long as more and more puzzle ideas keep popping into my head, you might even see Book 8 before the end of 2022!

And if you have any comments/suggestions about what you'd like to see in the next part of Peter's adventure, please let me know! You can reach me by e-mail at pj@pjnichols.com or by sending me a message through the contact page of my website (pjnichols.com).

Happy puzzling!

Acknowledgements

My mom, who answered every single "What if...?" question I asked while growing up. Her answers were all correct. *The sky didn't fall* and the *the sun didn't suddenly disappear.* Well, at least not yet, but... "What if they do?"

My dad, who is living proof that you don't have to be tall, strong, or get straight As at school to become a superstar. More than anything, he showed me how fun it was to make people happy. Everything I now try to do for my son I learned from him, especially the storytelling.

My three brothers: a "genius," a "creative mastermind," and an "athlete," who made growing up a true adventure, filled with countless fun memories.

My wife, who loves and supports me in everything I do, despite all of my quirks.

My son, whose curiosity in taking on new challenges inspired me to write this series.

Thank you to everyone who helped me along on my book writing journey. You are all awesome. I couldn't have done it without you.

About the Author

P.J. Nichols loves games. But not the kind you buy at stores. And not the kind you practice and practice and practice to get good at. He likes the games you think up and make by yourself.

No matter where he is, or what things are around him, P.J. will find a way to create a game. One where you race. Or one where you build. Or one where you think. Or maybe even one where you do all three.

Back when he was growing up with his three brothers in Canada, he was constantly making games. Neighborhood kids (and even some of their parents) would run over to join in. There was never a boring moment in or around the Nichols' house.

P.J. is sure that The Puzzled Series will have you rushing to think up games for your friends, brothers, sisters, or parents to try!

To find out more about P.J.
(and try some cool puzzles!) visit
pjnichols.com

Made in the USA
Columbia, SC
21 November 2021

49424275R00307